KILLING A COLD ONE

ALSO BY JOSEPH HEYWOOD

Fiction

Taxi Dancer

The Berkut

The Domino Conspiracy

The Snowfly

Lute Bapcat Mysteries

Red Jacket

Woods Cop Mysteries

Ice Hunter

Blue Wolf in Green Fire

Chasing a Blond Moon

Running Dark

Strike Dog

Death Roe

Shadow of the Wolf Tree

Force of Blood

Stories

Hard Ground: Woods Cop Stories

Non-Fiction

Covered Waters: Tempests of a Nomadic Trouter

Joseph Heywood is the author of *Covered Waters, The Snowfly, Red Jacket,* and *Hard Ground* (all Lyons Press), as well as *The Berkut, Taxi Dancer,* and *The Domino Conspiracy.* The Woods Cop Mystery Series (Lyons Press) has earned him cult status among lovers of the outdoors, law enforcement officials, and mystery devotees. Heywood splits the year between Deer Park and Portage, Michigan. Visit him at josephheywood.com.

A WOODS COP MYSTERY

KILLING A COLD ONE

JOSEPH HEYWOOD

LYONS PRESS
Guilford, Connecticut
An imprint of Globe Pequot Press

Lyons Press is an imprint of Globe Pequot Press.

Text design: Sheryl Kober
Layout artist: Melissa Evarts
Project editor: Ellen Urban

Map by Jay Emerson, Licensed Michigan Fisherman Emeritus

Library of Congress Cataloging-in-Publication Data is available on file.

ISBN 978-0-7627-9127-9

Printed in the United States of America

10 9 8 7 6 5 4 3 2 1

For Shanny (2002–2012),
Best in the Show called life.

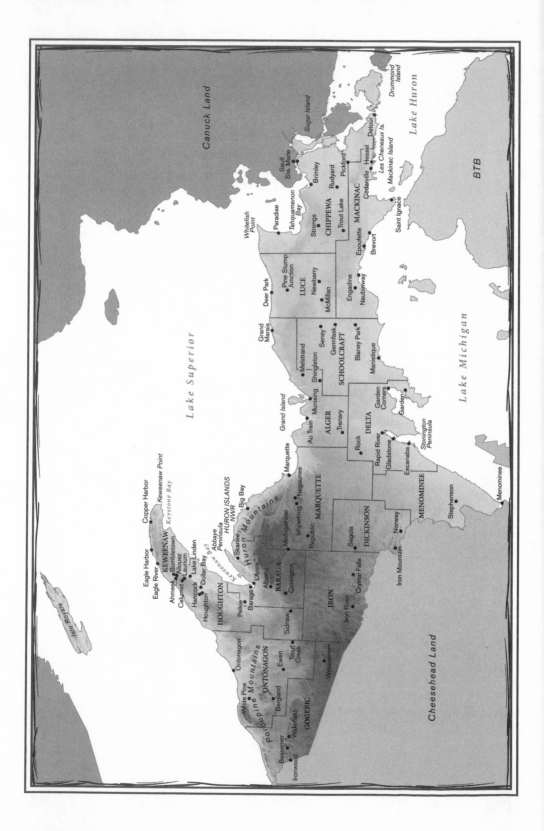

PART ONE

JANE RUNNING DOES

1

Sunday, August 3, 2008

DIMONDALE, EATON COUNTY

Chief Eddie Waco stared at the stiff cloth stripes Grady Service had dropped on his home office desk. New to Michigan, Waco was the recently appointed chief of law enforcement for the Michigan Department of Natural Resources. Last summer he had promoted Grady Service from detective to senior master sergeant—a new rank, which had made Service top NCO for the entire state.

Waco's home sat on the west bank of the Grand River, three miles southeast of Dimondale, the chief's property sitting on the borders of both Eaton and Ingham Counties.

"Retiring?" Chief Waco asked.

"Self-demoting," Service said. "The Mosquito Wilderness is open, and I want it back. I started there and I want to finish there, with my boots in the dirt. I'm sure you can understand."

The chief dangled the stiff cloth stripes between his fingers. "Sure, I can understand. But you haven't given the new job much of a chance—and what exactly do I do with these?"

"Bearnard Quinn's your man. Let him recommend his own replacement. It should have been him with the top job first time around. Not me. I'm not cut out for that committee and diplomatic crap."

"You haven't exactly worn out an office chair."

"Committee work would kill me. I can't stand not being in the woods."

"From what I've seen, you h'ain't been a whole lot behind a desk. Listen, Grady, you're the kind of man who stands up and says he's gonna do such and such, and the dang line behind you gets so dern long, nobody can see the end of it. You're a leader."

"I want my Mosquito back, Chief."

"It's not *your* Mosquito." The chief rubbed his eyes, looking weary. Years before, the two men had worked together on a difficult case in Missouri and had become friends. The chief had been recruited to Michigan to take the top job and infuse new thinking into the organization. Service knew Waco was a damn good man.

"Probably do you some good to put your boots in the dirt, too," Service said.

"Wun't take exception to thet," the chief said with a tired, flat voice. He looked tired, too.

The chief's home office was over his two-car garage. Service was surprised by piles of books, mostly nonfiction, not yet placed in what looked to be newly built floor-to-ceiling bookcases.

The chief studied him. "You work with that author yet?"

Months ago, the chief had gently ordered him to work with a man who wrote books about the department, but Service wanted no part of writers or journalists or anyone with anything to do with the damn media, unless they could be of use to him. "He was supposed to call me," Service said.

The chief sat back in his chair. "The man tried repeatedly, but apparently you don't make call-backs."

Busted. Service kept his mouth shut.

"Call the man and make it happen," Waco said.

"Just one day, right?"

"Several days, a week or two—whatever he wants. He's an ally, not a foe."

"I don't like civilians," Service said.

Waco sighed. "Just call him, Grady."

An old fart with hearing aids, a stutter, a cane, the writer was alleged to be painfully slow-moving and overly nosy. "Yessir," he said, with no intention of ever following through.

"The man's a vet," Chief Waco said. "If that softens the blow."

"Which war? Between the States?"

"Try to show some grace once in a while. It can work wonders."

"I'll take your word for it," Service said.

The chief shook his head and tossed the stripes to him. "Put them in your scrapbook. I'll call Quinn. And don't be taking that writer feller on some death march through one of your dang cedar swamps. He might just have to rescue yore big butt." Waco held a PhD, but he could talk pure and convincing backwoods when he wanted.

Service looked at the chief. "Thanks, Eddie."

"Git," Chief Waco said. "Some of us have paperwork to tend to."

"You could always do what I'm doing," Service said.

The chief glared at him. "Don't think I h'ain't considered it."

2

Wednesday, August 6

SLIPPERY CREEK CAMP

Lousy humid night to sleep, sheets sticking to him. Central Dispatch called him at 0330, night calls rarely presaging anything but bad news.

"Grady, it's Lamb Jones."

"Not a social call, eh, Lamb?"

There was none of the usual perkiness in Lamb's voice. She was terse, all business; this was unprecedented. Jones was the most proficient dispatcher Service had ever worked with: smart, spunky, determined, optimistic, in her late thirties, and not bad on the eyes. Lamb always insisted she was look- ing for a better job, which never seemed to materialize. Good thing. Her departure would leave a gaping hole in a critical function of the county's law enforcement chain.

"Two gorks at Twenty Point Pond," Lamb said. "CO Denninger is on- site with Sergeant Linsenman. She's freaking out and demanding that you join them ASAP."

Not good. "Out my door in four minutes, on scene in forty. Tell her I'm rolling," Service said, pulling on his pants.

He knew he needed a shave, but gorks wouldn't give a shit. *God, listen to yourself: Gorks! Gorks? People deserved dignity even in the ugliness of death, didn't they? What kid of a demeaning cop word is that? It doesn't even con- jure an image, only creates a shudder of revulsion on sound alone.*

"Troops alerted, Central?"

"Sergeant Linsenman's there; asked me to call Detective Friday. She'll rendezvous with you at US 41 and the old Peshekee Grade Road. Central clear."

Detective Tuesday Friday was his girlfriend of two years, a Troop homicide dick out of the Negaunee post. They lived (separately) together. Divorced, she had a son, Shigun, and a house in Harvey, outside Marquette. They split time between their homes. Often when he was on extended duty,

Service's 160-pound presa canario, Newf, and Cat, the cantankerous stray who had adopted him many years ago, bunked with Tuesday and her son. Service had lost the love of his life, Maridly Nantz, in 2004. His teenage son had died with her, but left a pregnant girlfriend. Service loved his toddler granddaughter, Little Maridly, named for his murdered girlfriend. He supposed he also loved Friday, and she him, but neither had so far used the word *marriage*.

He started the truck, reported into service with Lansing and Lamb Jones, his mind in high gear. *If it's red, it's dead*: This was August, venison meat at its tastiest. July 4 was when serious U.P. violators began to work in earnest. Even on still nights with swarms of mosquitoes and deerflies, Service could imagine them out there in his woods—poaching the people's animals, *his* animals, his *granddaughter's,* and the knowing cut deep.

He'd never wanted to be a detective in the Wildlife Services Protection Unit, and until a few days ago he'd had another job he'd not wanted, not just as a sergeant, but as the state's top NCO. *Damn joke.* All he'd ever wanted was to take care of the Mosquito Wilderness and eventually to retire. But life dealt shitty hands, and you had to play the cards you caught. Choice played but a small role in real life and seemed to serve largely as an illusion for pathological optimists and overreaching mouth-breathers.

From a selfish point of view, there was some good news in this call: Gorks and homicides were *not* the DNR's responsibility. Linsenman, it seemed, already had decided to push the case over to the State, which meant his girlfriend Tuesday Friday would catch it, in which case—*Dammit*—it would affect both their lives. The point now was that Denninger was demanding his presence, which is why Lamb Jones had bumped him. He wondered why Dani had asked for him instead of her sergeant, Willie Celt. Denninger was a relatively new CO, a competent, spunky woman who loved her work. She didn't rattle easily, and knowing this, he kept the accelerator to the floor.

Friday bumped him on the cell phone.

"You know where this place is?"

"Just beyond the butt crack of Bumfuck, Egypt. Technically it's just inside the Marquette border next to the Baraga County line, far northwest corner of the Hurons, south and a hair west of Mount Baldy."

"Sounds like Backwoods Valhalla."

"Definition of."

"Fastest route?"

"North up the Peshekee Grade Road, just past the river mouth west of Van Riper State Park."

"See you at the turnoff?" she said.

"Who'll be on top?" he asked.

"What a silly, shallow, and insecure man you are," she teased. "Move, Bucko. And hold that thought."

3

Wednesday, August 6

TWENTY POINT POND, MARQUETTE COUNTY

Five miles out of his camp Service drove past a mother raccoon and five babies flattened on the road, their blood black and glistening in his headlights, death by blind obedience to an obviously flawed maternal instinct—proof that mama did not always know best. She had made a gamble and all of them had died. Did animals think of family as refuge, the way some people did? Here was proof contrary. His own family experience further attested to that. What good was something that could be taken away as soon as it gained currency in your life?

He found Friday at the turnoff to the grade, and let her swing her unmarked black Tahoe in behind his unmarked Tahoe before he put the hammer down. They flew into the labrynthian maze of gravelly mountain two-tracks, Friday glued to his six, both vehicles spitting tombstone-gray summer rock bits in their wakes, raising clouds, and skittering dust devils into the night.

It was a half-mile hike from a small parking area to the pond. Formally called Rockgap Lake, it had been known locally as Twenty Point Pond since the head and antlers of a twenty-point whitetail buck had been found near the primitive campground back in the late 1950s. A hue and cry had gone up from the locals, demanding that the DNR find and punish the guilty! Who but an asshole would kill such a magnificent beast and not even bother to take the trophy horns? A kid then, Service had asked his father about the buck, which was being talked about everywhere. His old man had been a CO before him, a famous one, and not so popular with his son.

"You going after that guy?" Grady had asked his old man.

"*What* guy?"

"The one who poached the deer."

"What deer?" his father asked, half in the bag—as usual.

"The twenty-point."

"Chrissakes, who the hell says it was *poached?*" his old man grumbled.

Grady Service remembered being at a total loss for words until he managed to say, "But somebody just threw away the *rack.*"

His old man shrugged. "You can't eat goddamn horns, kid. Obviously someone wanted meat and didn't give a shit about the trophy. Use your fucking head, and think before you talk."

"That sounds crazy," Grady mumbled weakly.

"Are you some kind of hunting-ethics guru now?" his old man challenged.

"It just seems wrong—you know, wasteful," Grady argued, trying not to feel like he'd been written off by his father.

The old man sighed deeply and took a deep breath. "For the sake of discussion, how about we say that theoretically there's a near-starving family up on the Northwest Road, and that buck dressed out at close to three hundred pounds, meaning a good hundred and fifty pounds of meat, and said theoretical starving family can't eat no fucking horns. How about we say that, ya know, for purposes of a so-called fucking *learned* discussion?"

Grady knew then that his old man had killed the animal and given it to a family in need. He wanted to run away, but knew he couldn't back down.

"Was the deer shot at the lake?"

"Theoretically, but I'd guess it just might've been shot miles away and the head was dumped at the camp—you know, to theoretically keep assholes from swarming to the area where there actually might be other big bucks— theoretically speaking."

"But now hunters will swarm Rockgap Lake."

His father grinned. "There's a lot of dumb clucks running around the woods, kid. Most of the slobs don't hunt more than a hundred yards from their damn trucks on account they're afraid some bogeyman will eat their incompetent asses."

Before his old man died, Grady learned exactly where the old man had found the monster deer, and he had gone there himself, looked, and seen other trophy animals. This information he'd kept to himself since, not even telling other COs. It wasn't the sort of place hundred-yard hunters would stumble on, so why help them?

Meanwhile, Rockgap Lake morphed inexorably into the legendary Twenty Point Pond, and over the years COs had written countless tickets to cheaters and idiots looking for phantom giant bucks there. That was the thing about hunters, Service reminded himself: You could kick them into action with no more than a half-assed rumor of a trophy of any kind. Some hunters just couldn't restrain themselves, like it was some kind of weird damn disease, this drooling over antlers and Boone and Crockett scores.

Marquette County sergeant Weasel Linsenman was standing off to the side of a small tent, which Grady Service noted had been placed by someone who knew a thing or two about camping, situating it behind a rocky ledge to help shelter the structure from prevailing winds.

"Unfuckingbelievable," the Marquette County sergeant greeted Friday and Service.

"Where's Denninger?" Service asked.

"Tromboning her guts over in the woods, eh, and before you start trash-talking that girl, let me tell you, I had my turn hurling, too."

Service squatted at the fire pit by the tent, touched the ashes. No embers, ashes cold. But he could smell bacon or something fat in the dregs. A fire in this weather? *Weird.*

Friday turned on a flashlight, tugged on blue latex gloves, eased back the tent flap, and shone her light inside.

Service stood behind her. "Okay to lean over your shoulder?"

"Go for it," she said.

Flies were buzzing, the fetid smell of death and decay pressing. An air mattress covered the entire floor area of the two-person shelter. Remains of two unclothed bodies were side by side on their backs, their legs and thighs pulled up and back in gross exaggeration, synchronized death, something reminiscent of a Hollywood slasher movie. Females, both of their chests open, hearts gone, heads and hands removed, upper-arm muscles ripped down to stark white bone, pinked under the flashlight beam.

Friday shone her light on a corpse, calmly said, "No buttocks, either vick. And not much blood, considering the extent and nature of the wounds."

Her composure amazed him.

"Dump site?" Service remarked, his first thought having been that wolves or coyotes had gotten to the remains. "Wolves been here, maybe?" he said out loud to Friday. "Some kind of animal."

"Based on?" she said.

"Guts, butts . . . that's where wolves usually start. Other muscles come last. Don't know why, just is."

She said, "There should be hair, DNA, something left inside the tent, tracks outside. I thought wolves didn't attack humans."

"Not saying an animal attacked, but it might have fed off the meat available," he said. *Animals might have fed here, but no wolf did this—at least not one that fit his predator/scavenger profile or experience.*

"Look around for animal evidence?" she said over her shoulder.

He stepped outside and began looking around, careful to stand in one place and let his eyes move, rather than risk ruining evidence.

"You call your homicide people?" Friday asked Linsenman as she backed out of the tent.

"I did, and I told them I was calling you, too, because it was my guess you'd prolly end up catching the case. They said to call them if you need their help, but it's your call from here on, far as they're concerned. I thought it best to keep this as straightforward and uncomplicated as possible."

Service's friend Linsenman was a great cop, the kind of man you could always depend on, even when he didn't relish being depended on.

"Thanks for that," Friday said. "Dani found them?"

"Yeah."

Service went looking for the young CO, found her sitting with her back against a mossy stump, clumsily smoking a cigarette, coughing.

"They tell you about crap like this at the academy?" Service asked.

"I'm not in the mood for half-baked philosophy. There's nothing funny about this sicko shit," she said.

"Sorry. Friday's here. She wants to talk at you."

"Not a problem. I'll be right there," Denninger said.

Service watched Friday and Linsenman use a roll of yellow plastic tape to cordon off the crime area.

"Call the ME?" Friday asked Linsenman.

"She's en route, I expect."

"She?" Friday asked. "What happened to Myslewski?"

"Today's the deputy ME's first day. Myslewski announced that he'll retire in September, and she's gonna work with him until he leaves. None of this has been announced to the public."

"Her name?"

"Dr. Kristy Tork."

"Never heard of her."

"Hired out of Mount Clemens or some McMansionless scum pit between Flintucky and Detwat. Word is she works great with cops, and she's swum through a bunch of hi-viz cases downstate."

Service could see cop-think asserting itself and Friday immersing herself in professional mode. Her duty hat was snugged down tight: Preserve the site, get the medical examiner to the scene, summon the State Police crime scene team to collect forensic evidence. At this stage, you had to block out the horrifics and run your crime scene checklist. This was still early in the what-how-and-when stage. Motive wouldn't become an issue for a while—not until other essential questions were settled. He knew the missing heads and hands were problematic to the case, but Friday said nothing about them. As a good cop, she would focus on what she had, not what she didn't have. Amend that: Not just a good cop, a *great* cop.

Service had seen more than his share of dead people, but murder wasn't a DNR concern, much less his job. *Thank God.* Even so, he and other conservation officers encountered enough baffling and strange human behavior and corpses to understand that almost any and all things were possible. Nothing was too extreme or unimaginable.

The possibilities spanned human diversity. Satan whispered "Why don'tcha?" to an imaginary dog who, in turn, whispered the same thing to a nutcase, and *kabang,* psychic shit overflowed from an inner cesspool with severely negative karma for fuel. There were lots of folks in the world and woods, oddly bent and hearing voices, most just trying to hang on, but a few inevitably losing their grip. Friday was good at her job—logical, orderly, unflappable, and even-tempered. Hell, she was good even in her postcoital Jell-O mode, which was a wholly altered state of being (and which, he reminded himself, there'd not been much of recently). She'd been gone for a long week to a seminar in Lansing.

"Hey," Linsenman said. "Loan me a ciggie."

"Loan? You don't smoke."

"Until tonight. You know why most rural homicides aren't solved?"

"Enlighten me," Service said.

"No dental records, and all the DNA's identical."

Service felt himself smiling. "Is that profiling? If it is, I remind you it is against the current laws of the land, Sergeant. And it's downright sick."

"Hey, it's also nearly universally true. Where's that cig?"

Service handed him the pack, and Linsenman lit up. Friday walked over to them.

"We'll wait for the ME," Friday told the two men. "When I told my mother I wanted to be a cop, she screamed 'Why?!' I told her I liked the notion of helping people. Then, she yelled 'People?! Most creatures you meet won't want your help, and most of them are incapable of being helped.' This was the central precept of my mother's family—that there are two distinct classes of people in the world: those few who might reasonably be defined as human, and the greater part by far who were born hopeless, and not worth thinking or caring about."

"You're not like your mother," Service said.

"Sometimes I wonder if she's the one who understood reality, and it's me who doesn't get it."

"Relax," he whispered.

"This doesn't turn your stomach?"

"I've seen a lot that has turned my stomach, and this is as bad as it gets. Everyone dies; only the timing and method are up for grabs. At least there aren't any little kids."

She nodded solemnly. "What about guilt?" she asked.

Weasel Linsenman said, "As flies to wanton boys are we to the gods; they kill us for their sport. Weird dude named Shakespeare wrote that shit, like, five hundred years ago."

Service grinned. Weasel's depth sometimes astonished him.

Friday said, "When my mom and stepdad died, it occurred to me that somehow I was responsible—that my words, said in anger years before, had drawn death to them, like a bad-luck magnet. It's taken a long time to understand and accept that I bore no responsibility. They were killed by a Northwest L-1011 that had been improperly deiced. It lumbered off the runway from Detroit Metro into a thick, freezing mist and promptly crashed on I-94, killing everyone on board and eleven more luckless people on the ground, including my schizoid mother Eve and her latest husband, Luke. They were in her new red Mercedes.

"'Drinking' Eve used to ask other drunks how they would characterize a tornado picking up an eighteen-wheeler filled with pigs and dropping it on a synagogue; when no answer came, 'Anti-semitic' Eve would cackle and say, 'Intelligent design.' I asked her once, what if God was last in his drafting class? That cost me a four-week grounding one summer, but it was worth it. I still wonder if it was God's intelligent design to drop an L-1011 on all those poor folks. It seems to me that God and Mother Nature together kill a helluva lot of innocent people in ice-cold blood."

Service was almost relieved when Denninger joined them.

"When did you find them?" Friday asked.

Denninger looked at her watch. "Three hours ago."

"You looked inside the tent?"

"The smell told me I had to."

"What brought you out here?"

"There's a little brook trout stream near here. It's a magnet for both visiting and local assholes. This time of year the water never gets above forty-eight degrees. I'm not sure where the trout migrate from."

Service smiled. They were a long way from anywhere, but it was no surprise that Denninger would be out, about, and poking around, searching for miscreants in remote locations.

The Upper Peninsula was as much a state of mind as a piece of geography. Usually you knew the troublemakers in your area, or the people you regularly contacted in the line of duty. Or at least you'd heard of them. Below the Bridge, or BTB, as they say, everyone was a stranger, even your neighbors, and every encounter was potentially lethal. If your mind wandered, you could be quick-dead. In some ways, that was less true up here.

Outsiders thought of Yoopers as antisocial loners, but they weren't. They could be gloriously gregarious when the mood or need struck. Mostly they were private people; they didn't want to *be* alone, they wanted to be *left alone,* a fine line between the two. Collectively they had no use for rules and laws written by gasbag political flatlanders five hundred miles away in Lansing. Service understood the draw of the lifestyle, and his job. Unlike others, this work wasn't a stopover en route to something bigger and more lucrative. This was what he wanted, all he had *ever* wanted, and he was glad to have it back.

The bodies were removed by 10 a.m., overseen by new Marquette County medical examiner, Dr. Kristy Tork, six feet tall, with the build of a ballerina, the voice of a truck driver, and the vocabulary of a sailor on Hong Kong liberty.

"Fricking gorks, even up here," Tork said, shaking her head. "Who knew?"

Jen Maki, the lead forensics technician for the Michigan State Police, was with the doctor, blotting perspiration from her forehead with a yellow Cub Scout bandanna.

Tork said, "Lopped off their heads and hands, dug out their hearts. I'm guessing we'll find semen in their cisterns."

"This wasn't about sex," Friday asserted.

The doctor responded calmly and in a measured voice. "I don't mean to imply it was, Detective. But when men get to doing this sort of shit to women, it seems their dickie-doos are invariably involved in some way. Standard operating procedure to look for pecker tracks. Obviously the perp doesn't want the remains easily identified, yet I'm asking myself—if I'm trying to prevent identification, why would I take heads and hands and leave a leg with a tattoo? What's *that* all about? I mean, Jesus-on-a-Popsicle-stick. My guess is that our Jane Does are Native Americans, and the perp may be a major candidate for the rubber-room short bus." She banged the heel of her hand against her forehead. "Forgot the tat! Duh!"

"Evidence for Native Americans?" Friday asked.

"Skin tone, hunch—can't say for sure. I might could be wrong, but blood will tell. Tattoo on the one might eventually help. Stylized bear or a dog, not sure which, but I guess prolly a bear. Has a back hump."

"How often are you wrong?" Friday asked.

"Me? Lots of times, but mitochondrial DNA sequencing is never wrong. It doesn't lie or get confused the way we animated carbon units do."

Service didn't really understand the science or its nuances, but he'd noticed more and more young officers using animal DNA as a tool in making various cases. He told himself repeatedly that he needed to get up to speed with younger officers, especially in his detective role, but there had never seemed to be time, and now his detective days were over and he could immerse himself in the Mosquito Wilderness. *You were smart to turn down the top sergeant job. You aren't qualified.*

"Native Americans are problematic," Service announced to Tork.

"Meaning?"

"They live in a closed society and move around a lot. There are more Indians in Detroit than in the rest of the state combined. They're hard to trace, and they're basically uncooperative with white cops. A daughter visits her mother in Bay Mills or Hannahville for six months, then one night she books it to Detroit or the Dakotas, Southern Ontario, or the planet Neptune for a year or two without a damn word, and nobody even inquires, because that's just how it is. It's noble to be so free and to move around on whims, but for cops with cases, it's a pain in the ass. No offense, but I hope you're wrong on this," Service concluded.

"Ditto," Jen Maki added.

"I'm just the messenger," Dr. Tork said, noisily peeling off her gloves.

Service looked at Denninger. "Is there a vehicle?"

"Not that we've found."

"Somebody drop them?"

"Or whacked them and ganked their wheels," the young CO suggested.

4

Thursday, August 7

MARQUETTE, MARQUETTE COUNTY

The morgue and medical examiner's office were in the Marquette Regional Medical Center's emergency department complex, between College and Magnetic Avenues. Service said good-bye to Denninger and followed Friday only as far as the complex. He knew she wanted to attend the autopsy, as did Linsenman.

"How was your seminar?" he asked Friday before they entered the morgue.

"You coming in for the autopsy?" she asked, dismissing his question.

"Not a chance," he said. "See you at your place later?"

"Yep," she said distractedly. *Her head's buried in the case already.*

Service drove to Friday's place, relieved her sister of kid-care duties, and checked to make sure Friday's son, Shigun, was asleep.

When Friday got home, Service handed her a glass of white wine. They sat on the bed, undressing, and performing nightly rituals.

"Feebs think they have all the answers," she said with a derisive snort. "They don't even have all the damn questions yet. I picked up some good tidbits on DNA, though. The feds want to set up a national DNA bank similar to AFIS."

"Must be nice to be able to print money," Service said with a snort. The State of Michigan was broke and sucking fiscal carbon monoxide. AFIS, the Automated Fingerprint Identification System, had been pioneered by the FBI; major city cop houses had adapted the system to create local crime data banks, which helped to catch some criminals, but missed most, and cost taxpayers a bundle to maintain. The cost of a national DNA bank, he guessed, would make the AFIS look like chump change.

"So damn young," Friday said suddenly. "Eighteen and twenty. Jesus! Messy work on their necks, done in a hurry, machete or a hatchet. Hacked off heads and hands. The heart deal is really weird. I mean, what's *that* all about? I think he knew what he wanted, but I don't see any finesse at work. We may have us a power boy, a real grank-and-crank. I'm thinking we should do a statement for the media, the usual drill. Found two bodies of unidentified young women, approximately eighteen to thirty years of age, discovered yesterday in a remote location in Marquette County. Cause of death not yet determined, but foul play is suspected, and the investigation is under way, yada yada. Do I mention animals might have gotten at the remains?"

Service considered the critter what-if and rejected it. No real evidence. Wolves or coyotes were possible, but not likely. He could tell that her mind was absorbed in the case. Granks were killers who tore apart victims. "Leave out the animal part. No proof."

"I'm keeping everything on the table with me for the moment."

"No task force?"

"Not unless forced," she said. "It's a sad world when people begin to verbigate nouns," she added.

What the hell was she talking about?

"Linsenman checked between toes, and what was left of the arms. No tracks."

"They could be play-for-pay girls," Service offered.

"A possibility lacking evidence."

"The lab will mine all the cavities."

"Meaning vaginas, not teeth?" she challenged, clearly not pleased with his word choice.

"I hope Forensics can match the hatch," Service said. "Unsubs complicate everybody's life."

"Ya *think?*" Friday yowped at him with a half-growl.

"We're not going to fool around tonight, right?" Service said.

She tilted her head and looked over at him with blank eyes. "What did you say?"

5

Friday, August 8

TWENTY POINT POND

Denninger called on his personal cell phone at 0400. "Can you get loose?" she asked.

"Shouldn't you be back in your own house by now," he said, "getting— what's it called—oh yeah, *sleep?*"

"I found something you should see."

"Tomorrow?"

"Now," she said. "Please?"

He heard the pleading in the young CO's voice, pushed down the covers, said, "Soon as I can get there," got out of bed, and began to dress.

"Who was that?" Friday asked.

"Denninger."

"This case?"

"Don't know yet."

He kissed the top of Friday's head and went out to his Tahoe, wishing he'd gotten real sleep. Two 0400 wake-ups in a row was a decidedly crappy trend. He'd once challenged Friday on how obsessed she became by her cases, and she had looked him in the eye and said, "Pretty much like looking in a mirror, ain't it?" Right now was a case in point.

Denninger was parked in the lot with the trail that led north to Twenty Point Pond. She was standing behind her truck, tailgate down, a coffeepot on a small burner.

"You can't work twenty-four, seven," he said.

"Sure I can, and do, same as you. They just don't pay us for it."

"What have you got?"

"Coffee first, then we'll take a walk."

Walk, to a conservation officer, could amount to anything from a few hundred yards to several miles.

"South, I bet," Service said.

"You know your geography."

"Fields to the south, good grasses to attract bait."

Bait was a CO term for deer feeding in a field, where they served as magnets for violators. "Been lots of busts up here," Service added.

After coffee, they hiked to the crime scene and Denninger led him beyond the camp, taking him in a giant loop back to the south. She shone her flashlight in the dirt, showed him three huge canid tracks.

"Seen anything like that before?" she asked.

Service knelt, measured with his hand. The tracks were a good seven inches long, five wide. "If that's a wolf, it's the biggest sonuvabitch I've ever heard of," he told her.

"C'mon," she said, striding off to the south across a field of basalt, the smoothest he had ever seen. Strange geography: Basalt was rarely exposed to this extent, at least in this area.

"Laurentian Plateau, Canadian Shield, whatever," she said. "We're on the very eastern edge of it here. Keweenaw's part of it, too. The animal crossed this rock field, stayed on the hard surface maybe to hide its tracks," she said, and started moving down the sloping rock until she got to a gigantic white pine that had blown over, exposing its massive root-ball. Denninger pointed. "More tracks."

Service looked. *Geez. What does she want? Wolves are stealthy and cautious but don't hide their tracks.* "Okay, you found tracks; what about them?"

"They're the sideshow," the CO said, and lit the bottom of the root-ball with her light. Service saw something smooth and shiny, reflecting light. "Plastic?" he said.

"Look closer," she said. "I think they're gun cases."

He looked at her. "Did you look?"

"Didn't want to until I got you here to witness it, so we can keep the chain of custody untainted."

Serviced asked, "What's this got to do with the gorks? Anything?"

Denninger said, "Something, nothing—who the hell knows? Crime scene techs found an empty box of .308 ammo down by the parking lot— presumably the victims' or the perp's, or maybe it fell out of a vehicle. I don't know. Boot tracks from the parking lot led me to the cache. Let's see what we have before we jaw more."

"Fair enough," said Service.

Denninger handed him her digital camera and snapped on latex gloves. "I'll be the talent, which in TV lingo means the body in front of a camera."

"Whatever," he said. He couldn't help liking the live-wire Denninger, who had nearly lost a leg to a deadly wolf trap early in her career.

She pulled the package out from under the root-ball and undid the shiny cloth, revealing a hardback weapon case, locked, of course. It took her less than ten seconds to spring it with a tool from her pocket.

Grady Service stared at the two weapons. "Serial numbers?" he asked.

She gave the rifles a thorough examination. "Erased," she said. "Acid."

"That ain't good," he said.

"More here," she added, pulling out another package, smaller, unwrapping it and quickly picking another lock.

Service stared and lit a cigarette. "Night scopes. You know what we've got here?"

"Trouble?" she said.

"Those rifles used to be called M40s by the Marine Corps. Remington manufactured them *only* for gyrene snipers. They made fewer than twenty-five hundred of them, and outside military custody, you'd have an easier time getting rough sex from the Virgin Mary than laying your mitts on one of those jobbies."

"Scopes come with them?"

He looked and declared, "I'm not familiar with these optics. We'll check into it."

"You ever seen one of these in the hands of a violator?"

"These are relics, but they're the real deal, and I'm betting they're worth a small fortune to collectors." He failed to mention that he had on occasion been a sniper in Vietnam and had used the same weapon.

"If the rifles belong to the victims?"

He had no answer for her. Just shook his head.

She said, "Maybe it pulls us into it as well. Could be they were making a delivery or something?"

"Don't speculate," he said. "Not our business."

"Or someone came to get the rifles, and the deal turned bad?"

"You don't know that, and absent prints, you can't link the weapons to the vicks."

"Grady," she said, "that wolf approached the camp, circled, came to this spot, and moved on. Curious how the animal's trail mirrors our route to this spot. Maybe the victims stashed the weapons. It sure wasn't the wolf. This is freshly disturbed soil."

"It doesn't matter," he said. "We'll get Friday out here. This is *not* our business. More likely it'll be ATF or FBI—if the weapons are involved."

Denninger stared at him. "What if I told you there's some talk of a dog-man being seen in far western Baraga County. Bar talk says there's even a bar bounty out on the damn thing."

Dogman? This was the Michigan version of what the French called a *loup garou*—a werewolf. From what he remembered, the dogman was the fictional creation of some downstate radio disc jockey. "We don't need this kind of shit," he told her. "You're pulling my leg, right?"

"No joke, Grady."

"Shit."

By training, conservation officers could deal with just about anything, but if you really wanted to get them talking, all you had to do was ask about UFOs and other semimystical supernatural phenomena they'd encountered in the woods. Real or not, the dogman was one of those things that made some COs cringe while fascinating them at the same time. Service was certain all such fantasies were just so much crap.

"Do we take the weapons to Friday?" Denninger asked.

"We don't *do* homicides. If the weapons belong to her vicks, and her case, she can take them, and if not, she can pass them to whoever catches the weapons case."

"My gut says this is all in the same stewpot," Denninger said.

Grady Service shuddered. "You don't have a gut," he told her.

In fact, Denninger was a hard body who slaved to maintain it. His own scarred gut was suggesting the same connected mess. It was not something he cared to think about. Not that he believed such junk, but a lot of nut-job civilians would, and if this became public, all hell would break loose as every self-appointed monster-hunter in the state (and the country) would probably arrive in Michigan, trying to bag the alleged beast. Especially if there was a bounty on it.

"You need to find out for sure about that bounty: who, how much, when, why, everything."

"You?"

"I'll call Tuesday and wait here for her."

• • •

An hour later he was feeling dozy when he sensed he was being watched. Instinctively he remained perfectly still and began to scan the surrounding areas with his eyes, but nothing looked suspicious. After fifteen minutes, the strange feeling passed. *Not a wolf.*

Shakespearean lines filled his mind: "Or in the night / imagining some fear / How easy is a bush supposed a bear!"

The lines made him laugh. *Yeah, probably a bear prowling around.*

Where the heck was Friday? He stepped past the root-ball to urinate, looked down, and saw more of the giant wolf tracks. "Geez," he said out loud.

Friday arrived, took photographs of the weapons cache, and they carried and loaded the rifles and scopes into the patrol unit.

"Any theories to share?" she asked.

"Nothing supported by evidence," Service said. He decided to tell her nothing about the wolf man until Denninger got more information on the so-called bounty.

Friday wore latex gloves and hefted one of the rifles. "This thing's heavy, and would be even heavier with one of these scopes. Our vicks don't look strong enough to handle them."

"Could be irrelevant," he said. "May have nothing to do with Twenty Point Pond."

"Then what?"

He held out his hands and rolled his eyes. "It's the U.P., eh?"

Friday looked at him. "I bet you're glad you're not on this case."

"Like, *totally*," Grady Service said, grinning.

6

Saturday, October 18

NEGAUNEE, MARQUETTE COUNTY

Yint's Eat Healthy Eh-Café was poorly named, the emporium's fare so fattening you could clog arteries just by reading the menu. Service ordered a cinnamon roll and Friday curled a lip in revulsion.

"At my age sugar goes straight to my hips," she complained.

The waitress, a part-time college student at Northern, and a granddaughter of the owner, Helmi Yint, said, "Try the *pan kaka*. They're, like, Swedish, hey? You put your maple syrup on top of her."

Service and Friday both laughed. "Just coffee," Friday said.

Service loved his fellow Yoopers. "Put your syrup on top of *her?*" he mimicked.

"Good plan. File that for future consideration," Friday said in a low voice.

There had not been much closeness lately, and it sometimes felt like they were slowly drifting apart, largely because they were both so busy—Service reestablishing his presence in the Mosquito, and Friday with the two-gork case. COs were reporting an influx of road hunters, and there was a major jump in tickets for loaded weapons in vehicles, but most of the dopes so far were locals. Dogman-related? He hoped not.

The two Marine sniper weapons had landed back on his desk after being turned down by the FBI, ATF, and the US Marine Corps, all of whom said they had more important things to deal with. With no serial numbers, there wasn't much he could do, although he had called an old Marine buddy by the name of Prince.

Prince had been his platoon sergeant in Vietnam, a straight-backed, foul-mouthed, born leader out of the Blue Ridge Mountains in northeast Georgia. Prince was calm and patient, a born teacher with unerring judgment of men and situations. The Gunny had given Service's black platoon mate, Treebone, the nickname "Chocolate Bunny," and the first time Service heard this, he had expected a fight, but Tree had only laughed. Service respected and trusted Prince, the kind of NCO who was the bedrock of the Marine Corps, and all uniformed services.

Service and Treebone left Vietnam and the Corps, but Prince had stayed in and retired at an exalted super-senior gunnery sergeant rank. He now lived in southern California, not far from Camp Pendleton.

"Gunny Prince," said Service.

"Bet you never thought you'd be addressing me that way," Prince shot back.

"Standards slide; Semper fi."

"Semper fi. What the hell do *you* want?"

Service explained the situation—the rifles and scopes, ammo, all of it, along with the lack of leads.

"Well," Prince said after listening, "them's some real primo weps y'all's got, and in the long-gun market, you might could trade a brace for a heap of pussy, money, or both."

"There's a market for such?"

"There's a market for everything, Service. What the hell kind of a cop *are* you?"

"The serial numbers are gone. How do you trace something like this?"

"Rumor mill, old jarhead under-radar bullshit streams, and such, and like that, and so forth, and like that. You know the Suck."

"Pig in a poke?"

"The polar opposite of the odds of contracting the black clap in Saigon. You want me to make some inquiries?"

"Affirmative. I'm sort of at a dead end here."

"No promises."

"Anything might help."

He had already related this to Friday, and she had just shaken her head and said, "I think you invented networking, Service." She had asked for the meeting at Yint's this afternoon, and he had no idea why. Tomorrow he intended to drive to Houghton to see his granddaughter and her mom, whom he considered his daughter-in-law, even though she and his son Walter had never married. It had been sleeting for three days and this morning had turned to a heavy, slippery wet snow. He hoped roads would be drivable the next day.

Friday seemed pensive.

"You okay?" he asked.

"Yes and no," she said, lost in thought. "Almost three months, Grady, and we have bupkis for evidence, nothing on the vicks. The DNA finally came back: maybe Indians, maybe not. Tork's taking another look, new samples. There's not a damn thing we can use to point us now or later, assuming there is a later."

"There's always a later," he told her.

"My boss told me with state budgets as they are, MSP may be cutting some detective positions, and I'm low dick on the totem pole. I talked to my union rep, who said I should just suck it up and be glad I have a job. Let's hear it for moral support and brotherly love," she said bitterly.

"You're too good to chop."

"Seniority isn't about performance," she said. "There's no semen in the vaginas and stomachs of the vicks. That's not good for down-the-road use. No evidence of a struggle, no traces of intoxicants or drugs. Makes me wonder if they weren't willingly tied together. This one is weird."

She's venting, rhetorical mutterings. Service knew to keep his mouth shut while Tuesday tried to shape her thoughts. She liked to think out loud. He didn't.

"Outrage is waning," she went on. "Newspapers are folding left and right, and nobody gives enough of a shit to track something like this and keep the anger alive." Service knew that an intense emotional response often kept public interest high in certain crimes, and sometimes brought leads that led to case breaks, but the same so-called outrage could also interfere with cases, depending on how circumstances manifested themselves.

"Maybe details should be released to renew public interest?" she asked.

"It's only been three months," he said, trying to reassure her.

"It feels like three years," Friday grumbled, rubbing her eyes with the back of her right hand.

"Ask me, releasing details is a mistake," Service said. "Details can make people flip out. It's a small miracle we've held all this so tight this long."

Helmi Yint stood before them, interrupting their conversation. "Sixty-seven was the worst," she said. "My brother drove snowplow for the county. Snow up to the bloody eaves by mid-December. We had to tunnel out to the bloody roads just to put the kiddies on the school bus. Stayed like that 'til well after April Fool's. Sixty-seven, she was a beast, eh."

Service looked up. Yint was sixty, a stout matron who had buried three husbands, all loggers, and, through it all, had somehow kept the small restaurant alive and raised seven children, all good kids.

"You hear 'bout Martine Lecair?" Helmi Yint casually asked Friday.

Friday shook her head.

"She just packed it in last week, took her twins out of school and skedaddled. Nobody knows where she went off to, or why. Good job like that—in the U.P.'s best school system, too. Makes no bloody sense. Why would she call her principal and tell him she was resigning for personal reasons? Just like that, done deal. I can't even imagine it. Had it too good, maybe, too easy—state insurance, union protecting your butt, summers off, all that good guv'mint candy. Not hard living like the rest of us up here, that's for sure."

White prejudice against tribals was a given, and Service knew there also was a certain degree of envy and jealousy for teachers in parts of the U.P., and statewide. The same held true for state employees, who some citizens considered overpaid, underworked, and unduly pampered. *Citizen assholes.*

Service vaguely knew Martine Lecair—a pretty, vivacious woman about Friday's age.

"Guess that's how Indians are," Yint said. "State paid for her education with our tax money, and this is how she repays us?"

"I doubt it's personal," Friday said, her voice edged.

"Well, I *take* it personal," the restaurant owner said.

When they got up to leave the owner added, "Better put youse's chains on. When she gets this deep and wet early, youse'll need chains to move around. That's how it was in '67. Youse could hear chains on the roads in the middle of the day—like bloody ghosts in some cheap movie. It got spooky, I can tell youse. And here it is snowing again, and it ain't yet Halloween."

In the entryway they bumped into Trooper Harry Yawkey, a longtime road patrol officer.

"Road conditions?" Friday asked him.

"Salt and sand down, and not too bad yet, but getting there, eh. She's been pretty quiet. Last night there was a helluva fight at Tooley's, no permanent damage, human or property, but Kline had to taze *and* gas some jerkbait from Traverse City."

Felton Kline was a Negaunee city cop in his early sixties, an amiable man who could usually small-talk troublemakers out of bad intentions.

"Guy was playing grab-ass with one of the local ladies and her old man took exception and the scrap was on. I backed him up," Yawkey said with a laugh. "Hey, who knew the human head could hold *that* much snot."

"Sunny days and cloudy days," Friday said, "and they've each got their points."

"True that. You hearing they might cut some Troop detective positions?" Yawkey asked bluntly.

"Nah, they'll go for road cops first, especially in low-crime areas, Harry. Like here."

It was sometimes argued privately in Lansing and around Michigan that state troopers in the U.P. had much smaller workloads than their counterparts below the bridge in major population areas.

The Troop started to say something, but Friday stopped him. "Go home, Harry. You old road toads need all the sleep you can get."

"You develop anything yet on them girls you found skinned?" he asked.

"*Nobody* got skinned," Friday said forcefully.

"You know how rumor runs," the Troop said, unsympathetically. "Hell, given that Halloween's coming, I figured you'd do something to try to pre-empt the annual shitstorm."

Outside in the snow Friday looked at Grady Service. "Annual shitstorm? Do you know what he's alluding to?"

"Probably nothing," Service said. So far the dogman thing had not crept into the public light, and Denninger had gotten nowhere in her investigation of the bounty rumor. He still had not mentioned any of that stuff to Friday, or anything except the large wolf tracks near the crime scene.

"The transverse of 'probably nothing' is, inferentially, 'possibly *something*,'" she said. "You want to spill?"

"Nothing to share."

"Do I detect an implied *yet?*"

"If and when there's something of substance, you'll know right away."

"You promise?"

"Hell, yes."

"Snow's bad. You want to bunk with Shigun and me tonight?"

"Nobody to take care of Newf and Cat," he said.

"Dog, cat, kid, us—we need to tie us a damn knot of some kind and stop living like a coupla half-ass Hipsy-Gyps. You love me or not?"

"You know I do."

"Say it out loud like a big boy."

"When you're forced to say it, it doesn't mean as much."

"Humor me and say it anyway."

"I love you."

"And you want to jump my bones."

"*That's* a fact."

She patted his face. "Another time. It's not safe to fool around and drive when it's snowing."

"I never heard that before."

"Well, you can't say that anymore. How about we get together this weekend?"

"Another meeting?"

"Not the kind we just had," she said. "I suggest you rest up, Bucko. We are *way* overdue."

He started to ask her about Martine Lecair, but she'd shown no real interest. By contrast, he heard alarm bells in his head, though he had no idea why.

Knot. She means damn marriage? He suddenly felt light-headed, wondered why his legs felt shaky.

7

Tuesday, October 21

MANITU RIDGE, BARAGA COUNTY

The Lanse Indian Reservation was near L'Anse, the Baraga County seat. Some tribal members lived near Zeba on the east side of the bay, but most were on the west side, near Assinins, north of Baraga. A small, largely unknown concentration lived southwest of Baraga near a place called Manitu Ridge, which some locals called Old Indiantown, though, as Service understood it, the name lacked any current official (or historical) standing. Ramshackle houses were spread out along the rim of a steep canyon with the Blood River meandering below toward Lake Superior. Little or no Keweenaw Bay tribal casino money reached Ridge residents, and from what Service had heard, this was a bone of contention among some.

Sergeant Willie Celt had called that morning. "You know that thing Denninger's been trying to run down for you?" the sergeant asked Grady Service.

"Yeah."

"Word is you might want to talk to Kelly Johnstone up to Manitu Ridge."

"That can't be good," Service said.

"Is what it is, man. Denninger says she'll go with you, if you want."

"I'll give her a bump. Thanks."

"Who pinpointed Johnstone?" he asked Denninger when he reached her cell phone.

"Willie heard it from his cousin in Ontonagon County."

"The bounty thing is spreading?"

"Until Willie called me, I hadn't heard anything but the talk back in August and September, which I couldn't pin down. Willie said he heard Johnstone knows something about Martine Lecair cutting out."

Service had been troubled by Helmi Yint's odd news about the teacher, Martine Lecair, and had let all Upper Peninsula COs know they should listen for any information on the Indian woman, or the dogman bounty.

"I hate rumors up here," he said. "They either turn into a goddamn crown fire, or smolder underground for months, waiting to blow up."

"Don't whine," Denninger said. "Rumor is an integral part of the human condition."

"You sound like a bluehair know-it-all," he said.

"Whatever," she said.

"You know Johnstone?"

"Yeah. I don't think our souls meshed."

"Welcome to a big club," Service replied. "She's not overly friendly. I've sort of known her for a long time, but last time I dealt with her was five or six years back, and she was downright nasty." Kelly Johnstone served as the unofficial leader of the descendants of an alleged band who insisted their ancestors had lived since eternity on the Manitu Ridge property, separate from the Keweenaw Bay people, therefore constituting their own separate and distinct tribe, culturally, historically, and genetically. As far as Service knew, history didn't support such a claim, but Johnstone and her followers resolutely continued to press their right to separate federal recognition, presumably to make way for their own casino and its dedicated profit stream. Assuming there would be profit. From what Service had heard from various feds, only about one in twelve Indian casinos made money.

"What's the Lecair woman got to do with the gork case?" Service asked.

"Dunno," Denninger said.

One look at the Ridge made most people shake their heads. Why anyone *ever* gathered to live up here made no sense. How they eked out a living was even more difficult to discern. The Ridge, as it was known, was a distinctly depressing place, as bad in some ways as the Cass Corridor in Detroit.

Johnstone lived in two house trailers joined together by a jury-rigged communal room with a huge woodstove.

Ridge people heated with wood they cut for themselves, which is why huge forest areas near the community were long gone, which led to bank erosion and an inordinate number of fires in dwellings. Fresh snow covering the abundant flotsam and jetsam made the area look almost pristine and pure, which was an illusion.

Service knocked on the door and waited with Denninger. There was a small leather bag on the door knocker, the bag decorated with dyed porcupine quills and some black feathers. *What the hell is that about,* he wondered; *some kind of weird symbol?*

Although Johnstone lacked any formal education, she always struck Service as wise, practical, tough, and street-smart. She definitely seemed to have the respect of the people she led. Her age was impossible to guess.

This high on the rim of the Ridge, the snow was heavier than it was two hundred feet lower; window and door screens were still up, and snow and wind had combined to create odd-shaped sculptures on them.

"We've got our *own* tribal game wardens," Johnstone greeted him when she pulled open the door. "You got no jurisdiction here."

Great start, Service thought. *Why does she come out swinging?*

"Dial it down, Johnstone. You don't have federal recognition, and this area isn't even part of the Keweenaw Bay property that does, so you're subject to state law and peace officers here."

"You'll address me as Chairman."

"Okay, *Chairman* Johnstone," Service said, "we'll play it your way." *For now.*

"What the hell do you want?" the woman asked, ignoring Denninger.

"Mind if we come in?"

"No, I got the flu," she countered.

"You want us to call a doctor?" Denninger asked in a saccharine voice.

"I want you to mind your own damn business, girlie. I can take care of myself." Johnstone started to close the door, but Service boot-blocked her.

"The air out there is cold," Johnstone complained.

"This won't take long," Service said. "We heard Martine Lecair packed up her kids, quit her job in Negaunee, and left the area. Any idea why, or where she went?" Later he would be asking himself why he had thrown Lecair into the mix right away. He would never find a satisfactory answer other than some weird instinctive thing that pushed the words past his inner filter before he could think them through.

"That ain't the business of no white woods cop."

Still in my face. "We're curious—and a little concerned."

"I guess you heard what curiosity killed."

He could hardly believe what he was hearing. "Are you threatening us, Chairman Johnstone?"

"Just stating facts," she said. "Private people's business is private. This ain't your business."

"Her job and all . . . I just wondered about the suddenness, you know—if she's all right? She's not in some kind of trouble, is she?"

"No more'n anybody else," Johnstone said, flashing a crooked eye.

Fear? Anger? He couldn't read her with any precision. "We're not butting in. Just wondering if we can help."

"Can't help you," the woman said.

Can't or won't? No idea where she went?"

"She don't live here," Johnstone said. "People are free to choose, run their own lives how they see fit."

More attitude. When disaster struck, Indian survivors sometimes claimed that events had "overwhelmed" them, a Native American version of "Shit happens." The inference seemed clear: So much in life was beyond one's control; why even think about the future? Live for now, not tomorrow. It was an alien way of thinking for some whites, and a reminder that dealing with tribals was often complicated, and almost always frustrating. Hell, he could even sympathize with them.

"Heard rumors the tribal council's wanting to hire you when you retire from the state," Johnstone said.

"I heard that, too. But you know how rumors are."

"Rumors that stay around usually have some truth to them," Johnstone said. "Good you keep that in mind."

"What about the rumor of a bounty on a dogman? You hear that one?"

"Go away," the woman said, and stepped back.

Getting nowhere, being stonewalled, and she just tried to bribe me in a very subtle way. "All right, we'll be getting along. Thanks for your time. Hope you feel better."

"Will or won't," Johnstone said. "Have to deal with what is, not how we want things to be. Hope don't help nobody."

He sensed that perhaps she was trying to tell him something without saying it, and this seemed out of character for the uber self-contained Kelly Johnstone. *Or did I imagine it?*

As they walked toward their trucks, Service asked Denninger for her impressions.

"A prickly, rude bitch."

"You get the sense she was trying to tell us something?"

"You mean, like, we should go fuck a rolling donut? That sort of thing?"

"Not quite," he said. "When we pull out, I'm going just beyond the county road. I'll pull down a two-track and walk back so I can see her trailer. You want to pull off further east and wait for me to bump you?"

"You think something's up?"

"Not sure." His gut was churning. He thought of the old cop joke about how much you could learn about paranoia by following people around.

Having walked back to the woods near the street with Johnstone's trailer, he watched the house, wiggling his toes in his boots to keep his circulation flowing, making a mental note to switch to heavier insulation tomorrow.

Suddenly, Johnstone was outside her trailer. She got into an old Jeep, started it, and hurtled down the street. He called Denninger on the 800-megahertz. "Rusty brown Jeep rolling your way. It's her."

"You want me to follow?"

"Keep it soft." Too closely, and Johnstone would get spooked.

"On it, Twenty Five Fourteen. You heading for Houghton?"

"Right now," he said. He could hardly wait to see his granddaughter, Maridly.

He telephoned his late son's girlfriend, Karylanne Pengelly. "I'm leaving L'Anse. You need grocks or anything?"

"No, thanks, we're all set. Want to talk at your granddaughter?"

"Put her on."

He heard the phone fumbled, then an exuberant shout, "MY BAMPY!!" He hated the moniker, but Little Maridly refused to change it, being every bit as stubborn as her namesake, Maridly Nantz.

"Hey, rugrat."

"You *gut* anything today, Bampy?"

He had taught the little girl to fish, and she loved watching him clean out the guts. He had no idea why. "Just a dragon," he said. "But he was just a little sucker."

"Ain't no dragons," Maridly said resolutely.

"That's right."

"But they's dogmen," she added.

"What did you just say?"

"Dogmen—but they ain't bad, just scary. Dogs are nice, Bampy."

"*Aren't*, not ain't."

"I like *ain't* better."

"Who told you about dogmen?"

"Dunno," she said. "I just know, *okay?* Mum, Bampy's being a *cranky*-pants."

"Are you being cranky?" Pengelly asked, coming back on the line.

"What the hell is that baloney about a dogman?"

"Somebody reported something up in Keweenaw County. Everybody around here is talking about it. It's just talk," she said with a dismissive laugh. "You know how it is in these parts."

She was too green and positive in her outlook to understand what "just talk" could signal, and lead to, in the Upper Peninsula.

Denninger called as he drove into Houghton. "Johnstone drove to Baraga, went into the hardware, was there twenty-seven minutes, came out with several packages, and drove directly back to her house. I'm taking my horsie to her barn," she added.

"Thanks," he said.

"You want me on her regularly?"

"Just a drive-by now and then, see how much time she's away or there."

"Clear."

8

Wednesday, October 22

TWENTY POINT POND

"Your girlfriend got an amended report," Denninger said out of the blue. Service had asked her to meet him at the crime site again.

"When?"

"She called me this morning, asked me to ask you to call her."

"I guess you took your own damn time about telling me," he said.

She batted her eyes and vamped. "Yeah, I guess I kinda, sorta did."

"What about the report?"

"Only two DNAs."

He shrugged, thought. *Shit.*

"Remember what Sherlock Holmes said."

"I'd guess whatever the guy with the pen put in his yap," Service replied. "Holmes wasn't real. What's the point of tying up your vicks if you're not going to play hide-the-sausage?"

"Uh, you may be so advanced in age that you've forgotten condoms?" she quipped.

"Bullshit. Two DNAs: This case is going nowhere."

"The two DNAs are Native Americans, eighteen to twenty-two."

This caught his attention. "Doc Tork was right."

"Going nowhere is going somewhere," Denninger said.

"What the hell does *that* mean?"

"I don't see locals for this," she said.

"Like *that* narrows the field."

"It's a start, and we know from history that granks don't stop. There will be more bodies. We can count on it."

"Not us; Friday. This is *her* case. We don't want a damn thing to do with it." Service touched the tip of his forefinger to his forehead. "*Septum pellucidum,*" he said.

He'd read a book called *Ecstasy of Joy Touch: Fixing the Self.* This had been right after Maridly and Walter were murdered. He couldn't sleep then, needed something to help him face reality, and not booze, his old man's choice for comfort. He'd played with the Joy Touch technique, and it had helped him when his stress levels went up. It had been a while since he'd felt the need.

"Pudendum *what?* What the hell does that mean?" Denninger asked.

Service explained how the brain had pleasure centers, and how you had to imagine petting them.

"If you say so," Denninger said, smiling.

"The report—that's all Friday had for me?"

"Oh, I think she also said something about going to Grand Rapids."

"When?"

"Today, I think. I don't think she gave me an ETA."

"Did she say she wants me to go along?" he asked.

"Not sure," Denninger said, still smiling.

Service touched his forehead again, said, "Repairing damage."

Denninger quickly added, "She said something about how there's a substantial population of Indians in GR, including some of the former Ridge crowd."

He kept his finger on his head, pressing gently, a neuronal solderer run amok.

"You ever worry about short-circuiting that thing?" Denninger asked him.

"Happens regularly," he said. "It's part of the ritual."

Denninger's face lit up at the same time the thought struck Service.

"Did you say *ritual?*" she asked.

He nodded.

"Not trying to hide their identities," she yelped. "He took their heads, hearts, and hands . . . It's got to be some kind of ritual shit."

"Religious or psycho?" he countered, thinking about what they were saying and seeing no way to connect it to *any* kind of reality.

"That must be one hell of a channel you tune into," she said.

"It used to have great cartoons, old-timeys, not the goody-two-shoes kids' crap on TV nowadays. Or, the killer wants us to *think* it's ritual," he said.

"Times change, Rainman."

"Price is right, though. Keep your knees together and your mind on Jesus, my girl."

"Thank you for your advice, Sergeant."

"Not sergeant anymore," he said. "Just officer, same as you. I'm back in the Mosquito."

"Since when?"

"Late August."

"No fake? Nothing was announced."

"Bearnard Quinn moved to my old job, and Wildlife Resource Protection doesn't want dinosaurs, so here I am."

"Wow," Denninger said. "Welcome back to the working world."

• • •

He was headed back to Marquette and about to call Friday when Gunny Prince bumped him on his cell phone. "Got a lead, but it's thin as rabbit skin. Still, might could be something. Fella in Wayland, Michigan, claims he sold two M40s to a man name of Bird in Grand Rapids. I called Bird. He claimed the weapons were stolen last June."

"He file a police report?"

"Don't sound like it. The guy in Wayland is named Dog. You want his and Bird's addresses, phones?"

"Shoot."

Service pulled over and wrote the information in his notebook. "Thanks, Gunny; I owe you."

"Wayland near you?"

"Just south of Grand Rapids," Service said, "a long way from here."

He punched in Friday's speed-dial number. "You want company?"

"It's not your case," she said.

He explained about the guns and Gunny Prince's call.

"Dog and Bird," Friday said. "Too weird. I'll meet you up at Slippery Creek. Can you be there in an hour? I'll have my sis fetch Newf and Cat tonight and take them to her place with Shigun."

He was home in fifty-one minutes flat and found Friday playing with Newf, while the foul-tempered cat hissed disapproval from a distance.

"Denninger tell you the revised lab results?" Friday asked.

"She did. Could the explanation for all this be some sort of ritual?"

Friday stared at him. "I thought the same thing from the start. But what?"

"Point is," Service said, "maybe this guy's ignoring cops, doing his own thing, whatever the hell that means. It doesn't feel religious or psycho. Not quite."

"Maybe that makes some sense," she said. "Go pack and let's roll. We can talk on the way."

II

9

Thursday, October 23

GRAND RAPIDS, KENT COUNTY

Service knew Friday was having trouble getting the Indian connection out of her mind. There was no known connection between the dead women and Martine Lecair, the missing woman who wasn't even officially missing. She still had no clue who the Jane Running Does were, the term a joke courtesy of Kristy Tork. Granks, gorks, and Jane Running Does. Cops and MEs were subject to jaundiced views of life and humanity, and talked their own pidgin—a lingo that blended all sorts of odd connections, making it the ultimate hybrid, with virtually no sensitivity.

Why had Lecair boogied so suddenly, and does it even matter? The question remained, its relevance not at all clear to either of them.

They had driven to Gaylord the night before and stayed over in the Alpine Inn, and this morning, when her mind was briefly off business, they had made love like a normal couple. Breakfast was two Sausage McMuffins on the fly south. Back to normal.

"The guns you and Denninger found. What caliber?"

"Three oh eight."

"Is that good?"

He looked over at her. "What the hell do you mean, *good?*"

She rolled her eyes. "You know."

"Calibers aren't good or bad."

"Well, I'm sure not gonna *guess,*" Friday said.

"Tuesday," he said sharply.

"*What?*"

"You're in that zone you get into."

"I am?"

"You asked if the caliber was *good.*"

"I did?"

"Yes."

"What's the answer?"

"There isn't one."

She threw up her hands. "There ya go!"

There was no point trying to wedge her out of this. It would just take time for her to drift back to some semblance of physiological and intellectual reality. Not that this jaunt would give them any answers about the cases, but if they were lucky, they might start homing in on better questions.

Indians had their own word-of-mouth and cell-phone communications network, the modern version of smoke signals, and they used this to track comings and goings of relatives and friends who might be hundreds or even thousands of miles away. Tribals might not talk about what they knew to outsiders, especially cops, but they *would* know. Of that he was pretty damn certain. *The arrogant little twerp who invented Facebook could have used Indian commo as his damn model.*

The Grand Rapids Inter-Tribal Council Center was in the hilly north-west part of the city, a depressed zone with boarded storefronts, iron bars over blacked-out windows, and broken streetlights. The center was in a block-long brick building that appeared in another life to have been a school. There were no pedestrians on the street and no traffic. Cold air, but no snow. The last ground snow had been in Gaylord. A couple hundred miles made a dramatic difference in weather and weather patterns, he knew. It made an even greater difference culturally.

A half-dozen pickups and beat-up vans were parked in a narrow strip of unpaved lot between the street and the building. Everything in sight needed paint. With the economy the way it was, nationally and in the state, he doubted anybody would be slinging paint anytime soon. They stopped at a reception desk to receive directions from an old woman with an enormous head and stringy gray hair that looked like it had never been brushed.

Early evening and the door was closed and it was dark inside. Friday leaned against a wall to wait. Service, being impatient and nosy, followed sound up to a second-floor gym where several men were gathered in the middle of the floor whacking huge drums with padded paddles. Now and then they chanted and sang a cappella. If there were words here, he couldn't make them out, but the sound made him think of a line from a song: "Sing a boop boop aboopa lopa lum bam boom!" He loved Sheb Wooley and "Purple People Eater," and the drums for some reason made him think of it.

Though there were no words, the beat of the drums and the starkness of the voices gave him a chill.

Friday waggled a finger from the gym door and he followed her.

Downstairs she said to the big-headed woman, "Rose Monroe's not in her office."

"I coulda told you that," the woman said.

"But you didn't."

"What you asked was, 'Where's Rose Monroe's office?' and I told you. You never asked if she was in it."

Service fought a grin. One of the first rules for copdom: ATRFQ. Ask the Right Fucking Question. This could be even more important in dealing with tribals, with whom the road tended toward strict cultural construction-ism of the passive-aggressive school.

"Is Ms. Monroe available?" Friday asked.

"No, she ain't."

"Will she be available later today?"

"She don't leave no schedule for nobody, her being honcho, and all." After a pause the woman said, "I'm Rose Monroe."

Friday and Service sighed and gave her their cards.

Service guessed she had played dumb to buy some time in order to find out about Friday. The issue was why, especially with no apology forthcoming for anything that had gone on earlier that day.

She led them to her office and opened the door. "You two are a long way from home," Monroe began.

Friday said, "I'm not even sure you can help us. You're very much of a long shot, or a blind stab."

Monroe said, "Sometimes we find ourselves doing things without know-ing the reasons why. That doesn't make them wrong."

"We had two murders in August," Friday said. "Two young women in their late teens. We haven't been able to identify them, and we still have the remains. DNA confirms they're Native American. I asked around up there, but got no leads. Nobody seems to know anything, but I'm thinking your organization has a lot of extended kin to our local folks, and I heard there were some Ridge people down here, so here we are, asking for help. One of the dead girls has a tattoo on the back of her calf—a bear or a dog. Our medical examiner thinks it's a bear, but I don't know. I have a picture."

She dug in her purse, handed the photo to Monroe, who looked at it without expression. "You got pictures of the dead girls' faces?"

"No," Friday said.

"Woulda been a lot cheaper to call me," the woman said.

"The truth is, we're desperate," Friday said. "I really want to get closure for two families."

Monroe looked skeptical. "Just what is it you think I can do?"

"Help us identify the girls, get them to their families."

"They're not from here."

Service thought: *Way too fast an answer.*

Friday was on top of it. "How can you know that?"

"I make it my job to keep track of our people," Monroe said.

Service guessed the woman was buying more time, trying to think about what she would say next, and he was trying to figure out why.

Monroe said, "Now that there's legalized gambling, most tribes see each other as competitors at best, enemies at worst. The truth is, there's not that much contact anymore, at least not like in the old days. We're going backwards in inter- and intratribal relations."

Friday said nothing, and Service knew she was letting silence work for her.

Monroe said, "What you're asking for isn't easy. Like I said, things are changin' in our community."

Use of the word *community* made Service grumpy. Nowadays everyone had a community, even men born with single testicles who loved grape-stomping on surfboards while shooting water pistols at rubber duckies in a three-foot surf. *Crap.*

Tuesday Friday asked, "What would *you* do? I don't want to leave those girls unburied."

"There're worse things," Monroe said.

"Do you want to hear where we are in our investigation?"

"If you like."

Service thought: *Weird response,* but he wasn't in second-guessing mode. Friday needed to play this thing out, and he listened as she gave her report, omitting only a few details.

Report done, Monroe asked, "No other problems?"

"What sort?"

"You'd know," Monroe said mysteriously, and quickly added, "I'll do what I can for you."

"Not expecting miracles. I just can't get those kids out of my mind. I feel like it's my obligation to close the case and find out what happened."

"How far are you willing to go?" Rose Monroe asked.

"We're here."

• • •

Service left the meeting with Friday feeling unsettled.

Before leaving, Rose Monroe had said, deadpan, "Some of life's hardest journeys aren't measured in miles."

10

Thursday, October 23

GRAND RAPIDS

It has been a long day and now it was night. Carnelian Bird, the man who claimed to have bought the sniper rifles and subsequently had them stolen, lived in a rambling old house across from the John Ball Park Zoo. His yard needed mowing and contained numerous signs: GUNOWERS HASS RITES. NO COMMIES OR SOLIKICITORS! TRESPASSIDERS WILL BE SHOT ON SIDE. The signage made Service shake his head. He ran into illiterates a half-dozen times a year, mostly older folks, sixty and up. It always jarred him.

He had called Bird's phone number, the one he'd gotten from Gunny Prince, gotten an answering machine, which said only: "Leave message." Service had done so, knowing it was probably a waste of time to try to see the man, but being this close, he hated to lose the chance, however remote.

"You think he's here?" Friday asked.

"Not until I saw all the signs. I'm guessing this is his fortress, and he doesn't evacuate the ramparts too often."

"Or go anywhere unarmed?" she said.

"Never unarmed," Service agreed.

The door opened even before Service could knock, and a cadaverous face stared out the cracked door at him. "You that cop what called?" the face asked.

Service nodded.

"Got ID?"

Service dug out his ID and badge and held them up.

"What's *your* name?" Service asked. *Two could play this game.*

"Bird."

"Carnelian Bird?"

The man nodded cautiously.

"Let me see your ID," Service commanded, reversing circumstances, and momentum.

"I don't carry it around."

"Go get it. We'll wait."

The man looked sickly and had a tremoloish, irritating voice, but shuffled back with a state ID card.

"What about your operator's license?"

"This is all I got. It's legal, right?"

People showing state ID cards often had had their driving privileges and licenses suspended, or had other legal problems. Service nodded. "You want to step outside with us?"

"Gon' stay right where I am, sir."

"Why not step out where we can talk?"

"See that place acrosst road?" Bird asked.

Service nodded.

"They let them wild animals out at night, and they prowl all over the neighborhood. All them cougars that folks talk about on the Internet? Believe you me: That right over there's your source."

Service thought about taking exception but looked into the man's eyes and saw that he wasn't all there. "Have you had problems with the animals?"

"Not so far, but then they know I know they be out there. I hear them roaring all night."

"Have they hurt anyone?"

"Nobody talks about it. It's a government conspiracy. You ask questions, the IRS will rain all over your parade."

"Have you had legal problems, Mr. Bird?" Service asked.

"Never," the man said. "Never never never, 'cause I ain't stupid, see? You piss off cops here, they haul your ass away at night." He made a slitting motion with his thumb across his neck.

Whackadoodledandy. "You have evidence of that?"

The man tapped his head. "I know what I know."

Service looked over at Friday, who remained remarkably expressionless.

"Mr. Bird, you bought two M40 rifles from a Mr. Truffle Dog, is that so?"

"Never heard of nobody named Dog."

"He claims he sold you two rifles," Service lied.

"Whoever he is, he's a damn liar."

"Mr. Bird, we're going to run a background check on you. If there's anything you need to tell me, now would be the time to step up."

"Step up ta what?"

"Like, if you're a paroled felon and possess firearms in violation of the terms of your parole."

"Din't I just tell you I ain't bought no guns from Dog?"

"You say that like you know the man."

The man blinked fiercely. "Hey, it's a common name, ain't it, like Smith! Check the dictionary, *Webster's New Codge,* an' like that."

"But you just said you never heard of anyone named Dog."

"Everydamnbody's *heard* of dogs, so I guess they've all heard the goddamned name. You paying attention? I just don't know no individual goes by that pa'tic'lar name. What's the problem here?"

"I'm trying to find the owner of those rifles."

"Why's that?"

"Well, they were recovered under suspicious circumstances."

The man looked surprised. "You saying they was found?"

"They seemed to be in the possession of two individuals, who were found dead."

"I don't know them girls," Bird said.

"I never said anything about girls."

"Young women, girls, same thing. Why this hassle?"

Uh-oh. Time to tighten the clamps. "Mr. Bird, if your attitude doesn't change pretty damn quick, we're going to call the Grand Rapids police and haul you downtown for a formal interview relative to two homicides."

"*Homo-sites?*" the man said, his jaw sagging.

"Brutal murders," Tuesday Friday added.

Bird stepped outside, both legs in metal braces. *Polio at some point?* Service guessed. *Something like that.* The man was stooped, used two wrist canes.

"You want to sit down?" Friday asked.

He rattled a cane. "These don't make me no damn invalid."

"I didn't mean to suggest that."

"Sure you did. They all do."

The eponymous *They.*

Service said. "Let me see your ID again."

The man handed it to him. Fifty-one years old, and the description fit, but he looked a lot older than his age. Service handed the ID card to Friday, who headed for her vehicle to run Carnelian Bird through her computer.

"Hey, you, gimme my ID back."

"You'll get it," Service said.

"I didn't know them girls," Bird said.

"No?"

"They was Dog's," the man answered, his voice reduced to a raspy whisper, his breath coming in bursts. The man was afraid. Service's instincts told him Friday was going to come back with some sort of shit on Bird, and he was turning cooperative in the hopes of softening the blow. "Okay if I call you Carnelian?"

"Carnie," the man corrected him.

"*What* two girls, Carnie?" Service asked.

"Sluts, I just tol' you: Dog's sluts. I don't drive no more. Can't work pedals, and I can't afford no fancy electronic gizmos and such. I'm on a fixed income. Besides, OWG has got tracking devices in all the cars of the handicapped, so they can keep track of them for the day."

What day? "Fixed income, as in Social Security?"

"And military."

"You were military?"

"Gunner on a Huey in Desert Storm, Eye-rack." He tapped one of his braces. "Them's what I got out of the war—hamburgered my motherfuckin' legs, and three friggin' Purple Hearts is all they give me, which ain't worth shit-all."

"You never heard the girls' names?"

"No."

"Can you describe them for me?"

"Whores, small, short black hair. Painted themseffs with the makeup of fallen doves."

Friday came back and Service leaned over. "There's an 'Officer Caution' on him," she whispered. "Felon: Exercise extreme caution. He did a major stretch for aggravated assault on a cop."

Service turned back to the man. "You armed, Carnie?"

"Jes' a lil' ole scattergun inside the door is all."

Which he wasn't allowed to have. "No handguns?"

"Not on me. I ain't licensed to carry."

"Have you tried to get a license?"

"Wouldn't do me no damn good."

"Why's that?"

"Army retired me on account o' my legs, and said my brain was totally fucking Mixmastered permanent, but that ain't true. They just wanted me out so I wouldn't tell the truth about the war. OWG, man: Those fuckers are behind *everything*."

OWG meant One World Government, a favorite conspiracy theory of the extreme political right lunatic fringe. It included government men in black helicopters and a plan for the United Nations to take over the world. Service had some international-relations thoughts of his own and wanted to point out to Bird that China already pretty much owned the US through debt, but he avoided the tangent.

"Did Dog know the girls before the gun show?"

"Hafta ast him," Bird said.

"These girls . . . they have any birthmarks, tattoos, anything special?" Service asked.

"Not that I seen. Ast Dog. I think he seen all of 'em, if you know what I mean."

"What did you drive to Kalamazoo?"

"Dodge truck with a camper in the bed."

"You stayed all night?"

The man nodded.

"The girls too?"

"I went to dinner with some of them showpeople, and the sluts stayed with Dog. Never saw them when I got back, nor the next day neither."

"You bought guns from him?"

"I guess, mebbe."

"M40s?"

"Damn right, with night scopes. For them damned beasts over'n to zoo. Man got right to po-tackshun."

"But the rifles were stolen?"

"Girls weren't there when I come back from dinner, Dog was drunk, and them guns was gone. I never even got 'em home."

The man named Dog had been drunk? "How much did you pay?"

"A grand each, cash, but Dog threw in beaucoup ammo."

"You've got a receipt?"

Carnelian Bird laughed. "Ain't no receipts for cash deals at gun swaps."

"Dog give you an explanation for the guns being gone?"

"I ax him, but he beat on me so bad, I just shut up. He said cunts done runned off with them, but I'm thinkin' he give them rifles to them to pay for they pussies."

"And you didn't call the cops?"

"They'd just pinch me. They all out to get me."

"I'm not," Service said.

"We done only just met," the man countered glumly.

Service looked at Friday, who shrugged.

"You know you can't possess firearms with your record."

"Don't got more. They got stole, 'member?"

"You have a shotgun inside the doorway."

"Since when is a shotgun a firearm?" the man shot back.

Service poked Friday, and they backed off the porch and headed for their vehicle; then he turned around and went back to the house momentarily, came out to the car, and got in.

Friday drove down the block and parked. "Boy," she said. "We probably ought to take a look around for Mr. Truffle Dog. Why'd you go back?"

"Had one more question; I asked him again about the tattoos—if either of the girls had a tattoo that looked like a dog or bear. He said one of them did. On her ankle."

Friday looked at him and raised an eyebrow. "Can this actually be working in our favor?"

• • •

Dog's house turned out to be a trailer southwest of Wayland, on pancake farmland in a sea of plowed cornfields. There were half a dozen chained, barking dogs near the house, and no signs of two-legged life.

Friday called the Wayland Troop post on her cell and talked to someone. Service didn't catch the name and could hear only her side of the conversation, which was short on information. Minutes later a Blue Goose slid up beside them. A female Troop got out. She had a long, splashy, bright red ponytail and extraordinarily long fingernails that glowed.

"Name's Delay," she said, introducing herself. "Lindsay."

"Friday, CO Service. You know Truffle Dog?"

"Prince of slimeballs. We know that fool, call him T.D., Total Dickhead."

"Got a history, does he?"

"Long as a giraffe's dick. Violent SOB, loves his guns. Funny how often those two marry up."

"Wife, family?"

"Nah. Was a time he had two little girls around here, but just for a year or two—his sister's spawn, I think. She was off serving a year plus for meth manufacture, and the kids landed with him."

"Arranged and approved by Social Services?"

Lindsay Delay laughed out loud. "Truffle Dog's an Indian, Detective. He doesn't willingly cooperate with or even recognize white government agencies."

"We are to tribals what OWG is to some whites," Service offered.

Delay nodded. "I hear that."

"Indian from where?" Friday asked.

The Troop shrugged. "Wherever he wants. Tends to move around."

"Somebody got names on the two girls, photos, anything? Details on him, what he drives, anything?"

"Probably in his jacket back in the barn," Delay said. "You want me to call my sarge, ask him to open files for you?"

"We'd appreciate it."

"Not a problem," the officer said, and went back to her patrol vehicle.

• • •

Delay's sergeant was a light-colored, wizened Hispanic man who looked like his last meal had been several years before. His uniform hung off him like a flour sack. The whites of his eyes were yellow and pink.

The officers introduced themselves. "Old T.D. up to tricks?" Sergeant Alizondo asked.

"Not sure yet."

Service looked through the jacket with Friday perched by his shoulder. "Seems to have spent about half his life inside," Service said.

"Most like him get taken out of the gene pool somewhere along the way," Alizondo said, "but T.D., he seems to have some kind of protective mega-mojo whenever he's inside."

"Mojo?"

"Inmates call him Spook-man."

"You guys know he was dealing weapons?"

"No, but then, nothing about that fool comes as a surprise."

Service leafed through more pages. "Not exactly pedaling guns legally," he told Friday. She said to the sergeant, "At one time he had two girls living with him. Are their names in the file?"

"Gotta fetch us a different jacket," the sergeant said, "but unless you have a warrant, I can't let you see what's in this next one. I *can* confirm the two girls were with him five years back. They were fourteen and fifteen, sisters. Kilani and Marlaeani Kit, his sister's daughters."

"Photos?"

"Can make you copies," the sergeant said. "But the photos are five years old, hear?"

"Were they placed with Dog by Social Services?"

"T.D. set that up on his own, and Social Services thought it was a sign he was turning his life around, so they let it ride."

"Your department squawk?"

"Shee-it. Why waste breath? Social Services does what it wants in this county."

"Any idea where the girls are now?"

"Can't help you. Try Social Services."

"No warrant to open doors."

"We all face challenges, and I don't make the rules," the sergeant said, and leaned over to them. "Social Services won't have no record on them girls. They washed they hands of all that, left them girls' fate to fate, hear?"

"Their fate may be that they were murdered," Friday said as the sergeant handed her some photocopies. She stared at them and passed them to Service. Neither of them could correlate the old photos with anything. Without heads, identification was going to approach the impossible.

"Social Services should have prints," Friday said.

"Prints for what? No hands. And maybe they'd cough up if we have a warrant," Service said. "I'm guessing. What we need is a break, not paperwork."

"What about the girls' mother?"

"Dead," the sergeant said. "Wrapped her car around a pole week after the State kicked her."

• • •

Later that night they drove back to the tribal center in Grand Rapids and found Rose Monroe walking away from the front door. The woman turned, scowled, and waved them away, but Service flashed his shield and she reluctantly turned around and unlocked the door.

"What is it you want now?" the woman asked.

Service explained about the girls, and at the end of his story showed her the photographs from the campground. The woman showed no visible emotion. "I can't help, and I got to close. We got rules."

"Think she recognized them?" Service asked as they drove away.

"Couldn't read her," Friday said. "Okay, now that this day is done, there's one lingering question," she said.

He looked over at her. Yeah?"

"Just how long *is* a giraffe's dick?"

The two of them brayed like mules.

11

Friday October 24

MACKINAW CITY, CHEBOYGAN COUNTY

It was after midnight. "So much for initiative," Friday said as she pulled into Mackinaw City off I-75. It had been snowing tapioca since Vanderbilt, and traffic had slowed to a crawl by the time they got to Indian River, thirty miles south of the straits. "I *hate* whiteouts," she carped, pulling up to the city police building. Signs on the bridge's approach announced it was closed, but not for how long. They went inside, brushing snow off their coats, and found Chief Minky Malette in his office on the phone. Malette waved for them to step in and sit, yelled at someone on the other end of the phone about closing the bridge, and how it had already made for trouble in town.

The chief hung up. "You two lost?"

"Stopping to get a room in the stable."

Malette guffawed. "Here? Dream on. We got no rooms left in town. You don't mind, though, I've got a holding cell. Use them for prisoners until we can ship them to Cheboygan, or wherever. Got two, and one's empty right now."

"Any port in a storm," Service said.

"I hate weather humor," Malette said.

"Good for local business, though."

"Screw the shopkeeps," the chief said. "They get profits, and we get to clean up behind the whole mess while the town fathers shrink our budgets every year."

Service called Station Twenty in Lansing to let the dispatchers know where he was, and Friday called her office in Negaunee.

Malette showed them into the cramped holding-cell area. One was occupied by a young woman with stringy black hair in a black leather skirt just short of the average male imagination.

"Like . . . you one of them or one of *us?*" the girl asked Friday.

"One of them," Friday said. "Above the bridge."

"That's cool," the girl said. "I stuck my old man in the kneecap with an icepick. Come home from work, see, and, like, I found him pounding doggy on my BFF? Guess I sorta freaked?"

"Should have stuck her instead," Service offered.

"Did," the girl said matter-of-factly. "Thirty-eighties, they tell me? I din't count, myseff? She, like, croaked? Minky, he say I murderize dat bitch?"

The girl looked fourteen, couldn't have been more than nineteen, definition of PWT. "Crime of passion," he told her. "It may not go so badly for you."

"But I done stuck dat ho thirty-eightie? You think dat a record? I ain't never made me no record? I get pissed, I ack out, they tell me? She fuck my ole man, she dis me, see what I'm sayin'?"

Indeed. The urban patois of a long-haul client of the state's social welfare system rolled off the girl's lips. Their fellow resident waved a piece of paper at Friday.

"You want see my baby? Like, they took her from me, dude. I miss my baby," she keened.

Friday looked frustrated and whispered to Service, "I gotta call my sis about the kid and the animals, and this is how bad my life's gotten, feeling bad for a hormonally driven teenage assassin. I sometimes disgust myself."

"Thanks?" the girl said to Service after Friday went to another room to make her call. "You want kneel down and pray thanks to the Big God Dude with me?" the girl asked.

"I don't think so."

The girl shrugged. "I always try to pray a lot?" she said. "I guess it just don't take. You want shove yo junk through them bars? I'll suck that big boy. I ain't much good at much, but I'm real good at that shit."

"Rain check," Service said with a wink, thinking, *This is a fellow earthling?* Someone leaving gorks in campgrounds, walking dead gorks in jail, bad omens everywhere for his granddaughter and Shigun. Thoughts of the future made him cringe for kids.

"But it's snowing and there ain't like nothing to do here, dude, sayin'?" the girl whined. "I guess I ain't so smart?"

"Thus endeth social intercourse," Service said.

The girl looked perplexed and grinned. "I know I know *dat* word, and I'm sure we ain't done that? Did we? But I guess we could?"

Service sighed and sat back. It was going to be a long night. More and more the world felt like it was on the verge of coming apart. Friday came back, rested her head on his shoulder, and was asleep before him.

12

Sunday, October 26

SLIPPERY CREEK CAMP

The recent snow was melting under an intense south wind, and Service was on the porch with Newf. Karylanne had brought his granddaughter down from Houghton. Friday and Shigun had come out from Harvey, and all of them had spent two days in some semblance of a family. It was early Sunday, and he and Little Maridly were making breakfast for the rest of the clan. Shigun, Friday's son, slept soundly like his mom. Maridly seemed to loathe sleep, a lot like her namesake.

The cell phone rang and Service had an inkling to let it go to a message, but after so many years of being available to others, he reluctantly answered.

"Grady, Lori. I'm very sorry to disrupt your pass time."

"I gave up trying to differentiate my time from the State's too long ago to remember," he said. "What's up, Governor?"

He'd met the governor years ago, when she was a state senator, just before she ran for the big job. They had been acquaintances since. Maybe even friends. The exact status seemed to vacillate, mostly based on his moods.

"I'm told that Tuesday's handling that ghastly case with the headless girls."

How does Lori know this? No details have been made public. Had this case climbed the State ladder up to the top?

"You want to talk to her?"

"No. I've been told you're also involved in the case."

"You know we don't handle homicides. I have what might be a possibly related weapons case, but we really don't know yet. *Possibly related* isn't the same as *related.*"

"I'm a lawyer: Don't split damn hairs, Grady. You hearing some dog-man talk up there—a reward, all that panic-the-public nutcase crap?" The governor was a member of the exclusive Huron Mountain Club and had a first-rate network of Yooper informants who kept her tuned in to goings-on above the bridge, politically and otherwise.

"Heard some," he said, "but it's been a while."

"What do you think?" the governor asked.

"Think about what?" *Why does she do this shit—come diving into law enforcement and cases without the slightest clue?* But he knew the answer: *She was in political hell, looking for anything to boost her basement-level public ratings.*

"Don't jerk me around," Governor Timms snapped at him. "I'm in no mood for your lip," she added.

"Okay," he said. "Here's my take: There's no such thing as a dogman, Sasquatch, skinwalker, vampire, werewolf, windigo, zombie, whatever. They are all total bullshit."

"Yet many people ardently believe in zombies and vampires," the governor countered.

"So what? They believe angels are real, too." Service affectionately patted his granddaughter's head and whispered, "Tell your mum and Tuesday and Shigun it's time to get out of bed. Breakfast on the table in ten minutes, max—and don't jump on Shigun," he added as she scampered away.

"Listen, Lori, people also believe in the damn Tooth Fairy, the Easter Bunny, and Santa Claus," he said in a whispered growl. "Belief does not bestow biological reality."

"The latter examples are benign, the former are not."

"They are *all* bullshit, Governor."

"All of those entities you mentioned," she said. "What do they have in common, Grady?"

"They're not real, and only kids, assholes, and jerks believe in them."

"You skipped over the fact that they are all animal forms."

"The Tooth Fairy and Santa Claus?"

"Don't quibble and don't patronize."

"I repeat: None of them are real, Governor."

"People *think* they're real, and perceptions matter. You're not listening to me, Officer Service."

"Because you're not making any goddamn sense, Governor. Your political advisors feeding you the dogman tidbits? Or did your people do a damn poll?"

"I did not call to debate or argue with you, Grady. I've talked to Chief Waco. You are to hunt down this creature, whatever and wherever it might be. And having located it, you will do whatever is necessary. Am I clear?"

"Because you and your crack political team have surgically parsed the situation and concluded a little crime might hurt your party's chances against the Republican candidate?"

The Republican candidate was a filthy-rich, squeaky-voiced man who had started chasing the office years before the election, spending millions of his own dollars, which disgusted Service. "Have you been drinking?" he jabbed for good measure. More and more it was becoming clear that buying political office was the route to power for some rich people.

"You fight dirty, Grady. You always go right for the throat. But this time that's good: I want you to go right for the throat of this damn thing, whatever it is. Find out who killed those women, and make it go away."

There was no turning her down if Chief Waco had already been pressured to sign on. "All right, but here's the deal: I pick who I need and want to help. And it's all on your budget bucks, not Chief Waco's."

"All right. Who are you thinking of?" she asked.

"My call, not yours," he told her.

"I'm just curious."

"Treebone, Glenn Noonan, and Allerdyce. Tree and Noonan used to be top detectives, and Limpy's the best man in the woods I know. Tree and Noonan will help Friday. Limpy and I will work our own angles. I shouldn't have to pull any other law enforcement," he added.

"You need more, you call them," she said. "You amaze me. You analyzed this and decided on a course in an instant. Your talents are wasted in the woods, Grady."

"Especially in a fricking, horseshit wild goose chase like this," he said. "My team, your budget, Governor."

"Carte blanche," she said. "Whatever and whoever you need. Just get that damn thing, fast. You have your orders," she concluded, and hung up.

Little Maridly was back beside him. "Was that Lori?" she asked

"It was."

"Is she coming to breakfast with us?"

"She'd like to, but she's busy ruining the state and forcing individual citizens to dive into trashbins."

"Is Lori the boss of me?" the girl asked.

"She thinks so."

The little girl's face hardened into a grimace. "I'm my *own* boss, Bampy."

"Good for you, hon. Your mum awake?"

"Yep, I jump-ed on her and tickle-ed her."

"Did she laugh?"

"No, she said a real bad word. Wanna hear me say it?"

"No." Grady Service smiled as Shigun came running from the bedroom, arms outstretched, and jumped to be caught. "Was Maridly nice to you when she woke you up?"

The boy smiled.

I've got the Mosquito Wilderness back and a great start on a patched-together family. Why the hell can't the governor mind her own damn business? Fucking dogman!

Karylanne and Friday padded in at the same time, both in long fuzzy robes and slippers, neither fully awake. Friday mumbled, "Coffee," and held out a cup. Karylanne did the same.

"We'll talk to you two when you get closer to the runway," Service told the women. To Maridly, "Get the platter. We've got to get food into these poor old women."

Ten minutes later the breakfast was on the table, and they were all working at it slowly. Service nodded for Friday to follow him to another room.

"I just got a call from Lori," he said when they were alone.

"I know. My boss called me from Lansing a few minutes ago, too."

"I didn't hear your phone."

"Vibrated. I'm leading the case, but you're going to work to find the so-called dogman angle. What the devil *is* a dogman?"

Service told her what he knew.

"You knew about this and never told me?" *She's pissed.*

"It seemed irrelevant. And still does. Hell, it *is* irrelevant. It's *bullshit.*"

Friday flashed a dark look. "Any chance said investigations will converge?"

"Only in our governor's zany political fantasy world."

"What else have you withheld?" she asked.

Service got his cell phone, pulled up a photo of the tracks he and Denninger had found near Twenty Point Pond.

Friday raised an eyebreow. "And *that* would be?"

"We're not sure," he said. "Could be a humongous wolf track."

"A wolf is like a dog, right?" she asked.

"This is *not* a dogman," he insisted.

"Then what is it?"

"I don't know yet."

"When will you know?" she pressed.

"I don't know."

"You haven't even started to try to find out, have you?"

"I have to do some thinking on it," he said.

"Where was that damn track?"

"By the rifle cache."

"And you never said *anything.*"

"Seriously, I didn't see a connection, and I still don't. Did Forensics find any animal evidence on the vicks?"

"No," she said.

"There you go."

"But the governor thinks differently."

"She wants me to hunt the dogman, which does not exist," he said. "It's all political posturing—all PR."

"So why does she want you chasing a phantom?"

"Our governor has gotten it into her mind that this thing is theoretically an animal, which drops it in the DNR's lap. Her thinking is not just stupid, it's twisted."

"She actually *said* the thing is real?"

"Pretty much."

"Did you piss her off?"

"I'm not sure. She hides her emotions like an actor."

"Duh: She's a politician," Friday said. "What's next for you?"

No time to think it through thoroughly. "Lori said I can have who I want, and it's all on her dime. The first thing I'm gonna do is pull Tree in."

Grady Service and Luticious Treebone had both finished college, Service at Northern Michigan University, where he had been only a fair student and a competent hockey player, and Treebone at Wayne State, where he had played football and baseball and graduated cum laude. They had both been on the verge of being drafted, so they volunteered for the US Marine Corps, met at Parris Island, and served together in the same long-range recon unit in Vietnam. They had been through hell together and had rarely spoken of the war since.

When they got back to "the world," they had both joined the Michigan State Police; two years later there had been an opportunity to transfer to the Department of Natural Resources, and they both accepted, but within a year his friend had taken a job with the Detroit Metro Police. He had retired a couple years back as a lieutenant in one of Metro's vice squads, and Service had bought a camp in remote Chippewa County for his friend, a place called North of Nowhere, where they could escape to hunt and fish. They had remained close friends for going on thirty years, during which time Tree's idea of wilderness had been unhappily reduced to Belle Isle on the Fourth of July. But now that he was retired, he was spending a lot of time at his camp.

Service couldn't remember the last time he'd thought about his two years as a state trooper in the Detroit area. The post had been on Grand Boulevard in the city. He wasn't even sure if the post was still there, much less still operating. The MSP had been forced by budget losses to drastically reduce the number of posts—manpower, too, but not as much—over recent years.

Detroit had been an incredible assignment right out of Vietnam and Troop school. Those had been the days of smack, and before crack cocaine. Actual zombies (not the living dead, but the dying-live) crawled alleys at night, whacking anything with warm blood, stealing anything that could be hocked to fuel habits, even prying gold fillings from teeth, the dead serving to keep the dying alive a little longer. They didn't call heroin "horse" for nothing; upkeep on a golden arm was steeper than maintaining Secretariat. And deadlier.

Service remembered when Sergeant Jack Creekmore one morning described to the shift a series of six killings that had left body parts strewn around three Detroit police precincts. Creekmore gave Service a piece of paper with a name: Arthurine Snowden. "See the woman," his sergeant said.

"Metro has its own homicide dicks, right?"

"Don't question me, rook. See the woman," Creekmore growled, and added, "Metro's got so many bent dicks they don't want no good leads to get shat upon. You the man, Service. Arthurine, she the woman, and she claims she got most righteous poop. We copacetic?"

"Yes, Sergeant."

Arthurine Snowden ran a news kiosk outside a black biker bar called Lazy Fare. She also worked numbers for a crew called B&B (for Black and Bad) and traded favors with the law. The Cass Corridor in downtown Detroit was filled with genetic defects, losers, mouth-breathers, and sundry bottom-feeders. They were predatory and omnivorous, consuming anything and everything, but they were not without their own rules and ethics.

Cass-peeps believed in let-live among their own crowd, a rather wide-sweeping definition, but mass and serial murderers attracted jazzed-up cops, which jeopardized enlightened self-interest. Snowden pointed him at an address with unspoken hopes that busting the murderous shitbird would return life to its abnormal shade of normal. Working Detroit, Service came to understand that even Hell had its own version and vision of normal. Enlightened self-interest was not the exclusive domain of suits, uniforms, and forked-tongue sky pilots.

Service found himself looking into darkness at a shotgun house in an area off Cass and Mack. The place was set on a block torched flat during the '67 riots. The frames of seven houses still stood, charred and falling over, several basements inhabited by nomadic subterranean life forms, which emerged only when the streets went deep-dark. Most of the block was over-grown with weeds and strewn with garbage. There were two '67 Pontiacs, stripped of wheels and everything salable, but left as rusting, burned-out hulks, like blown-up tanks on an old battlefield. Six months back he'd been in on a raid of a blind pig in the next block, and it had been scary from start to finish. And exhilarating, a reaction that bothered him for reasons he didn't understand. Certainly, he was no cherry to violence; he remained idealistic, believing police intervention would eventually turn the tide in Detroit. Now he knew better. *Don't fight a battle you can't win.*

Entering the building, he quickly found a body in a bathtub of con-gealed blood. He remembered staring and trying to decide what to do when a rawboned country boy with a fluffy red Afro and huge hands came through the door, swinging a double-bit ax. Service's reflexes saved him. He mostly blocked the downstroke, but the handle had glanced off his head, the blade nicking his arm, the blow jarring him and leaving him loopy. Somehow Service had knocked the assailant off balance, hitting him hard on the shin bone with his sap, the impact sounding like a crisp single off a Louisville slugger on a cool spring day. The wounded man crab-crawled away like a cockroach. Service couldn't follow, as blood from a head wound left him nearly blind.

Bad karma. Only then did it occur to him to call for backup. A beat cop named Noonan was first on the scene, checked him over, said, "Head's nothing serious. Tourniquet your arm, motherfucker, you'll live." Noonan had dead eyes, no meat on his body, all gristle, wired like he was on crank, weight 140 max, giving off deadly vibrations of a tightly wrapped krait on a night-hunt for warm prey. The snakes, neurotoxic banded kraits, had been common in Southeast Asia.

Service heard two shots just before the cavalry arrived in force. There were more body parts in other parts of the house, and especially in the old cellar, trash bags stuffed into fifty-gallon metal drums, in old freezers and fridges. The media had a field day with the gore, which was always their priority.

By the ambulance Service asked Noonan, "What was his name?"

"Gives a fuck?" the cop said. "Shitbag like that don't deserve no name."

Forty stitches to close the wound where the blade had grazed Service's arm, and twelve more in his head from the handle. It was standard operating procedure that all shootings got an Internal Affairs look-over, but this was ruled a righteous shoot in two days, and Noonan went back to the street.

Service had other negative thoughts that lingered, and he had gone to see the cop one weekend and got right in his face: "The perp was in a different room," he told Noonan. "I heard no warnings, only shots. The fucker was crawling away and had no weapon. He dropped his ax with me."

"You trying to make a point, asswipe?"

"You killed that man."

"Fucking eh."

"In cold blood."

"Scribble a note in the public service column," Noonan said. "No extra charge."

"It was murder."

Noonan picked up a paper bag, emptied dozens of black-and-white and color photographs on the floor. "You can't murder a murderer, ass-pump. But if you got your monthly conscience like some big State pussy, go right ahead and whine to them IA assholes, and let's see who's standing when this dance gets done."

Service had seen plenty of war dead and ugliness, but the shotgun house and the photos were his first real experience with seriously aberrant human behavior.

Weeks later he'd driven down to Metro HQ at 1300 Beaubien and found Noonan in one of the cheap, baggy blue suits that would become his hallmark. He had just been promoted to homicide detective. Service returned the bag with photographs. "He couldn't walk," Service said. "He was crawling."

Noonan said, "Yeah, in *your* direction, with a fucking knife. Thing like that ain't human."

Service held out his hand and hated himself for it. "What makes us different than him?" he asked Noonan.

"We still breathing."

"Whoever breathes longest, wins?"

"Fucking eh," the new detective said, and smiled . . .

"Kalina won't like it," Tuesday said, breaking his reverie. Kalina was Tree's longtime spouse.

"Doesn't matter. I need him."

"Maybe he won't want to. He's retired and out of the shit."

"Semper fi. He and I are brothers. He'll come, but I'm gonna go down and fetch him, find out who he knows in the Detroit Indian community."

"Today?"

"Tomorrow morning. Today is ours. Might be a while before we get another one."

She leaned her head on his chest. "You'll check in, okay?"

"Roger that, boss."

Bluesuit Noonan: Still alive and available? Semi-human? This case might be one where a true barbarian could provide a distinct advantage.

13

Monday, October 27

DETROIT, WAYNE COUNTY

Service had called Treebone from Rapid River the day before, and his friend answered, "Yo, Big Dog."

"I need help."

"What is it this time?"

"Some very nasty stuff."

"Where you at?"

"Headed south to your place, be there around seven."

"Cool. Dinner waiting."

"Tell Kalina I'm sorry to barge in. And pack your winter gear."

"Am I going somewhere?"

"Hell, maybe."

"Heard Hell was hot."

"Not the one I have in mind. There a head Shinob mucky-muck down in Motown?" *Shinob* was street talk for *Anishinaabe,* slang for Chippewa or Ojibwe.

"Huh. Been long time since I danced with that crew."

"I just need a name."

"Let me make some calls."

"Bluesuit Noonan still around?"

"Yeah, he's still aboveground. Owns a block of fix-it houses on Blackfish Avenue, safest block in the city, and he doesn't even grease city cops or pay for extra muscle. What you want with that crazy motherfucker?"

"I want to talk to him."

"You *sure?*"

"I think."

"Okay, I'll call the man, and check on the Shinob social scene. Seven, right?"

"Tell Kalina I'm sorry."

"Tell her yourself. She'll just yell at my ass. Hey, I heard you're back in the Mosquito."

"How'd you hear *that?*"

"I'm a cop, remember?"

"Retired."

"So they say," Tree said, and hung up.

• • •

Treebone lived in Grosse Pointe Woods in a small house he'd added to over the years. Manicured lawns, topiaries on neighboring lots, mansion estates flanked the cop's house in several directions.

Treebone came out of his garage and waved majestically down the street. "My people, man. Kalina's got fixings," Treebone said, grabbing at Service's bag.

"Leave it. We're pulling out tonight, right after dinner."

Treebone grinned. "Works for me."

They ate the finest jambalaya Service had ever tasted, but passed on alcohol.

Kalina wanted to know all about Tuesday Friday and her son Shigun, and Karylanne and Little Maridly. Service quickly grew weary of the social small talk, his mind already locking into the mission ahead.

They said their good-byes after dinner, and Kalina glared at Service the same as she had for as long as he'd known her.

The two men got into the truck and headed west on Jefferson, eventually pulling down a street that ran down to intersect the Detroit River. A creek ran behind the block.

"Last spring Noonan made a big case for your DNR boys. Locals were selling silver bass to a local eatery. He tracked 'em, set 'em up on a damn tee for your guys, but he was the true author of their legal demise. Your boys here love his ass."

"Legal demise?"

Treebone shrugged. "I've been readin' a lot since I retired; you know, self-improvement shit and such."

The houses along the block were freshly painted, lawns neat, flower gardens—it was unlike any part of inner Detroit that Service remembered.

They stopped at a house and Noonan ambled out and stared.

"Man, you still on the State payroll?" Noonan asked Service.

"So far. Nice place you got."

"Amazing what work and a little money will accomplish, eh?" Noonan chirruped.

Service said, "You hear about the two women in the U.P.?"

The retired detective nodded. "Saw some shit in the *Freep*." Slang for Detroit's *Free Press*. "What's a woods cop got to do with a double homi?"

"Governor's idea, and order: Hunt down the killer."

Noonan looked skeptical. "You shittin' me? The governor herself gave you *that* order? Didn't think she had the balls."

"Maybe not in those words. You believe in dogmen?"

"Depends."

"On what?"

"They shit on my lawn."

"How about you come help Tree and me run this thing down?"

"No fake?"

"Nope; governor's paying, and I get to pick my team."

"Gimme some time to pack. Cold up there?"

"We've already had snow . . . looks like one of those years. I'll provide snowshoes and other gear. I'm going to step outside for a smoke," Service said.

Several boys rode bikes up to the Tahoe and dismounted. A black SUV pulled up behind his truck; a man got out and came up the sidewalk and began shouting: "Noonan, you nasty, nigger-hatin' little motherfucker, come outside and face your accuser!"

Noonan immediately came to the door, asked, "Who the fuck you?"

"Latoma Brown be who I am."

"Brown? I know your old man?"

"You kicked him outten his house."

"*My* house, not his, and he didn't pay rent for one year, Brown."

"You don't cut no slack for black men."

"I don't cut slack for my goddamn mother. What's your point, slick?"

"Gon' cap your cheap, racist ass," the man said, charging forward, and suddenly he was on the sidewalk, flailing like he was drowning, the air gone out of him. Service helped the man up, his nose and chin bleeding profusely.

Service said, "You've got to be careful on concrete. Can trip you up real easy."

The man was dazed. An old man crawled out of the car, and Noonan saw him. "What's your son's problem, Brown? You and me parted copacetic, and here your boy comes up on me at the half-step."

"The boy just back from the Afghanistan, thinkin' he can put righteous whoop-ass on the world's problems."

Noonan said to Service, "Let's get him inside, clean him up."

The kids with the bikes were huddled by the Tahoe. Noonan yelled from his door and darted over to them so fast Service could hardly believe his quickness. "Okay, boys, curfew's here—time for home."

"Ain't no curfew," the largest boy said. "Mothafuckah."

"Fine, let's call it a prelude to your funeral instead," Noonan said with a huge grin.

The kid took an aggressive half-step toward him and immediately doubled over on the ground, grasping his package.

Noonan said calmly, "Next?"

No challengers. "Okay. Get this sorry piece of shit on home, and don't never come back."

Noonan looked at Service. "How long you think this party will last?"

"Days, weeks, months—don't know," Service told the retired detective. "You want to know what your pay is?"

"Couldn't give a shit," Noonan said, and went back inside.

• • •

As the Tahoe headed north, Treebone said, "Where're the Browns?"

"I hired them to protect the block while we're gone. Latoma is Crotch, Semper fi. The old man's gonna live in my place."

"Semper fi," Service and Tree said together. Noonan was a unique creature.

"You get me a Shinob yet?" Service asked as they headed north.

"Working on that," Tree said. "Gon' take a while."

• • •

Passing near Gaylord, where US 127 merged with I-75, Service's personal cell phone rang and he answered it. "Sonnyboy," a voice rasped.

Limpy Allerdyce. Most of the Allerdyce clan lived in a compound in southwest Marquette County, on a narrow peninsula between North and South Beaverkill Lakes. The area was a long way from civilization, not the sort of place you stumbled across by mere chance. With water on two sides and a cedar swamp on both ends, it was difficult to get to. There was a two-track from a US Forest Service road down to the compound's parking area, and then it was a half-mile walk along a twisting trail from there into the camp itself. In terms of isolation, the place was a fortress, which was just as well. Limpy's clan had poached all over the Upper Peninsula for decades.

Many years ago Service had challenged Allerdyce for poaching fish with dynamite. The CO had no idea where the shovel had come from, but it had caught him hard, breaking his right shoulder, and a subsequent shotgun blast caught him in the left thigh. He was lucky it was a slug, a twenty-gauge, that somehow missed the femoral artery. Allerdyce spent seven years in Southern Michigan Prison and came out professing to have changed his ways, which, over the years, Service was reluctantly beginning to believe. Especially since the old man had helped him solve several major cases and even saved his life.

The apparent fundamental shift in the man was hard to accept, or believe. Limpy was no accidental violator. He had few normal emotions, was a predator in human form, a demon, a shape-shifter, a crow pocketing a bauble at Wal-Mart, a wolf taking easy, helpless prey. Allerdyce, no matter what he claimed, was cold-blooded and calculating, a dirtbag who had for most of his life taken what he wanted with no remorse. In the man's twisted mind, all that mattered was what *he* wanted, and if you didn't agree, you were in deep trouble. The tricky old poacher claimed he had been Service's father's informant in the old days, and since his release from prison downstate, he had decided to do the same for Grady.

Owing such a person for saving your life was galling beyond words.

"What do you want?"

"Heard somepin," the man said.

"Like what?"

"Like some punk-ass high school kittles talking 'bout some Holloweenie party up in da Whorons."

The man slaughtered language in unbelievably cockeyed ways. "What of it?"

"Heard dis in bar over Amasa Hotel."

Amasa was a long way from the Huron Mountains. "And?"

"Somepin' sick go down, I t'ink."

"You know the place?"

"Mebbe."

"Call Marquette County and tell them. Ask for Sergeant Linsenman."

"I call *you*, not dat weasel," Allerdyce insisted. "He don't like me."

Service said, "I don't do kiddie parties."

"You know dat case, dose two dead girlies up Twinnypointpond?"

"Yes." *Now what?*

"Hear sick like dat, mebbe."

"And somebody was blabbing about this in the Amasa Hotel?"

"I heard it for sure, and I believe it, sonny."

"Where are you?"

"Your place, talkin' your dog. I really like dis mutt. I call your girlie, tell her I comin' oot here. I go his sis's, she give me dog and cat, eh."

"You broke into my cabin *again?*"

"Ain't no break-in. I got key."

"I didn't give you one."

"Had it made, eh," Allerdyce said.

"From what?"

"Last time I was out dere."

Service sighed. There was no way to change some behaviors, and inexplicably, both his dog and cat loved the old bastard.

"Where youse?" Limpy asked.

"Downstate, rolling north."

"Take 'er easy. We'll all be right 'ere. Stop, get bottle Jack, eh. Youse're low."

Great, Service thought, and broke off the contact. Something Allerdyce thought might relate to the case up at Twenty Point Pond? His gut fluttered. He knew this would somehow be something of substance, but not what. Not yet. Limpy always seemed to know what was going on all across the U.P.

"Who that?" Treebone asked.

Service said, "You brung a nigger into my camp?" This is what Limpy had said when Service took Treebone with him to meet the man in his camp the night he came home from prison years ago.

Treebone exhaled loudly. "That motherfucker Allerdyce."

"He's waiting at camp. You guys can catch up and make nice."

Noonan said, "Can I turn on the tunes? You two go on like couple of dried-up old women."

14

Friday, October 31

LITTLE HURON RIVER, MARQUETTE COUNTY

CO Dani Denninger rang Service's duty cell just before first light. "You know the DeJean family?"

He mumbled, "Yeah, Old Man Guy, his six asshole boys, and me go way back. Why?"

The DeJeans had poached Baraga and Northwest Marquette Counties for decades. Yearly fish runs seemed to mentally unhinge the family, like some strange genetic seasonal disorder. The family would haul out truckloads of salmon and steelhead, or walleyes, or northern pike, whatever was making spawning runs. And every year they seemed to try a new method. One year they tossed quarter-sticks of dynamite, stunning the fish. Another year they used two sixteen-volt car batteries to make a crude fish shocker. Another year they were using buckshot from twelve-gauge shotguns, marble-size pellets flying all over the woods and two of the boys catching wounds from them. The family's U.P. roots traced to Chippewa County more than a century ago, and patriarch Old Man Guy recognized no higher earthly authority than himself. In some ways Service could empathize with him. Change was getting harder and harder to stomach, for law-abiding citizens and criminals alike.

The one thing they used to be able to count on was that Guy DeJean and his boys were nonviolent and saw competition with the DNR as a dicey game to be played and enjoyed.

"Been a while since you've seen him; he's got ten sons now," Denninger said. "His youngest, Donte, called me last night and told me some high school kids have something sick going on up along the Little Huron, east of Bald Mountain."

"He say which kids, and define *sick?*"

"Negative. I let him walk last black-powder season on a tagging violation. Told him he owed me. I think this is the payback."

"Halloween," Service said.

"Go figure. The night when assholes howl at the moon."

Service felt himself popping awake. "I heard something similar from Allerdyce a few days back. If it's coming from those two sources, you'd have to think it has substance. You want help?"

"I got a real gut-twister on this one, Grady, maybe because it isn't that far from Twenty Point Pond."

Grady Service blinked a map into his mind. Allerdyce had offered the same observation. "I hear you. Be me plus three."

"Sounds like an army," she joked.

"It *is* an army," he said, no hint of irony in his tone.

She said, "You know the two-track right after you cross Big Erick's Bridge, right?"

"Yep."

"Keep on that until you get to the first major crossroad. The south leg is passable. Pull up to the south a half-mile or so and wait. The place we want is north, where a two-track cuts east over the river and a pair of culverts. I'll meet you, and we'll take both trucks down after dark. Seven work?"

"We'll be there. Allerdyce says he knows the way."

"I bet he does," she said, and hung up.

• • •

Treebone and Noonan didn't ask where they were going, or why. "No snow," Service told them, "but we'll be in the western Hurons right on Superior, so anything is possible. Dress warm."

Allerdyce had not been at the cabin the previous night and did not appear until morning, just as they were getting into the Tahoe. Service thought the old man might be trying to avoid Treebone and was surprised when Limpy walked directly over to Tree, and, sticking out his bony hand, said, "I'm real sorry what I call you dat time out my camp."

"Nigger," Tree said. "I'm certain that was the word you employed."

Allerdyce hung his head and mumbled "I'm real sorry" again.

Treebone said, "Apology accepted, you sawed-off, wrinkled, white trash motherfucker." The two men shook hands, and Limpy cackled.

They're both looney tunes, Service thought.

• • •

They were parked where Denninger wanted them, and Service monitored her signal working its way toward them on the Automatic Vehicle Locator. Denninger was running dark, just as they had, about five miles out and closing.

Eventually she drove quietly past them, turned around, and pulled alongside Treebone's window. "All sorts of fresh vehicle tracks coming in," she said truck to truck, through open windows. "I called the sarge; he's coming, too. Ought to be here soon. Willie says there's an abandoned trailer near the west bank of the river, about a mile south of the mouth, a hundred yards below the culvert road."

"You know the place?" Service asked.

"Not the trailer," Denninger said. "That's new to me. I usually work the river in the riffles and holes up this way. The river flows west and turns ninety degrees to the north just below the intersection we came through. It parallels the road north down past the culvert road and ends at the mouth."

"Does Willie want to lead the charge?"

"Don't know," she said. "But he knows this area."

Allerdyce said, "Trailer got put dere nineteen ninety-t'ree by Finndian fum over Sidnaw. Name was Tom-Tom Joseph or some such. Use as deer blind an' camp when fishy runs was on."

Service looked back. "You've been there?"

"Seen it, but never ast me in for coffee."

"Where's Tom-Tom Joseph now?"

"Tree fell on 'im two t'ousand six. Lived mebbe twelve hours, but too much busted up in guts to fix 'im."

"Friend of yours?"

"Perfectional pal, you could say, but dem was old days, not now."

They watched Sergeant Willie Celt on the AVL, his truck turning up the road and stopping. Then he was at Service's window, on foot. "There's a one-lane wood bridge with a two-track a mile south of the river mouth."

Service looked at the AVL map. "You think we should go on foot?"

"The DeJeans, high school kids, Halloween, salmon, and steelhead seem to me a pretty dicey concoction. There's sure to be booze and weed and speed and God knows what else. We'll probably need all our vehicles to hold prisoners, at least until we can sort out the assholes. I'm going to call Baraga and the Troops for support, see what we have. Probably too far for Marquette deps."

"Okay, lead us on down," Service said.

Denninger said from Treebone's side, "How about I slip down there first? I'll stash my ride and creep the place, give us some sense of what we're dealing with. Give me one hour before you guys roll?"

Celt said from the other side of the truck, "Works for me. Donte's tip wasn't that specific?"

Denninger said, "Something sick . . . here . . . tonight; that's about the extent of it."

"That damn family wallows in sick," Celt said bitterly.

Denninger said, "Donte's not a bad kid, and I'm hoping he's giving us the tip because his family isn't involved. You can't help what family you're born into."

"Think Old Man Guy will be there?" Service asked Celt.

"If there's fish, that sonuvabitch will be somewhere in the area. He can't help himself."

"Saw plenty of fish last week, all the way up to the upper crossroad," Denninger said. "Salmon are sort of playing out, but I saw some fresh chrome steel up high. I expect lower holes will hold a lot of fish. Gotta go."

Service checked his watch. Fifty-five minutes. He found himself thinking about Guy DeJean and his six—now ten—sons, the DFC, DeJean's Family Circus, some cops called them. *What the hell are they up to this time?* Whereas the Allerdyce clan was deadly mean and smart, the DFC tended toward playfully mean, and dumber than a bag of rusty nails.

Celt moved without saying anything on the radio, and Service followed. No lights, no moon. At least it wasn't snowing. "Tree, take Noonan down the west bank. Allerdyce, hang with me across the culverts and down the east bank."

Service could see the occasional glint of Celt's truck ahead of them. Nosing down the steep road, it dawned on Service that his new army had no radios, or call signs. He'd have to solve that tomorrow. They could probably operate on a special event channel and not step on other operations. *Details you should already have taken care of,* he chastised himself. *Good reminder why you didn't deserve stripes. You're no good at staff shit.*

They stashed their trucks side by side in thick underbrush and started downhill on foot through the woods, west of the two-track. In the distance they could hear the thump of music, voices, the usual din of a backwoods party.

Denninger's voice came up whispering on the 800 MHz. "They've got a bonfire by the river, weed clouds in the air, a lot of screaming. There's a couple doing some vigorous *unh-unh* in a white van out by the culvert road. I left them alone. The river's pretty loud: They won't be able to hear much. I'm at the end of a finger-rock ledge, and I can see the trailer beneath me. The fire's just west of the trailer, which they don't seem to be paying much attention to, at least at the moment."

"Moving your way," Celt told her over the radio. "Both banks. How many vehicles?"

"Twelve," she said. "That I could count. There could be more down toward the mouth, but a dozen was my quick tally, including the couple in the white van."

"Weps?" Service asked.

"Haven't heard or seen any, but that's not saying there aren't."

Celt again, "We're coming up on the first vehicles. Looks like most are clustered around the culvert crossroad, and north."

"That's affirmative," Denninger said. "Clear."

Service grabbed Allerdyce's down coat. "You got a red penlight?"

"Sure, sonny."

"Break off when we reach the vehicles. Write down license numbers, makes, and models. You got a pencil and pad?"

"Got one writes in rain, and won't wash away."

Service thought it was a weird comment, but had no time to ask why the old man possessed such a thing. "If the couple are still shaking the van, go easy around that one."

"An' after I get plates?"

"Wait here and we'll be back to get you. Okay?"

Allerdyce nodded.

Celt on the radio to Denninger: "You got NVD or IR?"

"Both," she said. "Infrared shows kids creeping over to the trailer, looking in, and going back to the bonfire. They just look in and scoot, don't say a word. Major weird. Clear."

Service stopped his team. "Everybody got good lights and fresh batts?"

The other three men patted pockets with their gloves.

"Don't turn on any lights until I do. I want to mix in with them before we bring the light of the law to their sad little corner of the world."

Allerdyce split off to collect license-plate numbers. The other four headed down the Little Huron River from the culvert, and almost as soon as they started north, the wind picked up in velocity and began to blow hard. In ten minutes they could see the faint glow of a fire ahead. Service and Noonan veered right to where the trailer was said to be. Service said on his radio, "Dani, we're moving to the trailer. Hundred yards out, maybe. Clear."

"Meet you there," she whispered. "From your east. Clear."

A sudden east wind was making a metallic tapping sound. At first, Service thought branches in the giant oaks and maples were scraping and banging in the wind, but this was definitely metallic, almost like an off-key cymbal. He saw the silhouette of the trailer ahead, and a door, top hinge gone, bottom hinge holding it in place but askew, the wind making it flap like a broken bird wing. The place stunk from twenty yards away, and his first thought was that it might be a meth lab, but the odor wasn't right—less ammonia than something else.

Fuck: I know this smell. Goddammit to hell.

The sides of the trailer were clawed, the wood bits chewed. A bear had been here. Service got to the trailer, handed his rifle to Noonan, took out his red penlight, approached the door, peeked inside, and pulled his head back. *Porkies have been in there: Two black turd piles two feet high—like termite mounds.* The interior had not been chewed and not devastated the way a bear would do.

He leaned in again: *Empty DeKuyper root beer schnapps bottle near the far wall. Fishermen and hunters: Lots of them are slobs. Somebody using the trailer as a deer blind?*

Service put a knee on the trailer floor and shone his light toward the end. Something white shone pink in his light beam. *Something hanging. A coon?* He used his hand on the old jamb to get to his feet and take one step toward the back of the trailer.

Fuck. Not an animal, he thought, gorge rising in his throat. *A kid.*

This time, the killer had left the head and the hands, but the feet and buttocks were gone. Jesus.

He felt light-headed and fought through it to maintain composure. *Do your job, do your job, do your job.* "Dani, you close?"

"Right outside."

"Come take a look."

She did as asked, and all she said was, "We have to secure this fricking site *now*."

They crawled past the porky piles to get out, and Denninger stayed by the trailer. Service and Noonan headed for the bonfire, and when they reached the clearing with the music and kids, they turned on their flashlights, announced "DNR," and kids scattered like rats under the sudden light, running in every direction, including splashing through the stream. Service could hear Treebone and Celt barking at kids scrambling through the woods on the west bank.

Twenty minutes later they had thirteen teenagers sitting on the ground around the fire. Celt said, "I'm calling backup again."

Service hotfooted it back to the culvert road intersection to find five vehicles lined up on the road, headlights on, engines off, kids standing in front of the vehicles with their hands, palms down, on the hoods, key sets prominently displayed on the hood of each truck. There was a backpack on the hood of the first truck, and Allerdyce was standing with his hand on it, smoking a cigarette.

A red laser occasionally flashed down from the woods to the west, sweeping across the teens attached by their hands to their cars. Allerdyce seemed unconcerned by the light, but it made Service edgy.

"What's going on?" Service asked.

"Cripes, I got all dem plates and den I hear what I took for grope-motion down dere, so I stand myself near first truck, wait see if drivers come out. I put Donte up in dere in woods wit' laser, tole him sweep 'em once I got everyt'ing horgalnized."

Service blinked, trying to process what he was hearing. "Donte? What laser light?"

"DeJean," Limpy said. "'Member? Was in woods when we come down, and after youse'd gone, he come out. Ast he can help. Tole me what's down dere. I hope ain't true."

"It is," Service said.

Allerdyce made a snarling sound. "First kids get to truck, I lighted 'em up, tole 'em turn off motor, put on headlights, get fuck out, make line up on front, put keys in front on hood, keep hands on metal. Dat's when Donte-boy swepp 'em wit' red dot. I tole 'em, 'Youse guys'll seen dem cop shows on the TV, you know what dat red dot is.' Den dey do what I tell 'em, see."

"You tell them you were a CO?"

" 'Course not. Just said, DNR will want ta talk all youse."

"You threaten them?"

"Just tol' dem dat TV t'ing, eh."

Service had to swallow a laugh.

"After da first truck crew did what I say, t'other four din't argoo and di' what I tole 'em."

"How many people?" Service asked.

"'Leven, not count pair still bunny-humpin' in white van. God, talk 'bout lastin'!" the old man said admiringly.

Grady Service shook his head. "You ever drive one of our trucks?"

"Nope, but I sure rode in plenty wid cuffs on me."

Service handed him his spare key. "Take the Tahoe back up to the inter-section. Baraga deps and a Troop are coming to back us up. Park so your headlights point down the north road. Turn on the blue lights when they approach. You know how to operate the lights and siren?"

"I figger it out, don' youse worry none, sonny." Limpy handed Service his notebook. "Plates an' makes, an' like."

"Git. We've got work to do here."

Allerdyce took off with unexpected alacrity.

Service went truck to truck, gathering the detainees, and stopped the group at the van. He knocked on the sliding side door. A boy opened it and Service said, "DNR. Get your clothes on. You two will have to come with me."

The boy and girl dressed and got out and the boy leaned close to Service and said, "Thanks, man. The bitch was, like, scrompin' me dead, sayin'?"

Service cringed: English was becoming a second language even among English speakers.

They marched the group across the culvert berm and down the east bank to the bonfire.

He called Tuesday Friday on the cell phone as he escorted the group to the fire. "I don't know how long I'll have a signal. We're on the Little Huron, couple of miles north of where it dumps into Superior. It's a child this time. Butchered and nasty. Baraga deps and a Troop are coming for support. I alerted your Troop crime scene crew, and they're rolling. If you cut up the Peshekee Grade Road off M-28, you'll hit Arvon Road. Just stay on that until you hit Skanee Road. You can save a lot of time, but with this cold snap, the deer are starting to chase, and hormones have replaced brains."

"Normal males, then," she said. "One hour plus."

He walked her through directions west of Big Erick's Bridge, and told her a CO truck was in place to mark the correct road at the intersection.

"What shape's the scene in?" she asked.

"Ugly, but Denninger closed it off immediately to limit spoilage."

"Our boy's work?"

"I'm thinking that. Only thing is, this time he left the head and the hands, but the feet are gone."

"One hour plus," she said again.

Service, Noonan, and Treebone separated the kids and began talking to them one at a time. Denninger stayed with the main group, keeping an eye on the trailer. Celt took off down the road to check for other vehicles and to look for anything at the river mouth.

They quickly learned the party organizer was the young male from the van. He claimed to be sixteen but looked older. The girl with him claimed to be eighteen, but other kids said she was fourteen.

Service took the boy off to the side. "Where's your wallet?"

"In the van, dude."

"Your name?"

"I want my lawyer."

"How old are you?"

"Sixteen, man."

"You *have* a lawyer at your age?"

"Got no choice, way youses hassle peeps in the woods."

Denninger bopped over, whispered, "Daly DeJean."

"Says he's sixteen," Service said.

"Bullshit. Early twenties." She went back to her post.

"You're Daly DeJean?"

"What if I am?"

"Well, Daly, you're twenty-something, not sixteen, and the girl's fourteen."

"Dude, dat bitch *swore* she was eighteen. She's got ID, man."

"Look at her, Daly. She's probably still playing with Barbie dolls. Twenties and fourteen equals statutory rape."

"Dude," DeJean keened. "She give it up like she's t'irty. B'lee me, I ain't first one pork dat shit."

"Ten bucks a head to look at a dead child? What's wrong with you, DeJean?"

"Didn't do no such."

"Evidence and witnesses say otherwise. It's a felony to not report a dead body, and there's all sorts of other shit going down here. You provide the drugs and booze?"

"No, sir."

"It's a crime to move a dead body."

"Like hell!" Daly shot back.

"You check that with your lawyer?"

The boy said nothing.

"*Contra bonos mores,*" Service said.

"Dude, I don't know nothing about no bones."

"It means 'against good morals,' " Service explained. "You can be indicted for preventing a burial, for exposing a body, for preventing an inquest. You want me to go on?"

"But I didn't *put* the thing there, man."

"Then how'd you find it?"

"I want my lawyer. I ain't got nothin' more to say to you."

"Sure you do. You just don't know it yet."

The other officers gathered bits of meth, weed, beer, schnapps, box wine, and such an assortment of other prescription pills they'd need a reference book to identify all of them. DeJean was the only one over eighteen. Several gave names, recanted, and opted for mute.

Celt came back, puffing. "Guy DeJean's truck and boat trailer are parked at the mouth. There's a gun case on the floor, covered by a blanket, and an empty box of slugs."

"You open the door?"

"Door panel's rusted away. I could see through the hole."

"Boat?"

"Sea Skiff he runs all over hell. Lake's rough as dickens."

"He that nuts?"

"One year, when Superior froze over, I busted him and some of his boys eight miles out on the ice in their trucks. They think they're bulletproof."

"What's DeJean want?" Service asked. "This river's got plenty of easy fish."

Celt said, "There's a small stream just west of the Huron Mountain Club on their property. Dumps underground from Pine Lake. Only a half-mile long, but it piles up with early steelies and coaster brookies some years. Three feet wide, max. You can scoop 'em out with a net, but I don't think he's after fish. I've been hearing rumors of a jumbo bull moose in the marshes over by Huron River Point."

"Is he that crazy?"

"No, he's that greedy. I guess it can work out to be the same. Guy's been busted for recreational trespass at the club before. They get him again, it'll be criminal trespass. I already called Jocko Shannsky, the club's security boss. One of the club's two-tracks will take him almost all the way to the moose area and creek. He's rolling now."

"Can he handle DeJean?"

"Retired Troop, good man."

Denninger joined them. "What a mess. I think we ought to haul all these kids out to Big Erick's campground, call their parents, let them collect their nasty little asses, and haul them home. I say we write MIPs for those we can identify and verify, haul the rest to jail for failure to provide proper ID and seeking to avoid identification."

Service called Allerdyce on the radio. "Twenty Five Fourteen, partner. There's a Troop SUV en route. Follow her in. We're gonna need the Tahoe to haul bodies."

"Ten-four," Allerdyce cackled over the radio.

So much time with cops, the old man knew cop codes. What a joke. Service shook his head and looked at his watch. Midnight. Damn long night ahead. *Need to change my call sign. Not Twenty Five Fourteen anymore.*

They decided to march all the kids out to the bridge crossroad to wait for backups to start hauling them away. Meanwhile, Denninger began writing tickets, and Willie Celt stuck Daly DeJean in his truck in cuffs.

Jen Maki, the Michigan State Police lead forensics tech, was first to arrive and took possession of the site and the body. "ME's not far behind me. She was visiting her mom in Covington," she said.

Two Baraga deps and a Troop in his blue goose rolled in. Then Marquette County sergeant Weasel Linsenman and a second Marquette deputy in his personal vehicle arrived.

Service saw Tuesday approaching and the Tahoe right behind her. Service waved and went over to Limpy. "Where's Donte DeJean?"

"Took 'im oot wit' me, drop 'im off. Why?"

"Nothing. Thanks; you did good." Merely saying the words to Allerdyce threatened to gag him.

Police milled around the crime scene, and Dr. Kristy Tork came over to Service. "You want to step aside for a few?" she asked.

"Bring my people?"

She shrugged, took him to where Friday and Jen Maki were waiting, both wearing blue latex gloves. The ME said, "The cut patterns on the ankles and buttocks leave little doubt this is the same guy, although he did leave the head and hands this time."

Friday said, "He probably wants us to identify the vick."

Tork continued. "Very little blood here. I'm guessing she was killed and bled out elsewhere, dumped and mutilated here. She's relatively fresh, I think. Four, five days max, but that's just a guess."

"Chance of a copycat?" Noonan asked.

"Never say never, but not in my opinion. The cut patterns look identical."

"What else?" Tree asked.

"Female vick's five or six, give or take. Native American. Won't guess at cause of death, but I sure hope it happened fast."

Silence. No gork jokes this time. A child was dead. This changed everything.

Service contemplated the situation. Who found the body, and when, assuming the killer and finder were different? The first two victims remained unidentified, but this was a kid. Young women could run away and not be reported, but a missing child? *Highly unlikely anyone would ignore that.*

Celt bumped Service on the 800. "You want to come back up to my truck with Detective Friday?"

"On our way."

Tork stepped back and lit a cigarette.

"Stunt your growth," Service said.

"Bite me," she countered and looked at her watch. "Zero six hundred. Not that long until we have light."

There's light, and there's light, Service thought.

• • •

Celt met them. "Shannsky has Guy DeJean in custody. Caught him with fifty steelies, six coasters, and two cohos in his boat, but the boat was unattended, and he found DeJean trying to quarter a bull moose with a chain saw."

"He resist?"

"Shannsky said the old guy was too tired from so much work. He just sighed and put up his hands. Jocko's taking him to the Club's security building. Linsenman has dispatched a dep from Marquette to pick him up. I told them to make sure they bring the gun, net, fish, and some moose meat as evidence. DeJean's already asked for a lawyer."

"Conditioned response," Service said.

"What do you need?" Friday asked.

Service said, "Limpy sweet-talked Daly into letting us search his van. We found a thou in cash, meth, about a pound of weed, all of it creatively stuffed in the spare tire storage area."

Friday said, "I confronted Daly, talked about felonies, and he asked me if these are instead of, or on top of, the body charges, and I told him all of the above. He announced he's got a story to tell, and here I quote, 'to that big prick, Service.'"

Service pulled the boy out of the truck. "You got something to share?"

The first thing Daly DeJean said was, "Gimme smoke, dudes. Like, please?" Service lit a smoke for him. DeJean said, "Dudes, wasn't me found the body, swear to God."

"Which god—Pluto?"

"Pluto, like Mickey Mouse's bro?"

So much for cute.

"Say what you've got to say."

"I did not find that body, or move it, or nothin'."

"You already said that," Service said. "Get to your point."

"Name's Nepo, lives out to Sands Station, nort' of the old air base."

The former K. I. Sawyer Air Force Base was now Marquette's airport. "North of the county airport on County Road 553?" Friday asked.

"Couple of yellow house trailers parked back in red pines. Blue garage."

"Who is Nepo?" Friday pressed.

"Downstater—Rockford, I think. Dropped out fum Northern."

"You're telling us this dropout named Nepo found the body, not you."

"Right on, dude."

"I'm not a dude," she said.

"Yes, sir."

"I'm not a sir, either."

DeJean looked flustered and said nothing more.

"When did this alleged miraculous discovery take place?" Friday asked.

"Week ago, dude. Twinny fort, twinny fit, like dat. Dude said he was out here snagging salmon, ya know? Wandered up on the body in the trailer, said the blood even looked wet, and he got hell out of here. Like, it scared shit out of him, man."

"Where's Nepo now?"

"Probably drunk. He was bad shook."

"So Nepo found a dead child and told you about it. Why would he do that?"

"I wasn't only one, dude. He probably told others, too. He don't know how ta keep his mouth shut. I don't know why he told me. I don't hardly know the motherfucker."

"But you saw it as a profit opportunity," Friday said coldly. "Pay to see a butchered dead kid, dudes, It's party time!"

"Hey," Daly DeJean said, grinning demonically, "this here's the US of Pay."

Service fought the temptation to flatten the young man.

"How long you been bringing people out here?" Friday asked.

"Just tonight. I figured Halloween would get 'em out. Guess I was right," he added. "My old man says I got me a good head for bidness."

15

Saturday, November 1

SANDS STATION, MARQUETTE COUNTY

It turned out that Sean Nepo was no stranger to law enforcement: Two convictions for assault, a DUI, and once charged with attempted rape, charges dropped, reasons not specified. He'd spent less than ninety days in jail, all of them in Marquette County, and his last known address was as Daly DeJean had called it: two yellow trailers in Sands Station with a blue garage, like some sort of weird van Gogh painting, only dulled down by reality and decay. Friday had a photo of the man, from his last stint in jail: six-four, 167 pounds, reddish straw-blond hair, scorpion tattoos on his neck.

There were no vehicles parked anywhere near the trailers or garage. All of the doors were open, and the buildings were empty. The trailers were set one behind the other, connected by a four-foot walkway. The front door to the northern trailer was ripped away, bent, twisted, and hanging in tatters. There was mud scrubbed with snow scabs, no grass.

"No need to replace the screen with winter coming," Treebone said.

"You reading the deal here?" Service asked his old friend.

"I saw the tracks," Treebone said. "Looks like Nepo's had him a four-legged visitor."

"Tuesday," Service said.

"Bear?" she said.

There was a large pile of fresh scat by the front porch. "Looks like," Service said.

"Still in there?" she asked.

"We'll soon know," Service said. "Tree, take the south entrance door, rear trailer. Tuesday, stay here. Noonan, you take the west end, set up between the trailers so you can cover both end windows. Allerdyce take the east end."

"Ain't got no gun," Limpy reminded Service.

"No teeth neither," Treebone growled. "Make a face at the sonuvabitch."

Allerdyce grunted, then grinned.

"Be ready, Noonan," Service advised.

"For what?" the retired Detroit detective asked.

"Something big, black, and in a hurry," Treebone said.

"Just like home," Noonan said, walking west to get into position.

The team members had handheld 800-megahertz radio units, courtesy of the Negaunee State Police post commander, who had been faxed an order personally signed by Governor Timms.

"South side?" Service asked, keying his mike.

"Closed, secure," Treebone reported.

"East and west?"

"Fine and clear," came the responses.

"Entering," Service told them. He stepped to the north door, looked inside. "Near total destruction in here, and it stinks bad."

"I can smell death way out here," Noonan said over his radio. "Strong."

Service stepped inside, his Remington shotgun in hand. He heard the animal, but never saw it as it ripped its way through the back trailer's west window, then *whomp-whomp-whomp-whomp-whomp-whomp!*

Friday on the porch shouting, "Cease fire, cease fire!"

Grady Service found Sean Nepo in a bedroom, a shotgun sort of across his chest and right shoulder, only the top of his head gone, brain and tissue bits sprayed on the wall and ceiling, blood and tissue everywhere. Hands still in place, but feet missing. It also looked like the bear had been chewing on the body. The bedroom stank of shit, both human and animal.

"Got Nepo," Service said over the radio. He heard Friday coming up behind him, something on the floor crunching under her boot.

The dead man had black hair down to his ass, and a heavy, wiry black beard. He wore a black Megadeth T-shirt; unlaced black-and-white checked tennies were on the bed by his legs. His feet were gone, bone tips glistening white in the poor light.

"Description and photo showed him as reddish-blond," Friday observed.

"Too much fun for him. Maybe he needed a change. Who shot out there?"

"Noonan," she said. "Bear. You'd better come see."

"He okay?"

"May need to change his skivvies," she said. "Five slugs into a very big animal. It collapsed with a paw on his boot, tore the leather down to the steel toecap."

Bears rarely left human dwellings the same way they came in.

"You talk to him?"

"He flashed me the okay sign. I asked if he was really okay, and he said he was 'just dandy,' but I watched him trying to reload, and he was dropping rounds on the ground."

Friday moved to the bed, looked at Nepo's body, took out her camera, began taking photographs. "Suicide?" she said.

"Your call, not mine," Service said.

Friday used her radio to call the medical examiner and State Police forensic crime scene team.

Service looked behind Friday, saw Allerdyce creeping silently through the rubble. "Get out of here, old man, and don't touch anything."

"Just wanna help," Limpy said.

"Then get outside," Service said.

"Hurt my feelin's," the old man said.

Service shook his head. "You've none to hurt, so scram."

Treebone said over the radio, "Everything good to go?"

"Noonan shot a bear, and Grady found Nepo," Friday answered.

"That don't sound so sweet for the subject."

Noonan came in, tiptoed to the bedroom, looked at the body, clucked several times like an anxious chicken, said nothing, and withdrew.

"Crime scene and ME en route," Friday told them.

"Got a theory?" Noonan asked.

"Suicide seems obvious," Friday said.

"Seems like, but maybe not," Noonan said.

"Explain."

"Wait for techies," he said, clucking again, which annoyed Service.

The conservation officer looked at Noonan's bear. Big, fat, old, teeth worn to yellow nubs. "Whew," he declared out loud. "Why'd you let it get so close?"

"I didn't. He just wun't go down. Thought I was going to have to reach down his fucking throat and tear out his fucking heart. Damn thing didn't know he was dead."

"They can be like that," Service said. "Next time, put all your rounds into the head," and he tapped his forehead to show the man. "There."

"Gee," Noonan said. "I'll try to remember. How big, you think?"

"Four hundred plus, could push five."

"That good?" Noonan asked.

"Dead is good, size irrelevant in this situation."

Friday was inside when Dr. Tork showed up.

"Good God," she declared. "Y'all are like the Four Horsemen of the Apocalypse, your wake spewing bodies. Where's *this* poor soul?"

Service pointed at the front door and watched her march inside.

"We part of this soiree, or not?" Noonan asked.

"We'll have our chance. Be patient," Service said.

"Forensics and techie shit aside, this ain't fucking rocket science," Noonan said.

Friday eventually came back outside as Jen Maki and her technicians went inside to join the ME. "Small freezer in the kitchen," Friday said in a subdued voice. "Three hearts in plastic containers."

"Here dieth the beast, by its own hand," Treebone declared.

"Bullshit," Noonan said. "Ain't no suicide. Been staged to look that way, but it's not the real deal."

The ME came outside in time to hear, looked at the smaller man. "Care to share your opinion, little man?"

"Sure, sweetcakes. The spatter-splatter pattern ain't right. Anybody can see that. Man lays down, puts shotgun barrel *under* his chin, the blast takes some face, top of the anterior skull, middle to frontal lobe. But the posterior plate's gone on this guy, his chin hanging down like a drool string. He ain't no suicide."

Kristy Tork went back inside, came out ten minutes later, and went directly to Noonan. "What's your background?"

"Homicide, retired, Detroit Metro."

"You have a name, little man?"

"Noonan," he said.

"Kristy," she said. "I think you're right." She turned to Friday. "Staged suicide make sense to you?"

"Suggests somebody's gone to a lot of trouble to help us conclude this is our grank from Twenty Point Pond and the Little Huron. There's bear hair all over the bed and body. I don't know what to think. Time of death?"

"Fast as we can get it," Tork said.

The ME stayed close to Jen Maki and her people. The others went outside and gathered. Linsenman showed up with thermoses of coffee and a sleeve of Styrofoam cups, told them he'd talked to old man DeJean, who denied any knowledge of the dead child, or his son Daly's "nefarious activities."

"Nefarious? Great word," Treebone said.

"Can we get to the fucking point?" an irritated Noonan asked. "My ass is freezing. I need real food. Some asshole whacked Nepo, big fucking whoop. Are the hearts from the previous vicks, or not? Are they even human? Aortal openings are almost diamond-shaped, and those don't look human to me. If they aren't the vicks' hearts, some dumbass went to a helluva lot of trouble to convince us the shit trail ends here. If the parts don't match, we may have upped our body count by one. Either way, this is bull, and I need some god-damned food."

"Bear chewed dead guy some," Limpy told the others.

Friday looked at the man, went to her briefcase, took out a folder filled with crime scene photos, and handed them to the old poacher, who went through them slowly.

"Ain't no critter done that," he said after he was done, pushing the folder back to Friday.

"You're sure?" Friday asked the violator.

"No critter I know of."

"Good," Service said. "Maybe we should use this opportunity to get out to the public, get rid of the dogman red herring right here and now."

"Or," Friday countered, "allow for the possibility of a dogman—or some other kind of creature, yet to be determined or identified."

Service couldn't believe what he'd heard. "Jesus, Tuesday, you're *inviting* chaos," he said. "It's absurd."

"Perhaps," she said.

"No, I *know* it is," Service said, "and so does Limpy. Let's see what the vet can tell us."

Friday blinked and then stared at him. "What vet?"

"The one we need to look at Noonan's bear."

"We need a vet?" she asked in a doubting tone.

"Did the bear chew on the corpse?"

"It looks that way."

"If you think a bear gnawed on Nepo, a vet has to take a look and do a necropsy on the dead animal, the whole nine yards. That's SOP when an animal is suspected or accused of mauling or killing a human." He remembered when he'd killed a bear that had killed a three-year-old girl in the Eastern U.P. The local vet had retrieved the child's hand from the animal's stomach.

"Can't *you* just take care of it?" she asked.

He nodded. "It's your case. You want this done by the book or not?"

"You know the answer to that," she said.

"Then we need to get a vet here, let them do their thing, look for hair samples and so forth and so on, and send them in for tox work, just like human evidence."

"Seems redundant," Friday said. "An animal can give us cover," she argued again. "On the upside, our perp may believe we've been diverted. If rumors are floating a dogman, fine, let's give them one. Let them all talk dogman."

What the hell is wrong with her? It's insidious, but she has a point.

It just wasn't one he planned to accede to. "Repeat, invites chaos. You want to pull a public fake-out on this deal, then you need a vet here to confirm evidence and our story. You can be damn sure reporters will ask every possible question and draw whatever conclusions they think they can, and to hell with the impact. I'm telling you, if we even hint at a dogman or any kind of so-called 'creature,' we're going to be swimming in assholes and cameras from legit big-time media, and never mind all the half-asses and Internet shit. Some hunters wig out over a big deer; what do you think they'll do with a mythical creature?"

"Are you overstating to make your point?" his girlfriend asked.

Her tone pissed him off. "Hell, no. I'm telling you how it is, no more, no less. You must have a vet you work with," Service said.

Friday went into the trailers, and after talking to Dr. Kristy Tork, came back out shaking her head. "She's already called a vet—also by the name of Tork."

"Tork, like her?" Service asked.

"Her daughter Annastasia. She taught at Michigan State, now practices in Trenary. Should be here anytime. She's worked homicide support in the Lansing area. Her mother confirms a vet is *de rigueur* if animals are involved in any way. You were right," she said, looking directly at Service, who was smart enough to keep his mouth shut.

Anna Tork was thirtyish, blonde, thin, big-eyed, and vibrating with life. Mother and daughter hugged momentarily and disappeared back inside the trailer. The younger Dr. Tork came out ten minutes later and asked to see the dead bear. Service and Noonan showed her. She carried a large black tackle box, which she opened, peeling out a pair of latex gloves and putting them on.

"Can you guys help? I need this old fella over onto his back in a semi-sitting position. I want good access to the viscera and the helping hand of gravity when I start exploring and digging around."

Service called for Treebone and Allerdyce, and the four men together barely managed to get the dead-weight bear up into some semblance of a sitting position. "Jesus," Tree complained. "This old guy needed to be on Weight Watchers."

Anna Tork knelt in front of the bear with a hunting knife, scraped it on a whetstone several times, and began. She unzipped the animal like she had done it countless times. "Look at the thickness of the fat layer," she told them, pointing.

Service looked down and saw a three-inch layer of glutinous yellow tissue.

"This is one *big* animal," the vet said. "You guys put him on scales?"

"No," Service said.

"We need to," the vet said. "Jen Maki's got scales in her truck."

"You've worked with Jen before?" Service asked.

"No, but we're friends, and we trade publications and professional information."

Tork isolated the animal's stomach, severed the connecting tissues, lifted it, and set it on the ground. It was grayish-blue, shaped like a huge, slimy water bottle. She set aside her knife, peeled the wrapping off a new disposable scalpel, and looked around. "Hold this," she told Allerdyce and put his hand on one side of the stomach.

"Hold anyt'ing youse want, girlie."

"Is *he* a cop?" she asked Service.

"No," Service said.

"Thank God," Tork said, and waved the scalpel in a riposte near the old man's belly. "May have to give you more to hold if you don't act nice," she said with a snarl, and Allerdyce drew back before recovering his composure.

The vet deftly opened the stomach and spread it out. The stench was one of wet, hot ferment. She poked around the contents and looked up at Service. "Mostly empty, and nothing obvious, but we'll do tox, see what turns up. Not a lot of gastric juices for so big a stomach," she said. "And no visibile sign of human parts." She turned to the animal's head, rolled up its jowl, checked teeth. "Given the condition of his choppers, I'm thinking the boy would have trouble with a Jell-O diet, much less bone and meat. He mighta chewed with no result. We'll have two-way DNA."

"Well, it looks like something gnawed on the deceased," Service said.

"True, but maybe not this old fella," the vet said. She leaned close to look at the animal's eyes. "Advanced cataracts," she observed, not looking up at the men.

Service watched her touch one of the bear's eyes.

"I'm thinking this animal is either functionally blind or darn close to lights out," she said. The vet looked past the animal, saw Noonan's damaged boot. "You the shooter?"

Noonan nodded.

"My guess is, it wasn't a charge. He just wanted out and away, panicked, ran the wrong direction and couldn't see or smell. . . . Hey," she said, "*look at me, man.*"

Noonan did as ordered. She said, "If a bear goes into a human dwelling, it's committing suicide no matter what happens next."

Noonan grunted. "Something charges me, it dies—end of story. No remorse."

Dr. Tork the younger raised an eyebrow. "People included?"

"Especially," Noonan said.

The vet and the retired cop maintained eye contact for what seemed like a long time to Service. "Are we about done here?" he asked.

"Call it *finito*," Tork said. "I'll send samples to Michigan State to conclude the official necropsy, and another set to the US Fish and Wildlife forensics lab in Oregon, see what they come up with."

"How long for results?" Service asked.

"Honestly? When they can get to them. Great facilities, too much work, not enough qualified people, shrinking budgets; you all know the math. The times we live in, eh? When it happens, it happens."

Not the answer Service wanted. He asked the vet to come inside with him, caught Friday's attention, took her with them.

The body remained where he had found it. "The ME got some hairs here. You, too?"

"Yeah, wanna see?"

"No, but what are they from? The bear, the carpet, or Mr. Nepo?"

The young vet set her jaw. "Neither. One set might look canid to the naked eye, though the color seems off by a bit."

"Canid, meaning?"

"*Canis lupus,*" she said. "Best guess at this juncture."

"Wolf, but could be a dog," Service said.

"That's certainly one possibility," Tork said.

"There are others?'"

"Almost always," she said. "Let's wait for tox results and all the data."

"You can differentiate dog from wolf DNA with hair?"

"Usually. The mitochondrial DNA difference between dog and wolf is around one percent, which doesn't sound like much, but it is. By comparison, scientists believed for a long time that human and chimpanzee DNA differed by two percent, but we're learning more and more about the DNA of both, and now the diff is up to five percent and increasing, as DNA studies and capabilities increase. Having said all this, DNA generalities are virtually worthless for all but the most general, and therefore, meaningless, discussions."

"The odds are, there will be ambiguity and uncertainty?" he asked.

"Of course; this is science, not magic," she reminded them.

Service said, "The hairs Friday found are red. Are there red wolves?"

"Yes, of course—*Canis rufus rufus,* but none of them are left in the wild except for a small population along the Mexican border," said Tork. "The thing is, though, all wolf subspecies have some sort of known red hair tone. It depends on diet and habitat, and genetics, of course. *Canis rufus rufus* is smaller than *Canis lupus.* Are you aiming for a particular outcome with this line of questioning?" she asked.

"Not exactly sure," he said. How could he make Friday understand? He was frustrated in part because it seemed that Friday didn't understand the implications of a monster hunt. In fact, he wasn't even sure *he* had a full understanding, but it was a lot more than she had. The word that twisted in his mind was *frenzy.*

"Okay," Friday said. "We've heard from the vet. Now what?"

Service said, "We wait for DNA and tox results. We don't know anything yet."

"Does it matter?" Friday asked. "On the upside, an animal declaration would give us an edge, make our perp think we're diverted and off his trail. If rumors say dogman, that doesn't matter because we know our perp is a two-footer, not four-. He'll be glad we zigged instead of zagged," she reasoned. "Maybe it will affect what he does next, and how."

"Maybe for you," Service allowed. "But if you do that, the rest of us have to treat the dogman as a legit animal, and that won't be helping us *or* you. The whole dogman thing is bullshit, a figment of somebody's imagination. Ask the vet."

"Is there something going on here I ought to be aware of?" Anna Tork asked. "Did someone say 'dogman'?"

"It was said," Service said. "Yes."

"Interesting," Tork said. "Cryptozoology at its most insidious."

"More like cryptobullshit," Service muttered.

"Is it?" the vet challenged. "In the late nineties, surveys showed fifty-four percent of American adults believed in angels, and almost half in aliens from outer space. Earlier this year Pew reported a survey showing belief in angels is up to sixty-eight percent. There's no empirical data for such beliefs, yet people believe. What's the diff if you believe in Bigfoot or Christian dogma?"

"Are you defending fools?" Service asked.

"I'm defending the right of people to believe what they choose to believe, rational or not. At the base level, what religion is rational? Faith isn't rational. It's something else, and more compelling than facts for a lot of people."

"Look," Service said sharply, "that's philosophy, or whatever. We're talking about the possibility of making public a dogman's involvement in a series of killings, and obviously, *there is no dogman,* but Friday wants us to announce it in hopes that we can convince our perp that the dogman is the subject of our investigation, which may give us an advantage in hunting the actual perp."

"Who says there's no dogman?" the vet asked, and this brought sudden silence. "I can neither confirm nor deny such a thing. You can't prove a negative."

Service rubbed his head. "I'm going crazy."

"Nonsense," Tork said. "Rationality and good science demand that we calmly and deliberately examine everything, including apparent irrationality."

"And?" Tuesday Friday asked.

"New species, or those previously thought extinct, are still found from time to time," the vet ventured.

Service said, "In this country? *New* large mammals?"

"No, not here, not yet, but that doesn't preclude it from happening. We still have a lot of empty space, and that's invariably where they show up. Theoretically there are lots of possibilities we'd all like to ignore."

Service couldn't believe he was part of this conversation and wished he had kept his mouth shut, but at least the vet had taken samples and eventually there would be results. He prayed they'd be worth something. "I'm seeking substance," he said, "And finding vapor."

"What's your dogman look like?" Tork asked.

"No clue," Service said. "Never seen one. Nobody's seen one. They don't fucking exist."

"How about we let the toxicology tests come back. Meanwhile, I'll look at the dogman in my own way and time."

The ME approached with a bag of darker hair. "These were on the floor. After examining the deceased, I'm sure he had a form of hypertrichosis."

"Meaning?

"He was massively hairy," the ME said.

Service said. "So what?"

"Hypertrichosis, sometimes called werewolf syndrome."

Service clamped his jaws shut and walked away, leaving the women together.

"What's crackin'?" Treebone asked.

"I think we are about to birth a monster," Service said.

Tree nodded. "Deep . . ."

16

Tuesday, November 4

SLIPPERY CREEK CAMP

The situation at Sands Station deteriorated into a full-blown argument, with Service and Friday bellowing insults at each other before storming apart. "Look," she'd quailed, "I'm trying to find a murderer."

"Human, *not* animal."

"Goddammit, Grady, we're behind the curve and need an edge, even a small one."

He'd shaken his head. "Do you remember the story of the first thermo-nuclear weapon, fusion instead of fission?"

"No," she said with obvious irritation.

"Scientists made a miscalculation, which yielded the biggest goddamn bomb in history—*thirty times* more than the experts had calculated."

"We're not dealing with physics," Friday said.

"That's my point," he shot back. "This is about human beings, the most bloodthirsty, unpredictable creatures in the universe!"

Friday had exhaled loudly, barked "Asshole," got into her vehicle, and slammed the door.

Service, Noonan, and Treebone drove back to Slippery Creek in awkward silence. Allerdyce had disappeared at Sands Station, and Service wasn't interested in waiting or searching for the old poacher.

Camp was quiet all night, and when Service awoke, Allerdyce was in the kitchen, had made coffee, and was working on breakfast.

"G'head, make yourself at home," Service mumbled.

"Why youse got grumples?"

A young man with almond-colored hair came out of the downstairs bathroom. "Flush," Allerdyce ordered, and the boy went back and did as he was told.

Allerdyce pointed at a chair. "Sit."

The young man sat stiffly, head up, hands on his knees.

"Donte DeJean, meet Dickteckative Service."

"You the one who pointed us to the Little Huron?" Service asked.

The boy nodded.

"Youse got a voice, boy," Allerdyce growled. "Use it."

"Yes, it was me."

Service said, "You left before we could talk to you and thank you."

"DeJeans don't expect thank-yous from the DNR," the boy said.

"You turned in your brother. That took courage," Service said.

"Turned in the situation, not my brother," the boy corrected.

Service sat down across from the boy. "Care to explain?"

Allerdyce turned from the stove, said, "Tell da man what youse tole me."

The boy shrugged. "I seen it," he said.

"It?" Treebone asked, striding into the kitchen.

"You know," Donte DeJean said, staring at the hulking Treebone.

"You afraid of black folks?" Treebone asked.

"Ain't never seen one so big up this close," the boy said. "'Cept on the TV."

"Now you met a real one, not one on TV," Treebone said. "What did you mean you saw *it?*"

"The thing I saw," the boy said.

"Describe it," Service said, thinking, *Oh, God.*

"Hairy," DeJean said.

"Bear, wolf, cougar, moose—what?" Service asked. "Be specific."

"Two legs," the boy said softly. "Sort of like a person."

"Person in a fur coat?" Service ventured.

"Not like that," the boy said. "The fur looked real."

"You see this, whatever it was, near the Little Huron?"

"Once there, twice over by Ketchkan Lake, and another time up by Bull-dog Lake."

Tentative, not certain. Service tried to process the information and sites. Ketchkan was near where the actual twenty-point buck had been killed, a place that nurtured an extraordinary percentage of large deer and some moose. Service closed his eyes and summoned his mind map: It was all within a fifteen-mile radius, with Twenty Point Pond pretty much at the center. "Is seeing this thing at the Little Huron what got you to turn in your brother?"

DeJean nodded. "I guess."

"At the old trailer?"

"Near there, on the road, west of the river."

"Were you alone?"

The boy shook his head.

"Daly didn't see it?"

"I was with Sean Nepo, and he seen it with me."

"You and Nepo were there for what?"

"Fishing."

"But Nepo saw something more, is that it?"

"Yeah, and he told Daly."

"He didn't tell you?"

"No, I seen the thing and Sean followed it, and then he come back, grabbed me, said we had to get out of there, so we booked."

"Sean didn't tell you what else he saw?"

"No, he was toking like crazy. We bought beer and he dropped me at the old man's house, and he and Daly went off somewhere."

Noonan strolled into the kitchen, stretching.

"Hair color?" Service asked.

"Light," the boy said.

"Blond, white, gray—how light?"

"Sort of gray tips, real long hair."

"Size?" Treebone asked.

"Not tall, maybe five-ten, six foot, but big, like the Hulk, okay? I was fifty yards off . . . hard to judge exactly."

"Scrambled eggs, coffee, sausage links good for ever-body?" Allerdyce asked.

Service said to Tree, "Man, not monster."

The two men looked at Noonan, who nodded agreement.

"You see a face, feet, hands, details?" Service asked the boy.

"It was too far away, but I saw it didn't run as much as it hopped, and it didn't have no clothes, just hair."

"Hopped . . . like a kangaroo?" Noonan asked.

"More like a snowshoe hare," DeJean said. "Big jumps, covering ground real quick."

"This the first time you saw it?" Service asked. "At the Little Huron?"

"The last time I seen it."

"Four times, and you've never reported it?"

"Who to?" the boy shot back. "Not my old man. My brothers? I kept my mouth shut."

Service said, "Use your hand if you can, and show us how it moved."

The boy sat the heel of his hand on the table, fingers straight up, and nosed the hand forward in an arc, hitting on the fingers, and pulling the heel underneath to the original starting position.

"You saw two legs and two arms?" Service pressed.

"Yessir."

"Did Nepo know you'd seen it before?"

Donte DeJean shook his head. "Sean was real scared, and we didn't do no talking that day."

"Can you show us where you saw this thing—exact locations?"

"Not a problem," the boy said.

Service telephoned Friday. "We have a witness who alleges he saw whatever was out on the Little Huron."

"Well, hello and good morning to you, too," she said sharply.

"He claims four sightings of this thing."

"Description?"

"We're working on that, and we're gonna go check sighting locations. You want to come along?"

"No, I've got scut to sort through, waiting for tox results and all that," she said. "Who is this witness?"

"Donte DeJean."

"The one who tipped us on the Little Huron?"

"One and the same."

"You think he's credible?"

"We'll find out."

"Two-legged or four-legged?" she asked.

"He claims two-, but that's still up in the air."

"Let me know," she said, and hung up.

"Female problems?" Tree asked.

"More of a professional disagreement," Service said.

Treebone laughed out loud. "There ain't no such separation between personal and professional when you and your old lady are involved."

"Are youses gone eat, or I waste my time makin' dis grub?" Allerdyce asked.

Service called Denninger, and she told him the weather in east Baraga County was snowy, temperature dropping, northwest winds picking up to twenty knots, gusting higher. He knew they wouldn't be able to see anything in such conditions, but when the storm passed, animals would start moving and feeding again. With all the leaves down, they would have a really good look at the terrain, which was what he wanted. Little Huron, Twenty Point, Ketchkan, Bulldog: What did they have in common?

"What's the guess on how long this storm will blow?" he asked her.

"Twenty-four to thirty-six hours until it lays down."

"You working?" he asked.

"No, gotta go get some half-hard. I've been playing with dead-soft, but that just ain't cutting it; see what I'm saying?"

"Half-hard?"

She laughed out loud. "Jewelry wire, you moron. My new hobby. Who you voting for?"

"What're my choices?"

"Obama and McCain."

"I choose Teddy Roosevelt."

"He's not on the ballot."

"Don't I know it," he said. "Half-hard is wire, no joke?"

"No joke. Dead-soft, too."

"I'm tired of talking to you," he announced.

"You're sadly lacking in social skills."

"Been told that," he said, adding, "Bye" before closing his cell phone.

Noonan, Treebone, Allerdyce, and Donte DeJean were gathered at the kitchen table. "Presidential election today," Service told them.

"Absentee ballot for me," Treebone said. "Can't stand lines."

"No lines for me, either," Service said.

"Who you vote for?"

"Didn't. Lines are short when you don't bother."

"I don't vote neither," Noonan said. "What's the point? Damn politicians shake your hand before they're elected and shake your confidence afterwards. They're all slimeballs."

Limpy announced, "Secret ballot. Ain't gotta say my pick."

Treebone smirked. "Bet he isn't of color."

The boy said, "I'm not old enough."

"Snowing in the Hurons," Service told them. "We'll use today to outfit ourselves. I want to spend a couple days at Ketchkan and Bulldog, scout around. Each man needs a two-man tent, tarp and fly, thermal fart sack. I got plenty of extras. What kind of winter gear you got, Suit?"

"Good set of galoshes. It snow in the D, I don't go out, man."

Limpy spoke up. "Got plenty of stuff will fit 'im. I take Donte fetch his gear, grab mine for Noonan, be back dark."

"What about school, Donte?"

"Homeschool," he said.

"Really?"

"That's what my old man tells everyone."

Service looked at Allerdyce. "You know the country I'm talking about?"

"You betcha. Lots game up dose places, good birds, deer, moose, bear. Okay I bring my twenty-gauge, eh?"

Service shrugged. "Hell, we might as well have us an armed felon."

Allerdyce grinned. "I bring some bacon, too, knock us down some pats."

"You can't buy a hunting license," Service reminded him.

"Can buy," the poacher said, "just can't use legal, eh? You look nudder way when I get supper, okay?"

Grady Service sighed and spread out his hands. "Why not?"

What he thought was: *I'm going to game warden hell for this.*

17

Wednesday, November 5

KETCHKAN LAKE, BARAGA COUNTY

They took two trucks: Service's State Tahoe, and his personal Silverado. Ketchkan Lake showed on maps as nameless, a small body of water in the hills between Curwood and High Lakes, a mile north of the Huron River Road. There was a grown-over tote road that twisted up to Ketchkan along a meandering granite razorback. The snow had broken that morning, leaving six inches on the ground, wet and slippery. The temp was already in the low 40s and climbing, expected to reach 50 by afternoon, but drop below 30 that night.

Allerdyce and DeJean rode with Service. Tree and Noonan drove the Silverado.

Service knew the area somewhat from years back but parked and let Donte DeJean and Limpy take the lead going in. The boy stood on a ridge above Ketchkan and pointed at a rocky knob to the northeast. "It was below that high spot, headed down toward the lake."

"Same place twice?" Service asked.

"No; the other time was a bit north of here, closer to High Lake."

"Time of day?" Treebone asked.

"Both right in the middle, you know, like one o'clock?"

Allerdyce was hunkered down, shotgun across his thighs, staring north. Noonan was beside him in the same pose. *Monkey see, monkey do.* "You looking for a flat place to camp?" Service asked the poacher.

"Watching moose babies, but don't see mama."

"She won't be far," Service said. "They're born in May, June, will be with her for a year or so."

"Don't survive so good, moose babies don't," Allerdyce said. "Onny two in ten, mebbe. Dese two kittles look good, mebbe two hunert pound now. Dey down in red willow. I t'ink I go down dere, take look, get into popples, pop some pats dere." Then, he asked Noonan, "Wanna go?"

"Down in that fucking jungle? No way, old man."

"You camp up here?" Service asked DeJean as Allerdyce started shuffling downhill through a boulder field.

"There's a small rock tabletop just northwest of here," the boy said. "Can see High Lake from there, maybe a half-mile."

Service smiled. Donte had just described the same area where he'd camped long ago. It still amazed him how his old man had dragged such a giant deer out of this sparse, steep country. It struck him that Donte didn't sound like an older Yooper. MTV and YouTube and texting and all that other crap were erasing the Yooper way of speaking and replacing it—as in Donte's brother Daly—with an urban ghetto lingo that made the speakers sound like wannabe fools. Service didn't like it, but life was about change. What could you do but roll with it?

Finding the rock table, Service had them set up tents with flies, using rock spikes to hold them down. They would gather firewood later. Service, as always, had a supply of birch bark in his ruck, which would ignite even if wet, was the best fire starter he knew, and all free.

Limpy was stalking birds, so Tree set up the old poacher's shelter.

They heard five shotgun reports while they made camp, the shots spaced out, and by the time the tents were up Allerdyce came up the hill, breathing like he'd just gone out to the mailbox. "Better come see," he whispered to Service.

The two men hiked down to where the calves had been. A clear rill meandered along the base of a rocky embankment, and Service saw several ravens flap out of the heavy red willow that grew along the stream. Interspersed with willow were paper birches a few inches in diameter. The ravens had slugged their way out from the base of the birch trees.

"Water's pret skinny here," Allerdyce said of the small creek, and led Service across and into the willows where they got halfway to the rock wall before stopping. "Over dere," the old man said, pointing.

Service pushed past the poacher. It was a cow moose, but huge pieces of it were spread all around, like it had swallowed a bomb that had exploded inside it. "Seen this before?" he asked Allerdyce.

The old man said nothing, just shook his head with his mouth tight. The poacher's eyes were moving continuously, and Service could tell he was on alert, geeked by what he'd found.

When a wolf, coyote, bear, or cougar made a kill, the carcass would usually carry certain clues to help identify the predator. Cougars cached meat, and so did wolves. Bears generally didn't kill healthy deer or moose, only fawns, or they ate off carcasses. Coyotes pretty much stopped taking deer once fawns were dropped by early June and rarely ever attempted to take healthy deer. Wolves tended to eat everything from a dead animal—stomach, muscles, tendons, marrow, everything, small bones included. They also tended to rest near kills so they could feed at their leisure. This moose appeared to have been chewed on some, but mostly not; this scene was something he'd not seen before. "Any tracks or scat?" he asked the poacher.

Another head shake. "Ain't see this afore. She don't make no sense, eh? Youse find a kill, she tells you what happen, eh? Not dis. Dis don't tell shit."

Service agreed. "Look for scat and tracks."

"Snowmelt," Allerdyce reminded him.

"I know. Look close to the remains—logs, rocks, places where snow didn't get to," Service said. And then, after a pause, "What has the sort of power to rip a grown moose apart like this?"

"Beats me," the poacher said. "T'ing is, wolfies can smell mooses t'ree, four hundred yard away, eh? Wolfies close in, moose fight hards, kill a lot of wolfie. Healthy moose, wolfies leave 'em 'lone. Out west, Isle Boil, Canady, okay, wolfies eat moose dose places. Not up here U.P."

"Let's cover the kill site, grab samples: meat, hair, whatever we can find." Service pulled latex gloves and plastic bags out of his ruck, tossed some to Limpy.

"You send lapertory?" the poacher asked.

"We'll see if they're any smarter than us."

Service stared up the vertical bluff, twenty, maybe thirty feet up. *Cougar attack?*

He searched until he found the moose's head, and looked at the vertebrae. Cougars killed by breaking necks. *No evidence of that here. Not a cougar or a big cat.*

Limpy was on the far side of the remains while Service went methodically from clump to clump. He saw something whitish gleaming from griseous foreleg meat. He got down to a knee, felt the thing through his latex gloves. Couldn't move it. *Deep.*

He got out his pocketknife and loosened the object into a plastic bag. It was a huge, lethal-looking tooth, a cuspid or fang. He couldn't remember what terminology biologists used for various teeth. *Way too big for a coyote.* He leaned close to the leg joint and then to the meat, his eye moving from where the tooth had been until he found a second puncture wound, equally large, but no tooth in this one. He laid out a small tape measure and photographed the distance between the punctures. As he looked through his digital camera, he whistled in astonishment. If these were fangs, the width from one side to the other was nearly seven inches. The wolves he knew would measure two or three. *Totally fucking weird.* Not to mention disturbing.

Two hours later they went back to camp. As they hiked, Allerdyce asked, "You find somepin' dere?"

Service showed the poacher the bag with the tooth.

"Wolfie," Allerdyce said. "*Big* wolfie."

Service didn't tell the man what he measured on the bite width. It wasn't believable, even to him.

The tooth was interesting, the kill site unusual, to say the least. *But does any of this mean anything?* He had no answer. He showed the tooth to the others. "Tomorrow we'll spread out and cover this area, see if we can find tracks, scat, anything."

Later, Allerdyce brought him a cigarette. "T'ing kill dat moose ain't no normal wolfie," he said, shaking his head.

• • •

The next afternoon Limpy found Service, said, "Got 'nudder one."

No tooth at the second carcass, but the same violence as the first. And no tracks or scat, for any species, prey or predator. It was like the site was sterile, the carcasses dropped from a UFO, or maybe this placed was cursed.

18

Friday, November 7

BULLDOG LAKE, MARQUETTE COUNTY

They hiked out of Ketchkan at dawn, drove south to the Peshekee Grade, and to a small parking area for the trailhead up into the McCormick Wilderness. They hiked three miles north and uphill through the stone hills and pines, past White Deer Lake, which connected to Bulldog Lake by a thin channel. All the way they moved through mazes of SUV-size granite boulders spackled with pastel-colored lichen.

Grady Service pulled them together and passed around his camera, showing them the moose carcasses at Lake Ketchkan. "Be methodical," he told them. "Expect moose in the marshy wet areas, deer up in the hardwoods near cedar swamps."

"Where'd you make your sighting here?" Service asked Donte DeJean.

"At the bottom of this trail, where it leads across the channel."

"You were down there?"

"No, I was up here, but this was the closest of the four times. I think I surprised it."

"Why?"

"Took off across the channel, running south."

"Two feet?"

"Mostly."

"Show us with your hand," Service said.

The boy demonstrated, and this time Service saw that the motion was almost certainly four-legged, not bipedal. "We'll camp at the old logging camp clearing on the northwest corner of the lake—about a half-mile up the trail here. Limpy, Donte, and I will take the low areas, Tree and Suit, you guys take the trail north up into the hardwood stands."

With everyone headed for the campsite, Service ascended a steep promontory, found he had cell coverage, and called Cale Pilkington, wildlife biologist at the Marquette Regional Office, the man responsible for monitoring and managing the state's moose herd.

"Cale, Grady Service. I'm up in the McCormick Tract, near Bulldog Lake. Last couple of days I was camped at Ketchkan and found two dead cow moose, and saw two live calves." Service gave him the coordinates from his GPS unit. "We estimate two hundred pounds, give or take."

"Calves probably belong to one of the cows," the biologist said. "Size suggests six to eight months old. They could probably make it through the winter—if it isn't a blinger."

"What about wolves?"

"They're not an issue with our moose. We aren't aware of any wolf-killed moose so far. Isle Royale, sure, but here, I don't think so."

Service said, "I'm sending you some photos from Ketchkan. Let me know what you think."

"Okay. Seeing any big bucks up where you are?"

"Not a single deer, any sex, any age, any size."

"Deer carcasses?"

"None. Just seems like no deer, no tracks, no rubs, no pellets, no nothing."

"Weird. I've seen them yard up in some of those ravines."

"No sign of deer," Service reported. "And it's way too early for them to yard. Maybe we're not in the area you're thinking of."

"West or east of Ketchkan?"

"Mostly northwest."

"That's the area with the population."

"Let me know about those photos."

"You bet. You guys getting ready for deer season?"

"Sort of." *Deer season: What's today, the seventh? Shit. One week until the firearm deer opener.* Surprised to still have a signal, Service punched in Chief Waco's speed dial, and the chief answered his own phone. "It's Grady. I'm up in the McCormick on that case from the governor. Does this case take priority over deer season?"

"It takes priority over everything, Grady. By the way, there was a dogman report on the Detroit TV station this morning. It said the dogman was possibly linked to some recent U.P. killings, and the reporter criticized police for being so tight-lipped. You stay with your case; we'll cover your area for firearm deer."

"You know this assignment is ludicrous, Chief."

"She's the boss, Grady."

"She's micromanaging to shift attention from her job performance: She's a hornswoggling, thimble-rigging, political pinhead pushing pure piffle!"

"Spoken like a Hoosier from the hills," the chief said, laughing. "Just do what the boss wants done."

After a day of searching Service decided to move the team out at first light. Too much territory here, too few people, and not enough supplies.

That night after dark they were all at the fire getting ready to get into their shelters when an animal howled northwest of them, up toward Summit Lake, and on the same azimuth as Ketchkan. The quavering call lasted a good six seconds and burned into all of them.

After a long silence, Allerdyce managed to say, "Never heard dat sound."

"Wolf," Treebone said.

"Sure," Allerdyce said. "What kind?"

19

Saturday, November 8

PESHEKEE GRADE, MARQUETTE COUNTY

The others were loading the trucks when Friday called Service. "Where've you been?" she asked.

"Boots in the mud," he said, not liking her tone.

"We've got another one," she said wearily.

"Where?"

"Beaver Lake, Baraga County, between Parent and Worm Lakes. Best way there is off Old M-28."

"Campground?"

"No, it's a camp owned by some minister from Kalamazoo. He hasn't been up here in ten years, and the place is falling apart. Party house and vagrants."

"Officially abandoned?"

"Nope, just neglected."

"We're rolling," he said.

"You find anything?" she asked.

"Not really," he said.

Cale Pilkington called as Service was driving past Michigamme. "Service?"

"Here."

"Got those photos. Is this some kind of joke?"

"What do you mean?"

"Those moose are . . ."

"Fucked up?" Service suggested.

"I've never seen anything like it. I showed the photos to my boss and colleagues. None of them have ever seen anything like this. *Ever.* It makes no sense biologically. We don't know of anything that can do that to a live moose."

Service tried to think, but his mind was already moving forward to Friday. "The photos are legit, Cale; they show exactly what we found."

"Corroboration—scat, hair, tracks?"

"The spinal columns aren't broken."

"Okay, so we rule out cougar. That I can buy."

"I found a tooth," Service said.

"From the moose?"

"No, something stuck in a moose's thigh. Looks canid to me, but big."

"Wolf-big?"

"Twice that."

"Anything else?"

"Couple of months ago Denninger and I found tracks near Twenty Point Pond."

"Cast a mold?"

"Got photos. You want them?"

"Please. Dimensions?"

"Length is seven and a half inches, almost eight, splayed like fingers."

"Canid?"

"My first thought was whopper wolf."

"And now?"

"No opinion. I'll e-mail the photo in a minute."

"What about the tooth?"

"Show it to you when I can," Service said.

Then, he called Friday. "That vet, Anna Tork. Did she keep any hair samples from Sean Nepo's place?"

"I don't know, and I'm kind of busy. Where are you now?"

"Passing Three Lakes. Be there in no time."

She hung up.

Service called the biologist again. "Twenty Point Pond, mouth of the Little Huron, Ketchkan, and Bulldog Lakes—moosewise and deerwise, how do those places match up?"

"Not a lot of moose anywhere up there, but more at those locations than most places."

"Deer?"

"Good mast crops for fall, extreme isolation, minimal human interference . . . not a lot of deer, but conducive to growing some big ones."

"Low hunter pressure?"

"Probably nonexistent in all but Twenty Point Pond, and there aren't many deer there."

"What about Beaver Lake in Baraga County, south of Parent Lake?"

"Yeah, Haley Creek, Lateral Creek—lots of good swamp and moose food. That's pretty good moose country, not like those other spots."

"Thanks," Service said.

"What about that tooth?"

"Soon as I get a chance. You know a vet from Trenary, Anna Tork?"

"Know of her. She's fairly new."

"Give her a bump, ask her if she kept any hair samples from the Nepo crime scene. That's N-E-P-O crime scene, near Sands; got it?"

"I'll call her. And if she's got the samples?"

"Ask if you can see them, see what you think."

"I'm on it," Pilkington said, ending the call.

Service pocketed his phone.

"Pipple say ain't safe talk cellphony driving," Allerdyce said self-righteously. "Sonnyboy."

"Bite me," Service said.

20

Saturday, November 8

BEAVER LAKE, BARAGA COUNTY

The road to the small lake was flanked by a tamarack-fringed marsh beyond a cedar tree line on the east side, and a series of marsh ponds and low jack-pine scrub country to the west. Emergency vehicles were all nosed into the trees on the southwest part of the lake. Service parked and made his way through the maze to Tuesday Friday, who was sitting on a picnic bench staring off into the distance. The table was beside a small cabin that looked like it would fall over if a hummingbird crashed into it.

Service saw a grassy, open area across the lake, and some dwellings, signs of civilization, however small and remote.

"I'm guessing this is the other side of the tracks," he greeted Friday. "ME here yet?"

"Still waiting on him," she said. "Jerry Dove; you know him?"

"Nope."

"Lucky you. He's an officious, lazy little prig. The body's inside. Lucky us: Seems the perp left everything this time," she added. "He wants this one identified."

Or doesn't care, or this one's not connected, Service told himself.

One-room cabin, outdoor privy, well water through a red pump handle at a sink, ancient woodstove in the middle of the room. Old fireplace on one end. Some mattresses on the floor. Paper bags tacked inside windows, distressed wood board walls, spiderwebs in corners, piles of dessicated fly corpses everywhere, not to mention live ones buzzing over the female remains. The perp had left all the parts—just not attached to each other. Jen Maki and a tech were marking evidence against a string grid they'd assembled.

"Yo," Service greeted her.

"Back atcha," Maki said. "Can you believe I went to school especially so I could do this job?"

"I hear you," he said. But he didn't really understand. His work was a calling, not just a job. He'd assumed Maki's work was similar. "Look like the same perp to you?"

"They don't pay me to think about things like that," the woman said.

"What if they did?"

She shrugged. "Just as violent, but all of her parts appear to be present or accounted for. How do you add up all this shit?"

He had no idea, didn't care to push anymore, went back out to Friday. "Think we'll need another vet?" she asked, her tone edgy, words clipped, and charged.

"I was just following the rules, Detective. Nothing personal."

"It felt personal to me," she snapped, "like you were trying to tell me how to do my job."

"Not in the way you mean," he said. He didn't want another argument.

"I floated an idea and you kicked the shit out of me."

"I kicked the idea, not you."

"The idea was mine. You kick it, you kick me."

"Bullshit. You have to separate the dancer from the dance. You want me to keep quiet even when you seem to want an opinion, yes, B'wana?"

"Don't be an ass," she said, grinning. "Did you vote?"

"Absolutely."

She rolled her eyes. "And we're supposed to provide positive role models for good citizenship for our kids," she said.

"Did you vote?" he asked.

"Yeah, I was in line right behind you."

They both laughed. Service said, "I asked our moose guy to call Anna Tork, see if she kept any hair samples from Nepo's place."

Friday looked up at him. "Why?"

He took out the bag with the tooth and showed her the dead moose photos on his camera.

"This stuff relates to my cases how?" she asked, one eyebrow raised.

"Maybe not at all," he said. "But my gut tells me to press it. I heard there was some dogman coverage on Detroit TV."

"'Is legendary dogman on a U.P. killing spree? Story at eleven.' That kind of shit," she said. "God, what assholes."

"Where'd the story come from?" he asked.

"Unknown. No sources cited, much less alluded to, this being the golden age of sourceless news we used to call tabloid fiction."

"What kind of crime details?"

"Minimal: Four dead, some bodies mutilated, investigation a high priority, DNR involved."

"Four? They know about Nepo?"

"Maybe."

"This last one?" he pressed.

"I don't know, Grady. Good God."

"Got your way then," he said.

She looked at him and rolled her eyes. "Why doesn't it feel better?" she complained.

"Never does."

"This going to make it tougher on you?" Friday asked.

"Don't know yet. Maybe, maybe not. But how Nepo and this one get reported could make a difference. If it supports earlier rumors, we could be piling on."

She said, "I'm thinking we'll call this one a suspected homicide, but not the same as the others; probably different perp, different MO, no evidential links to previous cases. We'll call Nepo a suspicious death."

"You believe that?"

She waved a hand. "Does it matter? I'll just wait for the tox results to see what science can deliver to law enforcement."

"Are *we* all right?" he asked.

She nodded. "Peachy. We're just fine," she said. "There's a lot of pride and attitude in both these houses."

He nodded. "Truer words. Too much testosterone. This body staying with Baraga County?"

Friday smiled. "No, I want everything in Marquette to keep all the evidence close, and, by the way, you need a shower. Bad."

"I know. Uphill hiking and tent life—lethal combo on BO."

"You look at the body in the cabin?"

"Not piece by piece. Did the perp butcher her?"

"Probably."

"Anybody recognize her?"

"Not yet. We may issue a face photo."

"No ID?"

"Empty purse; it's with the evidence." She pointed behind her with her thumb.

Jen Maki and another tech had set up a table to record and coordinate each piece of evidence from the scene. Service went to the table, found a clear bag with a black purse, and picked it up. There was a smaller bag in the bottom of the bag. "What's this gizzy?" he asked Maki when she came outside.

"It was attached to the purse handle. Musta come loose."

Grady Service stared. It was the same small bag, with the same symbols as the one on Kelly Johnstone's trailer at the gorge. *What're the odds of that?* He waved for Friday to join him and she sauntered over.

"What?" she asked.

"See the little bag in here?" he held up the big plastic bag with the purse.

"Decorative," she said.

"I've seen another one just like it," he said, and explained.

Friday asked, "Should I call Johnstone, ask her what it means?"

"She's not the cooperative type."

"Maybe she doesn't like men," Friday said. "We all have days like that."

"All men, or certain men?" he asked.

"Both," she said.

Service opened the evidence bag and took photographs of the pouch.

"Outta here," he told Friday, who nodded, touched his leg behind his knee, and patted him gently.

21

Sunday, November 9

SLIPPERY CREEK CAMP

No call from Pilkington, and no answer when Service tried to call the biologist. Not a surprise; it was mostly COs who worked weekends and nights in the DNR. Limpy took Donte DeJean home and said he had to check his own place before coming back. This left the three musketeers, a nasty cat, and giant mutt.

Service awoke to gunshots and ran into the living room to find Noonan and Treebone on the front porch, pouring .40 caliber rounds into a target on a tree. He yelled, "Somebody declare war?"

"Just stayin' ready," Noonan said.

"It's Sunday," Service said. "Nobody declares war on a Sunday in the U.P. It's a rule. How about you get your butts inside and make coffee, not bulletholes."

A white Ford Ranger pulled up in front and Cale Pilkington, all three hundred pounds of him, squeezed out and waddled to the front door. He was carrying a brown leather briefcase, slung over his shoulder.

"Tried to call you," Service greeted the man.

"Range and reception issues. Remember when 'R and R' meant rest and recuperation?"

Service laughed.

Pilkington said, "I went to see Tork. She had extra hair samples." He tapped his briefcase. "What about that tooth?"

Service showed him to the table, got him seated, gave him coffee, introduced Noonan and Treebone, and handed him the plastic bag with the tooth.

The biologist put on rubber gloves and took out the tooth. "Jesus," he said.

"Freak, maybe?" Service offered.

"No, they've shot and trapped some massive specimens up in northern Canada, two hundred pounds plus, but the teeth of two-hundred-pounders aren't appreciably different than the choppers of an eighty-pounder. Freak size doesn't provide a biological explanation."

"What does?"

"Start with DNA, see where it takes us."

"Where?"

"Ashland," Pilkington said.

National Fish and Wildlife Forensics Laboratory in Oregon. "They'll take it? There's no crime involved."

"Scientists," Pilkington said. "We can't ignore something like this, even if it turns out to be nothing. This tooth and your photos will get their attention."

"We've got meat, hair, and some bone from both kills."

"Great; that enhances the package."

Service got the evidence out of the freezer in his garage, put it all in an ice cooler, and brought it to the biologist. "What about the hair?"

"She had quite a bit extra, four different samples. I'll send a couple of hairs from each batch."

"Turnaround time?"

"Not fast, but first we need to get accepted into the system and queue. We're talking weeks on the short side, months on the other end."

"Won't hold our breath," Service said.

The biologist finished his coffee, said good-bye, and left.

Treebone looked at his friend. "Where your head?"

"You were going to get me a name, the head street shinob in Detroit?"

"Down through a crack," Tree said. "Suit, you know the secret tom-tom for Motown Shinobs?"

"No, but I can find out quick-like."

"How fast?" Service asked.

"Drive down to D, ask Tonia Sorrowhorse?"

"Can't call her?"

"She believes all technology is from the devil or some such shit."

Service knew the woman from way back. He thought she was Oneida and Cree, tall, elegant, sinewy, uber smart (both book- and street-), and fearless, street name of Bambi. He'd first met her at an all-night honk run by a Delray bohunk, a placed called Stozely's. She hung there sometimes, but lived in a fortified house off West Jeff, the air there once sulfurous from nearby plant emissions. "How old is she now?" Service asked.

Noonan tilted his head and squinted. "No idea. We driving or staying?"

"Tree?"

"I go back to D, I got to see Kalina, she'll honey-do-list me. I'll stay right here. You boys have fun."

"Play nice if Allerdyce comes around," Service told him.

"Hey, we can talk about election results."

• • •

Noonan took a deep breath and scowled as they drove toward the bridge. "Clean air up here will kill a motherfucker," he complained.

"Fresh air, no pollution—light, sound, or air—great scenery . . . This is paradise, Suit."

"Man, I found this hooker floatin' titties up in the Rouge one morning. Somebody capped and dumped her. She got hung up in the effluent of the JAP, the Jestrom Avenue Plant. Chemicals turn her skin color of egg yolks. Water was all chartreuse, smell like old socks, blue smoke hangin' over the river. My idea of true beauty, not two fucking thousand different shades of green, like this shit up here. Others come see that body, they power-yack Olympic distances, even the damn EMTs. Me, I liked that shit. Good reminder what my job was. I hate Detroit and she hate me. Perfect marriage. Why destroy such good chemistry and balance? Bad cop is a great quality in a cop in a bad town, and D, she be the worst. Get back there, it'll be like fresh oxygen up my nose, man."

Service grinned. "Any reason to check in with 1300 Beaubien, let them know we're in their patch?"

Noonan said, "Multiple floors of assholes at 1300, all working political mind-fucks. Got four thousand cops on the payroll, and lucky to get five hundred to show for duty every day. Nobody give a shit, man. Call 911, you might get a response in eight hours—on a good day. Back in the seventies and eighties, all the city fathers blabbered on about Detroit Renaissance, and I think, What the fuck is sixteenth-century Europe gonna teach a giant clusterfuck on a death roll? Fuck that 1300 Beaubien shit."

22

Monday, November 10

DETROIT

Friday telephoned Service as they made their way south. "I've been trying to call Johnstone since I saw you Friday. No luck, no call-backs, no dice."

Service promised to follow up, and called Dani Denninger right away. "You been watching Johnstone's place?"

"Not in several days. I've been scouting, trying to get myself ready for the deer opener." This meant finding illegal bait and blinds, and other suspicious setups to visit opening morning. It was one of the busiest times of year for most game wardens. He couldn't blame her for making it a priority, and it was a reminder that he'd prefer to be doing the same.

"Check it out, will you? See if she's around. If not, ask neighbors."

"Something make you think she boogied?"

"Maybe. Also, look and see if there's a little bag hanging on her door."

"Like last time?" Denninger said.

"Yeah." *Good. She'd seen it, too.*

Noonan directed him into southwest Detroit, West Vernor near Marshall: Latinoland, Voodoostan, Geekville. Someone had spray-painted a wall: DETROIT: WHERE THE WEAK ARE KILLED AND EATEN. The people of the city had never had any false illusions about their burg.

His thought: *Finally, truth in advertising.* All he could think about was the old joke about how Detroit looked like Beirut. Bullshit. Beirut looked like Detroit, and was the worse for it. The city of soul had little left, had squandered most of what it had in the sixties, and never recaptured it. Diana Ross had cut and run, which should have rung alarm bells, but the city's leaders and denizens, then as now, were mostly blind to the obvious. Even if they had been able to read the tea leaves, what could they have done about major social upheaval?

A red van in front of them had a bumper sticker that read HAVE YOU HUGGED YOUR BITCH TODAY? *Not necessarily intended for dog lovers,* he thought.

Their destination was Lucy Rommey's joint, appropriately called Lucy's. Long ago it had boasted the best black bean soup north of Havana.

Noonan said, "Eighty-nine, Eulogio Protracio commence whacking people he found disagreeable, which pretty much took in everyone. He'd snatch 'em, put plastic bags from his old man's bakery over their heads, and suffocate their asses, drop the bodies near relatives' houses. Eulogio's other indulgence was PCP, which he popped like Jujubes.

"One Christmas morning I'm souping with Luce and I get a call: Some douchebag is down in the park half-mile away banging away with an AK-47, trying to off a buncha brothers and their Latin competitors. Park was DMZ, no violence zone, by agreement between two bent-ass crews, Latino Lords and the African Rangers. I run down there and what do I see but this asshole blasting away on full auto: It's my boy, Eulogio. I get up behind him, grab the wep, kick him in the balls, and beat his face so raw he pukes his spleen. Uniforms haul his ass away. That day I got points all the way around. Fine day, best day in long time."

"You are a violent man, Noonan."

"I might allow I got tendencies. You met Luce?"

"Couple times in the long waybackago."

"Let me do the talking."

• • •

Lucy's had not changed, but she had aged badly. She now sported a thick black bristle of a mustache, a majestic furry caterpillar over her upper lip.

"Suit," she said when they walked in.

Service felt her eyes on him. "Where you got off to, Service? Liberia?"

"U.P., Michigan's Siberia."

"Hear dat," she said, nodding.

Service was impressed by her memory.

"S'up, Luce?" Noonan asked.

"You know," she muttered, "stuff and shit, little this, little dat, like always."

"Could use some help, Luce."

The woman ladled dark soup from a cauldron perched on a massive stove burner, topped it with raw onions and slivers of red chilis. "T'ought you done retire, Suit, gole watch an' all dat shit," she said.

"Tru dat," he said. "Favor for a friend, here. Place ain't changed, Luce, eats good, smells good."

"Rent up ten ex," she said. "B'lee dat?"

"Everywhere," Noonan said. "Punks and zombies got all the bread."

Lucy chuckled. "What you want, Suit?"

Noonan asked, "Tonia Sorrowhorse still around?"

"Not by much . . . She been bit by Dr. Slim."

Service saw Noonan's mouth briefly hang open, as if he had been taken by surprise. Service knew Dr. Slim was AIDS in this neighborhood. It was a term he had never heard in the U.P.

"That shit be ev'where these days," Lucy said. "People won't even touch them folks when they die. Just leave 'em rot like dead wolf in woods."

Service was surprised at her reference. How did an inner Detroit black woman know that nothing in the woods would eat on a dead wolf? Worms consumed them, never predators or scavengers.

• • •

They drove to the address Lucy gave them. Same place Tonia had lived when Service had been a Troop. "Should have just come here in the first place," Service said.

"Lucy's the unofficial mayor of a big chunk of Detroit. We pay homage, she keeps her ears on for us. Rules of the road, man, matter of ghettocol." Noonan looked at the house. "This area a Ciz Seven, man."

"Meaning?"

"My first partner, Big George Ciz, he made his own scale of Motown badness, with Ciz Ten the worst. "

"So seven's good?"

"Under ten ain't synonymous with good," Noonan said.

An old man with yellowing hennaed dreadlocks answered the door.

"Tonia," Noonan said.

"You the Man?" the man asked.

"Not here, not no more. I'm an old friend," Noonan said.

"She ain't seein' no frens, my fren," the man said.

Noonan eased the old man aside. "Sorry, Pops, she'll see me."

It had once been an elegant house and was now on its last legs. Tonia

Sorrowhorse was in the parlor in a crank-up hospital bed, an IV in her left arm, oxygen tubes in her nostrils, the scent of decay and impending death deep in every pore of the room. Noonan sat on her bedside, kissed her forehead. "Bambi, baby."

The woman's eyes flickered. Yellow, rheumy, sunken, scared. "*Glenn?*"

"Heard you're feelin' poorly," he said.

She tried a smile, but failed. "Dead meat, Suit. Was prime meat, now soon gone be dead meat. Dr. Slim."

"I heard."

"Dr. Slim get you, too?"

"Maybe," Noonan allowed.

"Can't win 'gainst Dr. Slim," she muttered. "You want here, Suit? Do the nasty?" She grinned devilishly, stretching her lips tightly across her yellowed teeth and dark gums.

"You up for it?" he asked.

"Shee-it. That funny," she whispered. "You know I born ready, dig?" She took his hand and tried to squeeze, but Service could see she lacked the strength. "I done it all," she said.

As good an epitaph as any, Service decided.

"They take good care of you, Bambi, honey?" Noonan asked.

"Hopspits," she said. "Nice folks come dance with the dying." She stared at the IV drip. "They givin' me the good shit for pain. I flyin', Suit. Got Dr. Slim fum bumpin' shit, now they gi' me same shit fo' Dr. Slim. Tell me, dat make sense?" She closed her eyes, sighed softly.

Service watched Noonan squeeze the woman's bony hand. "We need information. We'll pay."

"You come, didn't you?" she said.

"Yeah, I'm here," he said.

"Then you paid enough," she said. "What you want?"

"We've got some nasty kills, no IDs, DNA telling us Indian blood. Who's Top Tonto these days, and where do we find him?"

"Dr. Slim turn snatch to snitch," she said. "Call him Speedoboy, aka Dwayne, last name unknown, works the doghouse, grabbing baby girls."

"Greyhound Station?" Noonan said.

She nodded. "Some say he take those little girlies, turn 'em out, work on the stree', but ain't like dat, Suit. Speedoboy, he help them babies, pull them out 'fore they get fucked up, put them on buses back home. Got a bad rep fum some, hear what I'm saying? Jealousy, envy, an' shit like dat."

"You know him?"

She nodded. "Bambi know ev'body, Suit. Your fren' there, he a State boy here one time, move to be fish cop."

Service was impressed at her memory, decided survival in a wilderness of any description was helped by a solid memory.

"Be careful, Suit. Speedoboy, he fat man, Ojibwe." She inflated her cheeks. "Like dat? Careful, dough. He fat, not soft, dig?"

Noonan kissed her and held her close until she seemed to be asleep. The man with the pink dreads was sitting on the stairs by the front door, smoking a pipe. "How long's she got?" Noonan asked.

"Hours, minutes. Only Jesus answer dat."

Noonan fished three one-hundred-dollar bills from his wallet, pushed them into the man's hand. "No pain. Get if off the street, you have to."

The man nodded, took the money, looked him up and down. "Bluesuit Noonan?"

"How'd you guess?"

• • •

The Greyhound station had been renovated since Service had left Detroit, or else it was entirely new. Decades of dinge had been replaced with chrome columns, huge glass walls and partitions, potted trees, carpet, red and blue plastic seating, all covered with fresh dinge. He instantly loathed it.

Speedoboy was the Man and easy enough to locate. He worked out of a black Astro van parked across the street. Noonan read the deal immediately. His teenage posse scouted arriving buses while the boss sat back. Eventually an enormous and obese man slid out of the van and lumbered slowly toward the terminal, legs apart, sagging in style (or fighting a rash, it was hard for Service to tell). Bodyguards followed and led, two lines, twenty feet from the man. Sloppy security. Noonan used an open flank to cut in, and Service followed right behind him.

"Speedoboy," Noonan said. "Bambi Sorrowhorse say you Top Tonto."

Fat but not soft; her characterization was correct, Service saw. The man had a thick corded neck, massive hands. Service flashed his badge. "We need to talk privately—about Shinobs above the bridge."

The man's voice was comic, high and slobbery, the opposite of his hard obsidian eyes. He led them into a public lavatory. A look sent his bodyguards out. Speedoboy stood at a urinal trough, grunting. "Got the bad p'ostate," he said. "Low manifold pressure. You a long way from home, fish cop," he said to Service.

"Bambi said you might help. She said you're a good man with a bad rep."

"She a ho."

"Got the Dr. Slim," Noonan interjected.

"It always somepin'," Speedoboy said. "What you want?"

Service told him about the killings.

"I look like Ast-the-Motherfuckah-Dot-Com?"

"You've got connections," Noonan said. "What we seen up there is ugly, man. We want to bury some kids, not leave their spirits wandering."

"I didn't make the world," the man said.

"No, but Bambi swears you've tried to make it a better place. This is like what you do for kids."

"People up north being ripped apart, chewed on," Service said again.

"I mebbe hear some shit. Dogman, right?"

Noonan asked, "You b'lee dat dogman shit?"

Speedoboy closed his eyes. "Windigo . . . You go talk wit' Father Bill Eyes."

"Macomb County Father Bill?" Noonan said.

"He the man."

• • •

The Macomb County Native American Center was just outside Mount Clemens. Air Guard jets thundered over the old Selfridge Air Force Base, now an Air National Guard operation. The center was run by a half-breed Cree priest, Father Bill Eyes. They found him playing basketball with kids half his age, twice his size, and holding his own.

They sat with the priest while he rested with a bottle of pale green fluid. "Gatorade—electrolytes," he explained. "As mysterious as the Holy Ghost. You have to take the existence of both on faith. Thought you retired, Suit," he said to Noonan.

"Did, but helping my friend here, Conservation Officer Grady Service. Woods cop up in the U.P."

"You a Catholic?" the priest asked Service.

"Raised one, but more Non-Pref now," he answered.

"What can I do for you?"

Service told him the story, adding the word *windigo*, but omitting mention of Speedoboy.

The priest invited them for a late dinner, but Noonan refused politely.

"The windigo is real," the priest said. "But let's define the word *real* in this context. It's not a myth or fairy tale. It scares the hell out of tribals—as well it should. Psychiatrists define it as windigo psychosis. Almost always hits males with families. They get into a spell of bad luck and begin thinking they've been inhabited by a windigo spirit. Makes them cold all the time, like they're filled with ice, and insatiably hungry for human meat. They sometimes turn to cannibalism, and start by murdering and eating their own families before reaching out to others."

Service had trouble processing what he had heard. "What's this thing look like?"

"Like any person. It's a mental disorder."

"Not hairy, like a dog or wolf."

"We're not talking about a werewolf, though the French concept of *loup garou* included werewolves *and* windigos, stretching back to the sixteenth and seventeenth centuries."

"How do people detect it?"

"Usually they don't until its too late and the killing begins. In some places there are elders who know how to identify symptoms, but they're dying out over time. It's possible to intervene early and stop it from progressing, but this rarely happens. Medical science can treat the disorder with a number of psychoactive agents, but usually the windigo ends up dead before any westernized medicos can get involved. The degree of fear this condition creates is difficult for a white person to appreciate."

"Happens in this state?" Service said. "I've never heard any such thing."

"Rare condition anywhere, never in this state, so far as I know. Mostly in Canada. I've heard of someone who's a true expert on the condition. Name is Lupo, Grant Lupo, a professor of aboriginal ethnology at Michigan Tech. I can find out how to contact him, ask if he'll get in touch with you and help.

He seems to know just about everything about this disorder from what I remember. Problem is that Lupo's got a bad dose of egomania. Late thirties, Hollywood looks; women cling to him like barnacles."

"How would one know if there's a problem?"

"Tribals won't say much to whites, so they'll keep it close in their own community. But you'll start to see amulets, manitu pouches—things to ward off the evil spirit."

"Pouches, like little leather bags?"

"Very common," the priest said. "If they start to become widespread, you can interpret it that the people think a windigo is operating. The bags will have small red figures on them, like stick figures. This represents the evil—the beast."

Service gave the priest his business card and thanked him.

"You know Father Clem Varhola?" the priest asked.

"May have heard the name; might even have met him once. Why?"

"No reason. Just priestly curiosity," Father Eyes said in an icy tone. "You think you might have this problem up your way?"

"Got something around L'Anse, just not sure what yet."

"Father Clement Varhola," the priest said, rolling his eyes. "Over in Assi-nins, north of Baraga."

"Someone we should talk to?" Service asked.

"Only if you have to."

• • •

A young Hispanic woman had replaced the man with dreadlocks at Tonia's house. She let them in without a challenge.

Tonia died just before noon the next day, with Noonan holding her hand and Service in a threadbare wingback chair faded from burgundy to skin tone. She was cremated the next morning. No funeral, no memorial service, no next of kin. Noonan placed obituaries in the two Detroit daily papers. "Tonia Sorrowhorse passed away peacefully. She did everything in life with grace."

Service decided that the extremely strange retired detective was one of the rarest of creatures: one who took friendship as a sacred pledge.

23

Thursday, November 13

BLOOD CREEK CAMPGROUND, BARAGA COUNTY

Travel was beginning to wear on Service mentally and physically. So much time in trucks, always moving; he had lower back pain and felt perpetually velocitized. As they headed north that morning, Friday telephoned.

"I've been thinking about our victims' feet," she said. "Why does he leave the heads and hands, but take some feet? It makes no sense. As I think about it, the victims so far aren't necessarily the type who'd be fingerprinted— you know, ex–special military, cops, or ex-cons—so the perp may feel safe in leaving hands and heads. Last night I was thinking about Shigun and that girl in Mack City, and it hit me: Hospitals up here take footprints of newborns and give them to the families as souvenirs. They have no official standing, or legal value as ID, but there are prints of every kid born in U.P. hospitals. Could be a back door in for us. Also, those hearts at Nepo's? They were porcine, which I don't get. Where are you?"

"Headed north to talk to Denninger. We had a meeting with a priest in Mount Clemens, and he told us about some stuff that may or may not relate."

"Care to share?"

"I don't know enough to share yet. This Father Bill Eyes is going to put us in touch with a Tech professor named Lupo who might be able to help us. Denninger called, and she wants to meet out at the Ridge, something relating to Kelly Johnstone."

"She's surfaced?"

"Don't know. Dani just said she wants us over there, so we'll collect Tree and Limpy and head over that way."

"Meaning Johnstone's still AWOL?"

"Apparently."

"She that important?"

"Can't say she's not; we do know that if something is going on anywhere in the Ridge community, Johnstone will know what it is."

"We'll talk later," Friday said, and broke off.

• • •

Blood Creek flowed into the Sturgeon River about two miles east of where the Sturgeon curled into Houghton County. The campground had been closed years before, too little use, too remote, too small. There were eight campsites on a steep rocky precipice, with a drop of at least one hundred feet straight down.

It was just turning dark when they all pulled into the campground entrance road and parked.

Denninger had not been able to find Johnstone, but she had found deerskin pouches on every door of every house and trailer she had checked in the Ridge community, and while the Natives refused to talk, much less explain, a citizen named Rodney Folsom called her to let her know he had heard from a friend that "untoward things were occurring out at the Blood Creek Campground." She pulled Service aside, told him all of this quickly as she studied the man sitting in her truck: blond, balding, beady-eyed, breathing through the mouth, squinty, with lizard-like brown eyes. She referred to him as Rod the Odd.

One look told Service her description seemed to fit. Mr. Folsom lived downstate, was chief financial officer for a multimillion-dollar trash company headquartered in Grand Rapids. The man had no specifics to share on the campground warning, but Denninger had persuaded him to come along. Service could see the man was both irritated and intimidated and trying to balance the two feelings.

Service heard him tell Dani, "I'm a CFO."

She said, "And I'm a CO. We share two letters in our titles, so what's your point?"

The man grimaced. "I did my duty as a good citizen, notified the authorities."

"You gave us no details. Do CFOs and accountants accept reports and balance sheets with no details or specifics?"

"Of course not," Rod the Odd said.

"There you go," Denninger said with a huge grin.

Service marveled at her skill in handling the man, who was obviously accustomed to giving orders, not taking them, especially from women.

"I asked you along so you can see what you reported. You *are* curious, right?"

"Am I in any danger?" the man demanded to know.

"I don't know. Are you?"

"You know how Indians are," he said.

"No, why don't you tell me about that," she said.

"Vindictive, a menace to civilized society, worse than radical Islamists."

"You lost me there, sir. Nobody will hurt you when you're with us."

"But you won't always be *with* me," he complained.

"True," she said, tapping her forehead. "Why didn't I think of that?"

They parked the trucks at the mouth of the one-time campground and went in on foot: Service, Noonan, Treebone, Allerdyce, Denninger, and Folsom.

"Where's your sarge?" Service asked Denninger as they walked.

"Sitting on Johnstone's trailer."

"You think she's coming back soon?"

"I got an anonymous call that she's gone hinkybird and is on the move constantly."

"Including her own hacienda?"

"That was the word."

"You know what those pouches are?" he asked her.

"No," Denninger said.

A trail led from the campground to the cliff. Service could smell the dregs of a fire. A pit was built not six feet from the edge of site number four, and dry deadwood had been stacked near the fire. Several peeled aspen poles had been placed in the fire circle, leaning into each other, tepee-like. A deerskin pouch was attached to each pole, and each pouch had a red stick figure on it. There were no footprints in evidence, but there were dark stains on the rocks around the pit. Noonan knelt, wet a finger, and swiped a rock, coming up with a red fingertip he lit with his flashlight. "The fuck is this shit?" he said.

Service nudged Rod the Odd, who jumped. "Ideas?"

"All I heard was there were some weird things out here."

"Heard from whom?"

"I don't recall. Hell, everybody's heard the dogman stuff. It's all over Baraga and L'Anse. You hear it everywhere—something about chopped-up dead bodies and such."

"Ojibwes up here don't go in for this stuff," Denninger said. "Most of them are Catholics and Methodists."

Noonan sniggered. "Means shit all. Santeros in southwest Detroit practice a form of voodoo combines African gods and R.C. saints. With religion, anything is possible."

Service said, "Let's separate, spread out, and sweep the area."

It was Treebone who made the discovery: a red wooden figure, five feet tall and sticklike, eye-popping red, with an eerily lifelike face. It had been flayed, singed, and impaled on a white pine stripped of its branches. A black cloth was attached to the figure's head, and snapped in a steady northwest breeze that smelled like snow was in the offing.

"Like a giant party favor," Treebone said.

Service stood close to Allerdyce. "Seen anything like this before?"

"No, I ain't."

"What does it mean?" a very shaky Rod the Odd asked in a quavering voice.

Denninger shone her flashlight around the damp ground. It had sleeted and rained that morning. "Just our prints. How did this thing get here?"

"Maybe it flew," Noonan offered. "Had a Santero priest one time tell me he could fly and shape-shift into other creatures."

"You believed him?" Tree asked.

"Fuck no. I was pinching him for capping his old lady and I told him, 'You gon' fly, motherfucker, this be the time.' He never moved."

Willie Celt called on the 800. "I've got Kelly Johnstone in protective custody. Says she wants to talk to you out there at the campground."

"Bring her," Service said, and wondered why.

• • •

Celt parked by the other trucks and led the woman to them. She was uncuffed, walking slowly and not talking. They met at the red effigy and Denninger lit it with her flashlight. "You've sure been gone a lot, Chairman," she said.

Suddenly Kelly Johnstone grabbed the effigy, ran straight to the precipice, and disappeared over the top into the night. No sound, no warning; just gone and over. Service and Allerdyce were behind her and heard only a dull splat as something struck the water below.

"Check it out," Noonan said. "She can't fly neither."

Willie Celt said, "We'll play hell recovering her body. Bad current, whirlpools, some deep-ass holes filled with sweepers and crap, snags everywhere down there."

"There an easy way down?" Service asked.

"None I know of," Celt said.

"Lot of heavity here," Allerdyce said to Service, who had no idea what he meant.

Service looked at Sergeant Celt. "Did you tell her we were at the campground?"

"Nope. She seemed to know that."

The sky began to spit ice pellets.

24

Friday, November 14

L'ANSE, BARAGA COUNTY

Service and crew took two rooms at the Hilltop Motel after the fiasco at the campground. County deputies put personnel there overnight, but no serious body-recovery effort could begin until they would have morning light, and perhaps the sleet and snow had let up.

A cell phone buzzing under Service's pillow woke him up. "What?"

"Cale here; sorry to call so early, but I wanted to catch you."

"You have. Who the hell is this?"

"Cale Pilkington, biologist."

"Sorry, Cale. We had some weird times last night. What have you got?"

"Nancy Krelle is a paleobiologist and anthropologist with the Oregon lab. She geeked out when she got the tooth we sent. She's seeking confirmation from a colleague at UCLA who works La Brea."

"The tar pits?"

"In the vernacular. Technically, the substance is asphaltum."

"Cale, *focus*. Please."

"Sorry. Dr. Krelle is four nines certain your canine tooth is a specimen of a very large *Canis dirus*."

"English, Cale."

"Four nines means ninety nine point nine nine, or almost one hundred percent probability the tooth belongs to a dire wolf."

"Like the Grateful Dead tune?"

"No, for real. They died out about nine thousand years ago."

"All but this one?" Service said. "How the hell does a nine-thousand-year-old tooth end up in a moose's thigh in 2008?"

"That is *the* question, isn't it," Pilkington said.

Service said. "I can't think. I need coffee. I'll call you back in thirty minutes, tops." He dressed and walked across the shared parking lot to the Hilltop Restaurant, which was just opening for breakfast, ordered a cup of black coffee to go, took it outside, lit a cigarette by the front entrance, and called the biologist back.

"Okay, I'm afoot now. Talk. You're not suggesting an extinct nine-thousand-year-old animal is alive and among us."

"*I'm* not, but Dr. Krelle says there's a chance. She says the crypto community has been talking like this was a likelihood based on reports of moose kills in Saskatchewan, all of them in the northern river watershed, big-time moose country."

"Creep-toe community?"

"Crypto, as in cryptozoology, the study of hidden animals—you know, legends and shit, like Bigfoot and so forth."

"That's real?"

"The study, sure. Even though some of the practitioners are lulucakers and nutsawillies, there are plenty of legit people interested in the subject."

"I don't believe in Easter Bunnies," Service said.

Pilkington said, "This Easter Bunny is about one and a half to two times the size of our gray wolves. Squatter build, wider, huge teeth and jaws. It lived exclusively off large game. When the large prey began to die off, the wolves died, too."

"There you go," Service said.

"Listen, please. What I'm going to say is speculative and highly theoretical, but that doesn't automatically render it inaccurate or impossible, then or now. Follow me?"

"I'm not sure. Keep going."

"The dire wolves were here at the end of the Pleistocene epoch—the Ice Age, if you will."

"Gimme a time estimate."

"Started twelve thousand years back, give or take, but we've recovered remains, and there are *a lot* of dire wolf remains. Suggests the wolves were still around three thousand years after that, give or take."

"People around then, too?"

"Heavens, yes. The first *Homo sapiens* dates to about two hundred thousand years back, and some of the most recent fieldwork has put man in the New World *possibly* as early as eighteen thousand years ago. Now understand: The dire wolves were only in this part of the world. They're not exactly wolves. More like a separate species, like a coyote or a hyena or something.

The common time for man here is eleven thousand years ago, which could put dire wolves and mankind side by side in North and South America, and we're pretty sure that man is responsible for the extinction of a great number of large mammals."

"Dire wolves included?"

"We don't really know. What you need to know is that there is anecdotal evidence of a dire wolf killed by Florida farmers in the 1920s, but no evidence or photographs, just several questionable newspaper accounts. There's some possibility that was *Canis rufus*, the red wolf, but we don't know. The reds were still being reported around the same time. And people still claim to see them, but it's not substantiated and they're considered extinct in Florida. Add to this the Inuit talk about *Waheela*, a giant white wolf, which some think is a relict *Canis dirus*, and the Sioux stories of *Shunka Warakin*, which translates roughly as 'one who carries off dogs.' Gray wolves, we all know, will kill any and almost all canid competition, so this Siouxan creature could certainly be a wolf. The thing is, if there's a relict subpopulation contemporary to the present, it's small and rarely encountered by man."

"Here, in the U.P.?"

"Well, we have some fine, isolated areas that theoretically could hold such animals if there was adequate prey. There are undocumented reports of three U.P. trappers bumping heads with a giant white wolf in northern Iron County in 1918. All of this is hearsay, but hearsay often has some basis in reality, even if we can't immediately find supporting evidence."

Service's brain was spinning. "Cale, *whoa*. What the heck is your take-home here?"

"I'm sorry, Grady. I'm so damn excited I'm about to wet my pants. What I'm saying is that we may have a dire wolf in the McCormick Wilderness. It may be indigenous, or it may be just passing through; we can't know that yet."

"You base all of this on one goddamn tooth?"

"A tooth *you* pulled out of moose remains. The moose didn't fall on that tooth. The measurement from the tooth to the other fang puncture tells us this is probably not a gray wolf, as does the horrific damage to the remains. We don't have anything that can do that to a moose . . . at least, nothing we know of."

"What the hell are we supposed to do, Cale? I don't even know what to think," Service said.

"Neither do I, Grady. I mean, is *endangered* in the same regulatory status as *once-thought-extinct?* I'm clueless on the implications of what we're supposed to do here. The only thing I'm sure of is that we can't say anything until we're certain. If we let this leak, every headhunting yahoo in the country will be up here trying to bag this thing. We don't need that sort of crap in conjunction with the deer-season opening. We already have enough wolves being shot by allegedly frightened deer hunters."

"The governor wants me to find this thing and kill it," Service said.

Silence from Pilkington. Then, "*Man . . . Why?*"

"What if it's killing people?"

"Listen, we think these things lived off carrion, not fresh meat they killed."

"You theorize. You don't know for certain, Cale."

"True."

"What if you and your scientific colleagues are wrong?"

The biologist gulped loudly and hung up.

Grady Service dumped his coffee dregs and lit another cigarette.

Dogman, dogshit, windigo, dire wolf, Waheela, Shunka Warakin, *five dead (counting Nepo), and now Kelly Johnstone—three people reported missing, including the teacher and her two kids. The governor wants me to hunt down the dogman. Given all this, what does that really mean? Am I under orders to kill an animal that might be the last of its kind on Earth? Is there even a link between the killings and this animal? No satisfactory answers. Even fewer satisfactory questions.*

Service felt like getting back into bed and covering his head with a pillow. "This gets shittier and shittier," he said out loud and headed back to the motel to get the others moving.

Friday, November 14

L'ANSE

The meeting took place at the L'Anse State Police post. Jerry Dove, the county's medical examiner, was tall and slightly bent, with a cigar-shaped head and a razor-thin aquiline nose. Noonan took one look at the man and whispered, "Dye that fucker green or blue and he's a dead ringer for a Muppet."

The ascerbic Dr. Dove had the antithesis of a sense of humor and lived up to Denninger's premeeting descriptor of a "prick practitioner."

"I do not want an explanation for the presence of game wardens at my meeting," the ME began. "I simply want them out of my sight. This is not a DNR case."

Baraga County sheriff Sulla Kakabeeke turned red. "Excuse me, *Doctor*, but they were witnesses to the suicide." The sheriff was new to her office, a retired State Police sergeant Service had worked with in her previous life.

"There is no suicide until I declare it so," the doctor said officiously. "*Nullum corpus, no regere.*"

"Dis guy don't spick no 'merican?" Allerdyce whispered.

"And who and what are you, sir? Identify yourself."

"Consultant," Service said quickly.

"Consultant in what area of expertise?" the doctor inquired.

"Search and recovery," Service said.

Dove crossed his arms. "All right, Mr. Consultant, tell us where we might find the alleged *corpus delicti.*"

Allerdyce didn't bat an eye. "You want body, she down dere Blood Creek."

"If said location is so readily known, why has the body not been recovered?"

Allerdyce said, "Mebbe 'cause youse stand up here in orifice pontious-piffleating 'stead climb butt down bloody cliff and do youse's job."

"I *beg* your pardon," the doctor snapped.

"He's suggesting that if you let us focus on body recovery, we can get things moving," Service said. "The body is in an extremely difficult location to reach safely, much less to recover. There's some chance, in fact, that you may have to descend with us to do your job, or you may have to authorize us to preliminarily declare death until we retrieve it."

"Do you know precisely *where* the remains are?" the doctor asked.

"We know where the body was last night—not where the river might have taken it overnight."

"In other words, it has not actually been located."

"No, not yet," Sheriff Kakabeeke said.

Dove coughed. "I see no reason to continue this charade. Go do your jobs and inform me only when it is time to perform my official duty." The ME departed without small talk or social grace and nearly collided with Tuesday Friday as she arrived.

"You guys piss off that man?" she asked, coming into the room.

"Local ME," Denninger said. "He lives in a permanent state of pissed-off."

"What's the deal here?"

Service explained.

"Suicide, cut-and-dry, seems to me," Friday said. "Did you hear the body hit?"

"Heard something," Service told her.

"Had to be the body," Treebone said.

"We *think*," Service corrected his friend. "But we don't know."

"Why am I here?" Friday asked. She looked weary.

Service hooked her arm and walked her outside into the parking lot where he lit a cigarette.

"There's no dogman," he said after a couple of hits.

"You know this how?" she asked.

"Is there any extraneous DNA in the remains?"

"In what regard?"

"Human or animal."

"No," she said, her voice trailing off. "What's going on?"

"You ever heard the word *windigo?*"

She nodded. "Somewhere, I think."

"How about *dire wolf?*"

This time she shook her head.

Grady Service said sheepishly, "That's all I got for now. We have to go find a body."

"You're sure it's a suicide?"

He gave her a quick description of the events.

"Hundred feet plus, straight down?"

"Have to rope down to get her, I'm thinking," he told her.

She squeezed his arm. "Be careful."

PART TWO

SKIRR OF THE IMPOSSIBLE

||||||||||||||||||||||||||||||||||||||||||||||||||||||||||||||||||||||||||||||||||||||||||||||||||||||||||||||||||||||||

26

Friday, November 14

BLOOD CREEK, BARAGA COUNTY

Six inches of fresh wet snow had fallen. The scene at the campground was chaotic, the entrance blocked by the Baraga County Search and Rescue (SAR) team's equipment and massive RV, multiple emergency vehicles, from fire department and county sheriffs to Michigan State Police, and a Bay ambulance pulling an elongated trailer. There was a steady flow of men and women in baseball caps, orange and electric-yellow Job Sight high-visibility vests, biking and climbing helmets, a rainbow of coats and colors and the clank of climbing harnesses and large bundles of ropes and lines. An ATV with four triangular tracks instead of tires pulled a blue, bullet-shaped Plexiglas trailer that looked like a stretcher on wheels. All together, just chaos, with a purpose visible only to those trained in the art of finding and recovering people, or bodies.

Carabiners rattled starkly with the sound of cheap wind chimes. Service and Allerdyce made their way to the cliff edge as Baraga County SAR personnel threw ropes down the drop, about fifty feet from where Johnstone had launched herself. Service saw that the SAR people had better anchor points where they had set themselves up. Any kind of high-angle operation was damn difficult even when everything worked right, and always dangerous: Gravity, temperatures, winds, light conditions, and weather consistently caused SAR team leaders to recalculate and make adjustments to their plans and equipment. Service saw portable klieg lights and generators being pulled up to the edge. He also knew this was strictly a recovery, not a rescue, and time wasn't pressing. Nobody survived the kind of dive Johnstone had taken. The lights suggested that SAR team leaders were expecting a lengthy search.

The incident commander, or IC, was fiftyish, retired Coastie Philet Ghoti, five-eight, no excess weight, gray eyes, an in-charge, no-nonsense bearing. "How many you got below?" Service asked Ghoti.

"Three so far."

"POD?" Point of detection.

"Have to see. One person, known launch point, it'll be PIW or POG."

Person in Water or *Person on Ground.* "We were here last night when she went over," Service told the IC. "We'll be close by if you need us."

Ghoti walked on. Allerdyce was seated by the edge, elbows on his knees, puffing a cigarette. "Youse notice somepin' last night?" he asked Service, not bothering to look up.

"Such as?"

"Hear onny one splatch down dere," the poacher said, using the cigarette as a smoky pointer.

"Right."

"Tink dere ought should be two, eh?"

The old man had a point. Service followed as Limpy began to shuffle along the ridge, stopping now and then, always peering over the edge . "Look dere, sonny," he said, squatting after fifty yards. There was a cluster of juniper on the side of the upper cliff. "Under dere—in da middle," Allerdyce said.

Service saw snow under the shrubs. "I see snow."

"Tracks," Allerdyce said, pointing, "Come t'ru dere, move our right, keep go dat way, I'm t'inkin'," the old man said, still pointing.

"You saying it's Johnstone?"

"Little tootsies, mebbe could be, eh?"

Allerdyce was over the precipice before Service could say any more, and he watched the man moving slowly toward where Johnstone had gone over until the overhang angle made it impossible to see him anymore.

• • •

An hour later Allerdyce popped back into view, now moving the opposite direction until he found a place to climb up. Service gave him an arm to help him to the top.

"I t'ink dat girlie, she hit flat grass table, mebbe eight foot down, den she t'row dat red t'ing over and we hear dat hit water." The conviction in the old man's voice gave Service a chill.

"Got a lot of fresh snow."

"She got nest down dere, lay dere while we was up 'ere, den later she move, eh."

"Climbed up in the ice and snow?"

"Yep, wit' gimp leg," Allerdyce said. "Drags left foot some, sticks to cover. Want me bust trail?"

"Got your radio?"

Allerdyce nodded.

"Go; keep me in the loop."

"Youse know da fact dat she know dat spot, mean she been here, mebbe plan dis t'ing, eh. Why'd she do dat?"

Grady Service had no idea, and went to find IC Ghoti, who was getting ready to put two more men over the side down to the creek.

"This could be a bastard, Phil. You may want to hold up for a while. I've got a man out looking at something now."

The incident commander looked at Service. *Bastard* was SAR jargon for a wasted search. "She's not down there?"

"Looking to find out," Service said. "One of our men found tracks, followed them back to where she landed and lay up. It's right below the launch point."

"Your man good at this stuff?"

"Probably a lot better than us," Service allowed.

He found Noonan and Treebone and told them what was going on, and the three of them went over to the trail where Allerdyce had disappeared and waited.

Denninger came on-site and joined them, heard what Allerdyce was doing, and said, "I'm leaving, Grady. Deer opener's tomorrow, and my hours are limited. Let me know if you need me."

"Where are you working tomorrow?"

"Glitter Creek, not that far from here. You guys?"

We're dry leaves in wind. "No idea yet," he said.

Why would Johnstone fake her death? Obvious answer: She's desperate to disappear. But why? And from what?

• • •

Two hours later, Service's 800 barked to life.

"Hey, dere, sonny, better come, 'bout mile an' half west youse, ole tote road crosses crick, dumps inta 'turgeon. No 'urry," the old violator said.

They found Allerdyce chewing his fingernails. "T'ink somebody wait up here wid truck. Catch 'er coming, give it to 'er den. I seen prints fum truck, hunnert yards back, mebbe."

"What kind of truck?" Service asked. "Could you tell?"

"For'n," Allerdyce answered, shrugged, took a breath, and added, "Looks it swurft over onc't, but I got good tracks for plasiturd gunk youse guys carry."

"Swurft?"

Allerdyce made a motion with the flat of his hand. The old man shrugged and said, "Show youse." Which he did.

Vehicle tracks only; no human signs of any kind. The truck had been parked. Had it been waiting for Johnstone? Unlikely anyone would accidentally come to this place. Whoever it was had either followed, or knew her plan, was maybe part of it, all of this prearranged, a conspiracy. Of what, why? What the hell was going on?

Service called Willie Celt. "You see any other vehicles while you were watching her place last night?"

"A small white station wagon pulled in two houses down from Johnstone's."

"How long after that did you see her?"

"Fifteen minutes, give or take?"

"Did you see that vehicle again on the way to the campground?"

"Nope, but I wasn't payin' much attention, either."

"You catch the make?"

"No, but it looked a few years old, not something new."

Service went over to Allerdyce. "How'd you know it was foreign?"

"Skins," the poacher said.

"Guess a make?"

Allerdyce chuckled. "I ain't no Hootdini."

Grady Service rubbed his eyes.

"We gon' eat tonight?" Noonan complained. "I can go without pussy for days, even weeks, but food I got to have every day, an' more'n once."

Service led them back to his truck, and Friday called as they pulled into the motel parking lot. He could tell by her tone she wasn't happy.

"The damn hospitals over here don't have footprint records," she complained. "They've never scanned them into their systems, or kept backup copies, even on disks. The woman in Records thinks some local churches used to come in and make copies for their own files, but she's not sure which churches, or when. What the the hell is wrong with people?" she said, adding, "I'm going home."

She had a cockamamie idea that she could match victims' feet to hospital footprints used as mementos. It had seemed an extreme and desperate long shot to him right from the start.

"We found Johnstone," he told her. "Not a suicide. She faked the jump and climbed back to the top after we were gone. Looks like somebody picked her up."

"Why would she do *that?*" Friday shouted.

"Got me."

"You think I should turn back to L'Anse?"

"No," he said. "Go home. Relax. Have a glass of wine."

Dinner at the Hilltop didn't help the group's collective mood. Allerdyce was with them for a while, but got a cell call, and later got into a brown truck and disappeared, not returning until almost midnight.

"Do 'morrow?" the old man asked Service.

"Probably head home."

"Opener, eh?"

"Like clockwork, every November on the fifteenth."

"Hear mebbe dere's crew up Black Crick Road, mebbe up ta stuff."

"Friends of yours?"

"Not 'zackly."

"Competition?"

Allerdyce cackled. "I ain't in dat game no more."

"What kind of stuff?"

"Timber, baits—youse know, all dat stuff goes 'hind lock gates."

"You know where this camp is?"

Allerdyce nodded and flashed an insipid grin.

Service came outside to have a smoke with Noonan. "That old fart's dangerous," the retired Detroit cop said. "I can feel it. I know a hard case, and I got me lots of comparitors."

Not exactly news. Real issue: What is Limpy now? Service couldn't say with any certainty.

He called Dani Denninger. "I know you and Willie have a plan tomorrow, but if I were you, I'd take a drive up Black Creek Road." Service gave her the name of the camp and its approximate location.

"I'll talk to Willie," she said.

"Let me know if it works out," Service told her.

27

Sunday, November 16

HANCOCK, HOUGHTON COUNTY

Grady Service telephoned his retired CO friend Gus Turnage to run down an address for him; it took about fifteen minutes. He didn't call ahead to the house. The man would be there or not.

The strange pouches were never far from Service's thoughts. No matter how hard he tried, he couldn't help wondering about the pouches surrounding the red effigy at the campground. Indians being snatched and killed and butchered. The other word he couldn't shed: *windigo. Jesus.*

Allerdyce had come back, and Service sent the poacher and Noonan home and took Treebone with him. Father Bill Eyes had mentioned the pouches and said he'd get a contact number for this Grant Lupo, but so far, no dice. Service kept the radio tunes blasting loudly the whole way, as if decibel level alone would crush the awful things they had seen, but he knew deep down it wouldn't work. Monsters, real or imagined, had to be confronted individually and face-to-face. There was no option in this. He also knew the word *monster* really translated to *human*, not to other species. Man was the only true monster in this universe.

They found the house, overlooking Mont Ripley Ski Resort. The old Quincy mine smelter and brick stack were almost directly below them on the shore of the Portage Lake Ship Canal; south, they could see the buildings of Michigan Tech. There was a Jeep in the yard, and Service parked behind it. It had patches of salmon-colored Bondo mixed with splotches of pea-green primer, ugly beyond description and only partially covered by fresh snow.

The man who came to the door was remarkably tall—six-eight, at least, Service thought—muscular, lean but strong, late thirties, with long blond hair that stuck out in all directions, a well-trimmed Vandyke with an orange tint. He wore a T-shirt proclaiming REMEDIAL CALCULUS DON'T ADD UP, faded jeans with holes in the knees, and unlaced logging boots reaching almost to his knees. Reading cheaters hung around his neck on a faded purple shoestring.

"We would have called," Service said, "but we ran out of time. We're looking for Grant Lupo?"

"That's me," the man said, stepping back to let them in. His handsome face had a used quality to it, leathery and shiny, as if it would soon crack like an unoiled baseball glove. His eyes, on the other hand, were almost animal-like. *Oddest eyes I've ever seen,* Service thought, pale green with the sparkle of peridot.

"Father Bill Eyes call you?" Service asked, showing his badge.

"Yeah, sure; I think I saw a message from Bill somewhere in my call-back pile."

"You didn't call back."

The man smiled. "See, the way it is, I get maybe fifty phone calls a day, and a hundred to two hundred e-mails. I figure if people seriously want to talk, they'll find a way. That saves my time, which is what matters most to me. It's not a perfect system, but it seems to work. You found me, right?"

Tree laughed out loud.

Lupo asked, "You guys want to do lunch? I did graduate work in NYC at Columbia, and I love how two-one-twos talk to each other. *Do lunch . . .* Is that a hoot or what? Happy horseshitisms from Great Gobshites of Gotham. I've got fresh venison stew. My recipe. I like wild game, about all I eat. Can't handle factory meat drowned in antibiotics."

Service knew Tree had never met a meal he didn't like and said, "Sounds good."

They followed the man down a long hall lined with dozens of rifles on racks, or slung on wooden pegs. The rooms they passed were stacked with books, or wooden crates filled with tents and sleeping bags and sundry out-door equipment, cardboard boxes, steamer trunks with LUPO stenciled on the sides in white. The house looked like a pass-through for a small transient army, and the kitchen looked like it had been decades since its last cleaning. When he saw it, Service mumbled, "Not hungry."

Lupo grinned. "This only looks like the Ptomaine Palace. I cook great. What I don't do so great is clean up."

The professor ladled rich, dark brown stew with floating cranberries into a red Styrofoam bowl and gave it to Tree, who sniffed it approvingly. Lupo looked at Service, who grudgingly nodded. *Damn stuff does smell good.*

They ate with black plastic spoons embossed with HUSKIES in yellow script. Lupo got a bowl of white onions and thin-sliced red peppers from the fridge and set it in front of them. "Recipe's got jalapenos, but you can't see 'em because I grind 'em fine to spread the seeds. I like things hot."

The concoction was thick and surprisingly savory, with a robust bite. The professor grabbed a paper bag from the floor, pulled out a flaky baguette, and tore it apart. "Fresh," he said. "Bakery in town's run by a psychotic Estonian who claims to have once been persecuted by the KGB. Could even be true, but nobody cares. His bakery is outstanding, and the world's not as neat or categorized as it once seemed. Beer or wine?"

"Neither," the officers said in chorus.

"On duty," Service explained.

"Beer with everything for me," Lupo said. "It's hard to spoil beer."

The man wrenched a top off a Labatt Blue long-necker and tossed the cap in the sink. "So what's the yank?" he asked, taking a swig. "People aren't usually in much of a hurry to see people in my line of work."

Service thought the professor seemed unusually energized, unorthodox, and earthy, and not at all what he had anticipated. His relative youth was most surprising, and for some reason disconcerting. He'd thought of expert academics as in their sixties or seventies—at least closer to his own age.

The conservation officer opened his briefcase and handed an envelope to Lupo. "We'd like for you to take a look at these; if you want to wait until after we eat, we'll understand, but we're interested in knowing your impressions."

Lupo put the photos on the table, raised an eyebrow, and took another heaping spoonful of stew.

"We think they're tribals," Service said. "DNA."

Lupo said nothing until he had gotten through all the photographs. He spent considerable time looking at each one. "Interesting," he said, returning the photos. "Where'd you get those?"

"Marquette County," he said.

Just "interesting"? Service thought.

"Recent?" the professor asked.

Service said, "The two older females in August, the child at Halloween, the other female about a week ago, and the effigy, just a few days ago, in Baraga County."

Lupo scooped another spoonful of stew. "They've been buried properly, I assume."

"No, the bodies are being retained as evidence in the investigations. There're no legal reasons to hurry. We've got them secured."

Lupo went through the photos again and pulled out one of the little girl from the trailer on the Little Huron River. "Where's this one?"

"With the others."

"I wouldn't mind seeing all of them."

"Why?" Service asked.

"I assume you want me to gauge whether or not you've got a windigo on the loose," the professor said. "There's no other reason I can think of for you to be here. I've heard about the murders and wondered, based on the dogman rumors floating around. You do know what *windigo* translates to, right?" Lupo didn't wait for an answer. "It translates into English as 'evil spirit that devours humans,' but this has been shortened to 'cannibal' over the years. I'd like to see the bodies. Every tribe in the north has its own version of, and word for, windigo."

"Sounds like a lot of hooey to me," Service said, adding, "We'll have to see about you taking a look at the bodies."

"People always need to believe in something," Lupo argued. "Consider transubstantiation. For Roman Catholics, communion is partaking in the actual body and blood of Jesus Christ. Literally, not figuratively. Is that not cannibalism?" Lupo grinned. "May I ask why the DNR is involved in this?"

"All agencies are short on manpower," Service said. "We're assisting the State Police."

"Now would be good for me," Lupo said, taking a last mouthful of stew and jumping to his feet. "But you can call after you talk to your handlers," he said dismissively.

Service and Treebone were outside when Denninger called on the cell phone, laughing. "Unreal. Forty tickets in all, and we took eight deer. All the blinds were big-time overbaited, all permanent structures just onto State land. My wrist aches from paperwork. One guy copped to three bears, including a cub. Another pal owned up to four wolves. And get this: Half the guys in camp didn't buy licenses, and never have. Yet not one of these assholes has a DNR prior. Makes you wonder how long this shit has been going on."

"No drugs?"

"Two pounds of weed, and sixty-one cartons of Indiana cigarettes to peddle. Three locals stopped to buy smokes *while* we were there. I called ATF and they're geeked."

"How much stuff did you seize?"

"Everything—wheels, rifles, all of it. You'll love the photos of the flat-beds and wreckers hauling away their trucks."

Grady Service felt a twinge. *I should be in the Mosquito right now, not chasing fucking bogeymen.* The thought that the Mosquito Wilderness was unprotected made his heart skip and blood pressure go up.

"Great job," he told Denninger.

"Fucking eh!" she said happily. "This feels like a big one for all the good guys."

28

Monday, November 17

MARQUETTE

Friday okayed Lupo viewing the remains, and Service was mildly surprised to discover they were being stored at the unofficial satellite morgue in Marquette, a facility he'd never heard of, which made him wonder how many other things he didn't know. The building had once housed iron-mining shipping operations. It was a sturdy brick structure covered with ivy, now dusted with snow. There were other buildings nearby, all of them with flagpoles and Green Bay and Northern Michigan University flags snapping in the wind.

Service and Tree came in the Tahoe, Lupo in his own Jeep. Friday wasn't there yet when the men went to the door and knocked.

The facility technician was an older man named Pellosio, who shaved his head and wore ankle-high duck boots and a black wool overcoat over a sharply creased charcoal-gray suit. "Chemicals get all over everything down here and destroy shoe leather," he explained, catching Service's questioning eye. "Rubber seems to last longer. But it won't be a problem for you folks. Gotta work in this crud for it to eat your kicks."

Pellosio unlocked a massive gray steel door by punching a long sequence into a keypad and jerking the door aside when the light flashed green. He stepped inside, turned on the lights, and waved them in.

Service saw drawers lining the walls of several long rooms. The place reeked of breath-catching chemicals, disinfectants, and God knows what else. There was a faded hand-painted sign by the front door that read DAHMER'S DINER. There were three pinwheel stars under the words, the stars fashioned from severed fingers.

"This work turns us all nutters," the technician said.

Friday told the man what they wanted to see and he shook his head. "The little girl is god-awful," the man said. "Horrific."

Service didn't need to be reminded.

The bodies were on gray metal mortuary trays in a locked room way in the back, and set aside under a sign—ACTIVE CRIMINAL INVESTIGATION UNDER WAY.

"Instructions from the ME are to not disturb the remains," Pellosio explained. "Ain't done nothing but keep our guests nice and frosty."

Friday arrived just as the technician pulled one of the trays out of its refrigerated compartment. Lupo bent over and reached down. Service handed him latex gloves and said, "I'm going outside for a smoke."

"No need; go ahead and smoke in here," Pellosio said with a sly grin. "We all do. Who's gonna tell?"

"I need to be outside," Service said. He hated shit with dead bodies, always had.

Lupo, Treebone, and Friday came out after nearly an hour, all of them rubbing their hands. "I'm starved," the professor said.

"After *that?*" Service asked.

"They're just remains. I guess I'm used to them. I'd think cops would be inured to all that as well."

Service guessed the man was testing them, and he couldn't figure out why. "It's not the remains; it's the fact that they've been murdered, and we don't have a single viable lead."

Lupo grunted sympathetically. "We academics hate unanswered questions, too."

• • •

The restaurant was called Autres Temps (Other Times) and advertised its specialty as molten BBQ Louisiana-style baby back ribs. Lupo asked for a double order and extra hot sauce, which he then doctored with a green bottle that materialized from this pocket. "Hmm," he said after one bite. "C-plus tops, even with the major saucing intervention."

"You wanted to see the bodies," Friday reminded the man. "Now you've seen them. What can you tell us ?"

"Can't say," he said, through a mouthful.

Friday said, "*You can't say?* You drive all the way over here and you *can't say?*"

Service could sense her thermometer rising.

"Life's a gamble," Lupo said. "A cop once told me that, and he wasn't half as good-looking as you," he added with a wink.

Service had to force away the urge to bitch-slap the smug asshole.

"That's it? That's all you've got for us?" Friday asked incredulously, her voice rising.

Lupo said, "Did you have extraneous DNA in any of these cases?"

Friday said, "No."

"Then you don't have a windigo. The thing is, baseline, we're talking psychosis, a possession, if you will—to put it in the vernacular. Technology aside, a windigo eats his victims uncooked. Logically and syllogistically, get a windigo, you'll also have his DNA. It's as simple as that."

"It looks like someone chewed on the remains," Service pointed out.

"Maybe," Lupo said. "But are we talking human teeth, or something else?"

"No endogenous DNA from any other species," Friday said.

"Are you telling us there's no possibility of a windigo?" Service asked.

"I neither said nor meant to imply that. Windigo is certainly *possible,* but not in any traditional sense. The cases I'm aware of all involve aboriginals, virtually all males, and they eat the victims with their own teeth. It is possible, theoretically and hypothetically, that someone fabricated a device to rip at flesh and simulate the human bite plate, but this might be a bittuva long-ass reach, eh?"

"*These* bodies?" Friday asked.

"Hypothetically, but you'd have to test flesh for metal fragments."

"High-quality steel doesn't leave fragments," Service pointed out.

Lupo said, "I assume that's true, but I thought investigators wanted to rule out all things that can be ruled out in order to keep focusing more tightly on what *can't* be ruled out."

Service could almost hear Friday's mind churning.

"If it were me, I'd employ a high-end metal detector to sweep the bodies and see what turns up. No ping, I'd surgically liberate tissue samples, put them under an electron microscope, and see what's there to see. I'd keep pushing until I'd exhausted all possibilities."

Out on the street after lunch, Friday said to Lupo, "Next time we call, I hope you'll have the courtesy of calling back."

"If I can," the professor said, with no hint of commitment.

Treebone coughed to disguise the word *asshole.*

Service looked at Friday. "Pompous jerk."

29

Thursday, November 20

HOUGHTON

Service had tried to call Lupo every day since the morgue, but once again the professor was ignoring calls, and it pissed off Service to the point where he decided to drive up to Houghton and grab the silly sonuvabitch by the scruff of his neck and shake some courtesy into him. Lupo's behavior was not helping Service's long-standing poor opinion of most academic types. The thing that galled him the most was that he was sure Lupo had seen something in the coffins and had held it back. *What had he seen, and why won't he tell us?*

But when Service drove to Houghton, Lupo wasn't at home. Next, Service called the university and got transferred to Lupo's department.

"He's gone," the departmental secretary told him.

"Gone?"

"Back up into the snow," the secretary said. "You know, his customary winter in the bush."

"Who's in charge there?"

"Professor Spar."

"Is he in?"

"*She's* in a meeting and can't be disturbed."

A set piece, delivered flawlessly, the answer to all questions and unwanted requests. *Classic gate-guard, verbal-foot-in-the-door security tactics.*

"Disturb her," he said, explaining that he was a cop and part of a multiple homicide investigation.

"Why don't youse just bite my head off?" the secretary groused.

A new voice came on the line, mature, clipped, sure. "This is Chairwoman *Dr.* Spar."

"Conservation Officer Service. I've been working with Grant Lupo, and we need to reach him, but your secretary tells me he's away."

"I'm not aware of any collaboration with the police."

She said the word *police* with a tone some might reserve for dog shit stuck to a shoe sole. "He's been asked to keep it confidential. Look," Service went on, "I don't want to be rude or pushy, but in five minutes I can have the Houghton County sheriff in your office, ordering you and all your bosses to do what we want."

"I don't care for your tone," Spar said.

"Back atcha," Service said. "Where *is* he?"

"Legally we can't say. As I understand it, he flies into Winnipeg and from there out into the bush to work."

"Where in the bush?"

"Somewhere on the Nelson Ojibwe-Cree Reserve."

"How far is that from Winnipeg?"

The woman sighed. "I have no idea, and if there's nothing more, I really do have more pressing business."

"How long is he supposed to be gone?"

"I really wouldn't know."

"What about his classes?"

She paused meaningfully. "Professor Lupo teaches no classes. He holds an endowed research chair." Her voice suggested that she disapproved of this arrangement.

"You've been helpful," he said sarcastically and hung up.

Service called Friday. "Tree and I are going to spend the night with Karylanne. I'm thinking I want to talk with Lupo face-to-face, but he's gone to Canada for fieldwork and probably won't be back until next spring, or whenever. Nobody seems to know for sure what the hell he does, where he is or what he's up to. It's a closely guarded state secret."

"Why talk to him again?" Friday said. "It seemed to me he gave us what he had. You think differently?"

"My gut says there's more, and Lupo might be a key." *To what, he had no idea.*

"I hear in your voice that you're gonna follow him. Are you traveling as a homicide dick or a creature hunter?" she asked.

"Seems to me circumstances are trying to make those things one and the same."

"When will you go?"

"We'll drive to Duluth tomorrow, and then fly to Winnipeg."

"What about your team?"

"Noonan can help you, and Allerdyce will do whatever the hell he does."

"You want me to keep Newf and Cat?"

"Please."

"Do you know where Lupo is?"

"Not exactly, but I used to be a detective, remember?"

"Vaguely," she said.

30

Sunday, November 23

MARQUETTE

A major snowstorm had dumped on the Great Lakes and turned out to be far more severe than predicted. Friday had called late the night before and said, "Lamb Jones is dead."

"When?"

"Just come back. Where are you?"

"Still in Houghton. The airport's closed. We couldn't get out. Suspects?"

"One in custody," Friday said.

"Is it like the others?"

"Come home, Grady. Please."

Her voice and the storm settled where he and Tree would go, but getting back was not easy. They met Friday at her office at 11 a.m.

"Bad over to the west?" she greeted him.

"Not good," he said. "What's the deal?"

"Lamb's body was found up on the Ice Train Plains near an old landing field. A high school kid had his dogs out, hunting snowshoe hares, and the dogs found her." Friday stopped talking.

"And?" he said.

"You'd better see for yourself."

• • •

Returning so soon to the satellite morgue disturbed Service. A small hand-written sign had been tacked outside the entrance: OUR DAY BEGINS WHEN YOURS ENDS. *What was it with people who handled dead bodies?*

Lamb Jones was on a mortuary tray next to the other four, the little harvest growing.

Service was not overwhelmed with the desire to see the body but willed himself to look. Lamb had favored baggy dresses and unisex clothing, so he was shocked to see that the forty-year-old had the figure of a much younger woman. A moment later he blinked as he realized her head was where it was supposed to be, as were her hands and feet. But Lamb's throat had been cut, her eyes gouged out, and there was a hole in her chest where her heart had been removed.

"He cut off the end of her tongue," Friday pointed out.

Lamb's pretty face was distorted by swelling, her lips crooked. "Who's the suspect?"

"Terry Daugherty," she said.

Service laughed out loud. "Terry? Jesus, Tuesday, don't joke." Daugherty was a longtime county deputy, flawed, but basically a good man.

"I *wish* it were a joke," she said. "Boomer was cleaning a cruiser, found bloody clothes stuffed under a seat." Boomer Andreson was responsible for maintaining the county's vehicle force and had a lot of work. The newest cruisers were three years old, the oldest going on ten years old, some barely able to operate. "Boomer took the clothes to Shirley Davis in Evidence. She found name tags and called the sheriff, and the sheriff called me."

"The body had been found by then?"

"No, shortly thereafter. All of this went down last night."

Name tags. Service wasn't surprised. Lamb Jones was known for her possessiveness, as well as her competence as a dispatcher. She put name tags on everything, including a mountain of paper clips she kept in a bowl on her desk. She wrote her name in microscopic print and Scotch-taped the labels to every paper clip. Obsessive for sure.

Everyone in the department teased her, but she was undaunted. "Name tags can be very useful," she would tell people. Ironically and sadly prophetic.

"The sheriff checked the duty manifest. The vehicle had been checked out to Daugherty. We tried to find Lamb, but she never made it to work. We went out to see Terry, told him what we found, and he broke down, said he didn't want a lawyer and refuses to talk to anyone but you."

"Me? I don't know him any better than others in his department."

"He says only you."

"What's Linsenman's take on this?"

"He says that the deps trust your integrity," she said.

"He's not a killer, Tuesday," Service said. Daugherty's reticence in physical confrontations was well known. On the other hand, he also had a rep for hitting on women, though formal complaints had never been filed. Mostly he was considered harmless, the sort of pushy, insecure male you ran into at every job.

"Nothing adds up," he said.

"We can only hold him so long," she said. "We have to charge him or kick him."

Service took a final look at Lamb Jones and found his mind drifting to asshole Lupo's sudden trip to Canada. He looked at Friday. "This one is different," he said.

"There are mutilations," she said.

"But it's not the same," he insisted.

• • •

Terry Daugherty was still in his civvies and came into the interview room at the jail with his eyes down.

"Terry," Service said.

"I *di'n't* do it," the man said, his eyes filling with tears.

Friday quietly left the the room.

"Lamb's clothes were in your cruiser."

Daugherty exhaled loudly. "I didn't to it, Grady. I swear to God I didn't."

"Was she in the car with you?"

Daugherty looked up with red eyes. "She was, but she was fine when I last saw her."

"Where and when was that?"

"Ice Train Plains." Until earlier today Service hadn't heard of the obscure spot in years. The Ice Train Plains was an isolated section of the Yellow Dog Plains, northeast of the McCormick Wilderness, and northwest of Marquette.

"Why out there?" Service asked. "In a storm?"

"*Her* idea. We used to meet at her brother-in-law's place on Lake Independence and take off from there. She had a thing for getting it on in patrol cars."

"You dumb bastard," Service said in a whisper.

"She wanted privacy, and the Ice Train is pretty private."

"You did her in your cruiser? Are you *stoopid*, or what?"

"Hey," Daugherty said, "it was more like she did me. It was her idea all the way. I wanted to use her brother-in-law's cabin at the lake."

"You two were an item?" Service asked.

"We kind of hung out for a couple weeks is all. It wasn't nothing serious, Grady. We were both just looking for some fun. Pure slam-bam short-time, that's all. Celia don't know," he added. Celia was his wife, mother of their four kids.

"Okay, you admit you were with her. Good. Just keep telling us the truth. You said she was all right when you left her. Tell me about that. At her car . . . at the Ice Train?"

Here Daugherty averted his eyes. "We were still out there. She got out to cool off, said somebody had been watching us and it creeped her out big-time. I got out to investigate, got my riot gun and followed tracks cross-country into some pines, but it was cold, I was pretty underdressed, and I was starting to freeze, so I backtracked to the cruiser. When I got there she was gone. Tire tracks, but no footprints. Looked like they had been swept clean right by the cruiser, mine included. There were vehicle tracks, so I figured she'd called somebody and split. You know how hinky-dink she could be. She was just like that, up and do whatever the hell she wanted." Daugherty looked at Service. "I would never hurt her, Grady. I couldn't."

"What did you follow into the woods?" Service asked.

"Tracks she'd pointed me to. I figured they belonged to whoever had been watching."

"Were those tracks still there when you returned?"

"I don't remember. I was so damn pissed she was gone, I wasn't seeing all that clearly."

"How long were you gone from your patrol?"

Daugherty shook his head. "Twenty minutes, thirty—I don't know."

She had called someone and been picked up in twenty or thirty minutes. Not likely, even if she could get cell service way out there.

"Did you go back to her car or her home, to see if she was all right?"

"I meant to, honestly, I did, but when I got into the patrol car, I got a call from Central. There was an eighteen-wheeler wrapped around another truck out on US 41, and the Troops were screaming for county help, so I rolled. By the time I was clear of that, my shift was almost done. I checked out and went home. Celia don't like me being late."

Service guessed Celia wouldn't much like him screwing a coworker, either.

Nonetheless, it seemed unlikely that Terry was a killer, and the mutilation of Lamb Jones aside, it seemed impossible that he had killed the other victims. "Did you guys have an argument?" Service asked.

"No," Daugherty said. "We just, like, did the deed, and we were getting ready to leave. She said she wanted to cool off and went outside. Everything went downhill from there. I figured she went squirrel and into one of her snits, and bugged out. Geez oh Pete, *everybody* knows how flighty she is."

Flighty enough to take off in the snow naked? Service wondered.

"Terry, you want to take a ride out there with us and walk us through what happened?"

"I keep thinking maybe I ought to get a lawyer," the deputy said.

"You know your rights, Terry. If you want one, just say so. But remember—I'm trying to help you. Maybe you should let this work first, then decide. I'll read you your rights officially and you can keep them in mind as we go through this. What do you think?"

"Okay; I know you're a stand-up guy."

Friday came back into the interview room. "For what it's worth, Terry, I also don't think you killed her, but you know the drill. You need to understand that we're going to pull all the evidence we can and let that talk. Even if you didn't kill her, you've got yourself in a bad jam. I can't believe a man of your experience would be so stupid as to knock off a piece in uniform in a patrol vehicle while you're on duty. It's ludicrous at best."

"I don't want to go to prison," the deputy said disconsolately. "Or lose my job, or my pension. I have a family."

Service sympathized, but figured the job and the pension—hell, maybe even the family—would soon be history, no matter how the murder investigation went. Some mistakes weren't fixable.

31

Monday, November 24

MARQUETTE

The sun was up but hidden by clouds when Daugherty told Service to pull over. "This is about the place," the deputy said, looking around.

"It, or about it?" Service asked.

"I'm pretty sure it was here."

"Show us what happened," Friday said. "Walk us through it."

"Everything?" Daugherty asked, his voice breaking.

Service asked, "How long was she out of the vehicle in the snow, Terry?"

"Couple, three minutes, max," the man answered.

"And from the time you got out of the cruiser and came back?" Friday asked.

"Twenty minutes, max." *Earlier it had been twenty or thirty,* Service noted.

Daugherty led Service into the jack pines, heaped with snow. The storm had covered whatever tracks had been in the open areas. Service thought he saw remains of some tracks inside the jacks, but they were faint, and not worth much.

"How did you know where you were going?" Service asked his guide.

"It gets a lot thicker up ahead," Daugherty said over his shoulder. "Some of the old guys in my dad's crowd used ta hunt snowshoes in the brambles ahead. I got into the pines and, knowing what was ahead, turned around. I mean, what was the point? That crap is damn near impenetrable even in daylight, so I turned around. I was really shook up thinking somebody might have seen us—you know, in the cruiser. I wanted to run him down and appeal to his . . . hell, I didn't want us to get caught. Is that so hard to understand?"

In some ways it wasn't.

"You did her on duty time in a county vehicle," Service said.

Daugherty hung his head. Service looked at his watch. When they got back to Friday's vehicle, it had been twenty minutes, exactly.

• • •

There were four or five reporters at Friday's office when they got back, none with the intensity or skills of some downstate journos, but the young and aspiring ones up here could be overly aggressive when they thought they might have a story that could propel them to bigger jobs and far better pay in more lucrative markets. The word was that Noreen Seiche from the Marquette television station was one such ambitious specimen, so much so that the others called her "Sledgehammer" for her confrontational style.

Seiche was immediately on Friday. "What's the latest on the Jones murder? We hear you have a suspect in custody."

"Nobody's been charged," Friday said calmly.

"Does that mean someone is *about* to be charged?" Seiche pressed.

"It means exactly what it means. English *is* your first language, right, Noreen?"

"Some people in town are saying you don't really know what you're doing, and that your record with recent murders demonstrates continuing incompetence. Do you have a comment?"

Calmly again, Friday said, "Just that I heard the same thing about you, Noreen. I guess uninformed opinion is the last frontier of all free men."

"Bitch," Sledgehammer muttered to her camera operator, who looked to be about twelve.

Friday and Service went back to the offices that were off limits to civilians, and Service looked at a large county map on the wall. Friday tapped a spot. "Found her body right there."

"Other side of the swamp from where he allegedly stopped chasing the alleged peeper," he said.

"Almost three-quarters of a mile," she agreed.

"What have you got from the lab?"

"Semen in her privates, stomach, and on the seat. Jen Maki ran a quick protein analysis, confirming the fluids are Daugherty's. We're getting DNA, too, but that takes a while."

Service said. "He doesn't deny being with her. DNA won't tell us he killed her."

"I never said he killed her," Friday said, rolling her chair across the floor to her desk. "I'm tempted to recommend we kick him loose. The sheriff is going to suspend him with pay, pending the outcome of the department's investigation."

"Some people will be underwhelmed by that."

"I know," she said. "But I just can't believe he killed her. The evidence is circumstantial."

"Cases get made on circumstantial evidence all the time," Service reminded her. "Her undies, his semen, and he admits to what they did. A lot of cases get made on a lot less than what you have."

"Why would he kill her?" she asked.

"Maybe she'd had enough of his company and he took exception."

"Grady," she said.

"Look, Tuesday, you're still relatively new up here. Lamb was . . ." He looked around before finishing. "Lamb knew a lot of men."

"As in, knew them biblically?" she said.

"And then some," Service said. "I've always heard she'd go hot and heavy with someone for a couple weeks and cut it off, just like that." He snapped his fingers. "No warning."

Friday stared at him. "You would know this *how?*"

"Yooper telegraph, " he said.

"Firsthand knowledge," she said. "Is that what you're saying?"

"No way, and hey, we're not talking an exclusive club here. She had a lot of partners, and she was also the best dispatcher the county's ever had. I liked her, but away from Dispatch she talked about little else except men."

"You're suggesting maybe Terry couldn't handle it."

"I don't know; Terry did a lot of fishing, but I suspect he didn't get many bites. Then suddenly Lamb takes the bait. Personality like that and facing rejection, you never know."

"There was no sign of anger or a fight, Grady, on her *or* him. I really don't think he did this. And since Lamb's not Native American, it makes this case different than the others. So, what the hell?"

Service said nothing and went back to see Daugherty, who had already written a statement. Service asked him to do it again, starting from the beginning. When he finally finished writing, the deputy handed Service a pile of notebook paper.

Service read silently, "Lamb Jones had me suck her nipples." He winced and skipped down a couple of paragaphs. The report continued,

Lamb said, How come I got to take off all my clothes and you don't? And I told her, what if we got an emergency call and we had to roll? I'd be dressed and she could start dressing on the way. If we were both naked, where would that put us?

Service felt disgust. *How demeaning is this?* He kept reading:

She leaned her back against the mesh between front and back and laughed, said, I'd figured all the angles. She was in a good mood. I told her that was my job.

Lamb said, Somebody catches me bouncing on your manroot in the backseat of the cruiser, neither of us will have jobs anymore.

I asked her if she wanted me to take her back to her brother-in-law's place. She said, Hell no, this deal really turns me on! Lamb really liked being on the edge. What, the risk? I asked her, and she said, All of it, everything. It's like a fuck-me-Santa moment.

I asked her to tell me more and she got huffy. I like *doing* it, not talking about it, she said.

Me: But talking's half the fun.

Her: Not for me, but then I never been married.

I told her she talked a blue streak at the office.

She told me, I got clothes on at the office. I just don't like to talk with my clothes on the floor. Can we just do it again? Then she almost broke my zipper.

I don't know how long we were at it. The windows got all fogged and my clothes were all stuck to me. Lamb was collapsed half on me and half in the corner of the backseat, breathing like she'd just run a mile, said she was burning up.

I offered to open a window.

She said, No, I need outside. I got leg cramps.

It was no wonder. I looked at my watch. We'd been at it steady for forty-eight minutes, a personal record.

Lamb got out, and I told her she'd get icycles on her boobs, and she said that might feel real good. I told her she was beautiful and she told me I had always said that just to get her clothes off, and I reminded her she came to me, not the other way around, and the next thing I know I hear her yell, Jesus H, Terry. Somebody's out here!

I got out, opened the front door, grabbed my belt and weapon, made her get back in the front seat. It was real close, right over there, she said, and I could see tracks where she was pointing. I started the engine, turned on the spots, and spun them around, but couldn't see anyone moving.

I asked her how far away he was, and she said, It, not he.

I said, What the hell do you mean by *it?*

You see it, you'll know, she said.

I got my flashlight and went and looked around. There were footprints not ten feet from the front of the squad. From there they would have seen a lot and heard everything.

Service stopped reading. It was a classic witness report—poorly written, largely unpunctuated, just a bolus of words and feelings expelled onto paper. She says she saw something; he sees prints and starts backtracking. Service went back to reading.

I was shook up. Jesus, she was standing outside, sauna-naked, and what if somebody saw us. We should have used her brother-in-law's place. Or something. The tracks took me to where I showed you. Jesus, the nearest houses to where we were had to be like seven, eight miles.

What kind of tracks? Service asked himself, made a note, and kept reading:

Terry, let's just go, that's what she told me. I'm scared. But I told her it would be just fine, I'd just follow the tracks and deal with the peeper and everything would be fine, and when I came back, she was gone. I nearly had a heart attack!!

I got way into the pines, no parka, no pack, my sweat freezing, I had to turn back, and I figured if some asshole came forward and accused us, we'd just deny it, two against one. We could do damage control. So I expected the cruiser's engine to still be running, but it was off. I yelled her name, Lamb! And she didn't answer, and I got scared and went back to work. I figured she was a big girl and could take care of herself.

Service called over to the jail and asked for Daugherty. It took several minutes to get the detainee to a phone.

"It's Grady, Terry. What kind of tracks? Boots?"

Daugherty broke into inconsolable sobs.

Service stayed with his questions. "Pull yourself together, Terry. Boots?"

Daugherty said in a soft voice, "Unh-uh. Big animal."

Fuck.

• • •

A statement in the case file was from the high school kid named Collins whose dog had found the body. The way the kid explained it, his dog was way out in front and when he found her, she was chewing on the body, which he described as blue, with frozen white hair, like Cruella De Vil.

Service drove over to Friday's place. "You read the Collins boy's report?" he asked.

"Of course."

"Including that he found his dog feeding on the body?"

"There will be another DNA this time," she said. "Why?"

"About what you said earlier today . . ."

"I said a lot of things."

"About Lamb not being tribal? She was Sault tribe—I think."

"Well, shit," Friday said. "We didn't need that."

"Sorry," he said. "And who the hell is Cruella De Vil?"

She smiled. "Disney character, *One Hundred and One Dalmatians.*"

He shrugged. "What is *that?*"

"Do you pay attention to anything but work?"

Grady Service smiled. "You."

Friday smiled and shook her head, whispered, "Hopeless."

32

Tuesday, November 25

SLIPPERY CREEK CAMP

Two days before Thanksgiving, and Service had not found time to think about the holiday. Cale Pilkington had called the night before to announce that paleobiologist/anthropologist Nancy Krelle was coming from the lab in Oregon to examine the site where the wolf tooth had been found.

Service had called the Ottawa National Forest office in Ironwood and talked to USFS Special Agent Darcella Dacilente, who often partnered with Denninger and prowled the McCormick Wilderness Tract when she had time off, even in winter.

"Service," she greeted him. "You hear about Dani's massive deer bust?"

"She did great," he said.

Dacilente hailed from Anadarko, Oklahoma. "Hawn," the special agent drawled, "Dani told me all ya'll done handed her 'at case."

"Whatever," he grumped. "It got handed to me, and I just passed it on."

"Wassup?" Dacilente asked. Because of her initials she was known around Upper Peninsula law enforcement circles as Double D.

"How're snow conditions up in the McCormick, Ketchkan Lake country?" Service asked.

"I know a guy lives on Lake Arfelin off the Peshekee Grade. Talked at 'im yesterday. Got in mind to camp over 'at way at the end of the month. Old boy says there's a foot a white crap on the ground, and more was falling yesterday. I'm guessin' they p'obably got a little more up higher by Ketchkan," she said. "Off-piste should be no problem. All y'all headed up 'at way?"

Off-piste was ski jargon for "off-trail." "Maybe; not sure. Tomorrow, maybe."

"How long?"

"Don't know yet."

"Let me know if you stay and we'll hook up."

"D, how much time *do* you spend up in that country?"

"Probably close to a month a year between vacation and patrols. Why?"

"All around the area?"

"Pretty much. There's so much geographic and geologic eye candy up there, I like to move around."

"See many wolves or moose?"

"Some moose, more wolves, but not that many of either."

"Ever come across a wolf-killed moose?"

She chuckled. "Not in the U.P. Alaska, sure, Canada, sure, Isle Royale, you bet—but here in the U.P.? Nopers."

"If you get up there later this week, keep an eye out."

"Are you telling me you found a wolf-killed moose?"

"Two, we think. We're looking into it."

"Holy shit," she said. "Does Pilkington know?"

"Sort of. Why?"

"He did his master's thesis on canid predation," she said. *No wonder the biologist seemed so excited.* "Thanks, D."

"See ya 'round the mountain, Service."

● ● ●

Pilkington and his Oregon visitor pulled up to the cabin at seven that morning. Nancy Krelle stood six foot tall, wore loop earrings, had massive hands and feet, endlessly long legs, and a tiny waist. Her complexion was smooth and youthful with a tan that looked permanent, which suggested she spent more time outdoors than inside. Her voice was low and deep, and she seemed to have the thousand-yard stare typical of combat veterans.

Krelle and Pilkington came inside, and Service gave them coffee. Noonan and Treebone were introduced and immediately went elsewhere. Allerdyce was already gone, off to who knew where. The old poacher wasn't one for keeping people informed. Introductions had been perfunctory. Krelle had intense blue-gray eyes and a quirky speech pattern that immediately irritated Service.

She said, "Thank you for seeing me, will it be, possible to see, the site where you recovered the tooth?" Before Service could answer the woman added, "Forsooth to reach the truth we need to get out to sleuth the tooth." Then she said "Whoops," and blushed bright red.

What the hell was that? "Right now the weather's cooperating," he said.

Krelle said, "'Ting. Got tuck in my ruck and plenty of pluck to do this, hoping for luck, you got a truck?"

Service looked at Pilkington, who acted like everything was perfectly normal. "I have a truck. How long you want to be out there?"

"There. Couple days, I'd say, which for us will or will not pay, we can hike around for a couple days, look for predator and preys, hope our sky stays dry and gray, and I hope we can soon get under way."

"Not a problem," Service said, thinking, *What the hell is the deal with her?*

"Not…blem," the woman said.

"You think the tooth is legitimate?" he asked.

"'Sibly, but this is not yes-no at this point. It remains to appoint un petite point before the evidence we can anoint or disappoint."

"Before we jump off, can you tell me more about the dire wolf?" he asked.

"Wolf. No, we'll talk up there in thinner air."

Service saw Pilkington shrug. "We'll leave soon," Service told them.

Krelle said. "Soon's a boon, I know I sound like a fucking buffoon with all these rhymes my speech's bestrewn. Shit."

Service pulled Pilkington outside. "What the hell is *that* shit all about? She keeps repeating words and saying all those stupid-ass rhymes."

"Mostly she repeats last syllables of the previous speaker's last word," the biologist said. "Logoclonia with intermittent obsessive-compulsive rhyming disorder. She's not sick, although some of her symptoms mimic dementia. The speech crap aside, the woman is a polymath, like da Vinci. Krelle is preeminent in her field; she knows her stuff. Think about what she had to go through to get where she is," Pilkington said. "Patience, Grady."

"We have to wait for Allerdyce," Service told Pilkington, "but we should be shoving off soon."

Krelle said, "'Oon, I won't swoon if we depart soon, before it's up the rising moon, and you should dearly listen to my tune. All my thoughts are hard at first, like Viking runes, but in time your ear will get attuned."

Service found himself staring openmouthed at the woman, afraid to say anything that would launch her into another cuckoo spiel.

"The operative word here," Krelle said with an upbeat voice, "is that all this is intermittent; it comes and goes. Once we're in the field, a lot of this nonsense ends. Don't know why. It just does," she concluded, took a deep breath, and started up again. "I sometimes curse this damn fixation, which yields so little approbation, yet I know in my private ruminations, I hope this will prove a consolation, when we reach our final destination, there'll be a whole lot fewer such inclinations." She paused again, and added, "Please don't feel you have to speak. My disorder can make folks weak, to think they're with such a creepy freak."

Service continued to stare in silence as she droned on, looking more and more frustrated with each word.

"Hence," she said, "I suggest we dispense in the interests of mutual defense, of all words lacking immediate consequence." And finally, "To get me moving, no need to say a bloody thing, just show me the way and I shall spring, like your duly appointed underling."

Service couldn't help himself, said. "No shit."

"Shit," she said. "Let me not submit to your words to wit, for neither of us will benefit."

When Allerdyce rambled into camp, Service had him get his gear out of his pickup and load it into his Tahoe. They departed in silence, lest the weird river of rhyming words begin anew.

II

33

Wednesday, November 26

KETCHKAN LAKE, BARAGA COUNTY

Double D's source notwithstanding, the weekend storm clogged the mountains, making it difficult to get where they wanted to be. Service was still brooding about Lupo but decided he was wrong. The man didn't know anything, so why waste time and money chasing him to Bumfuck, Canada. *To hell with him.*

Limpy rode with Service, and Krelle rode with Cale Pilkington in his truck. The four of them hiked in heavy silence in light falling snow, their boots and walking sticks leaving grooves to mark their passing. Service took Allerdyce's pack for him and sent the old poacher ahead into the valley to find and mark the remains, while he led Pilkington and Krelle on to the north to set up their camp, Pilkington huffing the whole time and sweating profusely, but keeping up and not complaining. Krelle looked as fresh and untrammeled as she had that morning; it was clear she was a field veteran, and in good shape.

Service carried the seventeen-pound six-person REI-brand tent in a special case, belted to the outside of his operations ruck. At the campsite he quickly unpacked the tent and sent Pilkington to fetch firewood. Krelle assembled the tent-frame poles and helped him fit the poles into the geodesic shelter, steadying it with steel spikes. Tent up, fly in place, and snugged to the tent to shed snow, they put their inflatable ground pads and packs inside and hung a few items from hang-loops built into the tent's fabric seams. Krelle went to help Pilkington gather and stack more firewood and cover it with a small tarp.

Allerdyce trudged up from the valley when Service was alone and muttered, "Lotta snow; bloody t'ings're down deep."

Krelle came back before Service could respond, and, fearful of launching her into more of her annoying rhyme-drivel, he tried to keep the subject specific rather than conjectural. "The tooth we sent—real or not?" he asked her.

"Real? Define real. Yes, I guess, but I must admit there is some stress, that when I let it, makes me into a terrible mess. Not to hedge, but by that I mean something about the tooth puts me on edge."

"I found it in the dead moose. I sent the photos," Service said. "That's all I know."

"No DNA yet," she said, "but I suspect it will come back as gray wolf. Mostly."

"Mostly?"

Krelle sighed deeply. "Size says dire, shape says gray, but the gray and dire are genetic canyons apart—that is, not part of the same line of genetic descent. The dire wolf line died out and went nowhere. All wolves today come from a previous wolf line or predecessor genetic stock. Dires were only in the Americas, and grays were concurrent, crossbreeds possible, but not probable."

"Dires only in the Americas?" Service asked.

"Its genetic common ancestor crossed over the Bering bridges and migrated south into more temperate zones, and then mutated into the dire wolf. It would seem that whatever the antecedent species was, it did not migrate south in Asia, and thus they died out. The dire is strictly a temperate zone creature."

"Crossbreeding with grays?" Service asked.

Pilkington answered, "Not that we know of. We have coy dogs and wolf dogs, and coy wolves, but dogs, coyotes, and wolves are more or less in the same genetic silo. Dire wolves aren't."

"But we can't rule it out," Krelle said. "While not probable, many things are theoretically possible in genetics. The problem is that we have never had a valid dire wolf DNA sample, not one, though we've found thousands of skeletons and remains. We've got the advantage of accelerator mass spectrometry now—AMS—which allows us to carbon-date very small samples."

"Are we wasting our time out here?" Service ventured.

Krelle said, "Don't assume that. Show me the sites, and let's think and talk about tit and tat, and this and that."

"A solo dire wolf couldn't survive alone," said Pilkington.

"That's certainly one hypothesis," Krelle said. "*If* this is a genuine modern relation of a dire. But it also could be in the genotype of Alaskan gray wolves, which died out about ten thousand years back, plus or minus, about the same time dires disappeared, and frankly, the interbreeding of disappearing Alaskans with modern new wolf breeds makes some sense genetically."

"Were there dire wolves in Canada?" Service asked.

"Never been found there, or, for that matter, here in Michigan or the upper Midwest. The consensus is that they were warmer-climate animals. Specimens closest to here have come from Missouri, Indiana, and Ohio. Some from Kentucky, too, and east and west along that line, all the way from the Atlantic to the Pacific Oceans."

"In other words, chances are this is not some descendant of the dire wolf," Service said.

"Certainly not based on established evidence and accepted theory, but I prefer to let new evidence take us where it will. I also prefer not to be in a hurry to discount new information solely because it lies outside accepted norms. If not a dire, it could just as well be something equally new and heretofore unsuspected. You guys know you probably have two species of wolf in the state?"

Service said, "Just *Canis lupus.*"

Pilkington coughed and said, "Actually, there's a fair possibility that we have *Canis lupus* and *Canis lycaon,* the so-called Eastern Canadian wolf."

"They're here," Krelle said. "Pro-wolf groups are already trying to factor this into their campaign to keep gray wolves from being delisted under the Endangered Species Act. The recognition of a new species could muck things up for those who have to manage wolf populations. It sure wouldn't help."

"And if there's a third, heretofore unknown, species to go with those two?"

"A potential regulatory miasma," Krelle said. "But look at this another way: If there's two here, why not three?"

The men stared at her until Allerdyce broke the silence. "Youses want go look at bones while light's still good?"

Walking into the valley, Krelle stayed on Service's shoulder and whispered, "When you talk, I sometimes hear what I take to be an implied sneer, as if you think I'm wiggy or insincere."

The rhyming had returned. "No, ma'am," he said, and pointed at a boulder. "Take a seat."

She opened a thermos of coffee and listened as he gave an account of the recent killings and the state of the human remains. The color drained from her face with each new fact.

"Do you have photographs?" she asked.

"In my pack," he said. He took it off and handed an envelope to her.

She went through the photographs slowly, several times. "Wolves or even near-wolves don't do this," she pronounced. "The artuation in the moose photos is suggestively canid, but in the environment, one predator may start, and follow-on predation waves tend to scatter remains about. As for those poor people, I have never seen anything like that, never imagined anything like that, and I never want to *see* anything like it again. Why the heck are you involved in this?"

Grady Service told her about the dogman and the governor's order. Krelle closed her eyes and held her hands over her knees. "That's insane, panic, cheap political stunt, or all of the above."

Service agreed and kept quiet.

Krelle said, "I want to see where the remains were, even if they're gone now, and then I'd like to sweep north and look around some more."

Allerdyce showed them where the bones were, and then led them north into corrugated and eccentric country between High Lake and the head-waters of the West Branch of the Sturgeon River. Pilkington had not come along. He begged off, went back to camp, got his gear, and headed out. Krelle would ride out with Service and Allerdyce tomorrow.

They were in an open boulder area, fresh snow falling, when Service's eye caught movement ahead. He had just decided it was time to go back to camp and eat, and something had moved. A wraith, something low, dark, and heavy. Krelle was to his immediate right, Allerdyce ahead of both of them, the stiffening wind into all of their faces.

"Limpy," Service said softly.

The old man looked back. Service held forefingers to the sides of his head like ears or horns, held a hand behind him, parallel to the ground, a wolf tail out, unlike a coyote tail down. Then he put forked fingers to his eyes.

Allerdyce raised his eyebrows, questioning without language if he should move forward, but Service held out his hand, palm out, and lowered it slowly. Allerdyce, understanding the command, sank slowly out of sight.

Service touched Krelle's arm and they joined Allerdyce on the ground. Krelle lay close to him in silence and eventually said tentatively and almost inaudibly, "Pair of boulders, eleven o'clock, twenty-five yards."

Service turned to look her in the eye.

"I saw it, too," she whispered.

"Saw what?"

"Ochre-gray, brindle maybe, tail out—a wolf without doubt, but a wide, wide body."

"Species?"

"The legs were short, the stature squat, trunk bigger even than the largest grays we know of."

"Dire?" Service ventured.

"Off-the-wall hypothesis," she said. "We know climate change is pushing some species north and killing others who can't adapt. The rate for this is alarming, and not theoretical. We have records. Perhaps there was a remnant zootrope in isolation south of here, and it's migrating north, looking for new territory. Certainly population shifts are being driven by climatic change, and there are more places to hide, more forest now by far than in 1900. Wild habitat is available, especially for migrators who can carefully pick their way."

Allerdyce suddenly ghosted into their peripheral vision, close to them, whispered hoarsely, "Wolfie," and pointed.

Service said, "See if you can cut the track. We all saw it."

"We're not hallucinating," Krelle told the old poacher, who grinned happily and crawled away.

• • •

Just before dark the old man came back and led them forward, where he lit the snow with a small green penlight. "Fresh," Allerdyce said. "Real."

Service heard the air go out of Krelle when she looked down. "Good God almighty," she said.

Not a single set of tracks, but three different sizes, one the size of the tracks Service and Denninger had found.

Allerdyce chuckled, said, "Dis is fun, sonny."

Service couldn't tell if the old man was amused or shaken. He knew that he himself was taken aback, and so, too, was Krelle. He could hear her hyperventilating.

"We play hide-seek wit' dese guys, or head ta camp?" Allerdyce asked.

Service measured the largest track at seven inches long by four inches wide, and took photos, but gave no thought to plaster casts. That gear was back in the truck. They had a lot to think about, and he was not the least bit sure where to start. Or how.

A dogman is one thing, but what appears to be breeding wolves of a size never before imagined is another. This is an entirely different deal, with so many ramifications I can't even begin to sort them out.

Service herded his small tribe south toward their camp and tried not to look over his shoulder.

34

Thursday, November 27

KETCHKAN LAKE

They talked little during the night, lost in their own thoughts. Sometime during the hike back to camp Allerdyce killed four pats. *Walking in the woods with that old man is like touring Wal-Mart with a kleptomaniac,* Service thought. *And the old man, presumably, is on his best behavior. Jesus.*

Service also knew he was beyond making an issue of minor transgressions. *Hell, I gave a felon a firearm!* The old man was quicksand pulling him deeper, yet it was also inescapable that Allerdyce never seemed to rattle, rarely showed any negative emotions, and, in the woods, had few equals.

They were drinking fresh coffee at first light when Service's cell phone vibrated in his pocket. It was Tuesday calling. *Shit, today's Thanksgiving!* He hadn't even thought about it.

"I'm sorry," he answered.

She cut him off. "Don't even. I'm here, and I've got everything handled. Pilkington called here this morning, checking on you, and I got worried. I guessed you'd be out of there by now."

"We got delayed last night."

"You're okay?" she asked.

"Fine. We should be back late today or tomorrow morning, latest."

"Professor Lupo called from somewhere in Manitoba. He wants us to come to him. We'll be met at the airport in Winnipeg."

"When?"

"Quote, 'Soon as you can get your tails up here,' end quote."

"What did you tell him?"

"I told him we needed to discuss it. Karylanne and Kalina will look after the kids. Both can stay a week."

He couldn't believe what he was hearing. "You *want* to do this Manitoba thing?"

"No, but now my intuition is telling me Lupo knows things we need to know, and he's not going to tell us unless we go to him."

Service sighed. "All right, we'll pack up camp and head in soon-as. Book a flight tonight, whatever it takes to get there. Use the governor's budget line for this."

"Lupo said we'll be met whenever we get there, and we shouldn't worry about such details, but to bring warm clothes."

They made a few more plans, and Service hung up. He was afraid going to see Lupo would be a waste of their time.

As they hiked, Allerdyce said, "Girlie wants ta stay oot 'ere, sonny, look more. Ast me ta help."

The thought of sparks flying between the old man and Krelle made him cringe. Why did educated, presumably classy women feel inexplicably drawn to the old bastard? It defied all logic.

Walking next to Krelle, Service said, "About our companion."

"A fascinating man. He must've led a remarkable life."

"He's certainly held law enforcement's attention for a helluva long time."

"What about him?" Krelle pressed.

"Not all wolves have four legs," Service said.

Krelle sniggered.

"You've been cautioned," Grady Service said, and kept walking.

35

Sunday, November 30

WOLVERINE JUNCTION (WOJU), MARQUETTE COUNTY

On Thursday afternoon, by the time Service had gotten to Friday's, she had decided against the Alberta trip. When he asked why, she answered with a shrug.

It had been almost a normal weekend until stand-in dispatcher Billye Fyke had called. Friday put her on speakerphone. A body had been found north of Ishpeming in the Wolverine Junction country, hanging in a tree. She told them, "Chet Saville was out on his trapline at WoJu, and he found the body, eh? Trooper Anne Campau went out to the scene to check on it. Chet called Jack Igo and his dogs, and they took off tracking. Campau stayed with the body. When Chet and Jack got back, Campau was gone, and so was the body."

"What the hell is WoJu?" Friday shouted at the phone.

"Wolverine Junction," Service said quietly. "East of the McCormick Wilderness, north of Ishpeming."

"Reachable?"

"Easier on snowmobiles later in the winter, but we can probably do it. We'll bring snowshoes, though."

Friday said into the phone, "Do you carry, Billye?"

"No, ma'am," the dispatcher said.

"*Start*," Friday said. "This asshole has a thing for women."

Service could sense Friday rubbing against panic and fighting to maintain her composure. *She's right about one thing: This is an asshole—not a windigo, not a dogman, not Peter Fucking Pan.*

There were two dozen people scouring the area, mostly civilians. Jack Igo had even taken his dogs down deep into some of the local drainage ravines while they seemed to be on scent, but it had petered out at one of the many small streams that crisscrossed the area north of Ishpeming and was too deep to cross safely.

A family from Gwinn called in a missing person, their daughter Sarah Root, age twenty, part-time student at Northern, last seen Tuesday morning when she'd skipped class to snowshoe in the woods near Wolverine Junction, which was no more than an old marker on the old railroad line north of Ishpeming. The parents had provided a photo, and copies had been made and given to cops and first responders all around the U.P. It turned out the Root girl was married and separated from her hubby, who worked as a detailer at a used-car dealership.

Service had gone to talk to the husband, who turned out to be a blob bound for a career of victimhood. "Who'd want to hurt your wife?" he had asked the man.

"She sorta ain't my wife no more, eh?" the man said.

"Answer the question."

"Anybody who knows her. She's a lot like the total bee-otch, sayin'?"

The line in the report that stuck in Service's mind was that the girl was tribal, a member of the Keweenaw Bay tribe out of Baraga. Her husband wasn't. Body language said he was a dolt, severely undermotored for even the slowest of lanes, but not a liar.

Igo came back out of the woods and shrugged. "My dogs got nothing left in 'em."

Service asked, "What were they on?" He'd heard them singing, knew they had some sort of spoor. You could always tell by dogs' voices.

"Not sure, eh. Dose damn dogs, dey keep looking up in trees," he said. Then, to Friday, "How long youse want me keep dis up?"

"Until I say it's finished, Mr. Igo. You'll be paid."

Service pulled Igo aside. "You're done," he said. "Rest your dogs."

Friday's stare was blank and unfocused.

• • •

Trapper Chet Saville showed them where he had found the body twenty-four hours before. Saville, who had retired from the county road commission, spent much of his time in the woods. "Oot scoutin' for late bow, eh, an' I find tracks of big old bruiser. Follow 'im up dis country, find dat dam body, by Gott, make me sick, dat t'ing. I hike right out, call State Police. Anne Campau, she come. I know her way back. She look at body, tell me get Jack

Igo and dogs and find spoor. I get feeling she t'ink t'ing comin' back ta eat on da body, and she be waitin'."

"Campau told you that?" Friday asked.

Saville shugged. "You know how Trooper Campau is. She don't say shit wit' mout'ful. Just feelin' I get, her being bulldog an' all."

Service said, "You've skinned and butchered game all your life, Chet. Impressions of what you found hanging?"

"Campau, she call hit horrenderoma, and dat sound 'bout right to me. All my years, ain't never seen no human bean skinned out, and don't mind I never see again," the man said.

"Show us where you left Campau," Service told the trapper, who took them through the woods and showed them. The snow was badly chewed up. Service knew there had once been tracks here, but they were obliterated. *Had Campau been pacing, or was this something else? Impossible to read.*

Noonan was helping a crew near where the body had been found, and Tree was back in a vehicle, changing clothes to head into the woods. Allerdyce had poked north alone, but came shuffling back and pointed. "T'ree hunnert yards."

"Tracks?"

Allerdyce shook his head. "Look like it went oot road. Carry girlie t'ru trees, come down over dat way at road."

Through the trees? What now—King Kong?

"Without tracks?" Service asked.

"Wass dere, been smooshed, but trail lead from where body hang out ta road."

"Which road?"

The old man pointed. *Paved. Fuck.*

"Anne Campau's an experienced cop," Friday said to Service. "Not prone to dumb decisions."

Noonan was up in the tree where the body had been and yelled down to them. "Thank God," he said, "I was beginning to think we were chasing a ghost. There's ligature-like marks on a branch up here. Marks are deep," he added.

Service was thinking: The Root girl was said to be two hundred pounds. Such weight would leave a deep mark. He had moved a lot of bodies during his life, and one man didn't move two hundred pounds of dead, limp weight, much less hoist it into a tree all by his lonesome, unless he was one very strong son of a bitch, or used a pulley to make the weight manageable.

"Look for signs of a pulley rigging," Service called up to Noonan, who, after a few minutes, said, "You want to step up and take a look. Not sure what I'm looking for."

Service took five minutes to climb up and discover what he wanted. A place in a Y where a rope had been connected and something metal had banged into the bark, nicking it, telltale sign of a pulley setup. *Okay, our guy whacks the Root girl and lifts her up. Then what?*

Friday stood below the tree. "What's in your brain?"

"Get Chet."

Service climbed down. Saville wore a faded red-checked Stormy Kromer hat. "Tell us exactly what you saw when you got here," Service said.

The man rubbed his neck. "Body hangin' up dere."

"Head?"

"Yeah, head dere, but not no hands."

"Blood?"

"Not so much."

"Not bled out here?"

Saville made a face. "Din't look like 'er, eh."

"Another dump-and-display site," Friday said, and Service nodded. "You think windigos display their kills?" she asked.

"Doubt it," he said tersely, but reminding himself that he didn't know enough to make a reasonable conclusion.

"So what is this asshole trying to tell us?"

"He don't like In'din woman?" Allerdyce said, barging into the conversation.

"Chet, why didn't you try to stop Anne?" Friday asked.

The man grimaced. "Don't make much sense try argue with split-tail pack a forty-cal Sig, know what I mean?"

Service knew Campau. Not the kind to ask for help, thought she could do anything—a weakness and a strength for a cop, depending on the roll of the dice.

Friday talked to the sheriff's department and county SAR, and they agreed to call off the search for the night, reevaluate conditions and a plan in the morning.

The men went back to Slippery Creek, and Friday went home. Just before she left, Service noticed that she looked like she was losing weight. *Pressure's getting to her.*

Noonan, Allerdyce, Treebone, and Service returned to his cabin.

Noonan said, "I seen dingers of every kind. Serial killer in Highland Park dumped carved-up bodies in abandoned houses. An Eye-ranian exchange student raped old ladies, pounded nails right through their eyeballs, left baling-wire loops through that little piece of skin separates nostrils in their noses. Janitor in RenCen raped fifty women; when Metro cornered his ass, he screamed "Superman forced me to do it!" and he jumped out a window, twenty stories up. Didn't fly for shit. But this stuff up here, man, this is something all on its own."

"Word *windigo* mean anything to you?" Service asked them all.

Allerdyce scrinched his face. "Win-dago . . . t'ink mebbe I know dat one."

"Know it how?"

"Finndians out dere Sidnaw say long time back, dey had one dose t'ings out dere."

"You remember when that was?"

"During Big War Two, forty-t'ree, 'four, like dat, I t'ink."

Service called Friday. "The Root girl lived with her parents?"

"As I understand it."

"Who went to the home?"

"Not sure; I'll have to check. Why?"

"Allerdyce says there was some talk of a windigo around Sidnaw back in '43 or '44."

Service heard her sigh. "What exactly are we looking for at the Root family's house."

"Medicine bags on the doors," Service said, and described them.

Ten minutes later Service's cell phone vibrated. Caller ID said it was Helmi Yint.

"Helmi—hi."

"Martine Lecair," the Yint woman said. "You di'n't hear dis from me, eh, but it bein' said aroun' dat Lecair, she went out Arizona."

"Who's saying this?"

"Could be somebody seen some envelopes down dead-letter box, Baraga."

"With Lecair's name on them?"

"Nope, just Tucson. You find the Root girl yet?"

The grapevine up here was like lightning. "Not yet."

"You do, take good long look her soon-be ex, eh?"

"You know him?"

"Yeah. Holy-roller type, gon' save da soul of da world, and if you don't change, you be sorry."

"He try to change his wife?"

"Wunt s'prise me none."

Service called Friday again. "Helmi Yint just called, says there are letters in Kelly Johnstone's unclaimed mail from Tucson. She thinks they could be from Martine Lecair."

"I talked to the sarge at the post. One of his Troops found medicine pouches at the Root girl's parents' place. I assume you're heading for Arizona?"

"Better idea?"

She laughed in an odd way he couldn't quite decipher. "Take company," she said.

Tree had no interest in Arizona, but Noonan was game for the trip.

Service had first asked Allerdyce, who said only that he had "an impervious engorgement."

"Don't tell me," Service said, shaking his head. "Krelle?"

"Dose tall ones iss somepin', donchu know," the old poacher said. "She up dere Ketchkan wit dat fat-ass biologist. He come back oot after youse leaved."

"You were supposed to stay with them."

"I go up dat way now," the old man said, defensively.

36

Thursday, December 4

BODISON, ARIZONA

Service and Noonan flew into Tucson on Monday. Before leaving, Service made a phone call to former CO Carl "Cherry" Sisniega, who had grown up in a migrant family that settled near Buckley, outside Traverse City. Service had given him his nickname. Sisniega started out in Corrections as a guard and transferred to the DNR in law enforcement near Newberry. He'd married the daughter of a Hamtramck cop with a bushy mustache and a voice loud enough to shatter glass two blocks over. The wife's parents retired to Tucson, and Cherry's wife Miggy couldn't stand being without them, so Cherry resigned and moved west, ultimately catching on as a deputy in the Pima County Sheriff's Department, settled in, and never looked back.

Service had stayed in touch over the years.

"Big Dog, you *still* in the game back there?"

"Much as I can be. I'm headed to Tucson on a semi-cold case."

"Must got you better budgets than in my day. I'm workin' too, made sergeant."

"Got a partner with me, retired Detwat homicide."

"You both stay with Miggy and me, more the merrier; Miggy be glad to see you. You need help finding somebody, I jump in witch youse. People here ain't so quick to fuck with the po-lice like back there."

"You're sure you've got room?'

"Got oodles," Sisniega said.

"Tucson cops say *oodles?*"

Sisniega said, "You gonna see some oodles, my frien', sunshine and lotsa smiley-face people."

Which turned out to be an understatement. His friend's house was garish pink stucco, with two inner courtyard gardens and an ornamental rock garden outside in a desert landscape.

"What's the square footage in this palacio?" Noonan asked the man.

"Not quite four thou," Sisniega said.

"You on the take?" a skeptical Noonan asked.

"Just how it is here. They pay us enough to live like real people. Don't need no basements. You know how much a basement add to the cost of a house? Snows out here once every five hundred years. Miggy and me, we died and got sent out here to Heaven."

Cherry Sisniega's hair was almost all white. Miggy's was blonde, and she looked like she'd not gained two pounds in a decade.

• • •

It had taken three days to develop a lead. Sisniega drove the Michigan men to a section of town he called Poco Detroit.

Service couldn't quite envision the Cass Corridor: People in Poco Detroit were out in the streets, talking and smiling, walking around with no apparent fear.

"My people aren't like blacks," Sisniega said. "The blacks, you step on them, they go boom, like right now. Latinos, we got to simmer, get it up, boil it some more, then you get your boom. Right now for blacks, but takes a while for my people. Make it to the same destination, but different routes and speed. Don't get so much sudden shit out here."

"No drive-bys?" Noonan asked their host.

"Not so many like you got."

"You working on a psych degree?" Service teased his friend.

"No man, I just seen how it is. This is it," he said, pointing to a faded building the color of bleached turquoise. "You want me along?"

"Got cavalry with me this time," Service said.

"Don't make no paperwork for me, Grady," Sisniega said.

"Not a problem."

Sisniega said, "Once a shit magnet, always a shit magnet."

• • •

The apartment was on the fourth floor. Service and Noonan stepped over several dusky kids playing on the stairs and knocked on the steel door, which eventually cracked open. Service flashed his badge and palmed it before the man could take it in. "We're looking for a Wheat Kurdock."

"Why's that?" the man asked.

Service shot back, "Who're you, Mr. Kurdock's engagement secretary?"

"He ain't here," the suspicious greeter said sheepishly.

"But he lives here?"

"I never said 'at," the man said, and tried to slam the door, but Noonan blocked him and shouldered it open. "Jerk," Noonan said.

"I did not resist," the man whined.

There were a dozen people in a large room in various stages of undress. Noonan looked them over. "Yogi Berra class?"

"This is a nonviolent gathering," a woman said, holding out a spliff. "Hit?"

Service said, "We're looking for Martine Lecair or Wheat Kurdock."

Somebody to Noonan's right shifted weight, and he instinctively stepped in that direction.

"We're not local heat," Service said. "Got no warrants, no hassles intended."

Dead silence.

A thin man from Service's left scampered for the door, but didn't get four steps before Service had him facedown. "You want to calm down, or do I have to call the local badge up here? You Kurdock?" Service asked the man on the floor.

"I guess," the man said.

Noonan said with a snarl, "Foo', this is a yes-no question, not no damn blue book."

"Yes, Kurdock, Wheat. That's me."

"Let's step outside and talk," Service said.

"I prefer to talk here in front of my friends."

"You think you need witnesses?"

"One never knows," Kurdock said.

"Okay," Service said. "I'm okay with an audience."

Noonan turned to the man who had met them at the door. "Hey, shit-for-brains, I thought Kurdock wasn't here."

"Wasn't the last time I looked," the man mumbled with an insipid grin.

A woman said, "Make love, not war, amigos."

Noonan retorted. "Make silence, not sentences."

Service felt his shirt sticking to his skin. He hated heat. *This shit in December? God.*

"Where's Martine Lecair?" Service asked his subject.

"Marti moved."

"To where, from where?"

"Over to Bodison."

"Which is where?"

"It's a town out beyond the air base. You know, Davis-Monthan?"

"I'm anal-retentive. I need more detail."

The man got up, went to a table, got out a notepad, wrote something, tore it out, and handed it to Service. "She's not here," Kurdock repeated.

"If we don't find her in Bodison, we'll be back with the chili peppers," Service said. "Do you good to remember that, sir."

Downstairs Sisneiga said, "Took you guys a long time up there."

"Language barriers," Service said.

"Shoulda have tooken me along," Sisniega said.

"We wanted information, not war," Service said.

• • •

Service had seen many peculiar places in his life, but Bodison, Arizona, was unique: The town, such as it was, sat southeast of Davis-Monthan Air Force Base on the southeast side of Tucson. Martine Lecair, according to Kurdock, had been hired to teach at an "Academy for Indians," the school run by the Minnesota Ojibwe Missionary Society. What business did Minnesota have sending missionaries to Arizona? He knew Minnesota to have plenty of its own ugly, homegrown problems.

Bodison lacked trees except for a few scraggly specimens in pots. The surrounding area was desert, the dominant color, babyshit brown. It was only December and the heat was such that you could see mirages of water ahead on the pavement.

The missionary school was fenced in with double rolls of concertina wire strung across the top, and the fencing made Service wonder if the hardware was intended to keep students in or non-students out. That was the thing about fences: It was sometimes tough to measure intent. Nobody greeted or stopped them at the front gate, which suggested security was more a matter of low-grade image than reality. A sign instructed visitors to sign in, but not where. *Twenty-first-century communications deficiency disorder,* Service told himself. *It was a plague on the country.*

Noonan grabbed a janitor by a building. "Martine Lecair."

"Did you folks sign in at Admin?" the man asked.

Noonan said, "Not much sense of direction."

"Hopi Lodge," the man in khaki coveralls said. "Down the block beside the outdoor swimming pool. Ask there." He pointed.

Hopi Lodge had varnished brown elk antlers over the front entrance. They went inside and found several children in a hallway tapping frantically on laptops. "Anybody here know where Ms. Lecair is?" Service asked.

A girl stood up, smoothed out her pink floral smock, and stepped over to them. "Miss Lecair? I'll show you."

There was a woman sitting alone at a table in an outside courtyard, reading a book.

"Martine Lecair?" Service asked, looking around. There was only one escape route and Noonan was close to it. "We've come a long way to talk to you."

Lecair was an attractive woman with large brown eyes, a round face, and a major case of instantaneous heebie-jeebies. "I don't know you," she said tentatively.

He showed his badge. "No, ma'am, you don't, but I'm Michigan Department of Natural Resources Conservation Officer Service. My partner over there is Noonan. You disappeared pretty fast from Negaunee, and that's got a lot of people worried."

"The State sent a game warden all the way out here to tell me that? I don't understand." The woman's head drooped and she began to tremble. She said, "I lost one, won't lose the other one." Then, "I need to use the bathroom," and scrambled to her feet.

"Whoa—tell us what happened," Service said.

"Not now," the woman said, "I have to go now; I *really* have to go."

She looked back from the bathroom door, said, "I'm not going back. We're safe from it here in the heat." She stepped inside and Service lost sight of her.

He yelled into the opening. "I need for you to talk to me about your daughters."

"You're here," the voice came back, "which tells me it's still going on."

Women and johns. "Don't take all day in there."

The shot came seconds later and set all the kids in the nearby corridors and courtyards shrieking and running around in panic. Service and Noonan charged into the bathroom, saw the teacher's feet sticking out from under a stall door, got the door open, saw the blood and the wound. The woman had stuck a .32 snubbie in her mouth. Noonan said, "No cry for help, this." Two-inch barrel, the kind some cops called a Good-bye Special. The pistol had skittered into the adjacent stall. Service looked at the wall, above the body. There was a familiar red stick figure hastily drawn. The lipstick tube had rolled out into the larger room.

"Fuck," Service said.

A woman came into the bathroom and Noonan told her to call 911, tell them there had been a shooting.

"What about an ambulance?" the woman asked calmly.

Service felt her femoral artery. No pulse. Checked her pupils: Fixed and dilated. He shook his head.

• • •

Wheat Kurdock was arrested in Nogales four days after the suicide, caught trying to go *south* across the border, which struck the Border Patrol as somewhat against the flow of the majority of border crossings, putting the event into its own special classification and priority, which is why Sisniega managed to pick up on it soon afterward.

The three men drove down and were taken to see the prisoner.

"Don't catch many going south, Wheat—like, nada, dude," Sisniega said.

The border agent who sat with them had the neck of a bull, and Cherry asked him, "I know you, man?"

"Perez. Played linebacker for the Cards," the man said.

"I remember you," Cherry said. "Arizona sell you to Detwat."

"Death sentence," the former player said. "Thank God I couldn't pass the physical. I come back out here and got work right away. Decided it was time to do something with the rest of my life."

"You were a good player," Sisniega said.

Noonan added, "You passed the physical, you'd have been in the ass-end of hell."

"Tell me about it," Perez said.

"Once had a petition in town to change the team name from Lions to Hos," Noonan said. "Got seventy-five thousand signatures, more than can fit in the stadium. Border Patrol's a big step up from Detroit Lion," he added.

Perez left them with Kurdock. Service said, "Yo, Wheat, let me guess— you were rushing down to Cozumel for surfing season."

"I heard she committed suicide," Kurdock said.

For once, the media got a story right. "You must have a better class of reporters than we have."

"She was a very frightened lady," Kurdock said.

"She say why?"

"She refused to talk about it."

"And you weren't curious?" *How many thousands of people had he interviewed over the decades? It was like there was a set score they had to be guided to, same tune, different lyrics.*

"Of course I was curious. I asked her and asked her, but she was wrapped so tight she wouldn't say nothing. *Muckwa,*" he added with obvious disgust.

"You tribal, Wheat?"

"Saginaw Chippewa. Former."

"Mugwop?" Noonan said.

The man curled a lip. "*Muckwa*—Bear Clan. Stubborn as hell, born trouble, especially their women."

"Where are her kids?" Service asked.

"I don't know, man. She never said nothing about no kids."

"So you ran?"

"Little time in Mexico can't hurt the soul," the man said.

"She had two kids, Kurdock."

"No, just one," the man said.

"You just told us she never said nothing about kids."

"She didn't say nothing. I seen her with a kid one time, figured it was hers. You can tell, right?"

Service felt like the man was telling the truth, or his version of it. There were sometimes several versions and multiple follow-up adjustments.

Service showed the man a photograph of the dead woman and the red stick figure from the bathroom stall. "Any bells ringing?"

Kurdock stared at the floor, shrugged. "Windigo sign . . . about all I know. Supposed to keep the cold one away."

"Cold one?" Noonan asked, and Service let him.

"Right. Like a monster."

"She used lipstsick to keep away a monster?"

"*Muckwa,*" Kurdock said. "They believe all that shit."

"But you don't?" Service said.

"I'm Catfish Clan, *Manumaig,* on my father's side. My mother was *Ude-kumaig,* Whitefish."

"I'm a fricking Scorpio," Noonan said. "And everybody hates my ass. Catfish, whitefish, bat shit, bear shit, monsters: All this shit is ozone, like foreign zoo duty."

Service told the man, "Go back to Tucson and keep your ears on for anything about her kid, or kids. You hear something, you call me right away. Fuck time zones and all that shit, hear me?"

"Am I under arrest?" Kurdock asked

Noonan said, "Is English like your fifth language, asshole? You leave Tucson without telling Sergeant Sisniega, or hear something you fail to pass along, and we'll be back. Then you'll get to see a real monster."

"Yessir," Kurdock said.

• • •

Heading north Service looked at his friend. "Jesus, Cherry, can't you drive any faster?"

"Hey, this ain't like Detroit—like, we've got real speed limits."

"You know anything about monsters?" he asked his friend.

"Like Creeper from Black Lagoon and all dat shit?"

"Like the windigo."

"No, man, I don't know no monster like that."

Service telephoned Friday while they were in transit.

"Thought you fell off the edge of the earth," she said, teasing.

"Lecair committed suicide, and I was ten feet away, pistol in her mouth. We can't find her kids. She drew a lipstick figure where she died, red stick figure."

"Windigo?"

"Looked like it to me," Service said. "I didn't really get to talk to her. She went hinky right away, said something about losing one and not losing another."

Both of them went silent until Friday said, "Gut?"

"Only one kid made it out here."

"Grady, get her DNA to me ASAP."

Service said, "Damn, that fits. I'm thinking maybe she lost one kid there and ran out here to hide the other one."

"We have an unidentified child in the morgue," Friday said. "Maternal mitochondrial DNA is the genetic link to mom."

"I'll bring the results myself," Service said.

"I especially like the myself part," his girlfriend grumped. "It's about damn time."

37

Monday, December 15

KETCHKAN LAKE, BARAGA COUNTY

Grady Service was beginning to regret how he had tied up Noonan and Treebone by dragging them into a fool's errand. Part of him wanted to cut them loose and send them home subject to recall, but all of this had broken so fast and erratically that another part kept insisting he keep his reserves close and on the ready. This was the sort of lesson you learned hard in the military, and as a cop. Out-of-reach backup wasn't backup at all. His gut told him to keep the two men near, even if they weren't busy.

It was just after dark when he slogged through the snow into the camp between Ketchkan and High Lakes. There had been more snow as there always was higher up, but no major new dumping, and there was a nice fire going and a couple of lanterns hung on the tent.

Nobody greeted him as he stepped to the fire and shed his pack. No sign of Cale Pilkington. Krelle had dark bags under her eyes, and Allerdyce looked the way he always did: untouched by reality. Service lit a cigarette.

Krelle said, "You didn't get the memo? The whole world quit those things."

Pretty playful for as disjointed as she looks, Service thought. Krelle ran her fingers through her hair, looked at him with a crooked smile, her pupils growing, suggesting she was glad he was back. He immediately wondered if Allerdyce had been hitting on her, or if her eyes were simply reacting to fire.

He took two large thermoses out of his pack and set them down. "Dinty Moore beef stew. Heated it in a microwave at a Shell station on the way up here." He shoved his ruck into the tent, noticed Allerdyce sitting beside Krelle like an adoring dog. He nodded in their direction. "Have I missed something?"

Krelle took a digital camera out of her pocket, hit some buttons, and handed the camera to him. Three wolves in the first frame, all large, one of the three looking like it was inflated by steroids. He looked up at Krelle and raised an eyebrow.

"Keep going," she said, "Film at eleven."

He flicked through more stills until he came to a movie segment which he watched for almost a full minute. The three animals were running perpendicular to the camera, or sort of running. It was more like . . . *Jesus! It was just like that hand motion Donte DeJean showed us!* Hand straight up, up and over to fingertips, pull hand heel in, repeat. At the start of the movie when the animals moved, it looked like they were on two legs, but this was just an optical illusion, a snapshot from a sequence that made you see what wasn't.

Was this the source of the dogman crap? True, some disc jockey had created the whole deal as a prank, but the thing had persisted since the eighties. Had people been seeing these animals all along?

"What are they?" he calmly asked Krelle, who held her arms and hands out to her sides.

"The beefiest one has short legs," she said. "The other two are large, although their proportions seem more normal. Until we get some actual DNA samples, we're not going to know anything."

"Where'd you get these?"

Allerdyce said, "Sout' a High Lake, mile mebbe, place call High Crick, jess little piss crick is all, but lots beaver in meadow, some willow, moose sign."

"Any more moose carcasses?"

Allerdyce shook his head. "No time look, eh. Girlie dere, she want wolfie movies."

Krelle said, "Mr. Allerdyce's ways in the woods border on the supernatural."

Service didn't ask for an explanation. He already knew. "Eat some stew. There's fresh bread in my pack from the Huron Mountain Bakery. Who shot the movies?"

Allerdyce nodded almost imperceptibly as he dumped stew from a thermos into a pan and stirred it with his ballpoint pen.

"How close?" Service asked.

Limpy said, "Forty paces, mebbe."

"What are they?" Service asked.

"Wolfies, t'ink, but not like I seen 'fore."

"Behavior suggest anything?" he asked Krelle.

But Allerdyce answered. "Pack for sure, family mebbe; sure di'n't like my smell."

Service asked, "Can you find them again?"

"T'ink so," Allerdyce said. "You want me pop one?"

"No," Krelle squawked.

"I take one kittle from pack, old man an' old lady can make more kittles replace one dey lose."

"No," Service said.

The poacher rolled his eyes.

Krelle said, "Scientists do this sort of thing in the name of science."

"Yeah, I remember a bunch of black guys down south that science types let carry syphilis to the end," Service said.

"This is *not* like that," Krelle snapped.

"Wolves are still protected here," Service said. "All wolves."

"You're assuming *Canis lupus,* and we don't know that."

"It's a subspecies?" Service asked. He'd never really had a good grasp of species classification systems.

"In fact," Krelle said, "there are forty subspecies of *Canis.*"

"In my business, when we don't know what something is, we assume it should be protected," Service said.

"That's to be expected," the woman said, "even commended, but it is totally inflexible."

"How it has to be," he said.

Allerdyce intervened. "Want me track scat, hair?"

Service nodded, looked at the woman. "Where's Cale?"

"Home. He's not well suited to tent life in the snow."

Service liked Pilkington, thought he was a good man and did a good job with the moose herd. "We all work differently," he said in the biologist's defense, knowing full well that over recent years experienced state biologists had been forced out of the field and into their offices by too-small budgets.

"You don't have to live out here," Service said. "There are places you can stay and come and go up here."

"Mr. Allerdyce already kindly offered the same, but no thanks; I prefer to remain right where we are."

Service looked at Allerdyce. "No firearms."

Allerdyce cackled happily. "Don't need gun for dem wolfies. Dey won't bodder no pipples."

"I'll spend the night, head out in the morning," Service said. "Call if you get lucky," he added, immediately regretting his choice of words, especially when Krelle's face turned scarlet and Allerdyce's eyes twinkled. *Good God, it's already happened!*

38

Wednesday, December 17

ISHPEMING, MARQUETTE COUNTY

Champ's Funeral Home was just south of the infamous Yooper Tourist Trap on US 41 / M-28. It was a brick building, darkened by soot and smoke, and close to some ancient iron-mine structures.

Joan Champ had called just as Service was getting into his Tahoe that morning. There was also a text message that Allerdyce and Krelle had hiked north to High Creek just before first light. Tree and Noonan were at Friday's office and heading to Baraga County to check birth records at the hospital, and at local church birth registries. They were still trying to find information on Martine Lecair's twins. Service suggested they might have been born elsewhere, maybe in another state, and Friday said she was working that angle through various online databases.

Service waved as Noonan and Tree sped west past him. He pulled into Champ's parking lot and punched in Val Houston's phone number. Val had been a classmate of his at Northern long, long ago. Back when they were both students, she had also bartended at the Holiday Inn. She had gone on to New York City to Columbia Unversity and gotten her master's degree in social work. A Potawatomi, she had married an Ojibwe lawyer and moved to the Walpole Island Ojibwe Reserve in Ontario. Houston had once explained the Council of Three Fires to him, the confederation of Ojibwe, Ottawa, and Potawatomi tribes. The Ojibwe were the faith keepers, the Ottawa, the trade keepers, and the Potawatomi, the fire keepers, or "cheek blowers."

"Val, this is Grady."

"Let me guess—you miss me?" she said.

"You miss *me?*" he countered.

"Not so much after the first fifteen years," she said, and laughed out loud.

"You know me and communcations," he said sheepishly.

"Meaning no commo, at all. I don't suppose you're somewhere near Walpole?"

"Parking lot of a funeral home in Ishpeming."

"Not family, I hope."

"A case," he said.

"When did animals start being handled by funeral homes?" she asked. "Things that bad up there economically?"

"They are," he said, "but that's not why I'm calling."

Val Houston was a social worker at the reserve. When Service was a Troop, he'd once driven over to Walpole to see Val and her husband Briscoe. The island was almost all swamp, with mosquitoes the size of hummingbirds. She and Briscoe would talk about nothing but reparations from the United States and Canada to aboriginals. Service had lasted one day and departed. He had little interest in the past, his or theirs, or the issues that lay in the way-back-when. Yesterday was gone. You had today and tomorrow, especially today. Still, Val was a smart cookie, a straight talker, and a master at navigating government red tape. If anyone could find certain Native Americans, it would be Val. Why he'd not thought of her until now was beyond him.

"I assume you're looking for someone," Houston said.

"I am."

"Let me guess: female?"

"Yes, but it's business, not personal. One of your people."

"Walpolean?"

"No, Ojibwe, from up here. Teacher. She had twins, now five or six years old."

"Hold up, big guy: You *do* know Walpole's in Canada?"

"I know some tribal folks don't pay a helluva lot of attention to US or Canadian borders."

"Any chance the twins are Canadian-born?"

This had never entered his mind as a possibility. "Nothing pointing that way," he said.

"You said the teacher *had* twins. Meaning?"

"Suicide, offed herself. One of her kids was murdered, identity confirmed by DNA. The other kid is missing. We don't have positive ID on the missing kid; no name, nothing really. The woman's name was Martine Lecair. Don't know where she was born either, but we assume up this way somewhere." The mental picure of Lecair dead on a floor in Bodison persisted, along with the lipstick figure on the bathroom wall. He told Houston the story, about all the killings and bodies.

"Good god," she said. "It sounds like a bloodbath up there. How come it's not major news?"

"All tribals so far," he said. "Maybe they lack news value."

"And maybe you people sat on a lot of it, to keep the investigation close?"

"Could be a factor," he admitted. "You know anything about windigos?"

"Good *god,* Grady! Listen, I hope you're not buying into that windigo psychosis crap."

"A psychosis is real, right?"

"Listen to me, Grady Service. Here's the truth about the windigo psychosis: It was white anthropologists' attempt to rationalize murder by groups and individuals in situations where survival was threatened and food was short, too much snow to get out and hunt, and not enough summer and fall preparation . . . Hear what I'm saying?"

"Donner Party, Andes crash survivors?" Both situations had spawned so-called survival cannibalism.

"There you have it," Val Houston said. "Same behavior, different label; problem of white-skinned academics being blinded to the dynamic and wanting to give it a forgiving, dismissive new set of clothes. Tell me what you've seen."

He did, sparing no detail.

"Seriously, not a windigo, Grady. Windigo is about starving people desperate for food. Seems to me you've got a nutcase either trying to make a statement to the world, or hiding something else he's up to."

"He?"

She laughed. "Near hunnert percent, big guy."

"Social workers deal with this sort of thing?"

"Do you know how difficult it is to find missing Indian children?"

"No."

"Massive dislocation, drugs, violence, mental illness, poverty, kids ending up with grandfathers, uncles, aunties, cousins, distant friends, unofficial foster families. Many are sent away and keep moving. Finding Indian kids can be next to impossible, depending on the situation."

"People don't care?"

"Some do; many don't. Many can barely care for themselves, and this isn't some recent phenomenon. It's been like this for close to a century. This is Canada, Grady. Just like where you are, we get paid little and are expected to do everything. Give me some call-back numbers."

Service did, closing with "Do what you can." He put away his cell phone and went into Champ's funeral home.

A vaguely familiar shape stepped over to him in the reception area. "Speedoboy," Service said.

"Fish cop," the man said with a mouthful of gleaming white teeth.

"You're a long way from your doghouse," Service said.

"Where that motherfucker, Noonan?"

"On a mission. You two have a history?"

"Gangsta, that one. I come to help."

"Help with what?"

"You talk to Father Bill Eyes?"

"We did. I also talked to Val Houston."

"Cheek-blower social worker over to Walpole?"

"She told me the windigo thing is a bunch of hot air."

"She wrong, Service. Windigo is serious shit."

"No doubt. What do you want here?"

"Payback."

"Don't we all. For what?"

"Kelly Johnstone."

"What about her?"

"My ma. Heard she offed herself."

Speedoboy is Dwayne Johnstone?

"Heard there's a reward," the man added.

"For a suicide?"

"I hear she got whacked."

"Your mother gets whacked and you want a reward to find out who did it?"

"A man gotta live," Dwayne said.

"I think our definitions of living differ significantly," Service said. "What do you think you can do to help?"

"You lookin' for bitch called Lecair, coupla brats?"

Grady Service stared at the hulking form. "What if we were?"

"One of them is over to the Soo, man. Some cops you are . . . can't find a body one town over."

"You need a geography refresher, Dwyane. The Soo's a hundred and eighty miles east. You need to chill."

"Don't dis me, man. She had old man named Bernard. Way I hear it, she got tired of her old man and no money."

"So she took her kids to the Soo?"

"No, man, she split like a spirit. Her old man run to Soo, live out Sugar Island. So how much is this shit worth?"

"Bambi Sorrowhorse said you're a good man."

"Even good men need money," Johnstone said.

"I got nothing for you, Chief."

"Don't call me Chief."

"Got nothing for you, Geronimo."

Johnstone sputtered. "I be 'round. When you ready, we be ready."

"That's comforting, I'm sure."

The man tossed a small deerskin bag to Service. "They talking about that shit everywhere, man. I come see. Medicine bags up on the Gorge, out on the rez, too. Keeps windigo off," he added with a grin. "You don't gotta fuckin' clue what goin' down, do you, man?"

Grady Service said, "It's been real instructive, Dwayne. But your mother's not dead."

The man stared, blinking fast. "Say *what?*"

"You heard me: She's not dead. She's missing, intentionally, and we don't know where she is, or why she staged her own suicide."

"'Member, time come, we all be there," the man said.

"I'd be more impressed if you'd have been here before this shit started. Your mother's not dead."

"That ain't the word on the drums," he said, turning and walking out the front door.

Service called out for Joan Champ and she answered faintly, "Back here."

He found her in some kind of lab. There was a naked old man on the stainless-steel table in front of her.

"Artist at work?" he asked. The room smelled of chemicals and sanitizers, an unpleasant combination.

"That trooper you run with—you hauling her ashes?" Champ asked.

"Not your business."

"You see the fat boy out front?" she asked.

"I did. I'll wait outside if you want to talk."

"Five minutes, max," she said.

The next time he saw her, she was in a sleeveless black cocktail dress so tight he was sure she'd been poured into it. She had a cashmere overcoat on her arm and held it out to him.

"Be a gentleman?"

Service helped her into her coat and she looked up at him, winked, and said, "You a player?"

"Not hardly."

Joan Champ smiled. "Hey, I'm an unwilling mortician in the U.P. What's not crazy about that combo?"

"You called me."

"For the fat boy. We went to school together, long time ago."

"That's all you got?"

She smiled and nodded.

Service walked out ahead of her, got into his truck, and watched as her Cadillac fishtailed into the street.

39

Thursday, December 18

BEWILDER CREEK CUT, HOUGHTON COUNTY

Friday said over the telephone, "A pilot spotted emergency-signal panels in Bewilder Creek Cut. Any idea where that is?"

"Houghton County, somewhere east of Pori."

"Bad terrain?"

"If you like things populated, or flat."

"The Baraga County sheriff called Ranse Nodnol. He'll scarf you up at the Baraga airport to be his spotter. Denninger and Celt are already in the area with Grinda, Simon del Olmo, and Junco Kragie."

"Why so many DNR?"

"Too many old-timers on the Houghton County rescue outfit, and Sulla Kakabeeke and your game wardens are closer and know the terrain better."

Service didn't know Nodnol. "Fixed-wing or chopper?"

"Chopper—Huey. USFS leases it for fires."

"Get to Allerdyce on the 800 channel, tell him to dump Krelle at the Baraga office and get over to the airport to join Tree and Noonan. They're already over that way somewhere. Any radio traffic indicating an aircraft down?"

"Not yet. The FAA is involved and working their checklists and systems."

"You sure the pilot saw emergency-signal panels?"

"VS-17s is what I was told."

"What about signal mirrors, strobes, lasers, GPS beacons—anything else?"

"Just two panels made into an X."

Translation: Medical assistance required.

"Is there wreckage?"

"No. Grady, get to the airport and help out."

• • •

Jesus, it was cold.

Ranse Nodnol was sixtyish, gray, and handled the bird with confidence. "Get lower?" Service asked.

The pilot nursed the cyclical, easing the Huey downward. "Get in back on the interphone and strap into the safety harness. I'm gonna sweep starboard, lift us, spin her one-eighty, and come down the other side. Hang on back there."

The gorge pines were above them. "We got enough altitude?" Service asked the pilot.

"Keep your eyes on the ground and let me worry about the sky," Nodnol said.

"The sighting was just above Greasy Grass Falls, and we're just beyond that."

"I caught a flash of color," the pilot said calmly. "Circling."

Service hung on to a strap as the rising machine pressed him downward. He stared out the open hatch. *How does somebody crash in this terrain and survive?*

Nodnol gave the rudder a tap and Service felt the machine drop into the steep ravine, where it immediately got darker. They stopped descending a hundred feet or so above the river, and Service looked out and saw the color. *Fuchsia, in an X.* "Got the signal. No doubt," he told the pilot. "Can clearly see the panels. Where's the wreckage?"

"We're too low to hover and play," Nodnol radioed. "I'll climb up so we can make several passes to see what we can identify."

They made six low runs, and Service marked the areas with his handheld GPS while the pilot did the same. They compared coordinates and they matched. Service took digital photographs before climbing back up beside the pilot. "This a USFS chopper?"

"Belongs to a Vietnam vet named Magnusson. Summers he leases it to the USFS for fire suppression. Winters he takes whatever work comes along. Sheriff Kakabeeke got the initital report and called me. I called Magnusson, and here we are."

Baraga County Sheriff Sulla Kakabeeke was a retired Trooper who had replaced the previous sheriff after a very messy situation. She was solid. "Bet she didn't even ask how much?"

"Nope, all she said was go fly."

"You related to Magnusson?"

"Brother-in-law. We crewed together in 'Nam, '70 to '72."

Grady Service understood such bonds.

They were back on the ground in fifteen minutes. Allerdyce was waiting with Treebone and Noonan, and an EMT from the Baraga County SAR team. The group had bags of equipment. Treebone handed him a list of weights of people and bags and Service handed it to the pilot.

"Our weight good to go?"

Nodnol quickly calculated, said, "Saddle up," and tapped gauges with a gloved fingertip.

They wore extreme cold-weather gear now, and the pilot went right down into the canyon, descending so low and close that Service felt like he could reach out and pluck fresh needles off the white pine and hemlock trees. *Not the best feeling.*

"Tallyho," Nodnol said tersely. "Ten o'clock, east side. Check LZ cold."

Service said, "We're not in Vietnam, Ranse."

"Roger, LZ cold," the pilot said. "For a change. Saw me a flat spot back there to put down this erector set, but I need eyes."

Treebone leaned out the cargo door. "Five, six feet right, eight to ten vertical."

The Huey slid right. Snow formed a cloud around the fuselage and filled the crew compartment with swirling angry snowflakes.

"Everybody hang tight," the pilot said with a clipped voice over interphone. The ship hit with a solid but not hard thump. The rotors continued to turn, the turbines screaming. Service and Treebone knew to wait until the pilot cleared them to move. First, he'd let the engines cool. Noonan and Allerdyce looked not just calm, but disinterested. The EMT looked ready to rocket into action. The good ones always did.

The engines began to unwind. Nodnol said over the interphone, "You're five hundred clicks north of your target—closest spot I could find in this light. At least it's on this side of the river. I'll sit here and await orders."

"Dismount!" Tree yelled.

Service and the others stepped down to the metal skid, then to the ground. Service reached in for packs and equipment bags and jerked them out. They put on packs and head lamps. The EMT's name was Sironi. "Your search," Service said.

"They call me Late Night," she said. "You see the panels?"

"Affirmative."

"How high?"

"Above river level . . . twenty feet?"

"Two teams," she said. "Two of you up the shoreline, three of us cross forty feet up. We should catch the panels between us. No wreckage, right?"

"None seen," Service said.

"We'll assume rescue, until evidence dictates recovery," Sironi said, opening a bag and handing each man a survival radio. "PRC One-Twelves," she said. "I doubt cells or your 800s will be worth shit down here." She pronounced PRC, "Prick."

They moved out as dark was settling, hiking slowly north for more than an hour, all of them sweating profusely and adjusting clothing layers to compensate as they went. They also had to work hard to not slip on the ice and rocks. Noonan and Treebone worked low, along the riverside; Sironi, Service, and Allerdyce walked the high route.

Limpy spotted the signal panels and immediately slid down to them on his behind, Sironi right behind him, yelling, "We've got a body under the panels—" and then a split second later, "*Shit!* She's still breathing."

Service joined them and looked. *Jesus, it was Anne Campau! How the hell did she get all the way over here?* Her uniform was torn and bloody. Sironi asked for help to pull Campau into the clear and wrap her in two extra large space blankets.

Noonan and Treebone saw the congregation of lights and clambered up. "Our path here was dicey," Service told them. "Yours?"

"Flat enough if you don't count ice."

Service toggled his PRC 112, called Nodnol. "Ranse, we've got one survivor, female, alive. We're coming south along the river with the litter. Call for emergency medical support at the airport."

Sironi assembled a foldable litter and knelt by Campau, examining her as quickly as she could. "No bleeding or obvious external injury I can see," she told the men. "Arm fracture, cheekbone, probably concussion; vitals are there, but real weak. She's hurting. I'll immobilize her head with a cervical collar," she said, ripping the foam brace out of plastic packaging. "Unconscious, breathing labored, skin cold, blood pressure low. We need to move quickly, boys, quickly but carefully. Our girl's on the edge. Do everything together. Steady trumps fast today."

Service nodded in the dark, sensing Sironi's competence and confidence. "You call all," Tree said.

"Lift on my lift," she said, "Two, one, *lift*."

Nodnol radioed, "I won't start engines until all pax secure."

It did not go as quickly as they would have liked, but the transfer got made, and Campau and Sironi got strapped in back. "You coming?" the EMT asked Service as the turbines screeched up rpms.

"No. Send food and coffee. Good luck, great job; thanks."

Sironi and Service bumped fists.

They all lay down behind cover as the lifting chopper pounded them with snow and ice chunks.

Treebone said, "Less than fifty-fifty." The chopper was quickly out of the gorge and beyond earshot, though Service could still feel some vibration in his bones. He had always felt helicopters long before and after others.

Sironi seemed to know her business. People up here valued space and privacy, but if you needed help, you could count on Yoopers to act without urging. This was the sort of rare place where people who had moved away fifty years ago still warranted a full-column obituary in the local weekly newspaper. *Once a Yooper, always a Yooper.*

He felt himself surging with powerful emotions. Gratitude, pride, a sense of being connected to others, the weight of duty and resolve—the kind of shit that made you glad for what you and others like you did for others.

"Okay," he said. "Let's go see if we can find out what the hell this is all about."

He forced himself to put Anne Campau out of his mind. *Nothing you can do for her at this point. Your part's done; it's up to others now.*

40

Friday, December 19

BEWILDER CREEK CUT

Ranse Nodnol returned five hours later with Sheriff Sulla Kakabeeke, CO
Dani Denninger, a large camp tent, and enough soup and sandwiches to feed
a small regiment. The sheriff jumped out and all of them unloaded before
sending Nodnol back to Baraga to stand by.

"Ranse took Campau on to Marquette," Kakabeeke told them when the
chopper was gone. "She was still alive when they unloaded her there."

"Why's Sironi called Late Night?" Service asked.

The sheriff said, "She was a medic in Iraq, got her sleep all screwed up.
Almost all ops there were after dark, so she worked nights and slept days,
her world inverted: Night is day and day is night. The name stuck. What do
we have here?"

"No idea yet," he said. "We never saw any aircraft debris from above. My
recommendation is that we get the tent up, eat and sleep, and hit this thing
hard in the morning when we can see." *Campau had been missing for more
than two weeks. How the hell had she stayed alive down here? Had she been
somewhere else most of that time?*

"Makes sense to me," Kakabeeke said. "We're sixty miles crowfly from
where she was last seen. Somebody want to enlighten me on how the hell she
got all the way over here from WoJu?"

Service said, "Or survived for eighteen days?"

Silence all around. Service said, "Let's get the tent up, eat, sleep."

• • •

The next morning at dawn was spent carefully examining the area for evidence, a wasted effort. Nothing was found. Service and Denninger focused
their attention on how Campau might have gotten into the gorge to end up
where she had been found. Her being alive seemed to buck all odds.

"Maybe somebody thought she was dead and dumped her over," Denninger suggested. "Even if she wasn't dead, she should have died pretty fast from exposure."

"We need to climb up and see," Service said. They were under the north rim. "How the hell did she get in from the north?" he asked.

"Same way we would," Denninger said. "Four-wheeler."

"You know this country?"

"Some. You can get fairly close to here on the old rail bed."

"The Escanaba and Lake Superior Railroad is still active?"

"Not really, but the infrastructure's still there. Rumor has it that ownership will make a formal abandonment request so the line can become a state recreation trail." Railroads all around the U.P. were dying, and it was good the old rail beds still found some purpose.

"Who climbs first?" he asked, staring up the iced rock wall.

"Hey, I can see you catching me, but not vice versa. If you climb first, we'll both end up crippled or dead. I'll take the lead on this, big guy."

She ascended with no further comment.

Two hours later she called him on the PRC 112. "I've got an abandoned Honda up here, very old model."

"Traceable?"

"We can try," she said. "But I'm gonna have to find an easier way down. The climb up got sort of freaky."

"Was the ORV hidden or just abandoned?" Service asked over the radio.

"Hidden pretty well. I smelled gas, which is the only reason I found it. I'm guessing it's stolen."

"Which means Campau was brought in on it with a one-way, the machine hidden, and the perp hiked out. Where to? You get the VIN?"

"I did, but this is an ancient sucker. I'm guessing it hasn't been registered in a very long time, and was probably reserved for private land use only."

Meaning it very well might never have been registered with the state.

"Do what you can," he told Denninger as they waited for Nodnol to arrive, to fly them back to the Baraga airfield.

Sulla Kakabeeke looked at Service. "This is the fricking black hole of Calcutta down here."

41

Saturday, December 20

MARQUETTE

Friday met Service at the trauma center. Willie Celt met Denninger at the Baraga airport, and the two of them headed back into Houghton County to return to the Cut from the north rim. Weather was quiet, no fresh snow falling. *Let it hold,* Service thought.

"Campau?" he asked.

Friday grimaced. "ICU—critical but stable, still unconscious."

"Touch and go?" he asked.

"The doc says way short of fifty-fifty, unless she starts showing some improvement soon. I went to an administrator for Lecair's school system, an HR man named Jalinga. He confirmed she had been an employee, but he won't surrender records without a court order. The usual fimble-famble legal mumbo jumbo. He's afraid if we get her records, they'll soon have a suit for privacy violation flying in their direction. Hell, I *begged* for a peek, but he wouldn't buy it. Said, 'The way I see it, we are both obligated to uphold the law.' He said, 'You bring a subpoena, you'll get everything we have. Until then, my hands are tied.' I told him we just want to know where Lecair's kids were born."

"Now what?"

"Get the subpoena. How the hell did Campau end up in south Houghton County? I don't get how or why, or why she's still alive for that matter."

"We think she was hauled in and dumped. Denninger found a stashed four-wheeler."

"What the hell is happening up here?" she asked.

Grady Service was too tired to think. "Go home, Tuesday, and sleep. You look wasted."

"Ditto," she said wearily. "The hospital will call when she comes back to us."

Service liked her optimism, didn't necessarily share it; he had learned early in life to not confuse hope with optimism. "Right."

• • •

Allerdyce rode out to Slippery Creek with him. "Where's Krelle?" Service asked.

"Big boy took her out his place."

Pilkington. "She been back out to Ketchkan?"

"Dunno. She wun't too happy when we pull out, tell youse dat."

"You want to go back up there?"

"Sonny, I t'ink dem wolfies et on moose, but di'n't kill 'em."

Service looked at the old poacher. "Spit it out."

"Found 'nother moose. Been shot, hey."

"Hunter tracks?"

"Nope, an' wolfies was just startin' on dat carcass."

"Were the other moose shot?" *Wouldn't we have seen evidence of shooting? Maybe not. They'd been so shocked by the wolf tracks.*

"I t'ink moose shot, but I go look, be sure."

"Moose shot and left, nothing taken by the shooter?"

The old man's head tilted. "Mebbe not shot for pipple grub."

Service rolled this around in his mind. "Shot for the wolves, to feed them—is that what you're thinking?"

Allerdyce opened his hands. "Just say what I seen."

Someone shooting moose to feed wolves? Who? Why?

"Any people signs?"

"I look long enough, I find," Allerdyce said confidently.

"Got any notions about who or why?"

Limpy Allerdyce wagged a forefinger. "Not yet, sonny."

42

Monday, December 22

SLIPPERY CREEK CAMP

Midmorning, a Michigan State Bell 430 helicopter powered its way into the open area in front of his house. Governor Lorelei Timms stepped gingerly from the flop-down steps and plowed though the snow toward the cabin where Allerdyce held the door open for her.

Timms peeled off black leather gloves and a forest-green toque, looked at Service, Allerdyce, Treebone, and Noonan, and asked, "Can we have the room alone for a few?"

Service said, "This is *your* team, Lori, all four of us."

Timms glared, but sat. "All right. What's the investigation's status?"

"Well, there's no more talk about a dogman," Service said. "That's what you wanted. That rumor's dead."

"Really?" The governor said. "What about the Michigan Tech professor on the radio today saying a thing called a windigo is on a killing spree up here. A fricking *cannibal,* for God's sake!"

Service closed his eyes. *Lupo.* "There's no such thing as a windigo, Governor."

"You said the same thing about a dogman."

"I'm right on both counts."

"You think this is about being right?" Governor Timms asked angrily. "Have you talked to the FBI, their behavioral analysis unit?"

"No, and I haven't called Ghostbusters, either."

Allerdyce reached for a cup of coffee. "Who *is* that?" Timms asked.

"Allerdyce."

"The one who *shot* you?"

Service said, "He's pulling his weight as a consultant. What do you want, Governor?"

"Consultant, are you out of your mind?"

"The BAU interviews convicted serial killers and relies on their information to catch others like them," Service growled at her. "This isn't about purity; it's about getting something done."

"People are still dying, citizens of our state, and I want it stopped. I *order* it stopped."

"Yes, your majesty," Service said.

Lorelei Timms glared at the small, gaunt figure of the old poacher and then at Service, who opened his mouth and closed it.

"I'm deeply disappointed in you, Grady."

Service said, "That sword's got two edges."

The governor stormed out of the house, and the chopper departed in a cloud of snow.

"I might could have been a bit more judicious in my word choices," Service told the group.

"You sure couldn't have done much worse, man," Treebone said.

Friday called. "You got your TV on? Turn to Channel 6 WLUC-TV Marquette for the noon news."

"The governor just left here. She's pissed."

"Watch TV," Friday said.

They watched a clip of Lupo's press conference, and after it was done, Service called Friday back. "You want us to go grab Lupo, find out what he's up to?"

"Was the governor really pissed?"

"'Disappointed,'" he said. "'Deeply so.'"

"Different emotions," Friday said.

"They sound a lot alike to me," Service said.

"You're such a guy, Grady."

"That your opinion?"

"Raw fact," she said. "Sadly."

• • •

Service went outside and placed a call to Special Agent Busby Adair, the FBI's latest Upper Peninsula resident agent. The U.P. was neither a plum assignment nor one of Dante's numbered rings of Hell but fell somewhere between those extremes. He and Adair had become friends after he'd helped the agent find a hunting camp to buy in south Marquette County. Adair had pledged to run interference with the Bureau's bureaucracy anytime Service needed it. *Time to find out if he'd meant it.*

Adair answered his telephone and Service said, "Help."

The agent didn't hesitate. "Say what, pal."

"Private talk with someone I can trust from your BAU outfit."

"Easy. Her name is Senior Special Agent JoJo Pincock, a real rock. When?"

"Sooner beats better."

"Back atcha," Adair said.

• • •

At dinnertime Lupo was on television in a longer segment than the one at noon. He looked more striking on TV than he did in real life, which seemed pretty remarkable.

Lupo said, "I was consulted sometime back by local police authorities." His delivery was confident, smooth, authoritative. The camera loved him.

"You're not normally a police consultant, right, Professor?" the reporter asked.

"That's true, but I deal with the dead," he said. "My subject is just a little older than what police normally deal with." He was smiling when he made the statement.

What's his angle? Service wondered.

"Why did they call you?" the reporter asked.

Had he scripted the reporter—controlled and set up the whole thing?

"Police in Marquette and Baraga Counties have been finding badly mutilated bodies, and the same kind of killings sometimes occur in rare frequencies among indigenous aboriginal populations."

"You mean Native Americans?" the reporter asked.

"Exactly," Lupo said.

"I don't think our viewers will understand the link. And I'm not sure I do, either."

Unexpected admission of twitdom, Service thought. Candor could be refreshing even from a fool.

"Think of it as an extreme form of psychosocial disease," Lupo explained. "If you will, a form of environmentally induced psychosis. For any number of reasons and complex factors, an individual may come to think they're possessed by evil sprits, which in turn convinces them they need to consume human flesh."

The reporter smiled. "Wouldn't that call for an exorcist—you know, like a medicine man?"

"Possession leads the stricken person to kill. He mutilates and often consumes his victims. Usually this begins with close relatives before he expands into his local community."

"Consumes . . . you mean, he *eats* the people?" Her face was rubbery and pliable.

Lupo nodded solemnly.

"There's a cannibal here. The police *told you that?* Why doesn't the public know?"

"You'll have to ask the authorities," Lupo said, "but I felt it my duty to come forward and share what I know." Lupo clearly loved the drama of his own voice.

"You're telling us two different county sheriffs and the State Police think a cannibal is on the loose around here?"

"I believe so, but as I just said, you'll have to ask the authorities to explain their thinking. I wouldn't presume to speak for them."

"But you just did, asshole," Noonan yelled at the TV.

Lupo added, "Considerable physical evidence supports my observation, but I would caution that there are other possibilities; so far, the authorities seem reluctant to confront any of the realities their own evidence suggests."

"You've seen such evidence?" the reporter asked breathlessly.

"I've seen some bodies."

"Can you describe them?"

"No. Talk to the State Police."

"Why haven't we heard anything about this?" the reporter asked the camera with an angry mask.

Lupo sighed. "I really don't know."

The wide-eyed reporter tasted blood. "There you have it, from one of the country's foremost experts. A cannibal is killing and eating Upper Peninsula

Native Americans, and the police are ignoring it. This is Bonnie Balat with Professor Grant Lupo."

"If it bleeds, it leads," Service said disgustedly. *Foremost expert on what? The shit's in the fan now.*

Service called Friday at home. "We just saw the whole thing. Now what?"

"Office tomorrow," she said, and hung up.

43

Tuesday, December 23

NEGAUNEE, MARQUETTE COUNTY

Some days were long and some just hard; this one looked like it would be a rasher of both—and then some. Reports and call-backs covered Friday's desk, and she sat quietly, obviously still trying to do a mind-sort on everything. In Service's world he could always duck into the woods to clear his mind. She couldn't.

One note said five shots had been fired before sunrise. A man who lived near the county road commission garage had seen an individual climb over the fence and had fired at him. But it was only the day-shift supervisor who had forgotten his keys and didn't want his wife to drive all the way out from Gwinn with the spare. No injuries. Thank God for buck fever. It made people miss.

A farmer from McFarland had seen a car with Wisconsin plates creep slowly down a private road. He'd confronted the driver, a large man who took umbrage, and a fight ensued, both men now hospitalized. Turned out the Wisconsin man was a mute, and lost.

By 11 a.m., a deputy called in to report that as of this morning, ammo sales at Gander Mountain were up 40 percent against all of last month. He'd checked three other shops and found similar situations. People were stocking up for war. Friday looked over at Service. "I don't like the implications. Deer season's pretty much done. Sales should be down, or flat."

A pulpie near Michigamme claimed to have found a blood-stained machete in the woods and called Channel 6. The station interrupted scheduled programming, and the same reporter who did the Lupo interview gave a breathless account of the bloody weapon, speculating that it could be essential to the investigation into the recent murders. The logger said he had additionally contacted a nationally syndicated TV crime program called *Blood Trails,* a show that featured unsolved murders, the bloodier the better. The logger claimed he would soon be telling his story nationally for pay.

To the highest bidder, no doubt, Service thought.

Several calls came from other reporters after the news report, and more than fifty "concerned" citizens called to demand to be told what was going on; Tuesday dealt with each person patiently, professionally, courteously, and succinctly, informing every caller there were no cases, cleared or uncleared, involving a machete, known, suspected, or otherwise.

Naturally the Channel Six reporter eventually called, asking "Isn't it your duty to examine the machete?" Friday stuck to her statement no matter what question got asked or how the questioner tried to come at her. The media wanted a voice and a face; they rarely cared what the voice actually said, as long as it filled time and space. The public was equally undiscerning.

"Could've been a machete," Service reminded her at one point.

"*I know that, goddammit!*" she snapped at him. "But until Tork tells me so, it isn't. Capisce? I already had someone visit that asshole logger to give us the weapon, but he refuses to surrender it until we get a warrant to force the issue, or until he's done using it on TV and with reporters."

He nodded like a chastised schoolboy.

A pair of cross-country skiers reported seeing someone acting suspiciously on the Ice Train Plains, the area where Lamb Jones's body had been found. Friday took this call herself. The suspicious character turned out to be a sickly moose calf stumbling around a jack-pine plantation. Nobody asked how a moose might be mistaken for a human. Once the media dove into a story, the wheels of reality tended to come off fast. People saw what they wanted to see, or were afraid of; same thing. And some unscrupulous or clueless wannabe reporters and editors alike tended to opt for the spectacular over accuracy.

Celia Daugherty called to report Terry got to drinking and had beaten hell out of her, but she didn't want to press charges. Friday sent Trooper Sal Nechamkus to find Daugherty and get him under control, and not long after that Daugherty was in jail. *Life's just too much for some people.*

Linsenman found a deputy named Fordell in the locker room of the county cop house using a Swiss Army knife to score the top of .40 caliber Smith & Wesson rounds, creating dumdums, which on impact would cause the lead to fly apart in several directions and create massive wounds. Such ammunition was against international law. The man was suspended without pay pending investigation and sure to get some unpaid time off. He was also told he would catch all the shit jobs when and if he came back on duty. Naturally the Fraternal Order of Police came running to their brother officer's aid, but not too strongly; mostly they went through the motions to keep members appeased.

Grady Service just shook his head. Some cops acted like the whole world was out to get them, when their own lack of judgment or stupidity was almost always what brought on trouble. He had no sympathy for Deputy Fordell.

The final straw came when Billye Fyke came in to report to Friday that all the secretaries and clerks in the office had uncased, loaded shotguns in their personal vehicles.

Service went out and took the weapons and delivered a tongue-lashing in the process. He decided enough was enough. "We're going back to camp," he told Friday.

Noonan had been with him the whole time, never said a word as the phones rang and rang. It was barely noon when they left, silent and disgusted with some of the stupid ways the public behaved.

44

Tuesday, December 23

HUMBOLDT JUNCTION, MARQUETTE COUNTY

Linsenman called as Service was leaving Friday's office just after noon. "I was so fucking pissed at that numbskull Fordell, I forgot to tell you there's a four-eighty out by Humboldt Junction. Whoever schmucked the poor bastard really give him a thump. A pulpie spotted the body twenty-five feet off the road, other side of plowed snowbanks."

COs rarely employed police codes, and Service had to search his memory. *Four-eighty . . . felony hit-and-run?*

"You call the Troops?"

"Yep, here anytime. There are tire tracks out into the snow. The victim was walking way off the road. The driver was either drunk or deliberately went after him."

"You sure?"

"I've seen too many to know this one ain't normal," Linsenman said.

"You're there now?"

"Yeah, with Deputy Kline. He's up at the intersection looking for potential witnesses. Some sort of delay with the ME, so I'm waiting."

"Why call me on a four-eighty?"

"Did I tell you the vick's Indian, and he's got one of them little bags on him?"

Shit. "Rolling," Service said. He stepped back inside long enough to tell Friday and earn an explosive "Fuck!" and then he and Noonan raced west on US 41 / M-28 to where M-95 cut south to Crystal Falls.

Service placed a call to Houghton detective Limey Pykkonnen, his friend Shark Wetelainen's wife.

"There's a prof up at Tech, name of Grant Lupo. Can you go grab him and haul him in as a person of interest in multiple homicides?"

"For real?"

"I'll be there as soon as I can. Let the asshole stew some."

"You should talk to Shark," the detective said.

The Shark, otherwise known as Yalmer, was his longtime pal. "Why?"

"Just talk to him, okay?"

ME Kristy Tork had still not arrived when Service got to Linsenman and the scene. The body had been covered but lay where it had landed in the snow. The blood spatter was large, indicative of high-impact speed and a solid hit. The deceased appeared elderly, no identification, deformed left hand. The windigo charm bag was on a string around his neck. The man had been struck so hard his viscera were strewn ten feet.

When Tork arrived the three of them checked the site and verified death. Jen Maki was en route with the evidence team.

Felton Kline came back and waved at his sergeant, who held a hand up to tell his dep to stand by. Kline was an average cop, neither good nor bad. He did what he was paid to do, and not much more, but he always backed up other cops, which was enough to ask of some people. "Anybody see anything?" Service asked him.

"Nope, just old-fart coffee klatches, eh? Half-blind, half-deaf old codgers; they got to yell across the table to hear each other's bullshit. Restaurant owner and gas station manager said nobody special had been through last night or this morning. But the Indian did have coffee at the restaurant."

"When?"

"Six, when they opened."

"What time did he leave?"

"Didn't ask that."

"Do," Linsenman said, joining the conversation.

Friday arrived, talked to the ME, and came over to them. "Rigor's not max, which suggests under six hours. The doctor did a rectal temp, got same result." Friday looked at her watch. "Call it one, now less six hours, we're talking ballpark of zero seven hundred on this deal. There should have been just enough light to see."

"Snow showers here," Service said. "On the body, and he was dressed almost all in black, hard to see. Snow then would have made it more dark than light."

Friday looked at him. "Somebody had to be looking for him to even see him off the road like this."

The other two nodded agreement. Friday looked at Service. "Tribal, but at least he has all his body parts, and we'll have a shot at prints."

She took the pouch from around the man's neck and put it in a clear evidence bag.

Noonan grumbled, "Sherlock Holmes never had to deal with such horseshit. Cult, voodoo, hoodoo, weirdoo, Santeria, apocalyptoids—we got all that shit down in Detwat. But them folks don't go 'round killing people like this. Their fare is goats, chickens, snakes—other stinky, crawly shit."

The retired Detroit cop leaned close to Service. "You think about bending some FBI ears? They ain't *all* assholes."

He had. The rest of the cop world had assets and toys galore, and lots of people. Not his outfit. Friday hated the Feebs.

"Saturday in Green Bay," Service whispered to Noonan, who nodded.

45

Tuesday, December 23

HOUGHTON/CHASSELL

It was late afternoon when Service parked on East Houghton at the county jail, and found Shark Wetelainen waiting for him. "Limey said you seemed kinda amped, might forget to call me. I seen that Lupo guy on the tube, all that BS about windigos."

Wetelainen was an outdoor freak and secretive about his spots, even with his closest pals. He managed a small motel to finance his hunting and fishing.

"You got something for me?" Service said.

"Dunno, maybe. My grandpa used ta skid logs cut by Kraut POWs down to Sidnaw and Pori. Sidnaw mostly had Afrika Korps guys, but at some point a few Waffen-SS guys moved in; these were the hard cases you had to watch real close. Sidnaw opened winter of '44. Don't know where the Kraut POWs were before that, but the army was concerned about the SS boys, and early on some of them refused to work and began various sabotage campaigns. One day the guards hiked a bunch of them back twelve miles in a snowstorm, just to remind them who was in charge. After that they worked okay."

His friend loved to tell stories. "And?"

"Well, the army boys figured winter would stop a lot of escape attempts, but those SS guys were tough fellas. One day the guards hauled a big old dead bear back to camp in the back of a truck, let prisoners get a good look. Big old boar, she'd go close to five hundred pound, eh. Had come out of a den, and some loggers had shot 'er out where POWs were working. This gave the guards an idea to put fear in the Krauts. Army boys tore up the carcass real bad, let the POWs see that, told them the area was filled with big bears, which ruled the forest, but this big fella, he run into a windigo." Shark paused. "Friend of my gramps come up with the story of the windigo, Finndian, told them Krauts about evil spirits and shit, cannibals, windigos kill and eat people, deer, bears, everything. Not one attempt at escape till spring, but those two guys got caught over by Kenton. Kraut prisoners talked about windigos all the time, didn't want any part of the damn things—and it was all made up," Wetelainen concluded with a laugh.

Service stared at his friend. "Did the locals believe the windigo story?"

"Don't think so, eh. Was just bamboozle-line to keep POWs inside the fences."

"Thanks," Service said, suppressing a smile.

"That Lupo," Shark added. "What's his problem?"

"Not sure," Service said.

Detective Pykkonen joined them, and Service asked her, "How'd Lupo handle being detained?"

"No problems; he's poised and way too slick. Argued a little bit, but said, 'Okay,' and that was it."

Lupo was in jeans and a jean jacket, what Yoopers called a Canadian tuxedo, unlaced logging boots, and an old Montreal Canadiens ball cap. "Ah," the professor greeted Service. "Had a feeling you might be involved in this charade."

"Charade?"

"As in my bogus incarceration."

"You have a big mouth," Service said pointedly.

"Just doing my job and exercising my civic responsibilities the way I see fit."

"Like trying to stir up and scare the shit out of the public?"

"No, *you're* doing that by hiding the truth from the public."

"You held back information when you saw the bodies in Marquette."

"Did I?"

Service said nothing.

"I invited you and the other detective to Canada to see for yourselves."

"A bit more detail and information might have gotten us on a plane."

"You have a closed mind," Lupo said.

"Is that your professional opinion?"

Lupo shrugged.

"What exactly did you want us to see in Canada?"

"Remains of a windigo, its burial site."

"From when?"

"Two years ago."

"Can't say I remember any news coverage."

"There wasn't any. The Nelson River Cree handled it quietly, and in their own way."

"Handled?"

"Man was too far gone. They had to kill him."

"Two years ago," Service said, "out in the bush. That's all you have?"

Lupo reeled off seven or eight more cases, all older.

"That's Canada," Service said. "Not here."

"But all the cases are documented in various scientific literature."

"Why did you go to the media?" Service asked.

"I want to help. You didn't accept my invitation to come see firsthand evidence."

"How can you help?"

"I can lead the hunt."

"Is that a fact?"

"I did it in Nelson River. You would have learned this if you'd come up to the reserve."

"You led the hunt to murder a man?"

"Windigo—no longer a man."

"And the Mounties thought this was all right?"

"They were not informed. It was reserve business, not the provincial government's, or Ottawa's."

"Like I said," Service told him, "that was Canada."

"We broke no laws. Windigos are common in Ojibwe-Cree beliefs," Lupo said.

"Say we agree to your help in some role . . . what then?"

"I get exclusive publishing rights to the case at its conclusion."

"Even if you fail?"

"I won't fail. Experienced windigo hunters are few and far between."

"Publishing rights . . . you're going to write a book?"

"I already have. It will come out next year. I'll add this to the case histories, perhaps feature this hunt, shape some of the book narrative around it."

"You get the rights and we get your expertise in return. That's the deal?"

"We can arrange a modest consulting honorarium, and per diem."

"How much?"

"Nothing outrageous."

"Got a number in mind?"

"One thou a day, plus expenses with a cap, and a modest bonus when I take the beast."

"What kind of bonus?"

"I'm thinking ten."

"That's a lot of money."

"Face facts: You're between a rock and a hard place. Without me, the windigo will keep killing."

"A windigo is a human being possessed by an evil spirit?"

"Simplified, yes."

Grady Service glared at the man. "You know who is doing this?"

"I may have some notions," Lupo said.

Serviced exhaled. "That's not good enough. Give me something concrete."

"Jill and Dorie Moulton."

"Who are?"

"Your first two bodies. They're Rose Monroe's nieces, from Nelson River; they've been coming down here for years. They came last spring to see Martine Lecair."

"How can you be sure?" Service asked.

"Dorie's tattoo. And I knew them both."

"Both born in Nelson River."

"Yes."

"Records there?"

"The tribe has them. Probably copies at the First Nations office in Winnipeg as well."

"You knew this and never said a word."

"I needed time to think about it."

Service paused. "I can't get it out of my mind that Canada's Canada. Apples, oranges, like that?"

"You have a windigo here now. And it's not the first one."

"Bullshit," Service said.

Lupo smiled. "Sidnaw, 1944."

"Documented?"

"I'm certain your army will have records. They handled the problem."

"Your source on this?" *Thank God for Shark.*

"There are many."

I bet there are, asshole. "Did your sources smile when they gave you the information about the Sidnaw case?" Service asked, and stood up. "Thanks for the names. We'll check them out, but no go on the consultant deal."

"You'll regret this," Lupo said.

Service looked the man in the eye and started to leave the room, heard Lupo ask behind him, "Can I go now?"

"That's up to Detective Pykkonen," Service said over his shoulder and closed the door to the room. Limey was waiting and said, "I can make the calls on those names for you."

"Check around, see what Lupo's financial situation is. He seems a little eager for cash."

"Posthaste?"

"Definitely. Tell him he can't leave town unless he clears it with you. Tell him we're weighing the consultant deal versus charges for conspiracy to interfere with an investigation by withholding evidence. And tell Shark thanks."

"Every now and then the old hubby coughs up a gem," she said. "You think Lupo's involved in this thing?"

"Hard to judge, but let's try to keep close tabs on him for a while."

Shark was outside, contentedly puffing on his pipe.

"Tell me again how the windigo thing came to be in the POW camp," Service said.

"Old game warden down there, Hans Kohler, his grandpa come over from Germany in 1920, hated the Kaiser. He was the one brung the idea to his nephew Fritz, guard at the camp. Hans got the bear from the loggers, knew army was concerned about escapes; knew if anybody ran, he'd get called in to search, and that didn't interest him. Talked to his nephew, gave him the story of the windigo, brought the bear to camp, and it all grew from that."

"Your grandpa was in on it?"

"No, Hans told him later. Fishing chums, eh."

"Who told you?"

"Fritz, his nephew, the guard."

"Who else did Fritz tell?"

"Just me, old fishing chum. Used ta fish together, but artritis got 'im real good now. I still take game and trout to 'im. He knew all the great brookie spots."

"What do you mean, you still take game to him. He's alive?"

"Yeah sure, lives in downtown Chassell, ninety now; still in pretty good shape, you don't count arthritis. Got all his hair and choppers."

"The guard Fritz is *alive*."

"Just said that. You want to talk to him?"

Service looked at his watch.

Wetelainen interpreted. "Old Fritz is a night owl—listens to books on tape, watches satellite TV stuff, sleeps late mornings. Follow me on down, I introduce the two of youse. He lives right off 41."

• • •

Fritz Kohler had white whisker stubble, white hair, and looked twenty years younger than he was. Shark told the man, "Grady here wants to know 'bout Krauts and windigo. He's a CO, like your uncle Hans."

"You a nitprick, too?" the old man asked. "We used ta shoot deer now and den, for change of grub at camp, yeah? But Unc, he said dis wass wrong, ordered us stop. Dem boys find deer in yards, use Thompsons, kill whole bunch. Even I didn't like dat much greed. Told Unc. He followed 'em, caught 'em red-handed, arrested 'em, and JP t'rew case out on account dey army, an' it wartime. Unc tell 'em, catch 'em again, wun't be no trip to JP, he just beat tar outten 'em on da spot."

I'd do the same, Service told himself. "Who knows the real story of the windigo?"

"Yalmer, youse, couple chums gone ta see God."

"Were the camp officers in on the scam?"

"Just me. Unc tell me how tell story good, convince 'em all it real. Guards and POWs all t'ought it real enough, I guess."

"Anyone ever ask you about this? Maybe a man named Lupo?"

Kohler grinned. "Ast 'bout what? Old man like me don't 'member nuttin'. I seen dat Lupo bird on da TV. Loopy, ask me."

"You're all right with Yalmer telling me?"

"S'okay. He call me, ast okay first. I said sure, go 'head, happen long time back, eh."

"How did you end up at Camp Sidnaw?" Service asked the old man.

"Was twenty, army found out I speak real good German, send me Sidnaw. Most guards speak 'er pret' good, POWS didn't know dat. Helped us keep track of dose monkeys."

"What did you do after the war?"

"Move to Marquette in '46, went Nort'ern, got teacher degree, taught Houghton High '50 t'ru '85. History, social studies. Since den, substitute some, fish, hunt, hang out wit' da boys and have some chuckles. But dey all dying, eh? Me, too, someday."

Grady Service started home, amazed at the unimaginable history old people walked around with in their heads. What a waste. Then he thought about Fritz Kohler spinning his yarn and began laughing out loud. *This place, these people. My place, my people!*

46

Friday, December 26

NEGAUNEE

Christmas had been an abbreviated moment, hardly marked, just him and Shigun and Tuesday. Service and his team were gathered in the State Police post's conference room, ready to hear what Friday had learned.

Kristy Tork had sent prints earlier that week and results were back from the Integrated Automated Fingerprint Identification System (IAFIS).

"The hit-and-run victim is Wendell John Bellator, seventy-eight, of Nett Lake, Minnesota," said Friday. "He was a member of the Bois Forte Chippewa tribe, retired sergeant with the Nett Lake Police Department." Friday looked at the men. "Korean vet, Purple Heart, Silver Star, Combat Infantryman Badge. The Nett Lake chief told me Bellator was very low-key, but an extremely efficient cop."

"This Bellator lived on a rez?" Tree asked.

"The chief didn't say. No relatives. He's the last in his line. I got the feeling our colleague was telling me just enough to get me to go away."

"Surprise," Service said.

"The chief said the man's Indian name is Na-bo-win-i-ke, and that he was in Michigan on a hunting trip. I told the chief the regular deer season ended eighteen days ago, and he said, 'I heard that, too.'"

"The red wall," Service said. Meaning silence. Indians often had little use for white cops and their courts.

Friday looked at the men. "Anne Campau woke up this morning. She has no idea how she ended up where she did. The post CO talked to her. She said she got Chet Saville's call, went out to meet him, and sent Chet to get Jack Igo and his tracking dogs. Then she thinks she saw something under the tree where the body was hanging, so she moved over to it, and the next thing she knew, she was at the bottom of the canyon and there was a rotted pack with the signal panels at an old camp site. She rallied long enough to make a fire and set up the signal."

"Does she have any idea who grabbed her, or why?

"No, only that she thinks he came down out of the trees and knocked her cold. She thinks he drugged her, but tox panel shows nothing. Once she got dumped, her body metabolized whatever he used. There was some evidence of ketazamine, which suggests she got stuck with the trank, but it's just not possible to know." Friday looked worn out and frustrated.

"How'd she end up in the canyon?" Treebone asked.

"She said she was strapped to the back of the four-wheeler and came to and managed to throw herself off the thing, and then she scrambled like hell and went over the lip and fell into the gorge. There was a small bag of energy bars on the vehicle and she managed to get hold of those and take them with her. Stuffed them in her shirt. God must have been looking out for her. She could have been killed. Whoever grabbed her must have assumed she was dead and went on. She found the refuge where you found her, and prayed."

Doesn't exactly advance our cause," Service said. "What did she see under the trees?

Friday exhaled and shook her head. "That's all she remembers. Next item, the body out there that day is not Sarah Root. She took her kids downstate and she's still there. Campau confirms it wasn't Root because she knew the woman and had written two OUILs on her. The body is someone else."

Friday paused. "Next item, the ME says massive trauma is the cause of death on Mr. Bellator; time of death is zero seven hundredish, catastrophic damage on the victim's entire left side. He must have pivoted at the last second before impact. Walking along, his back to traffic, he might have sensed or heard something, turned, and *bam*. His left hand deformity is congenital. Also, he's got major scarring on his face, very old damage. Dr. Tork thinks the scar coloration indicates an old wound, but there are also some very large, nasty scars down the man's chest, and they don't look as old as the facial stuff. Tork told me the chest scars looked like they came from claws, or talons. I think she was joking." She looked around. "No comments?"

Service said, "Somebody needs to get out to Minnesota to gather information face-to-face from the dead man's tribal chairman."

"You volunteering?" Friday asked Service.

"At some point," he said. "I don't exactly feel it pulling at me."

"Next item: Jen Maki got paint flecks off the vick's clothes."

"Chrome?" Treebone asked.

"Blue paint."

"Miracle in the day of plastic cars," Noonan griped.

"She ought to have a solid shot at a manufacturer match," Friday said, adding, "She's working on it now. Last item: I'm going to release Lamb Jones's body for burial. Her mom and sister are coming up from Niles. Figure a week, maybe ten days from now, early January."

"Cremation and memorial?" Service asked.

"Don't know yet. She was Catholic, and her mom will have to find a place. Whenever it happens, we ought to be there to see who shows up," Friday said, and added, "I know Terry beat up on his wife, but I just don't see him as the killer."

Service agreed.

47

Saturday, December 27

SLIPPERY CREEK CAMP

There was a black Cadillac hearse parked against the snowbank along the road just beyond Service's cabin when he returned Saturday night. It was an older model with prominent fins and a bulging hump-like trunk. CHAMP'S FUNERAL HOME was printed on a square magnetic sign affixed to the side door. Lights were on in the house. Allerdyce, he expected.

Instead, he found Joan Champ sitting on a chair in the kitchen, her arms and legs crossed, frown on her face, body language Service interpreted as the fortress: No entry, me here, you there, keep it so. There was a small-caliber nickel-plated snub-nosed revolver on the table in front of her.

"I had to get inside," she said. "Your door was unlocked."

He doubted her story. "That piece loaded?" Service asked.

"Wouldn't be worth much without bullets," she shot back. "You'd think a cop would know that."

Service got his hand on the pistol and eased it aside. "What's going on?" he asked, sitting down. She was skinny, baby-faced, sensual in a way that was more than the sum of her parts. He looked around the house, saw nothing unusual.

"I could use that drink now," she said.

He hadn't offered. "Preference?"

"Strong hootch, poured stiff, if you don't mind."

He fetched a bottle of Jack Daniel's, found a glass, put it in front of her, and poured a couple of fingers.

She gulped it down and set the glass in front of her. She drank without coughing, flushing, or sweating. Down the hatch with no effect seen.

"Hit me again."

"Limit of one in this joint," he announced.

"That might be a mistake," she countered.

He had no idea what she meant. *Why is she here?* He was in no mood for company. "The whiskey?"

"Me coming here," she said, "considering your reputation with women. People tell me you're peculiar, the legendary rugged individualist, and you have a way with women—that they're drawn to you. Although as I look at you, I simply cannot imagine why. I thought I'd see you in an official capacity tomorrow . . . one might say that was my intention . . . but I happened to see your camp, you know, and it seemed like a safe harbor. I felt compromised. Do you mind my saying that?"

She's scared shitless. "I don't mind," he said. *First the fortress body language, now this, whatever this was, a half-baked come-on. Very serious crossed wires here, mixed signals, meaning extreme complications.* "You're safe here," he said.

"I spent the afternoon at work with my father," she said. "People think my sister and I don't know what's going on, but we do, we surely do. He'll never get better. I've always taken pride in my ability to deal with reality, the world as it is, not as I might wish it to be—you understand?"

Which reality is hers? "Better tell me about it," he said.

"Never mind that I've never known how I really wanted to be," she said, turning toward him. "I've been very, *very* naughty at times, I can assure you. The point is that when I got home tonight, the door was wide open. My sister is in Minneapolis, diddling her latest beau. I locked the doors before I left earlier today. Do you know the difference between a doctor and an undertaker?"

New page from a new songbook. He decided to say nothing.

"If you're dead, who cares?" she said, and let loose a sort of scared, yelping laugh. "I've never killed a customer; how about you?"

Shock for sure. He left her sitting there for a moment, eased over to the phone, and dialed Treebone, who had stopped at the Happy Hour Bar for a drink with Noonan. "You guys hit the point of no return yet?" he asked Tree. Noonan was with him.

"Both of us are having trouble gettin' off the ground," his friend reported gloomily.

"Call a county road cop and get over to Champ's Funeral Home in Ishpeming. Do it fast and quietly. Tell the deps no lights or woo-woos. There may be a B and E, and it may be in progress. I'll meet you there."

"On it," Treebone said, and hung up.

"Ms. Champ," Service said.

"Technically it's Mrs. Dragadis, but I prefer just Joan, like *I Married Joan* on TV, or that d'Arc tootsie of history, though I am certain my pain tolerance is considerably less than either namesake." She looked into his eyes. "I can assure you I'm no saint, and only technically a wife, legally speaking. My husband is a major in the US Army, currently in Iraq with his gun. We've never gotten around to filing the papers and so forth."

Rambling—volume of words as a shield, blocking out reality. "We have to go back to your place," he said.

"I'm not liking this insistence on the collective pronoun and must confess I lean toward never going there again. Like for-fucking-never. Can I please have one more snort?"

He poured her another shot of Jack. "We have to go check it out."

"May I offer another alternative," she said, starting to unbutton her blouse.

"No, ma'am," he said, tossing her coat at her.

||||||||||||||||||||||||||||||||||||||||||||||||||||||||||||||||||||||||||||||||||||||||||||||||||||||||||||||||||||||||||||||||||||||||||||||||||

48

Sunday, December 27

ISHPEMING

It was closing in on midnight on Saturday as they waited in the hearse while Noonan, Treebone, and a deputy named Berghuis went through the funeral home. The portable 800 crackled with static on the seat between them. Joan Champ stared straight ahead, showing no interest or emotion. Service wondered where her mind had gone.

"Grady, Suit. You might want to bop on in. We're in the basement."

"What's in the cellar?" Service asked Champ.

"Embalming. My dad calls it the beauty parlor. His business is everything to him. He was like an artist, really. Now hear this: I am *not* sitting out here alone while you go inside."

Still loopy.

Together they entered the basement, painted white with a white tile floor and intensely bright overhead lights. It was sterile, overwhelming. There was a small laboratory off the main work area. A sign on the door said AUTOPSY SAMPLES. A stainless-steel refrigerator was on its side, the door broken off its hinges and flung across the room, broken glass scattered everywhere, twinkling in the bright light. Stainless-steel containers were scattered about like discarded toys. No need to ask what was in the fridge. Every morgue and funeral home had one or more just like it, but Grady Service sensed he was missing something obvious.

"How much was here?" he asked Champ.

"Not that much," she said. "Two sets awaiting lab reports."

"Who?"

"Two elderly patients from Doc Rhine Poppo; you know, cancers he thought he'd arrested, but he was wrong. Doctors always seem surprised when they're wrong. Have you ever noticed that? No wonder they bill themselves as practitioners," she added, not looking at him.

He got her point.

"Doc Poppo wanted a post for curiosity as much as anything. Curing is a bit less exact than embalming."

The wreckage didn't seem to faze her. "I assume it wasn't like this when you last saw it."

"A place for everything and everything in its place. We've been well trained by Daddy," she said.

Be direct. "Did you see this damage when you came back from visiting your father?"

"I thought I was perfectly clear on that point," she said. "I got precisely and *only* as far as the open back door and departed immediately."

So she hadn't seen this. "Have you had break-ins before?"

"Two or three amateur tries last summer—jimmied doors, broken windows. They never actually got in," she said.

"Did you report them?"

"'Kids,' my dad said. Why bother? He said the cops have enough real problems to cope with. He's the mellow, understanding sort, very empathetic, believes some kids are hugely fascinated by dead bodies, the same way he was. I tried to convince him he's wrong. Did I mention I *hate* dead bodies?"

Talk about unstable and unhappy. "There were samples, right? And you have paper on them?"

Joan Champ nodded, took him to a freestanding metal file cabinet, manipulated a built-in combination lock, pulled open a drawer, extracted folders, and held them out to him.

"Anything unusual about the autopsies, the samples, or the patients?" Service asked.

"Not really. Doc just wanted the organs saved for later study."

"*Whole* organs, not sections?"

"Right. Livers, a kidney from each, the usual grisly mementos of the biz. He had permission from both families."

Why whole organs? Service wondered.

They left Deputy Berghuis to watch the premises and to await Jen Maki and her techs.

Service told Champ, "You'll be okay. Berghuis will stay tonight. Tomorrow we'll have a more thorough look around."

"Do you want a ride?" she asked.

He gave her keys back to her. "I'll ride with my guys."

"I'm never going back in there," she said.

"Where will you go?"

"Dunno. I feel fragile, violated or something. I refuse to live with the dead."

Oh boy, he thought. "You can bunk with us tonight, but the best I can do is a mattress on the floor."

He took back the keys and drove her to camp. When they got there, he dug a sleeping bag out of the storage room and placed the bag and the woman in the living area on couch cushions. He'd left the cabin unfinished for years, but fixed it when he fell in love with Maridly Nantz. After her death he had reverted to his old ways, letting the place go, but when he'd met Tuesday Friday, he put the place back in order, trying to assemble a real home.

Noonan and Treebone came in, looked at the woman, shook their heads, and went to bed.

"Do you enjoy your work?" she asked from her sleeping bag.

"Mostly," he said.

"I feel a kinship with you," she said.

"How's that?"

"Both of us clean up other people's messes. We both deal in the past, don't we?"

He'd never thought of it that way before, but she was already snoring. He left a lamp lit in case she got up during the night.

• • •

Explosions brought Service clawing his way out of bed, his ears ringing, disoriented, heart pounding. Cordite hung in the air, bringing him to a standstill. *Inside the house?* He had his Sig Sauer in hand. Joan Champ was sitting splay-legged on the floor, a large-caliber revolver with a long barrel held convincingly in both hands. Service moved toward her, and she raised the weapon and pointed it at him, her eyes wide and bulging.

"Easy," he said quietly but firmly. "It's me." He hugged a wall just in case. She was trembling, glassy-eyed.

"Service," he said, "Remember?"

"Outside," she said, rolling her eyes toward the window, half its glass gone and snow wafting in. He knew he had to get the weapon away from her, couldn't risk moving around while she was spooked and armed, but Noonan was suddenly beside her and talking softly, easing the weapon from her grasp. "Where'd this old hogleg come from?" he asked.

"Two's better'n one," she said. She had an uncanny way of interjecting unexpected logic at odd times.

"I'm not afraid," she told the men.

"I am," Service said.

Noonan said, "Forty-Four Maggie."

Joan Champ was doe-eyed and rigid. Service watched her draw her legs up into a fetal position.

"Your shots?" he asked her. "At what?"

"Of course. Outside."

Less precision than he'd hoped for. "At what outside?"

"Something lurking on the porch, near the window."

Not likely. The windows were taped with plastic for insulation, and they were airtight. You could barely hear a forty-knot wind from inside during the winter. He went back into the bedroom and got a shotgun and a flashlight, slipped on his boots, went out the back door, moved around the house, saw and found nothing out of place.

"What was it?" she asked when he came back in. "Did I hit it?"

"Nothing."

"But surely you found tracks?"

Needs justification, reinforcement. "I can't see that well in this light. The snow's picked up some." *Lie for a good cause, mutual peace of mind. He had found squat.*

"I know I saw *something*," she insisted. "I may be a coward, but I have superior senses, including my hearing."

"You have a permit to carry?"

"You bet your bippy," she said.

Not to mention a jacked-up imagination. He went to the basement to find plywood to seal the window.

A voice called thinly from outside, "Comin' in. Don't shoot no more."

Limpy Allerdyce came in, both hands held high. "I din't do nuttin'," he yelled to Service. The old man was deathly pale, eyes like Ping-Pong balls.

• • •

The house was cold when they awoke the next morning. The light outside was a dull gray, the kind of partial light that would serve as daylight for the remainder of the seven-month winter. A flow of air told him the window needed a lot more work and he'd better call someone competent to do it right.

"I'm really sorry about this," Joan Champ greeted him from her sleeping bag.

"No problem," he said.

"Does your shower have hot water?"

"Try the handle with the 'H' on it."

He made coffee while she was in the shower and handed her a cup when she sat at the end of the table with a towel wrapped around her head. "I got really spooked last night."

"Happens," he said. He'd been terrified more times than he could remember. Fear never went away. You learned how to tamp it down so it wouldn't destroy you or prevent you from acting. It was an ongoing struggle.

"People who work with bodies aren't supposed to spook," the woman said.

"Don't worry about it. Last night is over."

"Everybody knows something is dreadfully wrong up here," she said.

"Do they?"

"Murdered women and children are bad for tourism."

Lacking specificity; is she fishing for something? "You know I can't talk about cases," he said.

"You think I'm pushy?"

No good answer for that. He kept quiet.

"*Have* I been pushy?"

Nearing his limits. "Whatever. It's fine."

"You should learn to say what you mean," Joan Champ chided.

"I do try."

Pause, a sour face. "You saw last night, did you not?"

"I saw a lot of things last night."

"I mean my place," she said, "the sample containers."

"All over the floor," he said. "There are lots of disturbed people in the world."

"Granted, but eating human organs?"

"I beg your pardon?"

"The samples—something took them and ate them."

"Your imagination is overactive," he countered.

"I've been trained to observe," she said. "Same as you, I presume."

"I looked at everything."

"Don't play the fool," she said, studied him and exclaimed, "My God, you *didn't* see! Those trays contained tissue samples and organs!"

"I got that," he said in his own defense.

"No; there's always residual blood and some tissue on the stainless, but all of them were spotless."

"There's probably a reason," he said.

"No dirty towels or napkins, nothing on the floor but broken glass and stainless steel. Where did those naughty fluids go . . . *Where?*"

She had already demonstrated an overactive imagination. "Crime scene specialists will look at the lab," he said. "We were all pretty tired last night."

"I was beyond tired," she shot back, "but I know what the hell I saw. You ever see a pie pan licked clean?"

He cringed, trying to block the image, which fit, and might even have occurred to him, but in truth he'd not seen it, had missed everything. "I think we'd better keep this to ourselves," he told her. "There's already enough speculation."

• • •

Returning to the funeral home mid-morning they joined Jen Maki and her people, and Service read through Dr. Poppo's files on the elderly dead. One had an address on North Stone Road.

"This the Indiantown Manitu Ridge area?" he asked Maki. He still had trouble keeping road names straight out that way. He could remember landmarks like his own body parts, but not street and road names, especially when every damn county seemed to name the same road something different than the adjacent county, more evidence of the past wanting to screw up the present.

He'd insisted Champ come along with them, pulled a chair over to her. She smelled clean and soapy. "This woman was Indian?"

"Both were," she said.

49

Monday, December 29

GREEN BAY, WISCONSIN

The FBI meeting kept getting moved, but now it looked like it would actually happen that day. All along the string-out there were no explanations or excuses offered. Green Bay was 160 miles south, give or take, Austin Straubel International Airport the closest major commercial air facility to Marquette.

Senior Special Agent JoJo Pincock had called the day before, left a message that she would be at the Wingate Hotel on Airport Drive. She had been in Alaska for a week and was en route to the East Coast for New Year's with her family, but would hop from Minneapolis down to Green Bay and spend Monday night to see that they got adequate time. Service reserved two rooms for his team.

Friday got a confirmation on the identities of the two girls from Canada, which seemed to confirm Lupo's reluctant help.

On the way, Service told his guys who they were going to meet.

"Could this be the Pincock from the Great John R shootout?" Noonan asked.

Treebone jumped in. "She was Metro back then, on the force three years, in law school for two of them. Dispatch sent her to an office at John R and Mack, not far from Wayne State, report of a man brandishing a revolver, which turned out to be an AK-47, Chinese-made, fully auto.

"The office belonged to a lawyer named Pollini," Tree continued, "whom Pincock later learned had been laundering cash for an intermediary of the Micalezzi family of Rochester Hills. Mr. Micalezzi's internal audit of Pollini showed him a few lira short. The armed men were freelance contract poppers out of Bossier City, Louisiana. By the time Pincock arrived, Mr. Pollini had been dispatched to Wop Heaven, but he had a temporary secretary from Manpower who slipped away and summoned the cavalry. The whole deal was a botch right from the start. Pincock's partner was an old warhorse named Jethro Lally; he'd gone down in the first volley, not killed, but hit badly enough to decide to retire when he came out of the hospital. Pincock hit one shooter right away and managed to drag Lally out of the line of fire. Additonal help came pouring in, but the shooters were barricaded pretty good, and a couple of curious civilians wandered by the outside windows and got nailed. The negotiation team arrived with SWAT forces. Pincock shot a second killer, and the third man finally surrendered. Soon as she finished law school, the FBI made her an offer and she jumped ship."

"Cojones the size of John Deeres," Noonan offered. "Solid cop. Should've recognized that name right away. Snow up here must be freezing my fucking brain cells."

"Is that good or bad?" Service kidded.

"This place is hell compared to Detwat," the old detective said.

"Without Detroit, maybe you wouldn't appreciate this," Service said.

"I don't need to swim in the cesspool to know what's floatin' in it. This place up here is its own kind of scary."

• • •

They met Pincock at her room and Treebone opened a laptop for the briefing they'd cobbled together.

The senior special agent took a thermos out of an orange canvas bag emblazoned with the silhouette of someone floating under a parachute. The bag was labeled LIFE'S SHORT. JUMP OFTEN! Service wondered if she practiced what her bag advertised. She was tall and stocky with big, stone-steady hands.

Pincock was neither friendly nor unfriendly, just quiet and self-contained. Service introduced everyone, and she looked at Noonan and said, "Bluesuit himself."

The detective grinned and nodded. "Yo, JoJo."

Tree conducted the briefing, had all the incidents on maps and charts with data for each event. Service had no idea his friend was so accomplished in such matters, but he wasn't surprised. It had been Tree's idea to call them events, not cases, the term making them seem connected, even if they weren't.

"Kick off your kicks, Senior Special Agent. This will take a while," Tree began.

"I'll be the judge," she said. "Understand, gentlemen, this is in the way of a ghost stopover. I was never here, never met any of you; this never happened—unless, of course, fate determines it should have, in which case it did, and will."

"Fair enough," Service said, not understanding at all. "We're looking for guidance from fresh eyes."

Tree methodically marched them through everything:

Two dead women, no heads, hearts, or hands, only identified days ago as Jill and Dorie Moulton.

Body number three was a Lecair twin, around age five; body recovered with head and hands, but no feet.

Sean Nepo, all parts there except for his feet.

The next female victim, body number five, found in a Beaver Lake cabin with all parts there (just not attached).

Kelly Johnstone, faked suicide, reasons unknown.

Lamb Jones, her body (number six) recovered quickly—maybe part of this, maybe not. She didn't fit the pattern.

Another body (number seven), skinned and hanging from a tree, hands missing—still unidentified. After disappearing, Anne Campau was found alive a couple of weeks later, eight or so miles from where she was taken when investigating this body. Outlier?

Martine Lecair, legitimate suicide stimulated by what, they didn't know for sure. Definitely related.

The hit-and-run victim's story: Wendell John Bellator, aka Na-bo-win-i-ke, left on roadside; no signs of mutilation like the others, but clearly a homicide. Bellator was an Indian from Minnesota, retired cop, probably connected.

Parts of two bodies missing from a mortuary, possibly consumed.

It took the better part of three hours to slog through the details. Pincock rarely interrupted with questions, but continuously scribbled notes.

"That's it?" she said, when Tree had finished.

"Yes, ma'am," Treebone said.

She took out her cell phone, flipped it open, tapped in a speed-dial number. "Carol, this is JoJo. Change my flight to tomorrow afternoon, late." The agent closed the phone, pulled off her boots, and tossed them aside, launching each one with a sharp kick.

"Do you find murder intriguing, Detective Service?"

"No, ma'am, not especially."

"I do," she said, flashing her first smile. "It yanks my crank."

"You've got some thoughts on all this?"

"Boys," she said, "let's order us some food. We're gonna need fuel."

• • •

They ordered three pizzas to start and three more around midnight. Pincock ate the greater part of two of them while she tapped on her laptop, plugged into a cell phone, which was connected to an electrical outlet. Service liked how she ate, tended to judge people by this, how connected they let themselves be to food. She ate fast, but not like an automaton. He could see she liked flavor and texture and aroma, and didn't mind sauce on her chin.

Pincock said, "Terminology is always a problem in these atypical cases. We've got media calling all multiples 'serial killings,' when the majority are actually sprees. Serial killers plan. They're hunters who carefully stalk their prey. 'Sprees' whack whatever gets in their path. No plan, no obvious rationale. Serials tend to be intelligent. Sprees are lucky to get their shoes on the right feet, tendency toward real rockheadism. But we're starting to think of a third category, what some are now calling 'sequence killers.' Sprees usually get stopped pretty quick, while serials go on and on until they're caught, snuffed, or picked up on some other charges, and dumped into an institution—penal, mental, you name it.

"Sequence killers seem to present with serial characteristics and profile but combine some aspects of sprees. They kill for a while and then disappear by choice, not because of our heat. They seem to have an agenda, exogenous, not some twisted OCD, fucked-up childhood deal. Serial killers are sociopaths. Sequence killers, too, but they have a purpose, an intended outcome beyond satisfying some sort of inner demon or personal devil's voice. They aren't technically insane."

"Like terrorists?" Treebone asked.

She rewarded him with a smile and poked in his direction with a pen. "That's sort of the idea."

"Ours?" Service asked.

She sat back and rubbed a foot. "Could be."

"Your people are working on a profile of this new type?" Service asked.

"Very preliminary work only. It has yet to go through the bureaucratic and academic peer-review gauntlet, and some people in my line aren't convinced."

"You have examples?" Noonan asked.

"There's no perfect signal case that might declare or verify the paradigm. We have pieces of cases, like a sexual mutilator in Eugene, Oregon." She paused. "He looked like a serial at first, but the evidence wouldn't fit, and the suspect killed himself, so we never had a go with him. Certainly the brutality was there. He used a cleaver. But no scrapbooks of his clippings, no trophies, no anal assaults. Most serial killers seem to want to stick something up the back door, but not this one. In fact, there was no evidence of sexual activity, which we put down to condoms and good hygiene when no DNA sample was forthcoming."

"That seems to fit ours," Service said. "Bastard's invisible, leaves nothing."

"No," Pincock said. "He's leaving *something;* you just haven't found it yet. Backgrounds and intelligence are different, as well. This new group tends to be extremely intelligent and often well educated, IQs of 130 and upward. None from dysfunctional families, no history of abuse. Everything appears perfectly normal, assuming there is such a thing.

"I'm thinking there's something more, but I can't support my hypothesis with the evidence at hand. I've got fragments of maybe ten cases right now, but only three seem fairly clear-cut. A lot of bureau people don't agree with me, but we get paid to think independently. As long as my boss tells me to keep going, I will.

"All three cases involved a brother with a younger sister. No idea what's going on and certainly no explanations. But three cases of brother, younger sister, him with IQ over 130, brutal killers each, and no DNA left on the vicks. All three perps were teetotalers, people who appeared to fit into their communities, the sort of folks you feel comfortable calling when you need help. They seem to believe in civic duty and have high ideals, tend to *really* believe, and this may turn out to be part of the profile. They like to join groups, churches, Rotary, Lions, Eagles, Moose, all that stuff. By all measures, they seem like perfectly normal and well-adjusted people."

"Who happen to like to butcher people," Tree said.

"There ya go," Pincock said.

"How do you find them?" Noonan asked.

"It's been pure luck so far. Accidents, serendipity, but as soon as we look at the cases we can usually see some patterns, classic twenty-twenty hindsight. The key seems to be their process. Not the same for all; each one has his own laborious, carefully developed method."

"For example?" Service asked.

"The perp in Eugene was an amateur ornithologist. Led the local chapter of a group dedicated to preserving habitat for a certain rare songbird, ruby-throated mattress thrasher or some such hoo-ha. All birds look alike to me," she confessed.

"Me, too," Noonan said.

She continued, "He was simply extending his purpose, protecting habitat; a straightforward and socially acceptable goal knocked the balance bubble a bit off the level. Even his logic made sense in retrospect. Kill enough people in the target area and people will stay the hell away. You can't refute his reasoning." She looked at Noonan. "It worked."

"Indians and females are the general common denominators here," Noonan said.

"Don't get hung up on gender," Pincock said. "These people know what they are about. Says society: Women are weak and defenseless, and when the weak and defenseless are murdered, you tend to get public outrage, which attracts media, which cranks up more rage and fear. Media play is always critical to this type's agenda."

"Until recently, we pretty much had the lid tight on all this," Service said.

"Hard to judge if that's good or bad," she said. "The media is his message, to steal McLuhan's line. Without it, he may have to jack up his activity, or he might pack it in. That happens, too. We think our boy in Eugene ran a similar deal down in Amarillo a few years before: That time around, it was anti-nukes. He started killing Pantex workers, just women. The Pantex plant assembled atomic weapons for the military. We got into that one early and sat on the publicity and kept it capped. He got nowhere with his cause and moved on. Later we confirmed he'd lived in Amarillo. The killings started shortly after he moved there and ended as soon as he departed. Circumstantial and correlative, but very instructive."

"Which reduces us to Indians," Service said.

She closed her eyes. "That's my guess. You've got to find a way to go deeper. What's going on around here—what issues, problems, causes—see?"

"Ever do a case with Indians?" Service asked.

"Not yet."

"Any race tendencies in this new class of killers?" Noonan asked.

She nodded. "White; all odds say whites. You want cites?"

"Your word's good," Noonan said.

"Meaning a white man killing Indians for a perceived higher purpose," Service asked. "Higher for whom?"

"*Men*," she said, shaking her head. "I need a short nap and breakfast, and I'll take charge of food if you guys don't mind."

None of them did.

Service left the hotel for a cigarette. It was snowing. Cold. The FBI agent had turned out to be a lot different than his initial impression. As the night wore on, he had felt her loosen up. He found a pay phone and called Friday, who was with Anne Campau.

"How's she doing?"

"Better. She's starting to hurt. You want to talk to her when you can get here?"

"Badly."

"Where are you?"

"Green Bay," he said.

She laughed. "Shacked up with some voluptuous bimbo?"

"Foursome," he said.

"That was meant as a joke."

"We'll be back this afternoon, tonight latest," he told her.

"File a report?"

Meaning visit her. "Your place?"

"Yes, that's a reasonable plan."

"I'll have a smile on my face," he said.

"I will look forward to that."

Weird call, oddly exciting, yet less than satisfying. *Why didn't you tell her about the FBI?*

50

Tuesday, December 30

GREEN BAY, WISCONSIN

Back upstairs, early morning, JoJo Pincock with wet hair, food on a counter, all of them grabbing at plates of French toast and bacon slices. They ate near the counter.

"Cat got your tongue?" she asked Service.

"Vampires," he said, feeling like a fool. Champ's Funeral Home break-in was bugging him.

The agent smiled. "Don't be so quick to laugh or dismiss. Who's to say what's real? Some dickhead thinks he's a vampire and drinks blood. Who are we to say he isn't?"

"Psychotic."

"To be sure, but so what? The behavior's real as hell. Mythic physiology doesn't fit actual physiology? So it goes. Famous case: Guy thought he was being poisoned, his blood being turned into powder. He began killing pets to replace the imagined blood loss. Later he raised rabbits and injected their blood. But things got out of hand as he began going up the evolutionary food chain, snatching people. First he'd just draw blood and inject it later, but eventually he tapped into arteries and drank straight until the vicks died. Good for his health, not so much for theirs. Didn't take a wooden stake or a silver bullet to kill him. This guy was in the Tampa area. Some young cop caught him snatching a sixteen-year-old girl and wasted him with double-ought buckshot from a Remington eleven hundred. Was the guy a vampire or not? I've got no idea. Cuckoo? Bet your ass."

"Not a spree," Noonan said.

She tilted her head. "In some ways. He didn't really *stalk* his victims, just took what came along."

"Serial?"

She shook her head. "Outlier case, no category yet. I never really thought about them before so-called blood-drinker cases. You guys know about eusociality and the science debates over the role of altruism in evolution?"

They all shook their heads.

"Think about vampire bats. Voracious appetites, and if they don't eat enough, they die fast. But successful feeders have blood on their wings and let unsuccessful bats feed off that surplus to keep their overall numbers high. Technically this isn't precisely eusociality, but the point is that individuals cooperate to keep the group alive. Is that altruism, or selfishness? Science can't answer that question yet." She stopped and took a deep breath. "I'm not sure saving one's life at the expense of others qualifies as a higher purpose, but you may have something. I'm going to have to think about this."

They broke up after noon. Service walked her to her rental. She told him, "Serials and sprees are almost all under thirty-five. Men start to lose testosterone fast after that. Sex crimes: Are they about sex or violence and domination? No definitive answer. But our sequence types tend to be over forty-five, and there's definitely a lot less testosterone fueling the engine by then, serious depletion well under way. A sixty-year-old man and a nine-year-old boy have relatively equal levels of testosterone. This is an important fact. Mr. Sequence, I believe, uses the appearance of sex for his higher purpose. He's older, calmer, focused differently than most younger men."

"Our take-home is white, pillar of the community?" Service said.

She nodded and handed him a business card. "Bottom number is secure. Call and let me know your progress, or if you need support. Between us," the agent said, "books, movies, and TV shows aside, what we do in our outfit is as much necromancy as science. Look at the vicks, the methods, locations, timing, and how all of it relates. Or does it? We look for patterns. Figure fifteen thousand murders a year in the US since 2001. Estimates are twenty serials in that fifteen thousand, accounting for maybe two hundred kills a year. Hard to pinpoint two hundred out of fifteen thousand.

"Last year we had about a million law enforcement personnel, and twenty percent fewer this year. Numbers have dropped since 9/11, but Homeland Security and others have taken priority over all other law enforcement priorities. Since three thousand people died that day, we've had about a hundred and twenty thousand murders, but where does the focus go? On the three thousand. We're in a mess. We've got a lot of dedicated, effective officers, but there's no cavalry and no hierarchy of priorities."

She looked around and lowered her voice. "Last February there was a survey that showed fewer than half the students in this country could tell you when the Civil War was fought, and one in four thinks Columbus came here after 1750. Twenty years from now Americans won't know about Pearl Harbor or 9/11, and we'll still have a massive, ineffective, resource-eating security structure in place. Once we ramp up these things, they endure outside their original purpose."

Pincock got into her vehicle and put down the driver's window. "Want some advice?"

Grady Service nodded.

"Shoot if the chance presents. It makes the whole thing a lot easier to clean up."

"Bureau policy?"

"JoJo Pincock's Rule of the Road, learned the hard way."

Noonan came up to stand beside Service. "Government: She rents a car to drive a few miles from the airport?"

• • •

Allerdyce called as they were passing north through Crystal Falls.

"Sonny, I been up Ketchkan; t'ink youse and dose boys be good meet me dere, eh."

"Ketchkan?"

"Start dere."

"For where?"

"Slate River country."

"We can drive closer," Service said.

"Not to see what I got," Allerdyce said, and hung up, cackling.

Tuesday, December 30

HURON MOUNTAINS, BARAGA COUNTY

It was well after dark, and Allerdyce was waiting for them on the Huron River Road.

"Where's your truck?" Service asked.

"Stashed," the old man said. "Don't like no pipples see where I go."

Shared values. "Where we heading?"

"Up cross't Arvon Mountain, past old Black Bear Camp up top Slate River."

Service thought about the destination. "We could drive it a lot easier and faster."

"Bin t'ru dat. Wun't see nuttin' if go youse's way."

"How far?"

The old man made a chattery sound. "Unh, 'speck six mile, t'ink. Cut nor-wess up Arvon, down wess at Curwood, nor-wess over t'ord Slate."

This would be a tough slog in the snow. Service knew he should have rested them all for a full day. Everyone was dragging—all except Allerdyce, who had boundless feral energy. "Tent still up?"

"Stashed 'er," Limpy said.

"How'd Krelle act when you pulled her out of the field?"

"Weren't none too happy, eh. I told her I bring 'er back."

"She still with Pilkington?"

"She gone back Whoreygon. New Year's wit' her gran'kittles."

New Year's? Service looked at his watch. He'd not even thought of it.

Allerdyce walked beside him. "Followed wolfies all t'ru dis turf."

"Grays or the others?"

"See bot'."

"With Krelle?"

"Wit' and wit'out."

"More than the three on the camera?"

"Still jus' t'ree, but Donte say dere was five one time."

"Donte DeJean?"

"Dat little rascal up 'ere shootin' moose, feed dem big wolfies."

Service stopped walking. *Did I hear that right?* "He told you that?"

"Yep, he say dese new wolfies don't like hunt. Too slow. Dey follow grays, chase 'em off dere kills. Grays fast, get away easy, don't want fight new guys. Too strong, too tough close up."

"Does Krelle know this?"

"Nope."

"You're saying the DeJean kid is killing moose to feed the new wolves."

"I tole 'im, no more moose, shoot jus' deers."

"Are you crazy? You *told* the kid to violate?"

"Kid already vi-late. I jus' tell 'im what. Dere nuff deers 'ere for wolfies."

Jesus. "You expect me to ignore this?"

"Ast self, want new wolfies or no? Youse choose. Limpy don't give no nevermind dey 'ere, not 'ere."

"These are not gray wolves?"

Allerdyce shook his head. " 'Speck somepin' new, so I got close, got good look."

"Photos?"

"Onny what youse seen. Didn't want do more 'til talk youse."

"Except to tell Donte to shoot deer."

"Apples and cat food. Ain't same t'ings."

Allerdyce and discretion seemed an alien partnership. "The wolves are all around up here?"

"Dey run little offal terr-tree from old Arvon quarry downriver, back up where we camp. Dere turf cross two timberwolf packs eeder end."

"When Donte shoots a moose or deer, don't the grays grab for the carcasses?"

"Nope. Once dose new galoots grab onta somepin', dey don't give 'er up."

Somewhere in the back of his mind Service had been wrestling with the faint improbability of all the mutilated people being part of a scheme to cover up the presence of the new wolves. "We'll deal with this later," Service told the poacher. "What's on the slate you want us to see?"

"Youse need payshits, sonny," Allerdyce said, chuckling happily.

"You fucking people are ate-up, bag-drag, shit-pounding around out here in this damn snow shit," Noonan carped loudly.

Treebone hiked in silence, as he always did, be it in a jungle or a blizzard.

"We gonna make camp?" Service asked Allerdyce as they trudged along. Dark was closing in fast, days this time of year short.

"No talk, walk slow, listen," the old poacher commanded.

They took their lead from the old man, who slowly worked his way across the slate beds beside the river. Service heard voices below them and closed his eyes, trying to identify them.

Service wished Denninger were with them. This was her turf. He could see the glimmer of small fires below them and through the trees, and he could smell meat cooking. He fished in his pocket for his SureFire as they stood invisible in the dark tree line. Allerdyce whispered, "Dey out dere," and gave Service a gentle push.

He walked purposefully toward the nearest fire, saw people starting to take note of him and turn toward him. One person stood by the fire.

"Conservation Officer, DNR—what brings you folks out here?" He turned on his flashlight, aimed at faces. Saw one of them, felt his heart twitch: Kelly Johnstone.

"You're not easy to find," he said, recovering quickly.

"That was the whole idea," the woman said.

52

Tuesday, December 30

UPPER SLATE RIVER, BARAGA COUNTY

Service looked around. There were at least a dozen men, Johnstone the only woman. "Odd place for a get-together," the conservation officer said.

"Slate blocks sound," Johnstone said solemnly.

He knew Indians believed that most spirits hibernated in winter, which made it the only time of year the "other world" couldn't easily eavesdrop on humans. "I thought winter alone was a buffer," he said.

"Yes, but nothing can hear through such stone. Insurance," Johnstone said.

Right, and Kryptonite turns Superman into a ninety-pound weakling. "I get that you're here for privacy," he said. "What I don't get are the earlier theatrics."

An Ojibwe named Paul Wak approached them, said, "We ain't poaching or trespassing; you got no right to be here." Service had known Wak from the years when he had been a fire officer out of the Baraga office.

"Saw your fires, just stopped by to say hello."

"Leave us alone. This isn't your business."

"Public land, Paul. What kind of business are we talking about?"

Johnstone said, "We are going to go after it, hunt it, and kill it."

"I don't think so," Service said.

"You don't understand," Johnstone said.

All the men were carrying rifles. Service said, "Why don't you enlighten me."

Johnstone said nothing.

Service said, "*Any* hunting makes it my business. Am I making my point?"

"He's the one who found the girl," Johnstone told the others.

"That true?" a huge man asked. He was obese, built low and stoop-shouldered, long-armed. Long black hairs sprouted wild from his chin, and his face was pocked.

"Sad to say," Service said.

"Early kill," a voice in the group said. "The spirit was beginning to cool down, exploring its potentials and needs."

"Neat trick," Service said to Johnstone. "Your own public suicide."

"You didn't read me being there. I told the old violator to bring you here. You by yourself?"

Allerdyce. He felt a flash of betrayal. "Bullshit," he said.

Johnstone said, "Your girlfriend's sitting on some of the details we need to organize this thing."

"Lupo was on TV."

"Lupo's no friend of ours, Service. Lupo's about Lupo. You need to know how far this thing can go."

"How far *can* it go?" he asked. "I'd say it's way the hell out there already."

"You in a trading mood?" Johnstone asked.

"Try me."

"Tell us what the police know."

"In exchange for what?"

"What we know."

He didn't want to turn away empty-handed, and if there was a way to prevent further violence, he wanted to know about it.

"You need to know I don't buy the whole windigo thing."

"Food first," Johnstone said.

"Why me?" he asked.

She touched her chest. "*Gwa-ai-ak o-de-im-a.*"

He searched his memory. "Straight something."

"Heart," she said. "Straight Heart."

"Honest."

"They may put me in a rubber room after this one."

"One other thing," Johnstone said. "I'm still dead."

"I'll have to think about *that.*"

"It's essential."

"For now," he said.

"Indian people must think first of Indian people, you understand?"

"Yeah, I get enlightened self-interest."

"You're a good man, Service. Fact: Whites have their ways, and we have ours."

He lifted his 800 and said, "Chow's on," and his three companions filtered down from the tree line.

Service pushed Allerdyce backward. "She *asked* you to bring me to her?"

The old man nodded. "I t'ink prolly youse two talk is good t'ing, eh?"

"Anything else I need to know?"

"Not nuttin' I know."

"They got vehicles?"

"Yep."

"Go get plate numbers, descriptions, all that."

"Already done dat when I finded 'em 'ere. Dis iss fun, eh?"

Only Allerdyce.

Service got wild rice and chicken soup from a pot along with a couple of fire-cooked biscuits and joined Johnstone.

"Your son's around."

"You seen him?"

"We talked. He thinks you're dead, and he wants to help find your body for the reward."

Johnstone hung her head. "That's Dwayne," she said sadly.

"I heard some good things about him in Detroit," Service told her.

"I never seen no good in that one."

"He told me Martine Lecair fled the state and her old man went to Sugar Island."

Johnstone remained silent.

"Lecair's dead," he said. "Suicide. I was there." *Still no reaction.* "She intimated that one of her kids was dead and that she stashed the other one, but we don't know where." *Still nothing.* "Wendell John Bellator— Na-bo-win-i-ke."

"Killed by the windigo," Johnstone said.

"It was a hit-and-run," Service corrected her.

"Windigo guided it," she insisted. "No matter what cops call it."

"The driver's the windigo? I thought they ate their victims."

She shook her head. "You don't understand. Windigo is still human— thinks, plans, feels. I brought Na-bo-win-i-ke here to lead the hunt. He was the best, very experienced in these things. Without him we have no leader. With his death, others are afraid to help, afraid they'll die, too. Killing a windigo requires an experienced hunter who knows the tricks of predators.

These killings have to be stopped soon," she said, paused, and added, "and you're the answer."

"*Me?* Not a chance," he said.

"Too many fears here. We need a *louvetier,* a hunt leader, to supervise and direct the others."

"Not me."

"When there're more dead, perhaps you will change your mind," she said.

"Lecair's man—Sugar Island?"

"Yes, but he crossed the border. Martine was never with him."

"One of her twins is safe?"

"We think, but like you, we don't know where, or with whom."

He took out a cigarette and offered her the pack. They both lit up. "Let's get coffee. I'll take you through what we have," he told her.

"Smoking is unhealthy," Johnstone said.

"What in this life isn't?" he said. "Be quiet and listen."

When he was done, he asked, "What's the deal with Lupo?"

"Wants to be the hero without the risk," she said.

"He claims to know a lot."

"This is true," she allowed. "You must be at the meeting tomorrow."

"What meeting?"

"About these things—in Zeba. And you should talk to Demetra Teller in Palmer."

"Teller?"

"Curator of the Grun-Baraga collection."

"How do I find her?"

"On the road around Palmer."

"Address?"

"Large black-and-red sign, says GRUN."

"Why the charade at Blood Creek?" he asked.

"To break the creature's focus, misdirect it."

Did she say focus?

"Are you saying you're a target?" Johnstone didn't answer, and he said, "Someone picked you up after your stunt."

"All in good time," she said, and headed for another campfire.

They pitched their small tents near the encampment for the night. Service got on his 800 and called Denninger. "Where are you?"

"Home, pretending I'm human. It's a real stretch."

"Pass or duty tomorrow?"

"On."

"I'll be on foot. Pick me up on the grade road outside the old Arvon Slate Quarry at zero seven hundred."

"What the hell are you doing way out there?"

"I'll explain tomorrow."

53

Wednesday, December 31

ZEBA, BARAGA COUNTY

In the old days, there had been one umbrella tribe of Ojibwe divided into bands identified with certain locations. But federal charters, treaties, and other legal actions had turned what had once been local bands and extended family groups into sovereign tribes, a purely judicial creation of convenience. Johnstone had told him to be at the Zeba Community Hall near the reservation for a 10 a.m. meeting, but the place was empty two hours before that.

Denninger said, "Uh, we on like, a mission, or is this just a pleasure drive?"

"There's a difference?"

She made a snorky sound.

"I want to take the local temperature."

"White, red, or Martian?"

"Whatever."

"Big Ned's will be the place," she said. "We'll tell them we're doing our annual animal-trap survey."

"Our *what?*"

"Pay attention," she said. "You might learn something."

They pulled up to Big Ned's General Store at McComb's Corner, three miles from the Marquette County line. Service knew the place, had been there with his old man, and as an officer. Big Ned opened the store after World War II and ran it until Vietnam. Son Ned Jr. had been killed in Cambodia by a sapper with a hand grenade, and Big Ned died inside, sold out to a woman named Sandy Fakir, who retained the store's original name. Ned went off to Idaho to mourn and drink, and eventually asphyxiated himself in the cab of a county snowplow. Sandy Fakir was in her late seventies now and going lame, but she sat in the store every day and barked orders at several harried grandkids, who provided unpaid labor and couldn't wait to get away to college or join the military to escape her vise grip.

They bought cups of coffee and joined the leather-faced proprietor in her corner. "Doin' my trap survey," Denninger told her.

"And what the hell might that be?" Fakir asked with a wheeze.

"I find out how many traps are being bought from local merchants, which gives us a rough cut for year-to-year variations and animal populations. Comparing past records with trapper licenses, and the takes allowed by annual regs, with an estimate of local poaching numbers and the sheer volume of traps. It's a crude but effective measure."

"Bollocks," Sandy Fakir said. "Where did you come up with that lame story? You know they all violate if they think they can get away with it, eh, but to answer your fool question, I ain't sold a bloody trap all fall. Whole dang bunch is sittin' squeaky-ass tight in these parts, and you won't be findin' no redskins skulkin' their traplines neither, 'til this infernal trouble's passed on."

"What trouble would that be?" Denninger asked.

Fakir slapped her leg. "Hell, Dani, you talk like that, local citizens will think youse're the clueless blonde youse look like." Fakir lifted the corner of an afghan off the floor and picked up a twelve-gauge Remington with a chopped barrel. "That damn monster walks in here, he'll be leavin' here leakin' a whole heap of motor oil."

"You believe the stuff you're hearing?" Service asked the woman.

"Damn right I do. It's damn hard to spook redskins, so when the rest of us see that they're creeping out, we pay attention. Most of my grand-uns got some Indian blood, and I won't be givin' none of 'em up easy, even if they're clueless, useless little buggers."

"Your weapon's illegal," Service pointed out.

Fakir tsk-tsked him. "Who turned you into the nitprick? You seen this old blaster ten years back and it ain't changed none since. What turned you chickenshit in your dotage, Grady Service?"

Yoopers like Sandy Fakir weren't intimidated by laws on paper or lawmen in the flesh. Service looked down at her. "Just no sound-shots, eh?"

The woman smiled, revealing worn-down yellow teeth. "I always knock down what I shoot at, son. 'Course, neither do I plan on traipsin' around in the bush askin' for trouble with the rest of that gang of yahoos skulking around the woods hereabouts."

"Something we ought to know?" Denninger asked.

The store owner glared. "What is this: Let's-Play-Stupid Day? Ask your partner, girl. Ever'body knows he was up top on Arvon at the Indi'n pow-wow last night, and I 'speck you'll both be at the palaver over to Zeba later this morning."

Back in Denninger's truck she said, "What powwow on Mount Arvon?"

"I'll fill you in later. Let's get back to Zeba."

• • •

They found several dozen vehicles parked along the hill and people walking toward the hall, mostly men. Several shook their hands or nodded greetings as they joined in the procession.

"The DNR with us on this?" a man asked.

"We're just looking for restrooms," Service quipped.

"Piss outside," somebody said. "Most of us do."

He thought he recognized some of the men from the night before, but he wasn't sure. It had been dark, and Johnstone hadn't bothered to introduce everyone.

The meeting had already begun when Service and Denninger slid into the back of the old church. An elderly man named Nordine was talking. "This business has nothing to do with us. It's the business of the others." Nordine was white, sank wells in the area.

A man in a black leather baseball cap turned backward stepped out of the crowd from Service's right. He had a black leather trench coat that reached to the floor and trailed like a cape: Dwayne Johnstone, Speedoboy himself.

"You're all shit," Johnstone squawked at them, "Red men, white men—the hull damn bunchayas, old women." He held up his hand and bent his forefinger. "*Ko-ko-min-de! Ke-na-kash!*" He spat on the floor for effect.

The crowd rose with a collective snarl. Several younger men had to be restrained by elders.

Service tried to translate while he was making sure a war didn't break out inside the old church. *Something about a bent penis. No . . . a useless penis, probably meaning less than a man. Not at all like Indians to make such direct insults. It just wasn't done. No wonder everybody's so riled.*

Johnstone stood his ground. "You all flap your wings like frightened birds and jump at the sound of your own farts! Go hide, cower in your houses while I go and kill this windigo and *eat its heart*."

This was greeted with mass silence. Service leaned left to see better. Johnstone opened his coat and produced a street sweeper, a shotgun with a rotary barrel magazine—a serious weapon, as scary as it was illegal.

Speedoboy brandished the weapon over his head. "The Ojibwe of Manitu Ridge do not fear this thing. Go hide in your houses with the women while I kill it!"

Several men with Johnstone suddenly showed their weapons and Service bumped Denninger toward the back door. "Follow my lead," he whispered as they stepped out into the cold air.

Johnstone and his people came out, pursued by several men grumbling at them, and a couple of scuffles broke out. Service cut through the crowd and got Johnstone by his arm, slammed him against a tree, ripped apart his coat, and wrenched the street sweeper from him.

"Dammit, Dwayne, we all *get* it. If you want to lead the way, you've got to clear that with your mom."

"My mum?"

"She's alive; I talked to her last night. She's trying to do the same thing you're doing, but you two need to talk and cooperate, not work against each other."

"Where is she?" Dwayne asked.

"She moves around a lot. You'll have to wait for her to come to you."

"What about my weapon?"

Grady Service smirked. "Dwayne, ordinarily I'd cuff you and haul your sorry ass off to jail just for possession, so let it go; keep your mouth shut, and let's call it a push."

"Constitution," Johnstone said.

"Stow that crap. By treaty, you're a separate and sovereign country."

The dustup in the yard left a couple of broken noses and a lot of ruffled feathers.

"What the hell was that all about?" Denninger asked.

"It's about punk, freeway Indians is what it's about," he said. "That's Kelly Johnstone's son."

"No shit?"

He handed her the street sweeper. "Put that in the district's collection."

"Are you going to let me in on what's going on?"

He looked at her, said, "Let's grab a bite at the Pump and Munch, and I'll bring you up to speed."

"Johnstone's son is really big and fat," she said.

"His street name is Speedoboy," Service said.

"Ew," Denninger moaned.

54

Thursday, January 1, 2009

MARQUETTE

Service and Denninger had cornered Paul Wak after the Zeba meeting the day before and convinced him to call Kelly Johnstone with his cell phone. Wak had handed the phone to Service when it rang, who didn't beat around the bush: "You need to meet with your kid and make peace before he goes postal with this windigo stuff."

"I calm Dwayne and you promise to lead the hunt; is that what I hear you proposing?" Johnstone countered.

Damn her. "Hunt and apprehend."

"But you *will* lead," she said, and he could hear the satisfaction in her voice. It made him wonder if she'd sent Dwayne to the meeting just to provoke this response. *Geez, I'm becoming paranoid.*

"All right, yes—but find your kid and tell him to stop pounding the damn war drums." While he had her on the line he found out where she was staying and gave the location to Denninger, asking her to go visit and verify it.

"Officer Denninger will swing by to visit and will maintain contact. If you relocate, you inform her. One violation of this and the deal is off."

Service had radioed Treebone and Noonan and told them to hike out to Arvon Road, where they piled into Denninger's cramped Silverado. She dropped them at their vehicles on Huron River Road. Allerdyce had headed back the way he came, on foot, they said, and without explanation. Service had a pretty good idea what the old poacher was about. He was fascinated by the strange animals.

"Good you called us," Treebone said. "We were gonna bump you and ask for a ride. See, Noonan here can't handle backwoods treks."

"I find no joy in a potential broken arm or leg with every slippery step," Bluesuit complained. "When I gotta be out there, no problem. But if I don't *gotta* be out there, then fuck all this back-to-nature shit."

Service told them that if they wanted to head home for a break, they were free to do so, but to report back by January 10, latest. Neither man indicated what he would do. They had already missed Christmas and any New Year's celebrations.

Service drove to Friday's house where they spent a quiet night with no talk about any of the cases.

The next morning, she'd elbowed him awake before dawn. "Can we talk *now*, oh manly mute one?" she asked.

"You mean after?" he countered.

"You know how loopy I get afterwards," she said. "There isn't going to be an *after* this morning. Self-indulgence isn't a luxury we can afford."

"Okay," he said sleepily. The bed felt good.

"I went to Lamb Jones's house on Green Garden Road yesterday afternoon," Friday told him. "Jen Maki assured me that she gave it a good going-over, but something kept nagging at me to go back over there and look less for forensic evidence than for something else. Malcolm Quigley called me yesterday morning and told me he wants to take a murder case forward on Daugherty, and I told him I don't see Terry for this thing. You want to go with me to see Terry? Afterwards, we'll hit Green Garden again. There are some things I want you to see. I've got some ideas, but I want your reaction first."

Working New Year's Day. That fits.

Malcolm Quigley was the county prosecutor. Barely fifty, he had silky silver hair he brushed back into wings and wore gold wire-rimmed spectacles with quarter-size lenses, suggesting he needed to see only small portions of anything that crossed his desk. He looked more professor than prosecutor but had earned a reputation as a no-nonsense hard-liner with criminals. Surveys by the Michigan Bar Association showed Quigley's sentences to be consistently the harshest in the fifteen counties above the bridge, and third overall in the state.

Quigley had once taught constitutional law at the Cooley Law School in Lansing, had clerked with the Michigan Supreme Court, partnered in a moderately prominent firm in Troy that worked exclusively for automobile clients, and had come north to get prosecution experience to prepare him for a state or federal bench appointment, Marquette being just another career merit badge for the man. His brother Montgomery "Monk" Quigley commanded the Detroit police division that included SWAT and other special operations. Monk was overly aggressive, entirely tactless, overweight, overbearing, muscle-bound, and over-armed. Malcolm was trim and calm, smooth and diplomatic. Both brothers were political creatures with little sense of anything beyond self-promotion, poor models of so-called public servants. *Sleazebags,* Service thought. *Self servants, not public servants.* He couldn't stand either one.

Service took Shigun to Friday's sister's place, told her they'd pick him up by 4 p.m. at the latest, went back to Friday's, parked his Tahoe, and jumped in with her.

Daugherty and his wife lived in an old homestead on the west side of the Kona Hills, south of Marquette. During the Great Depression desperate people had fled cities, thinking they could prosper by living off the land in a U.P.'s alleged Eden. Reality dictated otherwise: Most couldn't handle the way of life, and they either died or headed south. The land here was spiny, the weather relentless, and most economic immigrants had lasted less than two full winters. Oddly, the old cycle was being replayed as the current economic woes of the state and nation crushed people. They still ran north—which remained a stupid choice eighty years later. Daugherty's place was left over from the first wave of economic refugees in the 1930s, one of many decaying homesteads spread around the U.P., testifying to the land's dominance.

Last time Service had seen the deputy's place, it was barely standing. Now it looked pretty solid, and it was obvious Terry and his wife had put some effort and cash into modernizing the place.

Celia answered the door, her eyes red and puffy.

Mrs. Daugherty had been pretty once, but life up here came only in jumbo size and tended to pound everyone. She was considerably younger than her husband, though that wasn't obvious at first glance. She was tall and sincere, with stringy blonde hair and a pockmarked ego. She worked as a teller for a drive-in bank near Harvey.

"Can we come in, Celia?" Friday asked.

The house was sparsely furnished, testimony to Daugherty's previous financial obligations. There had been a kid by a first wife, now in Rhinelander, and two by a second, a local gal. A large part of the deputy's paycheck was being garnished for alimony and child support. The house's interior suggested Celia was trying to maintain some level of dignity for them and hold up her end of the marriage.

Daugherty sat morosely on the couch, looking even worse than his wife, who followed behind them, saying, "He told me everything—all about what him and Lamb done." Her words trailed off and she sobbed. "*Everything . . .*"

"You said you'd help me," Daugherty said, looking at Friday. "I got a call that charges are coming down."

"Nothing's changed, Terry. It's in Prosecutor Quigley's court. You know that."

Daugherty sniffled and rubbed his eyes with his shirtsleeve. "Can't you do nothing?"

"If a warrant's issued, someone will have to serve it," Friday said.

The deputy gulped and groaned, his words deliberate and slow. "*But I didn't do it.*"

"He couldn't," Celia said, coming to her hubby's defense.

Friday looked Daugherty straight in the eye. "Bottom line, there's enough circumstantial evidence to make a case, Terry. C'mon, you *know* what the hell is going on. Quigley has certain political goals, needs feathers in his cap, and we've got too many unsolveds around here right now to let one go if he thinks he can get a fast verdict and put one in the win column. And you're a cop. There's no bigger feather than a dirty cop."

"*I'm not dirty!*" the deputy insisted, but looked away, took a deep breath, and said, "So that's it: I take the fucking fall, no matter what the truth is? What happened to justice?"

"Terry," his wife said softly, trying to calm him.

"It's all right," Friday told him. "I told Quigley the evidence alone won't carry this case."

"Jesus," Daugherty said with a moan, "what did I ever do to that asshole?"

Celia suddenly shook a fist in her husband's face and her own face flushed. "Did you do *his* goddamn wife?" she yelped.

Daugherty fell back against the seat back and blinked. "Did I do his wife?"

"She wanders," Celia said. "Both of 'em do. God, I thought everybody in town knew!"

Service nudged Friday. It would be comic under any other circumstances, but Celia and Daugherty had just brought something to the surface they'd not heard before. Daugherty's response to his wife's charge indicated that perhaps he *had* diddled the prosecutor's wife, which might explain Quigley's aggressive stance on this case.

"What am I going to do?" Daugherty asked Friday.

"Get a lawyer," she said. "The biggest prick you can afford."

"But I didn't do it," he said, sobbing.

Celia walked them to the door. "Terry can't help himself, really he can't. He just likes women, is all. I knew that when I met him. It's like diabetes. You don't stop loving somebody because they've got diabetes," she said. "Do you?"

"You hear that about the Quigleys?" Service asked when they got out to Friday's vehicle.

"Rumors—but you know how it is up here. It never even crossed my mind to connect Daugherty and Margaret Quigley, Miss Arm-Candy Trophy Wife."

"And now?"

She puffed. "Good God, Grady. I just don't know. Let's go look at Lamb's house."

• • •

The house was relatively new and small, built on two or three hundred yards of frontage on the Chocolay River, a weathered cedar deck facing the river with a great view of all the sweepers hanging out over deep riffle water along the west bank. Yellow police tape still ringed the house: POLICE INVESTIGATION—DO NOT CROSS OR ENTER.

They found everything dumped on the floor. Service said, "Was it like this yesterday?"

"Nope," she said.

"Doesn't look like kids," he said.

"Agreed," Friday said. "Somebody wanted to find something."

"Something you saw yesterday?"

"I don't know," she said, and pointed him toward Lamb's bedroom.

Closets had been gutted, drawers turned over, clothes everywhere. "Got your camera?" Friday asked.

"Yeah. Let's both take shots."

He got out his digital, set the lighting for cloudy day, and began shooting for the record. "Robbery?" he asked.

"Possible, but it somehow doesn't feel like that to me," she said.

"In this economy, B and E's like a plague," he said. You could almost measure the health of the local and state economies by the number and rate of camp break-ins. He stood looking at a pile of underwear—silk, sleek, scanty, everything so small it would compress into less than a handful—not the sort of thing you ordered from the Sears catalog.

"Lingerie," he said out loud.

Friday looked over at him and arched an eyebrow. "Point?"

"Lingerie—that's froggy for frilly scanty panties and such, not for everyday underwear. You know this sort of stuff's mostly for messing around, the other stuff for workaday. There's gotta be thirty sets of scanty pants here. Where's her other stuff? Most women I know, they've got maybe a coupla scanty-pants getups, but this?"

Friday said, "You *know* most women and the difference between lingerie and underwear?"

"That's a cheap shot," he complained.

"Good observation, Grady. I had the same one yesterday." She went into the closet and came out carrying a pile of catalogs: VICTORIA'S SECRET, FREDERICK'S SEX ON SATIN, AMOROUS UNDIES. "There's a whole arsenal of sex toys on the floor in there, too," she added.

"Well, someone was in here looking for something, and I've got to believe whatever it is, it is in this vein, so to speak. When you can't easily find what you want, you know what your next step is?" he said to Friday.

"Stop and think?"

"No, start ripping the shit out of everything." Which he did, with gusto.

An hour later they had a shoe box he'd found inside a tackle box, hanging from a nail in the cellar. It contained three savings account books and a safety deposit box key stuffed into bubble wrap, and a small red teddy bear with ESCANABA UPPER PENINSULA STATE FAIR 1992 embazoned on its chest. The accounts held $68,000 as of last month, at least two years' worth of Lamb's state income. Nobody could save that much and buy a house with frontage on one of the Upper Peninsula's best steelhead and salmon streams. Most of the deposits were in cash. One entry for five hundred was monthly, going back two years.

And there were photos. Mostly old Polaroids, one with Malcom Quigley posing nude with a nervous smile, his small erect penis twisted sideways like a diminutive Leaning Tower of Pisa. Service laughed out loud. There were other men, none Service recognized, all of them equally busted *in flagrante*. In one touristy photo with Quigley, outside, there was a sign in the background, distant but readable: CALUMET THEATRE. It was the old opera house from a century ago.

Who was Lamb Jones—really?

Friday looked at him, tapping one of the account books on the heel of her hand. Celia had said that both Malcolm and Marge Quigley wander. "We're gonna get ahead of this right now," Friday announced.

She placed a call to Limey Pykkonnen in Houghton, and put it on speaker. "This is Tuesday and Grady," she said. "Can you get us a number for the woman who runs the curling club up in Calumet?"

"Sure—Elle Papatros, nice gal, and married to a good guy" the Houghton detective said, then told Friday the number, and asked why.

"Not sure yet; maybe nothing," she said.

She looked over at Service. "Here's the deal. I know Quigley and his wife were separated once—at least, that's what people around town claim, two or three years back. We need confirmation. The Quigleys curl over in Calumet. I heard that at the cop house." Friday punched in the phone number and put the phone on speaker.

"Mrs. Papatros, I'm Detective Friday over in Marquette, and I've been asked to contact you regarding some personal information about Margaret Anne Quigley. I've got you on speakerphone because I have a sinus infection and can't hear very well. Some of the women over here are thinking about giving her an award for her volunteer work in the community, and they want to make it a big deal, but there's a bit of a concern."

"Yes, of course. How may I be of help?"

Friday paused. "There's no easy or tactful way to get at this. We'd like to involve Malcolm, but we're in a bit of a quandary. We've heard, and I'm afraid I can't tell you the source, but we've heard . . . well, we've heard the Quigleys are having some serious marital difficulties. Do you know anything about that?"

"Nonsense. My husband and I had dinner with Malcolm and Margie a couple of nights ago. Who's saying this about them?"

"Not important, but you know they were separated a while back, and we heard this and we just didn't want to embarrass anyone. We're trying to do the right thing. This is strictly between us."

"I understand fully," the woman said in a conspiratorial tone.

Service was aware that most people enjoyed gossip and intrigue, especially if they thought they were on the inside, or at least on the short list of those in the know. It was a human frailty cops often leaned on.

"I mean, they were separated before, so there's a precedent. We just had to be sure," Friday said.

"Oh, that ended a long time ago," the woman said.

"Two years, right?"

"More like three. It lasted almost three months."

"There was a girlfriend?"

"I wouldn't know for certain about that," the curling club president said, and lowered her voice, "but I did hear something about it . . . I guess we all did," she added. "I really don't know what's true. I know Marge flew down to Orlando and stayed with her mother, but she came back eventually and they patched things up, and it's been fine since then. I'm sure the rumor's just that. Every marriage crosses some rocky patches, if you know what I mean."

"Three years. That long ago?" Friday asked.

"I remember she missed two months of curling, December and January. I had a terrible time getting substitutes."

"I must be getting old," Friday said. "My memory . . ."

"It gets us all," the woman said sympathetically.

Tuesday Friday closed the phone.

"Scary," Service said. "Why do people tell perfect strangers anything?"

"Therein lies the premise for so-called reality shows," she said. "Which aren't. And besides, a cop isn't a perfect stranger. Our badges imply trust and neutrality in gathering information."

Friday looked at the back of one of Lamb's snapshots. "Eight p.m., December twentieth, no year. Portage View Retreat House." Service knew this to be a relatively new B&B near Michigan Tech, a little on the fancy side price-wise, aimed at well-heeled alums.

Friday called Pykkonnen again. "Sorry to bother you again."

"Yalmer's ice-fishing," the Houghton detective said.

"Can you get someone to check the guest registry of the Portage View Retreat House—find out if a Lamb Jones was there on December twentieth, three years ago this month?"

"Lamb, huh? Terrible thing. Good gal. You making any headway with the case?"

"Not as much as we'd like," Friday said.

"Sorry to hear that. Hang tight, I'll be back at you in a few minutes."

"That fast?"

"The manager's one of Yalmer's fishing chums."

This rationale explained a lot of social and political connections in Upper Peninsula social circles.

The call-back came twenty minutes later. Friday answered on speaker. "She was there, Tuesday; registered in her own name."

"For one or two?"

"Two."

Friday seemed more relieved than elated. "You're a champ, Limey."

"Hell I am, but I know how to take care of my friends. You need anything more over this way, give me a bump. Yalmer just came back and says you should 'keep Lard-ass out of trouble.'"

"I'll try," Friday said. "But it's a big job." She broke contact and looked at Service. "Lard-ass?"

"Shark humor."

"Lamb," Friday said wistfully.

"Registered in her own name, and for two. Smell like a setup to you?"

"We must not assume," Friday said.

"I won't if you won't," he said. "Now what?"

"Quigley, face-to-face. We need to back him out of our business until we need him."

Service understood why she didn't bother to call ahead. It was New Year's Day. There would be a party to watch college bowl games. Quigley had entertaining power brokers as his primary religion, and prosperity theology as his own personal gospel.

55

Thursday, January 1, 2009

MARQUETTE

They pulled up a circular driveway to a large house in the swanky Huron Woods development some locals snarkily called Hot Shot Acres. There were a dozen luxury vehicles parked along the drive, but Friday found a close space and squeezed in. The house had been built by a local architect but tricked out by an interior decorator from downstate, no local businesses used except for some subcontractors, out-of-the-gate choices that got Quigley off to a lousy start with the locals.

A well-to-do local who didn't spend locally was immediately a questionable entity in the U.P. Quigley soon realized his mistakes and corrected them, making sure to take care of locals first, in the courtroom and outside it.

The prosecutor opened his door with a Manhattan in hand. Holiday music in the background, people talking. Quigley looked at them and said, "It's football day—what the hell do you two want?"

"We need to talk," Friday said, stepping past the man.

"Can't this wait? I'll be in the office Monday."

"No, Malcolm. *Here, now.*"

The prosecutor yelled "Business" into the din of Christmas music, showed them into a small room off the foyer. It was filled with shovels and boots, chooks and choppers on hooks, a large plastic snow scoop. "You better have a good reason for this," Quigley said menacingly as he closed the door.

Friday gave him one of two photographs and Service saw him suck in his breath. "There you go, Mr. Prosecutor. What goes around, comes around. Portage View Retreat House, three years ago this month. You and Marge were separated and you were banging Lamb. I don't care if that caused the separation or didn't. That doesn't matter . . . yet. Could've been because, but that's speculative."

Friday handed the second Polaroid to the prosecutor, the one with his dicky bird waving in the air, and handed him photocopies from Lamb's bankbooks. "Lamb sure did like photos, Malcolm, but I guess I'm not telling you anything new. And why not? It was all in good fun, right? Eat, drink, screw, and be happy. Then one day good old Lamb says, 'Lookee here, darling,' and there was the incriminating picture. Instantly you could see in your own mind just how good a hold she had on your shorthairs. How am I doing?"

The prosecutor glowered, took a swig of his drink, and exhaled. "The bitch was a lot smarter than I figured, a damn slick operator. She didn't ask for five hundred forever, just that much a month for four years, enough to build her a nest egg, and not enough to bankrupt me or send me off the deep end." Quigley stared at Friday and said wearily, "You can't believe *I* killed her."

"Well, it's a helluva lot better motive than Daugherty might have."

"Yeah, and maybe the deputy wasn't so magnanimous when she sank her claws into his dumb ass."

"Actually, Malcolm, it looks to us like Lamb saw Daugherty strictly as short-term sport, and a freebie to boot."

The prosecutor glared at her. "In other words, the deputy walks."

"The way it looks to me, maybe you had somebody toss her place . . . looking for these, no doubt. I'm going to ignore that because you don't strike me as the type to kill, at least not with your own hands, and in that, you and Daugherty are a lot alike. All I ask is that you stay out of our way from here on in. If evidence develops that shows I'm wrong about the deputy, we'll run with it. Same if it points to you."

"Checkmate?" he said.

"Just check," Friday said. "For now."

"Deal," the prosecutor said.

"I put great faith in your pragmatism, Mr. Prosecutor."

"Life is a series of choices," he said. "Sometimes you win, sometimes you don't. For the record, she was strictly lowlife, but I never wished her any harm. I let myself get trapped—my fault all the way."

Right, Service thought. "And then your old lady told you that she went out and diddled Daugherty for some payback, and that meant you were double-fucked."

"I've never much cared for you *or* the DNR," Quigley said, avoiding Service's glare as he and Friday left the house.

Service wondered how many more local men there were in the prosecutor's circumstances. "You going to check her safety deposit box?" he asked Friday.

"You bet. Next week. I'll even ask Malcolm to sign the writ."

"I wouldn't want to be on your shit list," Service said.

"Astute observation," she said.

• • •

There was an envelope stuck between Friday's storm and inside doors, a note inside the envelope: Dear Sheriff: Martine Lecair was a fine teacher and lady. None of us can understand why she left us. Her employment and personal records are in the envelope. The birthplace of her twins is listed as Nelson River, Manitoba. God bless you. No signature.

"I'm guessing the secretary at the school office," Friday said after she read the note. "Happy New Year," she added. "Funny, even without Lupo we would have been pointed to Nelson River. The first three vicks were born there. Makes you wonder exactly what connection Lupo has to all this, doesn't it?"

"I'm headed to Nett Lake," Service announced.

"When did you decide that?"

"When I read that note. All this is Indian-related, and I haven't been able to get the hit-and-run out of my mind. Anything on the paint sample yet?"

"No."

"Yell at me soon as you hear something," said Service.

"We are owned by these damn jobs," she said. "You going alone?"

"Probably," he said. Noonan and Tree had both gone south and would not be back until the end of next week.

56

Saturday, January 3

NETT LAKE, MINNESOTA

Driving through snow was neither fun nor easy if you had to be on paved highways. Back in the woods, it could present some dicey moments, but you had more time to think and anticipate. Service planned to drive from Marquette to Duluth, and from there, eighty miles north through the toothy Mesabi range, downhill to the marshy boreal swamps of Nett Lake. He'd delivered Cat and Newf to Friday's to stay until he returned. When Tuesday worked, her sis took the animals and Shigun. Her sister was nothing short of a saint. Newf loved the kids. Cat just wanted to be included, and close to easy food. He tried to call Allerdyce but got no response and took off at zero six hundred, thinking it would be an easy six-hour drive, weather permitting—the eternal *if* of living in the north.

He stopped to eat in Ashland at a generic food emporium, where everyone wore a plastic badge proclaiming HI, MY NAME IS, like this was the surname of a large contingent of individuals with fragile likenesses; like the military—second name last, no middle name needed. HI, MY NAME IS MELODY was distinctly a product of the "hon" culture, but the food came quickly, and what more could you ask when you were on the road, hon?

He had passed several Minnesota state troopers driving brand-new Mercury Sables, and this made him think back to his days as a Troop, driving a Plymouth Fury with an engine powerful enough to put the thing in orbit if only it had possessed wings.

Rumor had it that Ford would soon dump the Sable into the automotive model dustbin. There was something downright wimpy about cop cars named for fur-bearing animals mainly used to decorate women. Cops belonged in Furies, scaring the shit out of themselves in chases. Hell, Sables lived only to be skinned. What kind of model was that for law enforcement?

North of Duluth was hilly, not technically mountainish, and he stopped in Eveleth at an eat-cheap tavern across from the the Hockey Hall of Fame.

His waitress made a point of informing him that she'd had frequent carnal knowledge of a number of Minnesota North Star players before the team's "dickhead owners" had moved their cheap team down to Dallas, and she had sworn off sports for sex since then. The joint was called The Dead Canary, and nobody smoked. He wondered if canaries had died from smoking in order to influence the law. *No smoking in bars. What the hell is happening to this country?* Sometimes he felt like an alien in his own land.

The switch from hills to swamp was sudden, and the PBS station out of Duluth was calling for eighteen to twenty-four inches of fresh Alberta snow over the next twenty-four hours. The area south of Nett Lake was already under a thick white blanket, with impressive snowbanks piled up and few people or vehicles out and about. The U.P. seemed almost overpopulated by comparison.

He had the road pretty much to himself, his tires cutting fresh tracks, snow fluttering around without serious intent. It was the granular stuff, coming in hard little pellets. Back home locals could wax poetic about the properties and significance of different kinds of snow. For him it was just a bunch of slippery white crap that made life more difficult. You either endured or you didn't.

Service reached Nett Lake, and pulled into an establishment advertising LIVE BAIT—AMMO—BEER—DEER—CORN-FRY BREAD, a one-stop shopping experience in a snowy swamp. He topped off his tank and went inside, found himself in aisles filled with some great winter gear at pretty good prices, and helped himself. He had all kinds of gear in the truck, but in the North Country, you couldn't have enough. Several pairs of socks and some twelve-inch Sorels with a tag claiming they were insulated down to minus-100 degrees. The male clerk had a baby face and a flashy gold earring.

"Chains?" Service asked.

"Back to the hardware," the kid said with a head jerk.

He added another shovel to his new chains and a folding track for traction in case he got stuck, and a box of chemical hand warmers. Unexpected bounty. He *loved* outdoor gear, as did most COs.

"Expecting trouble?" the clerk asked as he tapped prices into an adding machine with paper that draped down to the floor like a Gene Simmons tongue.

"How far to Nett Lake?" Service asked.

"In miles or light years?" the clerk asked.

Bush humor. "How about drive time?"

"Depends on your speed, don't it. You've got about nine miles to go."

Some sort of virus was loose upon the land, putting the smart-mouth on teens everywhere: MTV, shit like that. *Millenium Generation, my ass: more like the Moronic Generation.*

Service said, "How far to the nearest asshole, not counting you?"

The kid said, "Look in a mirror."

He couldn't help but laugh. The kid was annoying but quick. He'd probably end up as the CEO of some damn dot-com.

Out in the Tahoe he fiddled with the radio and finally found WELY, which was mostly static and billed itself as End of the Road Radio.

If population was sparse between the iron range and swamp taiga, it was nonexistent in the swamp itself. All road signs had been torn down or turned around to confuse strangers, the unspoken message: *Get Thee Lost.*

Nett Lake turned out to be a loose collection of buildings, trailers, shacks, snowmobiles, boats on rusty trailers with flat tires, and so forth, just like the U.P. Roads hadn't been plowed, but there were iced tire ruts marking the way, and in one area some kids had shoveled space in the street to play basketball. A backboard had been erected on the roadside, and kidlings in snowsuits and plaid wool jackets and bulky chooks swarmed each other and the ball, trying to dribble, pass and throw each other down, like in the old days when some tribes played lacrosse with human heads instead of balls, and called by some The Little Brother of War.

One small building was set by a cluster of trailers with a big sign announcing that a new tribal center would arise magically on the location. Smoke tendrils trailed from chimneys and merged with falling snow. Snowmobiles were abandoned as much as parked, pickup trucks, too. A black dog sat in a doorway and issued a laconic snarl as he walked by.

The woman at the tribal post office had a moon face and brown doe eyes. "Not open," she told him. "Sorry."

"Not here for mail," he said. "I need information. Where's your police station?"

"Chief's gone fishing today," she said. "You could talk to Au-da-ig-we-os. This means Crow's Flesh in our language," she explained. "You know about Ojibwe people?"

"Some," he said.

"Most *wabish* ask to talk only to the chief."

"I'll talk to anyone who can tell me about Wendell John Bellator, also called Na-bo-win-i-ke."

"Crow's Flesh, he can help you. I will take you."

"I'm Grady," he said.

"Lynx," the girl said. "It's, like, a kind of wild cat?"

She led him down a row of trailers and opened a door in a mudroom without knocking. She had an accommodating, sweet way about her, and a soft voice. There was a deer carcass hanging from a tree by the mudroom, and moose antlers were attached to a basketball backboard, antlers wrapped in twinkling purple LEDs.

An obese raccoon charged to greet him and hissed in a standoff. Lynx said, "Hush, you little bully," and the coon scrambled away. There were photographs all over the walls, some small, some large, some framed, some just tacked in place.

"Would you like something to eat?" the girl asked.

"Where's Crow's Flesh?"

"He'll be out soon. He's taking his nap. I think when you become an elder, your nap becomes very important. We have plenty to eat."

The coon came back and jumped up, sinking its claws into his pants and staring up at him.

"Biter?"

"Sometimes. She's not a pet. But she stays here a lot, and the old man won't scold her because he says he was also a biter when he had teeth—you know, glass houses and such."

Nice. Grady Service sat at a small table and kept an eye on the animal.

"What do you do for a living?" Lynx asked.

"I run around in circles," he said.

She giggled. "They pay you for that?" she mumbled, and left him alone.

• • •

Bowls of food were everywhere. Crow's Flesh wore a burgundy sweatshirt emblazoned with REDSKINS in a fancy gold script. The man had tiny hands and broken, yellowed fingernails.

Lynx scooped something from a frying pan onto their plates. Brown meat and gravy. The old man broke a biscuit, dipped it into the gravy, and filled his mouth.

"You two should talk, Grandfather," the girl said. "He's looking for Na-bo-win-i-ke."

The man nodded and pointed at Service's plate. "Moose. Eat first."

Moose was followed by greens with thick crisp bacon slices, heavily seasoned fish, carrots glazed in honey and brown sugar, baked sweet potatoes, dewberry cobbler. The old man ate steadily, rarely pausing, and never returning to a dish once he had taken a small helping from it. The girl brought raspberries in thick cream and apologized. "They're frozen," Lynx said. "Unthawed, eh."

Service laughed. *They even speak some of the same peculiar language as Yoopers here.* The old man grinned, showing perfect white teeth. Service guessed they were as false as his own, but the old man said, "You ever had the gas?"

Had the girl delivered him to a feeb? Indians loved practical jokes and leg-pulling, and you just never knew. He immediately felt bad about the thought. The pair had just shared all kinds of food with him. It was rare to have such hospitality from people you knew, much less strangers.

Crow's Flesh made a cup with his hand, made a drinking gesture, and Lynx brought a small brown crock and two glasses and set them in front of the men. "Whiskey from my grandson out east in the Virginias," the man said.

It was smooth. "Nice," Service said.

"Been expecting you'd come along," Crow's Flesh said.

"I didn't even know there was a here until a couple days ago."

The man smiled "*Ancekewenaw.* You got the troubles over that way."

The troubles, and not a question. He hated articles with certain nouns. Indian telegraph. "That so?"

The old man sipped his whiskey, smacked his lips with satisfaction, and pointed a crooked finger across the table. "You're tryin' to figure it out."

"You read minds?"

"Not so good no more, I don't." Crow's Flesh turned to Lynx. "He thinks I read minds." The two of them burst into laughter.

Service wondered what the joke was.

"Was only me and a deputy here for sixty winters. Now they got casino money and five deputies, a chief, *and* a second chief. I'm too old now, they tell me: Hunt, sleep, eat moose, venison, fish, drink, eat rice, talk, had my time. Up to young ones now. What kind of badge you carryin'?"

Service showed him and the man stared. "I like a simple badge. Plain and simple, no need for fancy. That's a fine one, for sure."

Service had always carried a second badge in his wallet, a replica, for kids. He took it out and gave it to the old man.

The man had Lynx pin it on and looked down at it with obvious admiration.

"Michigan game warden. You know Bois Fortes?"

"Heard of them."

"Means hardwoods in *we-mi-ti-go-ji-mo-win,* our word for French-talking. We lived on hard ground. Now we are here in the soft ground, with rice. It is a good place for us."

"Treaty?"

"We were never good traders," Crow's Flesh said. "Got cheated plenty." He grinned. "Few people know Bois Fortes. We are forgotten, yet we remember the old ways. Only Bois Fortes do this. We were peaceful people and had no time for war. Would you rather make war or"—he made a circle with one hand and poked a finger into it with the other hand—"go inside a woman?"

Service fought a smile and saw out of the corner of his eye that Lynx was watching for his response. "I know what you mean," he said, evading.

"The land was rich. Our brothers, south and west, they fought the *Nad-owe,* the *Nadowese,* the *Shaganosh, Wemitigozhi*—they fought everyone. My people, *sug-waun-dug-ah-win-i-ne-wug,* no fighting, no enemies, just put our things in our women." He poked the air again. "They called us *Wa-boo-shi,* rabbits—thought we were afraid, but here we are, and where are all of them now?"

The man nodded. "Black robes, they came here: French, Anglais, Canada-man, Americans, they all came. We lived the old way. Our brothers signed treaties and broke them. We signed and honored them. Our sisters married men like you and let them go inside them and our blood became pale. But we still lived the old way."

"Things haven't changed all that much."

"Yes. Are all whites the same, French and English?"

"Not hardly."

"Black people, skin the color of obsidian knives, they are all the same?"

"Definitely not."

"Indian people not same. Different. No Anishinaabe-Nishaabe, Bois Fortes, Leech Lake, Grand Portage, Bad River, Fond du Lac, Red Cliff, understand? We were all brothers once, one tribe, together, like one family, long ago. No more."

"Everything changes," Service said. He wasn't sure he was so partial to change either, and he shared the old man's obvious anguish.

"Bois Fortes, we believe nothing happens without a reason."

Service kept quiet.

"Sometimes there are reasons we cannot see. If we live in balance, all of us, no imbalance. If imbalance, then everyone is not in balance. How people act tells us if the life is good and proper."

"Boat rockers cause problems," Service said.

"I will take you to Lakotish The False," Crow's Flesh said.

"Lakotish The False?"

The man held up his hand for silence.

• • •

They drove an old Jeep Eagle about a mile west of the village. There was no wind. The snow came straight down, the ice pellets turning to edged flakes. The old man drove slowly but steadily, parked, and led him through a canopy of cedar, tamarack, and balsam to an opening in the natural tunnel of winter-dead plants.

"Light," the old man said. Service turned on his green penlight and moved it around, saw they were in an Indian burial ground, complete with spirit houses and some old white wooden crosses.

Crow's Flesh stood beside one such structure, six feet long, three feet high, holes drilled in the ends. "Lakotish The False," he declared. A small board had been carved with the name SAMUEL WARGUS LAKOTISH.

"I don't understand."

"Na-bo-win-i-ke was summoned to your country to hunt Lakotish."

"But Lakotish is in the grave. Did he come back to life?"

The man hissed. "No. *This* Lakotish, the False One, is dead, and his body is here in this grave."

"I don't understand. How can Na-bo-win-i-ke hunt Lakotish if he's dead? His brother or something?"

Crow's Flesh said, "Lakotish The Real did not want to be a warrior but became a soldier."

"And died?"

"There is a body in the grave," Crow's Flesh said.

Service thought on this. "But you're telling me it's not the *real* Lakotish in there?"

Crow's Flesh smiled. "Wrong man. Blue coats, they got it wrong, sent this man, Lakotish The False."

"Nobody here noticed?"

"Body burned, almost nothing left."

"So who is this, if not Lakotish?"

The old man shrugged. "Lakotish was afraid, but joined your army, trained, went to war, fought, and married a black robe. Then he died."

"The black robe died?"

Crow's Flesh nodded.

"How can you know that?"

"Spirits tell us many things if we care to listen." The old man touched his heart.

"Which war?"

"The bad one, in the jungle. 'Hell, no, we won't go.' 'Make love, not war.' 'Hey, hey, LBJ, how many kids will you kill today?'"

"Vietnam. What oufit?"

"Van Tri Soong, Special Forces."

"Green Beret, yet he didn't want to be a warrior?"

"Yes, Special Forces."

He's making no sense. "How old was he?"

"Twenty winters."

"What year?"

"Six and six."

"Who is Na-bo-win-i-ke hunting?"

"Lakotish The Real," Crow's Flesh said, "but Na-bo-win-i-ke is dead, and now you will hunt Lakotish."

"I don't even know him."

"You will," the old man said, and added, "Look for this, and you will know." He took a finger and pushed it against Service's spine. "This lets the spirit out to begin its journey on the road of souls," the old man said.

Crow's Flesh graciously gave him a cell-phone number and told him it would be all right to call him.

• • •

Back in his truck Service punched in Gunny Prince's number in California. The old sarge answered, saying, "We just had Jesus's birthday. Who the hell are you calling so close to my personal savior's birthday?"

"Sixty-six, grunt named Samuel Wargus Lakotish, Special Forces, Van Tri Soong, eighteen years old, died, no details known, though there might be a chaplain involved in some way." *The old man had said Lakotish had married a black robe. Chaplain? It was a good guess.*

"Where you at?" Prince asked.

"Orbiting in Minnesota."

"That sucks; what do you want?"

"Name, outfit, details. Could be the wrong body got sent home and buried."

"Happens every damn war," the gunny said. "Samuel Lakotish, that's the name?"

"It is."

"Them boys up in the Puzzle Palace on the Potomac don't work weekends nor this close to Jesus's birthday, or to the new year."

"The holidays are over."

Gunny Prince howled. "You're a pip, Service. My personal Jesus worked miracles, not me, but let's see what he can do you for."

Grady Service sat in his truck. Crow's Flesh had said, "Now you will hunt Lakotish." *Had the old man talked to Johnstone? Weird.*

57

Sunday, January 4

DULUTH, MINNESOTA

The Hotel Voyageur sat at the bottom of a long, steep hill. From his room Service could hear eighteen-wheeler brakes protesting the grade. There was a terrible snowstorm outside, and he had holed up rather than push on. Gunny Prince called back.

Specialist Samuel Lakotish of Nett Lake, 301st Special Services. Enlisted for three years in 1964, trained in infantry, switched to chaplain's assistant, and killed in '66. Killed, not KIA, a major distinction, that. Died eight months into his tour. *Switched to chaplain's assistant? Why?* Volunteer, not a draftee, yet Crow's Flesh said he hadn't wanted to fight. Finished in the ninetieth percentile of his class at Basic, won some sort of fitness ribbon that normally only freaks could qualify for. The man had some aptitudes. AIT for infantry, then two other schools, names omitted. *Damn government is worse than a cop house.*

How did a rifleman end up as a sky pilot's Sherpa? Some chaplains were chickenshit, to be sure, but there were plenty with gigantic balls and a hankering for living in the real and deep shit among their flocks. Standard fruit salad: National Defense Service Medal, Vietnam Service Medal, Vietnam Campaign ribbon, Combat Infantry badge, Bronze Star, no V for valor. M16 expert. *Odd damn background.*

"Efficiency reports?"

"His last one with the chaplain. High as you can get."

"Photos?"

"Active-duty personnel only."

"Who signed the efficiency reports?"

"A captain named Varhola."

"*Clement* Varhola?"

"Yep, that's the name I got," Gunny Prince said. "How the heck did you know that?"

The name Father Bill Eyes had mentioned. What are the odds on this coincidence?

"Not sure; can you have the records sent to me?"

"Not for a few days."

"That's fine. Can you also get me the name of their CO, the one Varhola reported to? And when Lakotish began his chaplain's assistant gig? What outfit was Lakotish in before that, name of his CO, all that."

"Text or call you back?"

"Call me, Gunny."

"Oorah, son."

• • •

Sitting at the bar, he telephoned Father Eyes. The priest said, "I don't know whether to be flattered or flabbergasted."

"Depends on how well you can spell," Service said. "How long have you known Father Clem?"

"Long time. We first met at a retreat in Oklahoma City."

"Last time we talked, I got the distinct impression you're not a fan."

"Too stiff. Believer with a capital B. You know the type. Got his calling directly from God."

"That's not par?"

"Hate to break your bubble."

"You met him at seminary?"

"No, it was after that, and after his tour in Vietnam."

"Where was he ordained?"

"Maybe Kansas City, St. Louis . . . wait, I think it was St. Looey, for sure."

"Any way to verify that?"

"Priests may work holidays, Service, but church bureaucrats don't. Why not just ask the man directly?"

"Prefer not to. You wouldn't happen to have a photo of him?"

"Actually, I do. I can shoot you a cell-phone shot. It's a group photo from the seminar we attended."

"Do seminaries have yearbooks?"

"Most do—just like real colleges. It's the College of Christ the Savior," Father Eyes said. "I just remembered that. Usually the people who come out of there are first-rate, socially, intellectually, and theologically. Clem stood outside the mold, and I guess that's why I remember him."

"St. Louis?"

"Brintwood, Rintwood, Brentwood . . . an inner suburb, something like that."

The bartender in the Voyageur appeared to be Indian, had a gray ponytail, skin the color of burnished maple. "Tribe own this place?" Service asked.

"Only place we own shit is on our own lands, of which Duluth ain't."

"Your tribe?"

"Cree. You a cop?"

"It shows?"

"Does now."

"You ever hear the Ojibwe name, Lakotish?"

"Jump bail and run?"

"Dead. He was Ojibwe."

"Never heard that name, but there ain't no letter 'L' in the old tongue."

"Your lingo?"

"Cree and Ojibwe are pretty close kin. I get by in both."

"No 'L', huh?"

"Could be Sioux maybe—a takeoff on Lakota—or it could be some strange dumbass knockoff from *akotewagis* or *kateshim*. Lot of funny stuff happens with Indian names. Frenchie meets an Indian, can't prounounce the Indian word, slaps an 'L' on the front like it belongs, and cements the ignorance gap."

"You mentioned a coupla words."

"Just popped into my mind, ya know. Barkeep boredom."

"What are they?"

"*Akotewagis* means something like 'got a weapon,' or 'armed and dangerous.' *Kateshim* means 'catechism,' the book the missionaries used. I'm no language guy."

"You seem to do pretty good."

"Might could be bullshittin' you for a good tip."

"I don't think so," Grady Service said.

"A philosophical cop."

"Have a drink on me?"

"What the hell," the man said.

Service opened his phone, looked at the photograph from Bill Eyes. Which one was Varhola?

The falling snow made him remember he'd soon have to start trailering his snowmobile behind the Tahoe. The snow was going to get a lot deeper, and snowshoes wouldn't handle some of it.

58

Tuesday, January 6

BRENTWOOD, MISSOURI

There were no further call-backs from Gunny Prince, and Service pushed south to St. Louis, a good eight hundred miles south across Snowberia and the tundra of Minnesota, Iowa, and northern Missouri. Somehow he managed to get a call through to the College of Christ the Savior, where some nameless factotum informed him that Monsignor Pilfpolf would see him today at noon. By driving all night Service felt he could make it and agreed to the timing, hoping snow and fate wouldn't intervene.

He called Friday as he looped around Minneapolis.

"Are you headed home?" she pressed in her professional voice.

"South to St. Louis."

"Is there a point to this road trip?" *Irritation in her voice?*

"Sources tend to talk more openly when you can look them in the eyes."

"Oh," she said. "The kids are good, I'm good, thank you for asking."

Lessons of life: Never jog in a minefield, never interrupt a venting woman. Let her calm down. "So what *are* you up to?" she asked after an interval of seething silence.

"Wendell John Bellator, aka Na-bo-win-i-ke, came specifically to the U.P. to hunt the windigo, which is in some way connected to the Bois Fortes and Nett Lake."

"Are you on magic 'shrooms?"

"Beats group Kool-Aid," he said. "Has Quigley backed off?"

"So far, and more importantly, Jen Maki says she's gotten some wood chips and bits from every site, only she can't identify the wood."

"Call the Marquette office, ask for a forester."

"I already have a call in. What happens after St. Louis?"

"Not sure yet."

"Would be faster to fly than drive."

"The truck fits my ass," he said, "and you know I don't like to fly commercial."

"What's in St. Louis?"

"A Roman Catholic college and seminary."

She laughed. "Makes sense. We're already damn near celibate."

"Sorry I'm not there," he apologized.

"I know. Just be safe, and let me know where you are, okay? And it might be nice if you also filled me in on your FBI meeting."

"Shit," he said.

"Shit, you forgot to tell me, or shit, I found out?"

"BAU agent named Pincock. She's trying to help us focus."

"Did she?"

"Too early to tell."

"Lupo's in the news again, and every crank in the Midwest is reporting the cannibal."

"Call Lupo and chew his ass."

"You know he doesn't make call-backs."

"Send Limey over to push him around."

"I'm not going to do that, Grady. Take care, all right?"

• • •

The college of Christ the Savior sat among cottonwoods in a community called Brentwood. The college had an assortment of old three-story buildings made from brown bricks. There was no grass on campus and only a few large, empty planters. It reminded Service of West Point for priests. All concrete, religion, and business, a professional army undergoing indoctrination and basic training for the lifelong battles to follow.

Monsignor Joseph Pilfpolf was a short man with weathered skin, short white hair, and thick eyeglasses. He was strapped to a wheelchair with a sign on the side proclaiming JOE THE JET.

"Officer Service?"

The man had an easy smile and lively eyes. "Monsignor. Thanks for seeing me."

"Call me Joe. I'm retired now, and I was never one for formalities. I was told you want to know about Clem Varhola."

"Do you know him?"

"Didn't go to school here with him, but I met him later. He's a good man with a natural talent and calling for pastoral life. Not academic and bookish like a lot of us. I never met a man with such a pure joy for people, and life," Pilfpolf said.

Service opened his cell phone, pulled up the Bill Eyes group photo, and handed the phone to the priest.

"Mind if I put on my cheaters?" the priest asked. Pilfpolf looked at the photo on the phone for a long time, squinting his eyes, then looked up at Service. "Is this a joke? Show me his picture and I'll be glad to confirm it."

"He's not in that one?"

"No. What's this about?" the priest asked. Grady Service laid it out for the man.

• • •

Service sat at a coffee shop afterward and called Friday, who sounded tired. "Something wrong?"

"Two more, Grady."

"Same area?"

"West of where we found Anne Campau. Decapitated, arranged neck to neck, legs and arms extended like a da Vinci drawing in an eight-point star. Total evisceration this time. Both bodies were found in a tree."

"How high?"

"Twenty feet off the ground."

"Jesus. Feet and hands?"

"No heads or hands. He suspended them with braided fishing line. They're displayed, Grady. Do windigos display their kills?"

"Could be, but this guy ain't no P. T. Barnum."

"It's a huge change in MO," she said.

He could tell she was desperate, and reaching.

"Tuesday, could you ask Kristy Tork if she's seen any small cuts along the victims' spines, say, three inches or so?"

"Why?"

"Something I heard in Minnesota, and it just now popped into my head."

"Okay. Are you in St. Louis and did you get what you wanted?"

"Got something, but not sure what. This case may have just taken a real strange turn."

She sighed. "Are you *ever* coming home?"

59

Friday, January 9

LARAMIE MOUNTAIN, WYOMING

When Service called Friday to tell her where he was next headed, she said, "Heading west is not coming home," and she'd huffed and hung up, giving him no chance to explain that Gunny Prince had discovered Varhola's CO had been Brigadier General Paul Revere Mindred, long ago retired, founder and current honcho of an eight-ball outfit called The Horse River Citizens Patriot Tea Party Militia. Mindred had commanded a Special Services battalion in Vietnam, Special Services being to Special Forces as tap dancing was to knife-fighting. The photograph from Father Eyes had drawn a blank in St. Louis. Maybe it would here, too. *Then what do you do,* he asked himself, and had no answer.

"General was Mindred's army rank?" Service had asked Prince.

"Nope, he retired as a light colonel as soon as he got stateside after his Nam eployment. Promoted himself to general when he started up his militia."

"Voluntary retirement?"

"Postwar reduction in force."

Called RIF, *a common occurrence after wars.* "He wiggy?"

"No, but there are rumored loose-cannon tendencies."

Service called Mindred from Lincoln, Nebraska, and though the man sounded gruff, he was amenable to a visit.

• • •

The militia compound was north of Cheyenne in the Laramie Mountains, south of the 9,400-foot Warbonnet Peak. The property was called Six Six Two and lay at the end of a long gravel road that terminated in a massive steel gate, with vintage World War II tanks on pedestals on either side.

A double cyclone fence topped with razor wire stretched all along the property line. Two men in white fatigues, white parkas, and camo berets stood guard at the front gate and called ahead when Service presented his credentials. The sign over the gate read HQ, 662 BRIGADE, HORSE RIVER CITIZENS PATRIOT MILITIA: OUR ARMS KEEP US FREE. The guards carried shotguns.

"Sir," the guard on his left greeted him when he rolled down his window.

"Name's Service. I have an appointment with the general."

"Sir, remain here, sir." The man took his ID and stepped into a small brick building sprouting various commo antennae.

"Sir, 'kay, I will, sir," Service mumbled. Military bookend language. The brick building was sandbagged, and Service could see two other sandbagged emplacements on rises in the distance. There was only a small dusting of snow on the ground, and it was mixed with dirt. He guessed tunnels connected the installations on the hills.

The guard returned. "Sir, five miles west, sir. Sir, you've got precisely fifteen minutes, sir. Follow the blue signs to the visitors' reception center, sir."

"What if I don't make it in fifteen minutes?" Service asked.

"Sir, you *will* make it." He didn't tack on a second sir this time.

Mussolini would have gotten off on this place: timetables, spit-shined boots, and all the gaudy attachments.

Near the end of his drive he passed an obstacle training course and a tower used to train parachutists, no airfield or aircraft in sight. There were sandbagged positions on nearly every hill, a lowlife boys' club caught in a war in their heads. Bizarre, but every militia outfit he'd come across over the years was pretty much the same mixture of efficient and pathetic.

The visitors' center was a white pole barn. Several Humvees had machine-gun mounts but no weapons displayed. Two small squads of men were doing close-order marching, no weapons apparent.

The center's interior was paneled in knotty pine, the furniture from Steelcase, and new. A woman in a tight-fitting white jumpsuit was behind a counter marked INFORMATION. A wall rack held numerous publications, FREE.

"Mr. Service," the woman greeted him.

He nodded. She was tall with green eyes and silvery hair. Her jumpsuit was seriously tailored, not some old thing off the rack. She wore white flats, definitely not your average mud soldier.

"Please accompany me."

They went upstairs to a large room with blue carpeting, framed photographs on the walls, racks of weapons along another wall, and behind a desk, a large eagle. The woman brought him a cup of coffee.

The general walked with the assistance of two aluminum canes, the kind with metal collars wrapped around the wrists. He was short with a potbelly, faded jeans, scuffed jungle boots, and a too-tight khaki shirt with epaulets. GI whitewall haircut, dull blue eyes, today's stubble beginning to sprout on his face.

Mindred fell back onto a couch with a grunt and pointed at Service's coffee. "Please," he told the woman, who scurried away.

"The docs don't allow me much fun these days," the general said as he watched the woman's behind. When she was gone he said, "They can take the snakeskin off the snake . . ."

Service had no idea what the man meant.

"Not that I could do anything with that if I happened to catch it," Mindred added.

The snake or the snakeskin? The general's voice was estrogenic, almost comical, but there was some military bearing to the man, a way of carrying himself that suggested he was a putz accustomed to being taken seriously.

"Sorry not to give you more warning, General."

"A lot of people out there write us off as extremists or lunatics, but the fact is, we're law-abiding, God-fearing citizens, and if the law comes calling legally and politely, we want to cooperate, even if their jurisdictions don't pertain."

"I appreciate that, sir."

"You're from the Upper Peninsula, son?"

"Yessir."

"Guard your land, Officer. I have it on impeccable authority that the One World Government plans to take away our wildernesses. I mean ta tell ya, ya can't have America without boonies, am I right?"

"You were in Vietnam, sir?"

"Weren't we all?" Mindred said gloomily. "Goddamned special services, national parks and recreation service in Vietnam, two years of herding doper split tails for USO shows, Bible bangers on the federal dole, the whole Hollywood grab-ass and pepperoni sideshow. Yeah, I was there. People these days ask me what hell is, I tell them it's being trapped in Special Services in a shooting war. I know morale's important, goddammit, but I say send the boys off to a whorehouse every month or so, and make sure they've always got hot chow and clean socks. Pussy, hot chow, clean socks, and ammo— what more does a man need to fight? It ain't complicated."

Ooh boy. "Sir, I'm trying to locate someone named Lakotish."

"That some kind of Moozlim handle?"

"I don't think so."

"Hell, they all reported to me, everything from Anabaptists to damn Mormons. Sky pilots, of course. I avoided them as much as I could, figured they knew their own business, didn't need me in their way."

"Lakotish may have worked with Father Clem Varhola."

Mindred grinned. "Exception to the rule. Clem was the best damn chaplain I ever saw, always wanting into the shit. The kids loved his hot-dog ass. Made a field tour once dressed as St. Elvis, swear to God, sang this song, 'Blue Suede Boots.' He was an original."

"Do you know what happened to him?"

"Same as the rest of us. Did his time and caught the Freedom Bird back to the World—not that it was worth coming back to by then."

"Do you know where he went?"

The general stopped talking when Ms. Jumpsuit brought him a cup of coffee, and he stared at a wall. "Hold your horses: Forgot that. Clem got beaucoup shot up in '66. The medics evac'ed him up to Jappoland for repairs. Never saw him again."

"Wounded in action?"

"Who the hell *was* the enemy there? I never did figure that one out. Our gooks or the damn commies' gooks? Clem was always trying to bail people out of jams. He had an assistant, wild as a March-damn-hare. We lost a shit-load of kids in '66. I heard something about how the two of them went down to some ville and it turned into a Vietcong shitstorm, got both Clem and the crazy kid who worked for him. Several attacks. Hell, my exec was with them that day and got a round that went in through his mouth and out the back of his head. Always told him he talked too damn much. Bullet never touched his teeth. I got a photo of that somewhere.

"Hell, it was weeks before we got everything straightened out again. Both Clem and his boy got hit. The kid was killed, burned up in a fire that consumed the whole ville. By the time I got details, Clem was up at the hospital in Yakota, I think."

"You remember the dead kid's name?"

"That name you threw at me—that sounded about right."

"Lakotish."

"Yeah. He was trained infantry, but ended up with Clem after a stint with an outfit in the bush. Heard he'd been a little overzealous, but how can that be if what you do is in your nation's interest? That's Uncle Sam: Train a man as a rifleman, then ask him to lug around a Bible."

"Have you got photos from those days, General?"

The general moved over to his desk and opened some drawers. "What am I looking for?"

Service handed the general his phone and pulled up the photo. "Anyone you recognize?"

Mindred studied the picture for several minutes and declared, "Be damned."

"Sir?"

"Fog of war . . . ever hear that term?"

"Yessir."

"Like I said, things were major fucked in those days. You issue an order and expect shit to happen, only it doesn't and nobody tells you. You never get anything sorted out; nothing's ever simple or clean."

The general rooted in another drawer and pulled out a photo. "Here you go, son."

"Father Varhola?"

"Him and his wallah."

Service pointed at Lakotish. "Varhola?"

"Hell no, that's the kid who got wasted. Clem's next to him."

"Lakotish?"

"Like I said, that name sounds right."

Service looked at the photo on his phone. It was Lakotish in the retreat photo Bill Eyes had sent to him. Not Varhola. *Holy shit!*

"There a copy machine I can borrow, General?"

"Sure, how many copies you want?"

"Just one."

Mindred pushed a button on the desk and the woman reentered. He held out the photo and minutes later the woman returned. Service bid farewell to the general and she led him to his vehicle and handed him the envelope containing the copy.

"You've got fifteen minutes," she reminded him. "You think I like being all the way out here in nowhereland with all these toy soldiers?"

He shook his head, started the Tahoe, and hammered his way out to the main gate, his heart racing. Only conclusion to draw now: *Varhola died in Vietnam, and Lakotish took his place. What the hell does it mean?*

Out on the highway Service headed south. He tried to call Father Eyes, but Gunny Prince called first. "Major Harry Axtall lives in Battle Ground, Indiana, plant manager for an outfit called Nocturne Solar Panel Systems. I called the major and told him you may call him, too. In fact, I want you to." Prince gave him the number and hung up.

Service pulled over and tapped in the phone number. "Major Axtall?"

"Just Harry these days. Prince said you wanted to talk about Lakotish."

"Yessir."

"I had him for half of '66. I was losing new brown bars every seventy-two hours, and some platoons got pretty disorganized. Lakotish was one tough customer and never gave me any problems, but one of my new Looeys stopped by one day with a bag full of Vietnamese hands and heads. Told me Lakotish had been freelancing at night, got caught by his platoon sergeant with the bag. Fricking mess. I called CID and then we got hit hard and lost a bunch of my men, and Lakotish fought like a damn demon. I would've kept him, but what he'd done was wrong, and we had reporters crawling all over the bush with us. Couldn't keep the boy. He told me he wanted a chaplain's assistant job to atone for his sins, so I got him transferred to Special Services and never heard of him again."

"He got caught with body parts," Service said. "What about the torsos?"

"Found some after the firefight."

"Lakotish kill them?"

"Nine or ten, all head shots. That kid could shoot the nuts off a flying mosquito."

"Anything else about the bodies?"

"Nothing jumps to mind."

Service started to end the call, but the former major said, "Wait—I think I remember that all his kills were stripped of their clothes and weapons and had cuts right along their spines."

"Before or after they were shot?"

"Didn't much matter to me."

"This have any influence on your decision on Lakotish?"

"Might have. That kid helped keep us alive, and when the shooting stopped it was water under the bridge."

Service called Friday. "You talk to Tork?"

"I did. All the bodies have spinal cuts."

"The killer's an Indian," Service said.

"A windigo?"

"More like a little turd who gets off on killing."

"Got a name?"

"Almost."

"Where to next?"

"Home."

PART THREE

THE KAISICK HOLES

60

Monday, January 12

HARVEY, MARQUETTE COUNTY

It had been a long, tiring drive from Wyoming.

Father Bill Eyes called back as Service drove past Sidney, Nebraska, and Service had been blunt. "You believe that windigo shit?"

"I generally believe what the church directs me to believe. To do otherwise would be impolitic."

"Is that a yes or a no?"

"Classify it as moral pragmatism. You need to head for home. The publicity from up north has the church on edge. The mucky-mucks have issued orders for priests in the trenches and all church personnel to steer clear of the media, on or off the record."

"Why would the church get dragged into this?"

"I'm sure you can understand why I can't go into that, but if you talk to a Ms. Demetra Teller, she'll no doubt help to fill in some of the blanks."

"The Grun-Baraga collection?"

"That would be her, and it. Yes, good, our minds are aligned. And Grady, I try to keep a clear head and an open mind. I assume good cops do no less."

"Why should I care about this collection?"

"It's complicated," Father Eyes said. "Adolph Grun was a Belgian Walloon who fled to the United States just before Pearl Harbor. He made a fortune in banking and land speculation. As a devout Catholic, Grun admired Bishop Baraga, and over the next fifty years created one of the five or six most important manuscript collections in the US, all of which he willed to Northern Michigan University, and with it a capital grant of many millions to build a facility for a permanent collection. But the church intervened and threatened to sue for Bishop Baraga's papers if the university made any of the collection public. Result: Demetra Teller was given the collection, and she alone controls access. There is a Father Baraga collection controlled by the diocese, but this is separate, and I imagine quite different."

"This isn't making sense," Service said.

"It will after you talk to Teller."

"If she lets me in."

"She will. My church warned me off contact with media, not law enforcement. Teller will see you."

Service felt cranky and seriously velocitized by the time he got back to Marquette County. Instead of heading south to Slippery Creek, he went directly to Friday's house in Harvey, let himself in, undressed, and slid into bed beside her where she lay snoring softly. Soon they were a cacophony in tandem.

61

Tuesday, January 13

PALMER, MARQUETTE COUNTY

The house was a mile up Anderson Road, just north of the old iron-mining village of Palmer. The air was frigid, but Service felt refreshed to be out of his Tahoe, if only briefly. There was a layer of broken clouds and a dappled sky. He had called Demetra Teller early that morning, and now, as he and Tuesday Friday walked toward the house, he saw her step outside to greet him.

"Cold out," she said.

"Not so bad," Service said.

Teller was well along in years, tall, thin, and slightly stooped, though there was a youthful air about her, despite baggy clothes and loose gray hair, the dowdy look of an aging hippie.

"Did we interrupt anything?"

"Not at all," Teller said. "I've been expecting you."

Service introduced Friday, and the woman led them through a cluttered ground floor to a door that opened to an elevator. She took them down two levels.

"Looks bigger once you're inside," Friday said.

"I live in an apartment on top, and it all seems small to me after so long."

The elevator opened into a small anteroom which opened into a room with couches and chairs and five orange cats. "My mouse patrol," the woman explained. "They think they own the place."

The animals stared at them, ears and whiskers back, low growls hanging in their throats. Service was glad he wasn't a mouse.

Demetra Teller asked them to make themselves comfortable while she brewed tea. "You sounded concerned on the phone," she told Service.

"Do you know Dr. Lupo of Michigan Tech?"

"As well as anyone can know him. Grant's not one to run with the herd, intellectually or physically. He tends to work alone, but his reputation is certainly growing in certain academic circles. His work is frequently referenced. Do you know Grant?"

"We've met." *Is she unaware of what's been on TV?*

"I've always been astonished by how worldly such an erudite man can be. And devilishly charming," she added. "If you know him, why are you here? He's seen everything we have. Some of it will be in his book. I doubt there's anything I can add."

"Ever heard the term *windigo?*" The word stuck in his craw.

Teller folded her hands. "Yes. It's impossible to know anything of northern Amerinds and be ignorant of their myths and beliefs. The windigo myth is predominant in most of the far northern tribes. Something like it also exists elsewhere, but essentially this is a story of the cold and winter and starvation and failure. There are references to windigos in *Jesuit Relations* and among various accounts from the earliest European explorers in the north."

"What do you make of it?"

"I don't. I'm the collection's curator, not a scholar."

"One doesn't need to be a scholar to have opinions," Friday said.

"Lupo is the expert, not I. He is deeply interested in Amerind spirituality and how certain religious beliefs can influence the mental heath of individuals and the groups to which they belong."

"He studies such things?" Service asked.

"His book is highly anticipated. It's said that Dr. Lupo has accumulated impressive data in his research, but all of it remains in his notebooks, which are not public."

"Have people approached him to see his notebooks?" Friday asked.

"I believe they have, but it's mostly an empty gesture."

"Why?"

"He doesn't actually live anywhere."

"He has a house in Hancock," Service said.

"Strictly a pass-through and landing pad. Professor Lupo lives out of a suitcase, which is not a lifestyle I would choose. People like him are not like the rest of us."

Conversation not going where I want. "Did you say his work is frequently mentioned in the scientific literature?"

"Footnoted in an astonishing array of fields, a true polymath, and you will run across numerous references to personal conversations and personal correspondence."

"But he has no home."

"I know. It's almost sad, yes?"

"What can you tell us about windigos?" Service asked.

"Nothing. That would be overstepping my professional and academic authority. But I can pull materials for you, if you wish."

"If you don't mind," Friday said, glancing at Service with a look that asked *What in the hell are we doing here?*

Teller started to leave them, but turned back. "I'm thinking it might be more . . . informative, to see for yourself."

"See what?" Service asked.

"The Black Letter Collection," Teller said.

"Which is what?"

"One of the Church's greatest secrets—a collection with everything reported from the New World, all of it stored now right here, and because of the volatility in some materials, generally unavailable to just anyone."

The woman took plastic packages out of a desk drawer and gave a set to him. "Linen gloves for handling manuscripts. Ordinarily I set it up so that no touching takes place, but given your urgency, we'll make exceptions this time. Are you familiar with *Jesuit Relations*?"

He was. "There's a copy of the set at the library in town," Service said. He had used the books in a case just last year. "Letters to the boss, from his priests out in the bush among the tribes."

"Exactly, but later all those original letters were collected in a central repository, which is in Cincinnati. Our benefactor, Mr. Adolph Grun, managed to find manuscripts the Church had never seen before. Some of these he passed to Cincinnati. Others he kept, and those are the core of the collection here. You have seen the various periodical reports by priests, but there are many, many other documents and special reports most people haven't heard of, much less seen. Bottom line: We have here information that exists nowhere else in the world."

"Baraga wasn't a Jesuit," Service said. "I think."

"You are quite right, but he was a star in terms of reports and orderly record-keeping. He was an erudite man of immense intellect and natural curiosity," Teller said. "Born an aristocrat in Slovenia, he took a law degree from the University of Vienna, was ordained in the Recollet order after that, and dispatched west, arriving here in 1830. Baraga studied the Ottawa tongue under a full-blooded priest named William Makateginessi. The newcomer already spoke French, German, Italian, Latin, and Illyrian. He learned English while he learned Ottawa. Later he became fluent in Ojibwe and authored an English-Ojibwe dictionary, the first time the language had ever been rendered to paper.

"He was a determined, hardworking man who traveled on foot, by boat, horseback, and snowshoes through the wilderness year-round, and during his travels he witnessed and reported many, many unsual observations and events," Teller explained. "After some years in the bush, Baraga was named Bishop of Amyzonia and Upper Michigan, serving in the Soo and Marquette. By then he had affected a lot of lives, leaving most the better for it. He kept detailed reports for ten years and suddenly stopped. Scholars have anguished over this sudden change, hypothesizing that some traumatic event caused him to lay aside his pen."

"And you've figured it out."

"I have an idea but can make no public declarations, and the Church has no official view on the question. The fact is that cannibalism, in whatever form, still carries a massive social taboo in most cultures. People don't want to think about it, don't want to know about it. Consider the continuing debate over Neanderthal remains in France and other parts of Europe. There's clear evidence of the butchering of human remains, from bones recovered from dated firepits."

She continued: "Naturally, modern people don't want to rationally discuss aberrant behaviors we can't bear to embrace, even in historical or evolutionary contexts. So here we sit, trying to evaluate ancient aboriginal practices in light of current values and mores: oranges and orangutans, more or less. Two plus two equals five-point-six, or something. We dare not think the unthinkable, which means we turn culturally blinded eyes to knowledge that potentially could help us to better understand who we are and how we got this way.

"I've heard many scholars argue vehemently against the evidence and point to cultural bias at the time. Jesuit fathers, for example, reporting on Huron and Iroquois torture and cannibalism, which, while true, may miss the whole point. Cultural context and history tells us that torture was commonplace throughout Europe at the same time, and in fact driven there by Church doctrine, which insisted that only the Church and God could determine right from wrong. Therefore, Church-supervised torture was considered a legitimate tool of State and Church, yet condemned in the hands of Native Americans. The Church subjected suspects to 'trials by ordeal.' If an accused survived, he was adjudged truthful in the eyes of God. If he died, he was guilty," she said.

"There followed a massive shift in philosophy exploding out of the Reformation. Suddenly legal experts and churchmen decided man could determine truth through reason, and without God's assistance, but torture remained the primary method of assisting the quest for truth. Only now, *man* interpreted the results. The Jesuits wrote quite a lot about torture, but they wrote very little about cannibalism, which is odd, considering how close the two practices were in some of these cultures." Teller stopped talking and looked at them.

"Still with me?" she asked.

"Mostly," Service said. Friday nodded.

"The fact that not much was written about cannibalism doesn't mean it didn't exist, do you agree?"

"Can't disagree," he said. "Baraga?'

"Yes, he had a lawyer's dispassionate eye for detail, but the Church, for all its presumed power and worldliness, was and is as vulnerable to cultural bias as any other human being or institution. The Vatican began to tighten access to certain materials it judged unacceptable to human exposure."

"Eyes and ears only," Friday said, "the term the American government uses to compartmentalize and control access to its secrets."

Teller began again. "Fairly early on, Rome decided to allow the creation of certain collections to be known under the masking rubric of 'Black', that is, *extremely* sensitive information. These collections are dispersed around the world, not centralized in Rome. The Church didn't tell its people to keep such materials, but also didn't say *not* to keep them—just made sure security was put in place when such materials came to light, which they have from time to time."

"Cannibalism," Service said, reading where she was heading.

"The beliefs and religious practices of barbarians and pagans. Secret organizations, inside the Church and without. Sanitation practices. Theories of disease causation. Magic. Sex. You name it," Teller said. "The Church has innumerable collections buried deep in the dark."

"But not Grun's."

"Not his. He had seen this behavior in Europe and decided to protect what he had taken the trouble to assemble. But herein is the great conundrum in the situation: None of this exists—not here, not in Cincinnati, not in Rome. And although it doesn't officially exist, we have here some letters that were never sent up the line, and we don't know why. Where Grun found them and their provenance remain a mystery, but they have been informally authenticated by various sources and methods. What you see today doesn't exist. Agreed?"

"Agreed. But why let us see them at all?" Friday asked.

"I think you folks need some help in clarifying what you're dealing with. I live up here, too. What you read here, you can use for your own purposes, but not as evidence or in any official public capacity. Subpoenas will get you only denials."

"Fair enough," Friday said.

Teller took them into a stark white room and brought them metal boxes that contained yellowing documents in neat piles. "We have about fifteen thousand items here, all originals and rarely used, so most work is with facsimiles. I'm giving you folks originals so you can see for yourself that this isn't some sort of hoax. What you will read is what Bishop Baraga believed he had experienced."

Service set a letter between them and they began to read:

To The Most Reverend Lord,
Bishop Edward Fenwick
Bishop of Cincinnati

Most Reverend Lord:

I find myself surrounded by the darkness and pall of paganism, most hideous and repugnant. I have come these seven days past to a place southeast of Ontonagon, finding here a scrofulous lot of savages invested in an encampment in a canyon along a river the color of blood. We have walked four days from Ontonagon, which sits astride the short of the Upper Lake. My guide in this arduous journey is Jashagashkadekoman, which in English would translate to Crooked Knife. He is of the Otchipwe of Fond du Lac, north and far to the west of our present position in the wilderness. He is a noted hunter among his people and held in the highest regard, a good and attentive Christian, with a wife and five babes, as reliable as any man can be.

The savages here at the River of Blood are unlike any so far encountered in my travels. The men, upon our arrival, were intoxicated and belligerent. They carry stout knives with which they slash and gash their fellow savages, and on occasion plunge the blades into their own flesh in the throes of inebriation. I have witnessed these same savages drink their own blood and that of their fellows. Upon our arrival, these frightening creatures had painted their faces black, a condition which put my companion into great and immediate consternation. He urged us to move on quickly, calling this place one of great and deep evil, advising we quickly repair to more favorable conditions in location and company. But I confess, I was tired, possessed of a small fever, in need of rest, and had no intention of moving because of my guide's troubled mood.

It is, My Lord, my impression and experience that savages often present a brutal first sight, but with time the imagined ferocity gives way to a gentler and truer nature, the truth of God being that we are all equal beneath our flesh. But this phenomenon was not to be at Blood River, whose inhabitants continued their regrettable behaviors. What we confronted, I would learn, were warriors of the Bear Clan, a warlike faction of the Great Otchipwe People, whom we have come to respect and love. The people of this clan are uncompromising, and their women and young maidens are such wanton and foul creatures as to preclude detailed descriptions. Like their men, they painted their faces black and dyed their naked breasts vermillion, and fornicated in plain view with any savage in whom the urge commanded. It is further my observation that the women of this clan, rather than accept copulation as a husband's right in God's plan for man's procreation, seek out partners for the act in which they claim to derive great pleasure.

The winter is early this year, first snow arriving on 27 September, and it now being November, the ground is covered with a blanket of snow five or six feet in depth. It was my hope and prayer, Lord, that by wintering here among these creatures I might bring God's light to them, but instead, I now find my own faith shaken, and apply to you as my Holy Confessor to hear my confession:

O My God, I am heartily sorry for having offended Thee. Over the days of our encampment there were regular bloody altercations, some of which took the lives of savages, or left them maimed and crippled. The clan was in vaporous frenzy when we arrived, and I expected it would slowly taper. I was wrong. It grew stronger, more violent and unpredictable, and I learned from my guide that the savages were in a frenzy over a windigo, which has taken residence among them, and whose identity is not yet known. The savages have at times begged my indulgence in forgiving their vile excesses, and they explained that they are powerless to behave in a more civilized manner until the monster that craves only human flesh is identified and killed.

It occurs to me that this may be a form of possession by Satan, and that the route to salvation might be a holy exorcism. Unfortunately, not knowing the beast's identity, and despite prayer, I was unable to judge if it had previously been a good and true Christian. On our fifth day, my guide and I were visited by a delegation, which begged me to bring the power of Christ to their aid, and to find and dispatch the monster lest it consume the entire clan. If I would do this, they agreed to give their hearts and souls to Lord Jesus.

I am hardly prudish, your Lordship. I remember well from the days of my youth in the gymnasium the debaucheries of the soldiers of Bonaparte; as they prepared to advance to battle they invariably entered into drunken and wanton behaviors. It occurred to me that what I was seeing at the River of Blood encampment was of a like ilk, but now I know I was badly mistaken, and that missionary priests being sent forth by the *Leopoldinen Stiftung* should be informed that one's learning under the tutelage of the Church cannot be used to extrapolate or interpolate situations in cultures of which civilized men cannot imagine. A missionary must accept what is, what presents to him, and act accordingly.

Last night the savages led us *sur les raquettes* over a crusty snow to a rocky promontory the savages call *wijiganikan*, the place of skulls. The river has such velocity below that normal voices a hundred feet above cannot be made out. Having hiked for several hours, we reached a grotto where we confronted a creature that defies my powers of language to fairly describe. I will say that it seems only distantly possible a human being, with sunken red eyes, and emitting a continuous flow of pink froth during its rantings and jumping around, the sounds being oddly childlike in tone, but with no discernible language. It caused me to wonder if the creature had suffered some sort of critical head trauma or mental infirmity; had we been in Europe, this thing surely would have been collected and safely established in an asylum. Torches showed the beast's grotto to be scattered with human remains.

I suggested that we apprehend the beast and restrain it with ropes, but this was rejected by the savages, who assured me that only death could remove the threat to their continued life, and that none of them dared kill it because they believed this could risk the creature's infirmity passing into their souls. My guide and I managed to rope the animal and subdue it long enough for me to drive a knife into its heart and deliver Extreme Unction in the hope that God would take pity on its pitiful soul.

Much thankful, our savages informed us today that, now clear of the windigo, they are preparing to move north to a location they call L'Anse, the head of the bay. They have invited me to visit them, which I intend to honor in order to instruct them in the ways of Christian living.

My Lord, I commit this confession to your judgment. I have committed murder in the coldest of blood and in violation of God's law. This letter will be carried east to the Soo and be taken by packet to Detroit, and from there overland to be delivered to your hands. It is my fervent hope God will forgive me. *Fiat voluntas dei*—Let the will of God be done. I am well physically, my Lord, but I fear the rending of my soul by this great sin I have committed.

I have no doubt that like all men I will be asked to atone for this abominable act on the Day of Judgment. In this knowledge I wish to spend the remainder of my life among these savages, to rescue their unconsecrated souls, with God's help. In our Lord's name I remain faithfully, Frederick Baraga, missionary priest.

Service looked at Friday. "Baraga killed the thing. Does it matter if he thought it was an actual monster, rather than a psycho?"

Friday had no response, and Service thought: *Pincock from the FBI told me to kill this thing if the chance presents itself. Seems like the priest led the way in this.*

"That puts us in a quandary, doesn't it?" Friday finally said.

"I think I know who we're looking for."

"Do I get to know?"

"When I'm sure."

"How much do you think the bishop's letter is worth?"

"Incalculable," Service said. "And I suspect if it became public, a large part of the world would talk about nothing else for a long time to come."

"You're thinking a man has done all this?"

"Absolutely."

"Not an animal."

"No."

"So you are free to wash your hands of it, if you want," she said.

"Man or animal," he said, "when it comes to tracking something in the woods and bringing it to ground, that's what we do."

62

Wednesday, January 14

MARQUETTE

Larry Holemo was a longtime forester, could have retired years ago, but kept working and never complained.

"Larry, we need help," Service said.

Noonan and Treebone were back and had gone with Service and Friday to the Marquette DNR office.

Holemo picked up the plastic bag that held the wood chips picked up by Jen Maki at the crime sites. The forester pushed his glasses up his nose. "*Pinus gloriensus,*" he announced. "Glory pine, rare as a beanstalk, thought extinct in the state and never abundant anywhere in the Upper Midwest. Prefers the climate further north. Technically, we're outside the tree's southern range limit, but plants, animals, and people don't pay a heckuva lot of attention to arbitrary lines drawn on paper. *Gloriensus* is a tough customer. Indians considered it sacred, used the sap for everything from glue to medicinals."

"What's it look like all grown?" Friday asked.

"You won't find it in an *Audubon Guide,*" Holemo said, and went to another cubicle, coming back with an old, dusty book. He also had a photo album and flipped carefully through the pages until he stopped and handed the book to Friday. "There ya go."

The sepia photo was faded.

"We once had a few thousand stands scattered around up here, but loggers tore through the woods and weren't particulary discriminating. The specimens in the picture are from northern British Columbia in the early 1930s."

Service looked at the photo and pushed it to Noonan and Treebone. "How big are we talking?"

"Twenty or thirty feet, tops. Likes extremely acidic soil and cold-ass temperatures, both of which limits growth around here, but there were some pockets. Nature gives and takes. Specimens in Canada have been aged between four and five hundred years. Nature doesn't easily kill them. Only man seems to do that."

"Pockets in the U.P.?" Treebone asked.

"Probably here and there." Holemo opened the photo album. "This one was near Bruce Crossing one summer."

Friday sounded exasperated. "A tree's a tree."

The forester looked horrified. "It's rare for them to grow alone like the one in this picture. Usually you find them all packed together inside a lattice."

"Lettuce?" Service asked.

"Lattice. Personally I've never seen it, but I've read descriptions. In areas where the species is abundant, they grow in colonies, and are almost always surrounded by thick groves of slippery elm, *Ulmus rubra*." Holemo took the book again and turned it. "The slippery elm likes the edges of wet areas, swamps, and floodplains."

Friday studied the photo. "The branches are grown together."

Holemo grinned. "And you won't find one unless there's latticing to make it stand out. When I was in school at Tech a timber cruiser claimed he'd seen *Pinus gloriensus* over the Kaisick Holes area, west of Sidnaw. But that was a long while back, and the guy was pretty much of a bullshitter. Loggers have gone through that area numerous times, so the chances of the species being there is low to nil, and this isn't the time of year to be looking around."

"Where in that area?" Service pressed.

The forester crossed his arms. "I don't have a clue. Sorry."

They stood in the entrance after the meeting. "Mount a search?" Friday asked.

Service had doubts. "Not without more evidence. Big woods, rare tree— those odds suck, and that turf is not exactly user-friendly."

"Lamb's memorial is tomorrow," Friday told Service.

"Where?"

"Church of the Wilderness Redeemer, Assinins, fourteen hundred tomorrow."

"We both going?" Service asked.

"Out of respect for Lamb," she said. "She was a colleague and a friend, and a good gal, never mind her predilections. Nobody's perfect."

63

Thursday, January 15

ASSININS, BARAGA COUNTY

The Church of the Wilderness Redeemer was made of red brick and sat on a steep rolling knoll overlooking the winter-gray waters of Keweenaw Bay. The church was new and not quite part of the old Father Baraga property, which had included a church, a convent, and a graveyard.

Gunny Prince had called to pass on details of the Lakotish death and autopsy done in Vietnam so many years back. No DNA, of course; DNA had barely been identified as the stuff of life then. Lakotish had been burned, his head gone, identity confirmed with dog tags on his boots, and a gold ring. The absence of the head and extent of fire damage eliminated certain identification, but for that day and time, Service knew, this was normal. More than a few families had gotten the wrong remains back then. Fire damage, of course, obliterated the possibility of fingerprints, but blood type matched Lakotish. Nobody tried to explain the whereabouts of the missing head, or how it was separated from the body.

Service listened, making mental notes, told himself that if nothing else, here was a perfect opportunity for an identity switch. Motive, of course, was a separate issue. He handed coffee to Friday as they headed west. "Na-bo-win-i-ke came here to hunt Lakotish, whom the army believes died in Vietnam. But Crow's Flesh at Nett Lake insisted that Lakotish's grave there contained someone else, not him. I talked to a couple different sources, one from the war and one afterwards." Service gave her his phone and showed her the photographs. "I think Lakotish is Father Clement Varhola."

Friday stared at him, her mouth slightly ajar. "That's one big goddamn leap!"

"Crow's Flesh told me to look for cuts along the spine, which is done to release spirits. Lakotish was with an infantry unit before his transfer to be Varhola's assistant. His old platoon sergeant caught him with a bag of heads and hands, and the army pushed him aside to get him out of the way. Some bodies were found with the spinal cuts."

"Grady," Friday said, "this is a stretch *at best.*"

"Varhola's body was burned, the head missing. They identified him by blood type, dog tags, a ring. Apparently the two men had the same blood type."

"Do you understand what you're saying?" she said.

"It's *him,*" Service said.

"I only hear piles of circumstantials."

"I think Lakotish is now the priest in Baraga. He's got Indians in his parish."

She took a deep, audible breath. "We have to go carefully, Grady. Physical evidence: We need to link him to the killings, but we can't even declare him a suspect yet. Between us, he's barely a person of interest, and even that's not for public consumption," she concluded, staring down the highway.

"We take it slowly, one step at a time," he agreed. "No more big leaps, let evidence provide the trail."

Friday said quietly, "Okay. Do you know Varhola?"

"I met him briefly many years ago when he was in Marquette."

"Impression?"

"Not great. Creepy, slimy type. To be fair, he was friendly in an awkward way."

"And now he's saying mass for Lamb," she said, then jumped subjects. "What about fingerprints? Varhola and Lakotish both had to be fingerprinted when they went into the service."

"My source is pursuing that," he said.

• • •

The church parking lot was full. Service and Friday slid into the standing-room-only crowd in back of the church. The congregants were mostly tribals, and Service wondered what the precise split was between the Bay's and Johnstone's community.

The priest stood in a raised dock. An image of Captain Ahab flashed through Service's mind. Father Clement Varhola's voice boomed out over the crowd, loud and precise, with no sense of emotional tie to the deceased.

Varhola began: "The way to God is through Jesus Christ. Without Christ we are all susceptible to evil. You take your children to the medical clinic to have them vaccinated. Christ is our protection against evil. He is the only way, His, the only path to truth. Those who do not choose His path are doomed to perish. We are all afraid. It is human to fear. Christ is peace, the absence of fear."

The last time Service had seen the man preach, the only time, he had been a preaching drone, a human tape recorder, spitting lines without emotion from a church reduced to rules shorn of all human passion. This was not the same man. Varhola expertly modulated his voice, his gestures were practiced, and he virtually dripped intensity.

Friday nudged him. "Impressive turnout."

"Since *it* came," a woman behind them said quietly.

Friday looked back at her. "Before that?"

"No reason to be here," the woman said.

They waited outside the church and watched mourners file out. It was snowing lightly and people opened golf umbrellas and hovered around the church entrance, visiting.

"Maurice Prendergast," Friday said.

"Huh?"

"*Umbrellas in Venice.* A famous painting."

"It snows in Venice?"

"Moron," she said, rolling her eyes, and walked away.

Moron? He was just wondering why Indians had so damn many golf umbrellas.

The priest came out and mingled with mourners, looked stiff in the cold wind, made his way over to Service almost immediately.

"Did you enjoy the memorial?" the man asked.

Service stared at him. Who *enjoyed* a funeral mass?

The priest didn't wait for a response, added, "Will you join us at the cemetery?"

"Can't," Service said. "Duty." *Where the hell was Tuesday?*

In fact, why were they even going to the cemetery? Lamb's spirit was gone, this whole thing ceremonial. Her remains couldn't be interred until spring when the ground thawed. Her winter would be spent in the back corner of a beer warehouse awaiting breakup.

"Pity," Varhola said. "Physical death reminds us poignantly of the glorious and eternal life that is to come."

"You're sure there's something after this?" Service asked, the words out before his filter trapped them.

"Oh yes, indeed," the priest said. "What matters for the living is how we prepare for the inevitable."

To his mind churches were exclusively otherworldly. *Eat shit in this world for a theoretical "something better" in the next. Piss-poor bet. A strange man, Varhola, his voice, mannerisms—everything about him makes my skin crawl.*

Friday miraculously appeared at his side. "Lamb was a friend?" Varhola asked her.

"Colleagues," Friday said, "and friends."

The wind was biting. Varhola pursed his lips and patted her arm. "Police are temporally anchored, too, wed to evidence. What you need is faith, like true believers."

Friday bristled. "Cop is what we do, not who we are. Same as priests, I would think."

Varhola bobbed his head. "Point taken. Actually, I see us both engaged in explaining the apparently inexplicable. There's a natural connection between our callings. We both live by the Book," he concluded, nodded, and walked on to talk to others.

Friday left again as Service watched the priest visit and circulate. He didn't seem nervous or jerky. Very relaxed. All of his instincts told him the priest was putting on a show. Children beamed at his attention. Priest: major authority figure, someone given trust immediately and unconditionally. Was it possible for a priest to appear so affectionate, yet . . . ? He refused to finish the thought. *One step at a time. Ease up and let your quarry come to you; don't charge it.*

Friday was in the truck. "You left early," he said.

"Needed to stretch my legs."

He didn't look at her. "We don't have a warrant," he reminded her.

"What do you guys call it—open fields doctrine? I don't like the man," she said.

"I can tell."

"I found the woman who spoke to us before the service. She said the church has been full only since the killings began. Before that, hardly anyone went."

"People have to find their guts where they can," he said. Service looked at her. "Gonna tell me what you found?"

"He likes to whittle; actually, it's more than that. He's a woodworker, one hell of an artisan. He makes totem poles, some of them thirty feet high."

"Rome lets its priests make totem poles?"

"This one does."

"What else did you see?"

"His workshop was open. Wind must've blown the door open, so I closed it for him. Most completely outfitted workshop I've ever seen. No religious items, a few clothes, no mementos; a very boring place."

"Fishing rods, fly boxes, anything like that?"

"Nothing like that."

Service remembered from the Marquette meeting years before that the priest was acclaimed as a true trout fishing fanatic. "He's got to keep his gear somewhere."

"Not in his workshop."

64

Friday, January 16

ASSININS

Allerdyce had shown up the night before at Slippery Creek, tight-lipped and untalkative. Treebone and Noonan had gone to see Jen Maki that morning to once again sort through evidence. Friday had gone to her office, and Service took Limpy with him to Assinins.

Swinging by Varhola's workshop several times, Service finally saw the priest, got out, and confronted him between the rectory and the shop. "Father," Service greeted the man.

"*Yes?*" came the response, sharp, clipped, annoyed.

"Bad time?

"Not at all, if you don't mind watching boring work. In my line, I have to use my time wisely."

Service and Allerdyce followed the man into the workshop, watched the priest slip on a green shop apron and pick through pairs of gloves. "Must be nice to have a hobby," Service offered.

The man had immense wrists and oversized hands. "My hobby is trout fishing," Varhola said. "Woodworking subsidizes the parish funds," he said, lifting a black block from a chest high shelf, lifting it only with his arms and moving it down the shelf a good four feet away. The priest continued. "I suppose the work has a certain therapeutic value, helps to get things out, the objects of frustration and such."

What happened to prayer for those reasons? "Difficult for some us to learn how to relax," Service said. The priest had not yet looked at him.

Varhola said, "I've always believed one can learn what one needs to know." He used a wooden mallet and a chisel to knock pieces of wood off a log, which had already been peeled and roughly shaped.

"Pine?" Service asked.

"Too soft. I do my work with maple, oak, beech."

"Heard about your totem poles. Do they have to be chemically treated after they're carved and assembled?" Service inquired.

"With a sealer," the priest said.

"You like wood," Service said.

"The Indians believe everything in existence has a spirit, and I think it's a sculptor's work to bring that spirit out in the wood, to make it visible. That's a lovely sentiment, don't you agree?"

"Seems like a pagan view for a Catholic priest. How does that square with Rome?"

"Rome directs us to follow orders. This doesn't remove our minds and free will."

The workshop was as clean and sterile as an operating room: nothing out of order, walls peg-boarded and covered with wood-handled tools.

"Nice tools," said Service. "You make them?"

"My predecessor did, Father Beauclerc."

"Where's he now?"

"Gone to his reward," Varhola said.

"Those tools are remarkable. What wood did he use?"

"Something exotic. I prefer common woods." Varhola looked up. "Is this visit about wood and carpentry, or is all of this a convenient metaphor?"

"Sorry, Father," Service said. "I just wanted to ask you if you've seen any changes in the recent behavior of any of your parishioners."

"For some, change is continuous, especially those with tortured souls. For others, it is not. I'm not sure what sort of changes you're interested in."

"You know about the killings."

"Everyone knows," Varhola said. *No reaction, no flinch; flatline all the way.*

"Are the people in your congregation talking about them?"

"I am far from kosher in my approaches, but I draw the line at abomination. Whatever they've learned, I'm forced to try to undo. I don't believe in evil spirits inhabiting human bodies."

"But Rome believes in demonic possession, exorcists, all those things."

"The church is large and encompasses a wide spectrum of opinions, not all of them with equal merit, intellectually or theologically."

Tinge of annoyance in his tone, just under the surface. "I'm just trying to understand," Service said.

"I have no time or sympathy for superstitions and their adherents. I'm trying to lift people to the simple glory and grace of God."

Service decided to go right to the heart. "Is it possible—for those who believe in such demonic possession—for such a thing as a windigo to exist?"

"I seriously doubt it."

"But you don't reject it out of hand?"

"Only in the sense that certain phenomena may be interpreted and embraced as messages from the other world. Erroneously, of course. People tend to see what they want to see." Varhola kept chipping away at the pole, not looking up, focused on his hands.

Vague response. "Possible in this case. Here?"

"Quite unlikely," the priest said, putting down the chisel. "I'm not an expert in such matters."

"What about Grant Lupo?"

"What about him?" the cleric asked.

"You know him?"

"He's been all over the television, hasn't he?"

"Have you met him? That's what I'm asking," Service pressed.

"Perhaps. I meet a lot of people, and my memory isn't what it once was."

"We all have our failings, Father. Have you got an opinion on the windigo?"

Varhola shrugged. "I think Lupo is a self-promoter."

"To what end?"

"The end of every self-promoter: glorification of ego."

"Or he might be trying to perform an actual public service. You know, in the public's interest."

"If the man has that kind of knowledge, why doesn't he move in to stop what's going on?" the priest asked rhetorically.

"He may very well do that," Service said. "With his assistance we've identified a suspect. We'll make the identity public soon, after we apprehend." *Pulled that out of my butt. Too far? How's he reacting?*

Varhola said nothing, gave no indication he'd even processed what he'd heard.

"I've always thought of the church as contrapuntal," Service said.

"You know music?" the priest asked.

"Not really, but it seems to me the church represents a refuge for balance against the irrational and inexplicable."

"I would generally agree with that, but much of what we Catholics believe is itself irrational—anti-logical, if you will. That's where faith comes in."

"Law enforcement has to continually measure the pulse of the communities they serve," Service said.

"My vocation, as well," Varhola said. "The shepherd's role . . . so your metaphor holds."

"People are scared, Father. Scared people do desperate things."

"I would agree."

"But the good news is that it will soon be over."

"That's very encouraging, I'm sure," the priest said.

Said in a flat tone, no emotion, and no follow-up questions, despite a virtual invitation to probe. "Closing the loop," Service said. "We have a profile and an identity. The killings are getting closer together. It's only a matter of time now."

"The end will no doubt be a great relief to all," Varhola said.

Service dawdled. "I wanted you to know in case you hear anything."

Varhola tensed. "You're not suggesting I violate the trust of the confessional?"

"Of course not. I'm just saying that if you see or hear anything that seems out of place or odd, give us a call."

"I can do that much," the priest said.

Service handed the man his card and one of Friday's. Varhola stuck them on a shelf, did not look at them.

Allerdyce, who had said nothing and had disappeared for several minutes, moved over toward the shelf with the large black block. It read QUINTAL on the side. Service saw the old man rest his hand on one side of the block. The hand tensed and withdrew in almost the same motion.

Varhola saluted with his mallet. "Be safe."

Allerdyce got into the passenger seat.

"You were quiet in there."

"Dat guy give me creepie-jeepies."

"You see the handles on his tools?"

Allerdyce produced a wood-handled chisel from his coat. "Like dis?"

"*Jesus.* Where'd you get that?"

"Ootside on ground. Saw stick up from snow."

Service doubted him. "We'll have to give it back."

"Was outside," Allerdyce countered. "Din't even know wass his."

"The wood looks the same."

"Yeah, I seen dat," the old poacher said, holding the tool out to Service.

"I guess we can return it later," Service said. There was a catch-bag between the seats. "Put it in there," the CO said, pointing.

"You see dat big sex toy in dere?"

"What sex toy?" *Is he serious?*

"Dat big black t'ing."

"That's not a sex toy."

"Is, too. Says 'quimtail' on it."

"*Quintal,* not quimtail," Service said. *Old fool.*

"You see how he move dat t'ing?"

Service had.

"I tried, cou'n't move it inch. Made metal, eh. Old creepie-jeepie, he move dat booger like iss marching mellow, eh."

"Heavy, huh?" Service asked.

"Real heavy, and I ain't weak. What means quimtail?"

Service had no idea and made a mental note to check when they got back to camp, but he grew impatient and called Friday. "Can you look up a word for us?"

"Of course. I'm not doing anything else." *Dripping sarcasm.*

"Q-U-I-N-TAL," he said. "Quintal. I'm guessing on pronunciation."

Service could hear her typing. "Got it. Means a hundred kilograms, about two hundred and twenty pounds. Why?"

"It's a thing in Varhola's workshop. Limpy and I saw him lift it with his arms extended and move it like it weighed nothing."

"What's the punch line?"

"There isn't one, yet."

She said, "Jen Maki called. The paint flakes are from a 1996 Volvo 850R."

"How many of them in the U.P.?" he asked.

"Seven we can pinpoint."

"Any link to Varhola?"

"Nopers."

"Shit," he griped.

"Varhola give you anything?"

"Not really, but to catch a big fish you often have to make a lot of casts."

"This isn't fishing," she said.

"There's plenty about it that is," he said, and hung up. Then, he turned to the old man.

"What was your problem last night? I thought somebody sewed your lips together. You ever hear of glory pine?"

"Sure, wort' more'n curly or tiger maple."

"Seen it?"

"When I was kittle. Real rare now."

"Where was it back then?"

"Middle Manistique, all along Menominee, an' some on down Esky. Likes floodpans."

"Floodplains."

"Right—low banks, river-bottom wood."

"What about up this way?"

"Ain't never seen none, but I know guy might know."

"Who?"

"Chenk, name a Ulupov."

"Czech?"

"Just said—Chenk."

"He still around?"

"Hard ta find, sneaks 'round."

"Like somebody else I know?"

The old man cackled. "Corbin Lake, last I hear."

There were hundreds of lakes in the U.P., perhaps thousands if you counted beaver ponds and such. Only some were named, and Service knew only a small portion of those. "Where's that?"

"Nor-wess Sidnaw, mebbe t'ree, four mile."

"This Ulupov would know?"

"If anybody does."

"You talked to Krelle recently?"

"Come back April, check for dens."

"Pilkington know?"

"Didn't talk ta fat boy," Allerdyce said.

"How do we see this Czech pal of yours?"

"Ain't no chum a' mine. Go dere, hope he don't shoot. Commie Reds drove 'im out, '68. Been 'round here since '71."

"Plays by the rules?"

"I guess. He don't like guv'mint."

"Do any of us?" Service asked.

Allerdyce laughed out loud and smacked the dashboard with his hand. "Youse jes like youse's old man!"

65

Saturday, January 17

WOLVERINE JUNCTION

Service called Friday first thing that morning. "I want to go back out to WoJu," he told her.

"Why—do you think we missed something?" There was a hint of defensiveness in her voice.

"Don't know, but I want to take Limpy, Tree, and Suit with me. If we missed something out there the first time, one of us might spot it this time around."

"Why now?"

"Campau said something came down on her from the trees, and Limpy made the same observation at Sean Nepo's place."

"I don't remember the Nepo thing."

"Limpy said it looked to him like someone may have come out of the trees. And did Campau mean someone *emerged* between the trees and the ground, or that someone dropped down *from* the trees?" Service asked.

"Reasonable question, I guess," Friday said. "That whole thing went right past me that day."

"It went past all of us, but it keeps nagging at me."

"I'll go see Anne and call you. Meet you at WoJu?" She asked. Then, after a pause, "Why would Varhola do—"

He cut her off. "Don't go there yet, Tuesday. Baby steps, okay?"

"More on the paint chips from the Volvo," she said. "Black undercoat, but Jen had the samples under an electron microscope and found evidence of white and green—like camo olive drab."

"Repaints?"

"She thinks."

"Which color we looking for now?"

"Probably white, she says."

Black, white, green? "Maybe he repaints to match the time of year. Glossy, enamel, what?"

"Flat or matte, like primer."

"To dull reflection," Service said. "We'll be out at WoJu. Tree and Noonan are already rolling, Limpy and me right behind them. We'll call if we trip anything."

• • •

Once on scene Allerdyce and Noonan got a notion to climb some trees near where the body had been, "Just to look around, sonny," Allerdyce had said.

Service overhead Noonan's voice: "You climb like a fucking spider monkey, old man."

Allerdyce: "Back in day, di'n't drive 'round, waste gas. Scout sign, climb tree, wit' twinny-two horny, turn on light, pop pop, put deer down, get down, t'row in truck, meat in larder, feeds kids, eh."

Service shook his head. *How many violators operated like Limpy, climbing around in trees while COs sat on their asses in their trucks, watching open fields near roads? Disturbing thought.*

"Pulleys," Noonan said from above.

"Wass ropes, look bark 'ere, all barked," Allerdyce said.

"You guys got something?" Service yelled up to them.

"Sonny, we t'ink mebbe guy use pulley, yank body up tree."

"Pretty good guess," Noonan chimed in.

"Old ground, this, but good to reconfirm," Service said. "Do us a favor?"

Noonan reached down and Service handed his digital camera up to him. "For the record."

Treebone stood nearby. "The deceased was a big woman, Campau and the others said. Even with pulleys, this wouldn't be so easy. Would take some real strength. Me, I couldn't do this alone, and neither could you, Grady."

Tree had a bear's strength, and his own was close to his friend's. "You thinking two perps here?"

Treebone shrugged. "Speculating is all."

Noonan came sliding down right beside them, but Allerdyce descended almost forty yards away. "How'd you get way the hell over there?" an astonished Noonan asked the old man.

"Iss like bloody sidewalks up dere," Allerdyce said matter-of-factly.

"Not for me."

"You a city sicker."

"Slicker," Service corrected.

"What I said," Allerdyce insisted.

Friday called. "The WoJu vick may have been identified," she began. "Norma Carlock from Pipestone Road. Neighbors just came forward to report her missing. The night of December second they heard a ruckus in the house trailer next door, a woman screaming. I'm at the place now. We've got dried blood inside, but not much. Her car's here, parked outside, covered with ice. No tracks. No trees near the trailer."

"The neighbors call it in after nearly six weeks. Makes you wonder how many haven't been called in."

"I don't even want to consider that, Grady. We've got a potential ID, and I'll take that. People are really spooked," she concluded. "You guys still at WoJu?"

"About to wrap up, head for the barn," he said.

"Get anything?"

"A theory, maybe." Although her report of no trees at the Carlock place didn't exactly contribute to the theory, so he clammed up.

"I guess a theory beats nothing," Friday said.

Service told the others about Carlock.

"Snitches," Noonan said quietly.

"Neighbors," Service corrected him.

"Call the bulls, you're a snitch," Noonan shot back.

Allerdyce lit a cigarette. "Carlock? T'ink I know dat fambly. Old man Gus used ta hang out over Kewadin, get self fried, steal purses offen old womens in parkin' lot."

"You one of his character references?" Treebone quipped.

"Was t'ief, not no carkature," Allerdyce said.

"*Ad rem,*" Treebone said. "To my point."

"What the hull youse talkin'?" the old poacher asked, squinting.

"Latin."

"T'ought we spick Englitch."

We're all getting loopy, Service told himself.

Friday called again. "Just talked to Limey. She's at Lupo's house. There's a body."

"Lupo?"

"She thinks. She's guesstimating height at six-six, six-seven."

"No head?"

"Nor hands."

"This one's strictly for show," Service said. "It's a message to us because he knows we'll get an ID off this one without the head or the hands."

"It's Lupo," Friday said. "He had a tat on his ass. Student who found him had seen it before, identified him."

"Time of death?"

"They only got there an hour ago. She's guessing less than twelve hours."

"Anyone in the area see anything?" There were no close neighboring houses.

"Canvassing now, but you know how isolated the place is. She'll forward everything to us."

"You headed over there?"

"No need. Limey's got it. She knows her job."

"See you tomorrow," he said.

Service tapped in forester Larry Holemo's personal cell number. "Service here. Where you at?"

"Bell Forest Products."

"Ishpeming?"

"Yeah."

"How long you there? I need to get your opinion on something."

"Half-hour."

"Meet us at the Westgate Shell on 41. We're north of town now, heading in. See you when you get there."

• • •

Holemo got there a half-hour later and they took him inside for coffee. Service showed him the "outside" tool from Varhola's workshop.

"Glory pine, no question," Holemo said. "Where'd you get it?"

"You know anyone who makes tools with this wood?"

"No, sorry, but that is definitely the handiwork of a highly skilled wood craftsman."

"We found it in the snow," Service said, and Holemo said nothing.

Service paid for the forester's coffee, went outside, and tapped in the phone number for Crow's Flesh in Minnesota. Lynx answered. "He there? This is Grady Service," he said.

"Yes, Mr. Service. I am walking the phone to him now."

"I dreamed you would call," the old man said happily, and Service cringed. He was no more comfortable with Native American spirituality than the mumbo jumbo spouted by white churches and creeds.

"Did you actually *know* Lakotish?" Service asked.

"Yes, as a boy, and until he went to become a warrior. I don't know him now."

"Was Lakotish a woodworker?"

"He carved wood as a boy, loved finding the spirit in each piece he made."

"Totem poles?"

Crow's Flesh chuckled quietly. "We *Anishinaabe* don't carve totems poles, except for tourists, but the word *totem* is from the Ojibwe, *o-doo-den-an*. The French heard this and called it *acoutem,* and the English changed *acoutem* to *totem.* When he was a boy Lakotish carved small, but not large, *o-doo-den-an.* Lakotish was a clever boy," Crow's Flesh said, "but secretive and difficult to warm to."

"Thank you."

Friday called again. "We're taking off. Jen says the attack took place in the kitchen area. We've got blood traces, but not a whole lot. There were spongy fragments in a crack in the kitchen counter. Jen thinks the material is neoprene, and she's guessing five to seven millimeters."

"Waders?" Service asked.

"Great guess. Or, a very old wet suit," Friday said.

"You're sure there're no trees near the trailer?"

"Not near, but there are some trees, and there's an old wooden ladder back there, leaning against a tree."

"Have someone climb up and look at the branches, specifically for abrasions and cuts, chips, signs of extreme stress that are not natural. Also, where do the trees lead?"

"Lead?"

"Never mind the last," he corrected himself.

Friday's next call came as Service neared Slippery Creek. "Bunch of marks, grooves, like something got dragged up and over," she reported.

"Better block off the whole tree area."

"You think our guy is Tarzan?" she joked.

66

Sunday, January 18

NEGAUNEE

Her sister unable to babysit, Friday brought Shigun to the office that morning. The kid went directly to Limpy, crawled onto his lap, and went to sleep. Service rolled his eyes.

Once again they pounded all the cases and evidence methodically, and Service presented their findings/theory from WoJu, all the while thinking more about the timing of Lupo's death, now officially a homicide, not yet made public. *I questioned Varhola about knowing Lupo on Wednesday afternoon, and a day later Lupo is a murder vick? Coincidence?*

Jen Maki and crew were back in the trees at Carlock's trailer. Service put her on the line with Allerdyce, who explained what to look for above the ground. *So damn many pieces now.* Service made a note to hit WoJu again, take yet another look out there. Carlock's license with the Secretary of State put her weight at 245. *Big woman: Pretty amazing for someone to move that much dead weight without some kind of help, mechanical or human. Of course, such strength wasn't totally unknown. Varhola had lifted and moved a quintal like it had been a loaf of bread. Boy.*

Not just WoJu. Service suddenly realized they also needed to look at the Little Huron River site differently. There were trees everywhere there, and in close proximity to the trailer where they had found the child's remains.

Service said, "I think we ought to call Senior Special Agent Pincock. She deals with this crap all the time."

Friday glared at him. "And I don't? I'm a homicide detective."

"That's not what I meant."

Not normal for her to be touchy like this. Pressure coming from her chain of command? He'd have to ask later, if he could remember.

Friday steered the discussion to Varhola, told the others, "He's a person of interest. We can get him in for a voluntary interview, but a prosecutor will need to be on board with that approach. There's no evidentiary link to him at this point."

Service said, "Our source at Nett Lake told me that the man Bellator came here to hunt Lakotish. I have one source who has identified Lakotish as Varhola. My read on this is that Lakotish switched identities with Varhola in Vietnam. His line infantry unit moved him over to Special Services after his platoon sergeant caught him with a bag of Vietnamese heads and hands. Bodies were found, too, many of them with cuts along their spines, same as the victims here. The real Varhola was found headless and handless and burned beyond recognition in a fire. ID was based solely on blood type. The two men had the same blood type.

"We've gotten wood chips from every body site, except Lupo's, and these chips are from a rare wood. Varhola has a workshop filled with tools whose handles have been made from that wood. The priest claims his predecessor made the tools and he inherited them. It should be possible to find parishioners who knew the previous priest and if he was a woodworker. The Bois Forte Chippewas think Lakotish is a windigo. It all fits, more or less."

Friday shook her head. "It's still all circumstantial and theoretical. There's no convincing physical evidence linking Varhola to the vicks."

"I'd still get him in here and talk to him," Treebone suggested. "Officially declare him a person of interest and see how he reacts."

"I think we should talk to Pincock," Service pressed.

This time Friday didn't snap at him. "You trust her?"

"I do." Treebone and Noonan nodded agreement.

"We need to hit all the sites again, look for neoprene traces, if that's what it is," Service said. "And find Varhola's fishing gear, including his waders." He took the tool Allerdyce had found and placed the plastic bag on the conference table.

Friday stared at the bag. "Explanation?"

"Limpy found it outside the priest's workshop. We're gonna return it to Varhola."

The State Police officer hissed. "Dammit, Grady, there's no warrant! This could fuck up the case!"

"It was found fair and square outside. There might be fingerprints."

"A good lawyer would get this excluded in a nanosecond. No link to Varhola."

"Even with prints?"

"A good lawyer would get them tossed as illegally gotten. And I wouldn't blame him." She looked Service in the eye, said slowly, "What tool?"

He took it off the table. They'd have to return it to the priest and apologize.

• • •

JoJo Pincock was waiting for the phone call. Service had alerted her the night before.

Friday went through the developments and the FBI agent listened.

"Moving on," Friday said, "Lupo was a big strong man. It would take someone with equivalent strength to take him down. Varhola is of average size at best, but very strong in the shoulders and arms."

Service then related the quintal episode, but Pincock seemed uninterested. "What did Varhola say about Lupo?"

"Self-promoter, glorifying his ego."

"That's it?" Pincock asked.

"We told him that thanks to Lupo, we have a suspect, and an arrest is near."

Pincock said, "Lupo's murder could be a gauntlet thrown at you. Tell me what else you saw when you visited Varhola."

Service related what he had seen, and Friday did the same. Then Allerdyce got up from the table and walked around, reeling off every item in the workshop like he was looking at a photograph in front of him. Service was fairly certain he was experiencing a perfect example of eidetic memory, something he'd heard of but never witnessed. *No wonder the old bastard was so good in the woods. He saw and remembered everything!*

When Allerdyce finished, Pincock said, "You have a highly organized killer at work. The priest fits the pillar-of-the-community portion of the profile. The eat-off-the-floor workshop shows organization, perhaps even a degree of obsessive-compulsive disorder. You need to put your suspect under a microscope. All your bodies have been dumped, the killing done at yet other sites. You need to find where those other sites are."

"Multiple sites?" Friday asked.

"I didn't mean to imply that," Pincock said. "With an organized killer, I'm thinking there's one secure site or area where he can come and go with relative assurance that there will be no interference."

"Off the beaten path," Service said.

"That doesn't mean in the boonies," Pincock said. "Could be an old building. Could be anything that others have little or no access to."

"Church land," Allerdyce said. "Churches and sky pilots up here got proppity all over place in U.P."

"That's a reasonable starting point," Pincock said. "Are you officially asking the agency in, Detective Friday?"

"Not yet, but I'm also not ruling it out," Friday said.

"That's cool; you can get ahold of me anytime. But would you permit me to make some inquiries from the Bureau? I'm talking low level with my own contacts, off the books."

"I don't know," Friday said. "Explain."

"If the Lakotish-Varhola switch is real and the evidence is there to support it, the army and Pentagon will be caught in a situation where they've been sitting on top of—and protecting—a possible serial killer, and mixing up the identity of war remains. The church has a problem, too. All of those problems with pedophile priests, and now a serial killer impersonating one. The DOD and Rome are a lot alike. They don't like airing their dirty laundry, don't even want to admit they have any, and the golden rule for both organizations is to protect the group first."

"They won't stonewall?" Friday asked.

"They will as long as they can, or if the issue goes the wrong way, but there are ways to encourage cooperation," the federal agent told them.

"I'm reluctant," Friday said.

"I might be, too, in your shoes," Pincock admitted, "but what if they're sitting on evidence that could help you clear the case?"

"The key word in that statement is *if*." Friday looked over at Service, who nodded at her.

"Okay," Friday told Pincock, "low-level, non-threatening, off-the-books contacts you know you can trust."

"Only the ones I use when I'm on a data-mining expedition," the senior special agent said.

Pincock still on the line, Treebone said, "He's impersonating and assuming the identity of another person—that's a Class B felony in Michigan, and probably every state he's been in. I'm guessing the multiple-state angle brings federal interest into the mix. If nothing else, we can haul him in on this and use it to squeeze him."

Friday said, "My intuition tells me there's more to this."

Pincock added, "Mine, too."

"Sounds like a duck," Treebone said.

"Not hearing a convincing quack yet," Friday said, terminating the meeting and the phone call.

67

Monday, January 19

MARQUETTE

They met in Service's old office in the regional DNR building everyone called the Roof because of its odd architecture. Between his office and the Forestry Divison, there were plat books for every county in the U.P., and all sorts of other maps, from topographical to harvest scans.

Over breakfast at the Roof, they debated going over to the Marquette County Register of Deeds office, but Service ruled it out, calling it a fishing expedition at this point. Besides, he wasn't sure Marquette County was anywhere in the solution. Last night he had sat down with his own maps and marked body-recovery sites, and it hit him that they were watching a slow, mostly western migration from where the first bodies had been found. Lamb Jones's abduction and Campau's were outside the flow in that sense, and so too was Norma Carlock, though her body remained missing. Lupo's murder? Hard to fit that in, too, but still the feeling persisted that events were moving westward. Where Carlock's body turned up might tell them if the trend was real or not. Maybe. His gut was telling him the answer was further west, probably not even in Baraga County, but beyond, in Houghton, Ontonagon, or Iron, but this was pure speculation at this point.

Friday joined them, and the first thing out of her mouth was "You think he'll kill again?"

Service hoped not but had no answer for her.

"You guys want me here?" Friday asked.

"Stay," Service said.

"What are we looking for?"

"Any property owned by the Church of the Wilderness Redeemer. It'll probably be abbreviated CWR, or something along those lines. Tight squeeze in plat books."

"Baraga County?" she asked.

"I'm guessing something west. Could be Iron, Onty, Houghton—just don't know yet. The body finds seem to be working slowly westward."

"Does that tell us something?'"

"Maybe if he has the safe place Pincock described, he may be working closer to it to keep from getting caught too far from his hidey-hole. The further from home he ranges, the more risks he runs."

Friday took the Baraga plat book; Service took Houghton/Keewenaw. Allerdyce took Ontonagon, Treebone took Iron, and Noonan took Gogebic, though Service thought that might be a bit too far.

Private land showed as white in the plat books. Last names of owners were indicated, along with a number representing the total acres owned by that person, anything five acres or more in size. Where lots were physically separated, arrows linked them. No sign of Varhola's name, or Lakotish, or the church.

"Leased land will show in the landowner's name, not the lessee's," Service told them.

"Leased?" Friday asked.

"Right; a lot of private land up here is owned by people who live a long way from here, so they lease out hunting or fishing rights to help cover their tax bills. That way there's no negative effect on their cash flow, and the value keeps appreciating. Lumber and power companies offer public right-of-ways, or get a tax break from the State if they list the land under the Commercial Forest Act, opening it to public use. You can hunt, fish, trap, camp, do whatever you want on most CFA land, and you don't need written or verbal permission. You can just go and do it, treating it pretty much like it's public land."

"But leases are different," Friday said. "Owners might pop in at any time. I doubt he's using leased property."

Her thinking made sense to Service. "No security."

"Probably not public land, either," she added. "Same concern. He's got to have privacy, a secure refuge, something he alone controls, a place he can be sure about, Pincock told us."

Service heard her. She was right. It had to be private property, and if not in the woods, something in a town.

Friday added, "It's got to be a place where he belongs, where he has total control, and a place where he blends in. If people see him, they'd think nothing of it because he belongs there."

Varhola's interest in trout fishing. "I'm gonna guess there'll be good trout water either on the property or close to it." The names of places in the plat book fascinated him. Flying Snake Lodge. Fat Jack's Deer Chops Club. Brasiere Bay Association. The Red Hot Antler Club. The Ecumenicals.

Actually, the plat said ECU. Service had to flip to the index of owners in back to find the full name, "Ecumenicals."

"What's this?" he asked, showing the book to Friday. She had no idea.

Service called Shark Wetelainen, put the conference phone on speaker, and asked him. "Plat book, extreme south Houghton County, property called the Ecumenicals?"

"Oh, yeah. What about it?"

"You know it?"

"Yeah, sure, some dandy little brookie cricks down that way. Methodists and Presbyterians bought the property together in the seventies for a rustic church camp for kids."

"What about bead-shakers?" Noonan asked.

"Catholics," Friday whispered loudly to the retired Detroit detective.

"Yeah, they once had a camp there, but run out of money to operate, eh."

"Where?" Service asked.

"Gimme a minute," Shark said, and came back rattling pages. He read off the township, section, and range. The area was west of Sidnaw and labeled DOM.

Service looked it up. Diocese of Marquette.

"Accessible by road?" Service asked his friend.

"Somewhere in there is dinky road, I guess, mebbe traces of old tote roads, but youse don't use 'em, they grow over, eh. The woods prolly took whatever was there. It don't take long for Mother Nature ta get her own way," he added, then asked, "Why the interest?"

"Filling squares on a case," Service said noncommittally as he noticed a 40-acre parcel marked R King Trust. To Shark, "What's R King Trust?"

"Oh, yeah, that would be Regis King Trust, pastor of the Church of the Holy Shepherd in Baraga."

"There's a church by that name in Baraga? I never heard of it."

"What's that church up in Assinins called?" Shark asked.

"Church of the Wilderness Redeemer."

"Yeah, sure, that's the one. Ownership, she got transferred. County don't pay much attention to land off tax rolls."

"You know that property?"

"Sure, pretty good trout there. Used to be three, four cabins, big lodge hall, but she all burn down, no electricity, no running water, no indoor plumbing. Supposed to be for Indian kids, but it cost too much to run, and the church let it revert to nature."

Service thanked him and hung up. "We need to go take a look at that land."

"It seems to fit what Pincock told us to look for," Friday said.

Service looked at the others. "Three veeks: Tree and Suit, Limpy in his, me in the Tahoe. Allerdyce will drop that tool back at Varhola's office," Service added, looking at Friday.

"No idea what you're talking about," she said.

68

Monday, January 19

SLIPPERY CREEK CAMP

Service dug two plastic bags of frozen venison stew from the freezer, thawed them in the microwave, and dumped the contents in a pan on the stove. Meanwhile, he mixed coleslaw with sliced almonds, raisins, dried apricots, hot pepper flakes, and green onion slivers. He dumped in most of a jar of Marzetti slaw dressing and mixed everything together. Two frozen baguettes went into the oven, and he put a case of Miller Lite on the front stoop to take advantage of nature's fridge.

Tree and Noonan tromped in behind him, muddy and tired, shed their clothes, grabbed beers, and flopped down in their long johns. Allerdyce came along later as Service was serving the stew. Limpy grabbed fresh coffee and joined them.

"Make your delivery?" Service asked.

Sharp nod of the chin. "Done what youse tole me."

Service watched the old man play with his coffee cup, sensed he had more to say. "Varhola there?"

"Up in house, mebbe. Shop, she was dark."

Service looked at the others. "You too?"

"Tire," Allerdyce said before the others could answer.

Service looked at the old man. "What?"

"Foun' tire."

"Where?" Service felt his blood pressure spike.

"Don't get crimp in youse's panties. Was out back behind woodshop."

"And?"

"Like tracks dat day out Bloody Crick."

"Where Johnstone's tracks disappeared?"

"I'd say."

"How do you know?"

"Jes' know, is all."

"What kind of tire?"

"Snow-skinny, wrote down name." He took slip of paper from his pocket. "Nookie."

"What the hell is a Nookie tire?" Service asked. The old man made him tired.

Allerdyce handed the piece of paper to Service. It read NOKIAN HAKKAPELIITTA.

"T'ink dat one dem 'pensive Finnlander tires," Allerdyce added.

"You think these were the tracks at Bloody Creek?"

"Wore real bad. Must'a got new ones."

Service looked to the others for help but spoke to Limpy. "Nokian equals . . . Nookie?"

"Could," Allerdyce said.

"How *many* tires?"

"Jes' one I found."

"Where exactly?"

"T'irty yard back shop, in willows."

"Badly worn?"

"Such t'in tread, she no good no more, 'specially for snow."

"You *know* this tire? I never even heard the brand name before."

"Seen in book one time, got Mork's Code pattern, letter F tread, dot-dash-dot."

Dot-dash-dot? "You mean, *Morse* Code?"

"Jes' said dat: dot-dash-dot."

"You saw the same pattern at Bloody Creek?"

"Yeah, just din't 'member till see dat tire back woodshop."

"Somebody sells these in the U.P.?"

Allerdyce shrugged. Service got his phone book, called Cully Klock, owner of Cheaper Tires in Gwinn.

"Cully, Grady Service. You ever hear of Nokian Tires?"

"Finnish company; what about 'em? Don't see 'em much around here."

"Who sells them?"

Service heard Klock loudly exhale. "Pretty sure Griz Harris will know. Owns World Tire Wholesale, down to Tee-Cee."

"You know Harris?"

"Met 'im coupla times."

"Has a store in Traverse City?"

"Yeah, over by the airport."

"Thanks, Cully."

Service called Elton Sape, a hard-charging CO in Grand Traverse County.

"Sape, Service. What you up to?"

"Clipping my toenails. Why?"

"Do you know the owner of World Tire Wholesale?"

"Sure, Griz Harris. What's that old fart done?"

"Nothing. We need his help on a case. Can you call him and ask if he sells Nokian Hakkapeliitta tires? If he does, ask him to go to his office and get a list of anyone in the U.P. who bought that brand from him in the past five years. Think he'll cooperate?"

"No problem. He's a good guy. He'll grumble and I'll grumble and then he'll do what we want."

"This could be real important, Elton."

"I'm all over that shit," the CO said. "Bump you back. Harris lives way out on the Old Mission. Will take him a while to get to town. Been snowing like an SOB here all day."

"Thanks."

Service rubbed his eyes and looked at Allerdyce. "Anything else from Blood Creek that you forgot to mention?"

"Yeah, I was t'inkin'—Vulva wagon."

"Vulva? You mean a Volvo picked up Johnstone?"

Allerdyce pointed at his stew bowl. "Can I eat? All dis grub get cold, eh."

The old man defied all categories. "Anything else?"

"Nope."

Service got out the plat books, stared at the Ecumenicals property in south Houghton County.

Allerdyce wiggled his fingers, his mouth full, and Service slid the book over to him. The old man chewed loudly with smacking sounds, said with a full mouth, "Used ta be cathouse on dat proppity. Compete wit dat cathouse over west Kenton, up hill from Jumbo, eh. Dat one burn down, jes' chimley left now."

"There was a cathouse on the property owned by the Ecumenicals?"

Allerdyce nodded. "Still dere fiffy-one, I come back Korea. Nice, clean girls."

Service studied the man. "You were in Korea?"

"Inch'on, took fiffy bit in side leg, took me up Nipland, fix me up, send me back my spittoon."

"Outfit?" Treebone asked.

"First Marine Divison, Fifth Marines. I get back down wit' da boys, fight nort' 'til Red Chinks join Red Gooks. Had pull back fiffy miles, fight hull damn way. Spittoon down to five men. Carry our el-tee last ten miles. Assopolis guy, twinny-one, no bullshit, fair, do your job, help your fuckin' buddies, helluva man. Cancer ate 'im dead nineteen and fiffy-nine. Survive chinks and gooks, onny den die cancer."

Service thought he detected a choking sound and some tears welling.

"Dey send me hospital We't Coa't. Gotted da ice bite fingers and toot-sies, last few days. Rifles frozed up. El-tee tell us tie K-Bars to mittens, fight by hand, keep moving. No warm food, whole mont', no good sleep, no clean socks, no baths. Cou'n't hardly walk. I come back U.P., go cathouse up dat proppity, fix me up wid big girl fum over Ironwood, good gal."

The room was still until Tree said, "*Semper fi,* you racist old motherfucker."

Allerdyce's head rolled like a bobblehead as he wheezed and coughed.

How long have I known this man? Never heard any of this, never suspected, which might now explain his old man's alleged affection for a fellow vet. Limpy Allerdyce: Brother Marine. Good God. Focus.

"Great big ole log cabin, burnt down, and dat was dat, had go elsewhere."

"When the hell were you born?"

" 'Round nineteen and twinny-nine. Join up Marines forty-nine when I twinny. Next year my butt over dere bloody Korea."

Allerdyce is seventy-nine? He looks older, moves around younger. "Other buildings on the property?"

"Not den."

"Been there since?"

"Once. Had t'ree new cabin, big barn."

"How long ago was this?"

"Long time back."

Service retrieved the plat book.

"You told me about a Czech—Ulupov, right?"

Allerdyce nodded. "Yep."

"What lake was that?"

"Corbin Lake, last I hear. Don't like dat guy," the old man added.

"Think we could talk to him?" Service looked at the plat, saw no property listed for anyone named Ulupov. Corbin Lake was a few miles east of the Ecumenicals.

"Ain't much of a talker. Likes ta shoot firs' sometimes," Allerdyce said.

"He own the property?"

"Dunno. Mebbe belonged some church in the way-back."

"Which church?"

"All same me, cross up top, Jesus guy down below."

Service called Friday and informed her.

"You gonna see this Corbin Lake guy?"

"He sounds like a real wood tick, and you know what they say."

She laughed. "No, enlighten me."

"Wood ticks have big eyes."

Elton Sape called back. "I'm with Griz Harris, and he wants to talk at you."

New low, growly voice. "Harris."

"Service."

"I sold one set of Nokian Hakkapeliitta tires last summer. I don't carry the tires here and had to order them. These are an old model made only two or three years. Had to get them from the home office in Finland."

"Customer's name?"

"Flirty, flitty broad named Jones."

"Lamb Jones?" Service felt his heart racing.

"Linda Jones, my 'puter tells me."

"Marquette address?"

"Green Garden Road."

Lamb for sure. "You remember her?"

"Don't tell my wife, but sure do. Good-looking, friendly, and offering it up, not that I could do nothing."

"She alone?"

"Nope, with a guy in a Red Silverado. Loaded the tires myself. Guy in the truck never said a thing, never introduced himself."

"Did she say the tires were for her?"

"Nope, something about getting them for her uncle."

"Did the uncle order them?"

"I guess, only I got her name wrote down, not no uncle."

"How'd she pay?"

"Cash money."

Who owns a red Silverado? He called Friday and told her about this development.

Friday said, "Quigley drives a Red Silverado. I'd better visit him tomorrow."

"We still in circumstantial land?" Service asked.

"Yes, dear, but we may be getting closer. What's your next step?"

"Hit the woods, try to talk to a wood tick."

Tuesday, January 20

CORBIN LAKE, HOUGHTON COUNTY

The temperature was pegged at 7 degrees, tiny snowflakes fluttering straight down, no wind to divert them, six or eight new inches on the ground, and more falling at a steady, leisurely pace. Friday called as they drove west from Marquette. She told Service that Quigley had acted like a wolf in a trap, head down, tail between his legs. Yes, he had driven Lamb down to Traverse City—as a favor. No, he didn't know who the tires were for, or care, but she might have said something about an uncle over near Covington, and yes, they had overnighted at a bed-and-breakfast in Harbor Springs.

"You explain about Varhola?"

"He said we lack physical evidence, but he'll push through search warrants if we ask and insist."

"Physical evidence, such as?"

"He refused to specify."

"Gaming us?"

"I don't think so. Where are you guys?"

"Limpy and I are east of Sidnaw. Tree and Suit are headed to other sites to look for more neoprene. Allerdyce and I will have to hike in to see the Czech. It's fairly high ground between Booth and Corbin Lakes."

"How far?"

"About a mile in and a mile out."

"Snowing?"

"Yep. Eight fresh down, more falling. We'll lug snowshoes on our packs, but I doubt we'll need them. There's not much of a base here."

"Call when you get out, and be careful."

"Got our 800s," he said. "We'll be fine."

• • •

Allerdyce wore a Marmot down parka, dull and black, with a pair of old bear-paw snowshoes. Service had modified metal bear-paws on his pack. He took the shotgun instead of the rifle. Not a bad load. He checked his compass, saw they were northbound by a few degrees above east. "Thought we were headed to Corbin Lake."

"Nort' bit fum 'ere, up on da high groun'."

Service guessed they'd find a cabin on the south exposure of a hill, and he was close. They moved along the crest of a long sharp ridge that ran east to west, paralleling cedar swamps and tag alders below them. "We get close, we'll pull up and figure out our next step," he told the poacher, who seemed to be able to maintain a hard pace no matter what. *Seventy-nine, my ass.*

The shack was small, made of logs aged black, had been in place a long time. Had a rotten-looking shingled roof with a steep pitch. There was a black tar-paper sweat lodge in a clearing just to the east. Looked like a dark Twinkie, and as old as the cabin. A long woodshed was piled with neat rows of firewood. Two other sheds, one metal, one with smoke tendrils fighting up into the snow. They weren't seventy-five yards away, and both put trees between them and any trouble.

Allerdyce took off his chopper and blew on his hand. "Las' time dis galoot got two, mebbe t'ree dogs in dere."

Service cringed. "I don't hear dogs."

"Best kind defend the proppity. Dey jes' suddenny dere, get youse by t'roat."

"What breed?"

"Wolfie crosses, last I seen. Bruisers."

Grady Service felt a chill. "We'll go in about ten yards apart. You call to him and ask him out." Service's boots felt like they were weighted with cement. *Fear,* he told himself. *Use it. Stay calm.*

The dogs came out of the tree line three abreast, ears back, heads up, ruffs swollen. A man came out of the larger shed, the one with the smoke, at the same time. Wiry, small, clean-shaven, faded camo, rust-colored Carhartt bibs, Pac boots, blood on his hands. The man ignored Allerdyce, made a clucking sound, and the dogs melted away.

"You are the big dee-en-arr preek, Service, the one they talk about," the man said. "Is about time you come finally to do your work."

"Sir?" Service countered.

"Yes, of course," the man said. "The holy impostor in the Kaisits."

"Kaisick Holes," Allerdyce interpreted, his voice a strained rasp.

Service knew about the so-called Kai-sits, but had never been into them. It was an area of deep sinkholes and foliage grown so tight it was dark as night even midday. It was said you had to belly-crawl to get through some places. "I am Service. What holy impostor?" He was glad the dogs had ducked away, but guessed they were close and watching events.

"The pretender from Assinins."

"A lot of people up there."

"Varhola, the priest."

"What about him?"

"Unspeakables everyone talks of."

"How does this concern the law?" Service asked.

"He brings the women."

Service felt his heart do a stutter beat. "You've seen women in the Kai-sits?"

"Yes, of course."

"Grown women or girls, and with the priest?"

"Yes, of course," the man said.

"Brings them where?"

"Old church land."

"Ecumenicals?"

"Yes, of course, but he prefer Kai-sits most times."

"You know where he takes them?"

The man nodded.

"On foot?"

"Has weehicle—Svedsky."

Swedish? "Saab, Volvo, something else?"

"Wolwo."

"New model or old?"

"They all look like square box. Old, I think."

"Square shape, you say?"

"Yes, like box."

"Color?"

"This changes. Now is white, long kind."

"Wagon?"

"*Jo.*"

"He drives them here in the Volvo?"

"*Jo,* he keeps parked here. Comes on four-wheeler."

"Why haven't you told anyone this before now?"

"I am telling you now."

Allerdyce coughed. "Comrade."

A knife magically appeared in Ulupov's hand, a deadly-looking Finnish *puukko,* and the two men stared each other down. Service went to the man, grabbed his wrist, and took the knife. "Let's get this little item out of the formula."

"This insolent pig has insulted me," Ulupov said. "I fought Soviets. I am good Catholic, not communist."

Got to calm things. "What did you do in Czechoslovakia?"

"Teacher of young minds."

"But you don't teach here. Your English is good."

"Is not important," the man said. "You come to do something about dem priest or not?"

Service walked over to his companion and gave Allerdyce a furtive push to create more space between the three of them. "Is there a license plate on the Volvo?" he asked Ulupov.

"*Ne,* he is keep on wall in shelter."

"But this is Varhola's Volvo?"

"Was Dede's first."

"I don't know Dede."

"Father Andre Beauclerc; his friends called him Dede."

"The priest before Varhola?"

"Yes."

"How did he die?"

"His heart stopped beating."

"Before Varhola arrived?"

"*Jo,* two years."

"Did Dede spend time in the woods, out here?"

"*Ne,* he was shepherd of his people."

"And a woodworker?"

Ulupov shrugged. "Dede had no skills. His people looked after him, and he watched over their souls."

"Did Father Beauclerc keep the Volvo at the rectory?"

"By the church, *jo*."

"But Varhola keeps it here. Did he build a garage?"

"Yes, of course."

Service triggered his 800 to talk to Friday. "Can you check with the Secretary of State on an emergency basis, see if there was an old Volvo registered to Father Andre Beauclerc, or to Varhola's church?" He spelled the late priest's name for her.

"I'll have Lansing run it."

"Don't know how our service will be out here for the 800 or the cells. We're sort of off the grid."

"Got a year or model?"

"Old is all we know. And white, but it changes colors."

"*Really?*" she asked, excitement in her voice.

"That's affirmative."

"Computers are having some problems today. Might be late before I can get through."

"Never fails," he said.

"Call you when I get something."

Service turned to Ulupov. "Can you tell us how to find this Volvo?"

"*Nemozny*—impossible. I must insist to show you."

Tuesday, January 20

KAISICK HOLES, HOUGHTON COUNTY

It was past 10 p.m. by the time they got back to the Tahoe. Service discovered he still had Ulupov's knife and tossed it in the way-back. He dug out MREs for them to eat, put water in a bottle in the flameless heater that would fire on magnesium dust, salt, and iron dust; he put the pouches in their boxes and waited for two meals to heat. He and Allerdyce would share, Ulupov would get the other one. The Czech moved with the same tireless gait as the old poacher and also wore snowshoes.

Allerdyce used a Pocket Rocket camp stove to heat water for instant tea and made a cup for each man, emptying a honey packet into each.

They ate quickly, without talking.

"How far from here?" Service asked the Czech.

"Six kilometers."

Service converted in his head. *Four miles.* "Terrain?"

"You want to drive close?"

"Can we?"

"Off M-28 we can get within two kilometers, all flat, easy walking there. From here, hills and very steep, deep cuts, not good walking."

They tossed their trash into the truck, got in, and drove west on M-28 to where Forest Highway 1200 cut south, but there Ulupov directed them north on a good gravel two-track. When they reached a Y, he had Service veer right, almost due north. Another half-mile and Ulupov said, "Okay, iss good here." There was an old tote road mostly grown over, virgin snow, untouched. "Two kilometers," their guide said, pointing.

A while later the Czech said, "Here."

Service stopped and called Denninger on the 800. "You outside?"

"For a while."

"We're west of Sidnaw. You see us on the AVL?"

"Got you stopped, engine off."

"Just a sec," he said, turning the key back on for a moment.

"Got you for sure."

"Yep. Come sit on our vehicle if you don't mind. If we need you, you can drive to us by following our tracks. There's three of us, and it's relatively flat and easy going to where we are now."

"Moving your way," Denninger radioed. "One Two One Niner, clear."

"Distance from here?" Service asked Ulupov, unslinging his shotgun.

"Half-kilometer, no more than one."

"Road?"

"Old."

The Czech led them forward to the west and down a steep defile. The tote looked like it went up to the trees and stopped. Ulupov kept them moving to the end and stopped. "I go no more. Your business, I must not do more." This said, the Czech turned northeast and briskly walked away. No time to argue.

Service tapped Allerdyce's shoulder and urged him ahead. "Let's see what we've got."

Ulupov was right. Finding the place with verbal directions alone would have been impossible.

The structure was roofed, low, hard to see even when you were almost on top of it. The two men stopped to slow their breathing. There was a clear space at one end of the building and an old door. *Garage: Not room for a full-size Ford truck, but high enough for a Volvo.*

"You go left, I'll go right, meet in back," Service said.

Allerdyce moved immediately. The snow was coming heavier. Service slid along the east wall, heard a dull sharp noise, and stopped to listen. *No more sound. Go slowly.*

He peeked around the corner at the end. Allerdyce said "Over 'ere" in a low, throaty voice. "Door on my side, window broked," Limpy whispered. "Somebody mebbe tried break in, eh."

Service shook his head in the dark. *Guess who.* "Tracks?"

"Nah," Allerdyce said. "You check in, I go bit nort', down trail."

Service couldn't see a trail, but said, "Okay, but don't get too far."

• • •

An hour later Allerdyce returned, sliding up to Service inside the garage with no sound. The Volvo was inside, locked. "Don't touch anything," he told the old violator.

"Din't."

Service had given the structure a thorough look. "Where the hell have you been?"

"Trail run mebbe two hunnert yard to trees, steep drop, den no trail. I know dis place, sonny."

"You do?"

"Heard of 'er, eh. Old Finndians Sidnaw hunt big bucks down 'ere, late in year when snow come and deers migrape south. Don't use no ground trails. Dey climbed up trees, lop off branches, make trails can be used all winter. Could go miles, I heard."

"*Up* in the trees?"

"You betcha. Got dose glory pines mixed all up with udder trees, all tangle to hell, mebbe t'irty feet up—can move okay up dere, I hear."

"Thought you didn't know if there were glory pines over this way."

"Said never seen, and I ain't," the old man said in his own defense. "Dis stuff run for miles. Can go long, long way. I t'ink youse tell me go climb up look 'round, follow me, and we meet up, okay?"

"No way."

"Just to look. Find somepin', I wait for youse."

Service looked around the garage, shining his light. He saw snowshoes on the wall, but no tracks. "Okay," he told the man. "But just a look-see, and if you find anything, stop there and wait. You've got your 800. Be on it."

Allerdyce nodded, left him.

Service used his SureFire to locate three old Michigan license plates nailed to a wall beam, got out his notebook, recorded the numbers and years. The most recent was 1982. There was a good four feet on either side of the Volvo. Not much overhead space, but side to side was good. Service moved up along the Volvo, checked the right front. Black specks on the dirt, lots of them. The headlight was shattered, plastic gone, the fender crinkled, the grill pushed in. Service took off his gloves, wet his finger, probed the black specks. *Blood. How fast does cold degrade DNA? No idea; another deficiency in my knowledge.* He took some specks for samples and put them in an evidence bag, took photographs of everything, and decided he had probably found the vehicle that had killed the Minnesota man.

A voice on the 800 said, "Youse up dere, sonny?"

"Yes."

"Okay, I been puttin' up dem bright eyes. Come morning, t'ink she still be real dark inside da trees—like monkey's ass at night. Put light on eye-tacks, find me easy, okay?"

"How will you see?"

"Don't worry, sonny. Not no problem."

Service guessed the old man had infrared and maybe even a thermal imager in his pack. "Youse use name your old girlie name, security challenge, okay?" Allerdyce said.

Nantz. Service almost choked on her name. Service toggled his 800. "One Two One Niner, Twenty Five Fourteen. You there?"

"Affirmative."

"I'm coming out alone. Bump Friday on the cell. Tell her I've got the Volvo. Have her collect Tree and Noonan, and Jen Maki. They should dress warm and bring bear-paws. Call your sergeant and tell him we need him here, too. If there are any overtime issues, don't worry. I've got it covered. Copy?"

"Affirmative, One Two One Niner, clear."

He was grateful Denninger hadn't asked any questions. He took a look at Allerdyce's tracks, dropped a GPS reading for the garage, and headed back to meet Denninger.

He found her parked by the Tahoe. He got into his truck and uncased his rifle, re-cased the shotgun, took off his pack, and put the rifle and pack in her backseat and got in with her. It was almost too warm with the engine running, the heat on.

"They're all rolling west," she reported. "Tree and Noonan are meeting Friday at Humboldt, will follow her. May take a good two hours. Willie will be here soon. Whole western and central U.P. is getting clobbered by a storm. They're saying twelve to sixteen more tonight. What the hell is going on?"

He filled her in as best he could, then went over and started the Tahoe and turned on the lights so incoming vehicles would have a target to shoot for. If necessary they could put both trucks' spots into the treetops as a signal to the help coming.

"You think this is the hit-and-run vehicle?"

He gave her the evidence bag with the black flakes from the garage. "Make sure Maki gets these. Might be blood."

She tucked the evidence bag into a larger bag on the seat beside her, and Service wrote a note saying he had transferred evidence. Dani signed it.

"How'd you get onto way the hell out *here?*"

"Not sure myself." *Intersection of weirdness maybe. I feel old and drained.* He took a deep breath and exhaled slowly.

"I've got plenty of fresh coffee," she said.

"Bless you," he said.

He called Friday on the 800. "You remember the woman we talked to, from the East Coast?"

"Affirmative."

"I'm going to give you a name, one time only. Got a pen?"

"Go."

"Uniform-Lima-Uniform-Papa-Oscar-Victor, no read-back, break."

"Got it."

"One more word. Nationality is Czech, that is Charlie-Zulu-Echo-Charlie-Hotel—copy?"

"Affirmative."

"We need all available information—wake people up, rattle cages. How're the roads, break?"

"They suck."

"We have the vehicle," he told her.

"On the way," she said calmly.

"Hurry," he said. "Clear."

71

Tuesday, January 20

KAISICK HOLES

Jen Maki looked half asleep, mumbled "Blood" when she saw the evidence bag from the garage.

"DNA still good?" Service asked.

"Maybe. Is this all you got?"

"No, there's a lot more on the vehicle."

"We should be okay, but I can at least get a blood type. I've got an ABO sample kit. That ought to give us some direction. The vick was AB negative, which is about one percent of the population."

"You don't need a fresh blood draw?"

"Ordinarily and ideally, sure, but if I can get enough, I can liquefy it and test that."

Celt had been first to join them. Then Maki, Friday, Treebone, and Noonan.

Down in the garage they helped Maki set up her equipment and add extra lighting. Jen Maki grinned when she saw the blood on the Volvo, and fifteen minutes later announced, "AB negative—certainty of ninety percent, worst case."

Service looked at Friday. "Call your people, have them pick up Varhola for questioning. If he's not there, have them sit on his place. You think Quigley should hear about this?"

Quigley will hear, but it's lousy cell coverage here; I'll have to move," she said. "Where's Allerdyce? I haven't seen him," she added as she walked toward her vehicle, Service beside her.

When he explained where the old man was, she said simply, "Have you got enough people?"

"For this. Bump me on the 800 if they grab Varhola."

She patted his rump and jogged toward her own Tahoe.

Service briefed the others on what lay ahead. Only Treebone had a question. "You trust Allerdyce?"

"No choice. We'll hike down to the tree line. Bring your snowshoes, tied to your packs." Service handed his shotgun to Tree. "Limpy's marked the way. Everybody got their IR? There are tack markers. They should show up like spotlights under infrared. We don't move from one tack until our point finds the next one. Dani, you're point, then me, Willie, Suit, and Noonan. Slow and easy. Added security: Our challenge word is 'Slow.' Response word is 'Roller.' Slow Roller—everybody got that?"

"Allerdyce?" Tree asked.

"He knows."

"He armed?"

"Not with a firearm. He knows how to be invisible. Let's go. I'll take point to the tree line and Dani will jump to the front from there." She was younger, far more nimble.

• • •

The marker was easy to see. Service climbed up and gasped at the walkway built from tree to tree across connected and intertwined branches. Two-by-fourteen cedar planks were installed end to end. Dani came up behind him and moved down the catwalk until she found the first up-top marker.

"Got it," she said.

"Stay right there and let me get the rest of them topside with us and up to you before you move out again. You good?" he asked.

"Never better."

Denninger turned back to Service, who estimated that they had traveled three hundred yards on the catwalk before it branched. The right angle was the same planking as what they had already covered. The left branch was aspen-pole bundles, three or four each and bound with wire. "Stay right," he told Denninger, turned, and passed the word back.

Two minutes later Service heard Dani say "roller" and Allerdyce was suddenly there, swinging down to them from the branches above. Service noticed Limpy was shaking. "You all right?" he asked the poacher.

"Fiffy paces here, hit intersex. Go right twinny, dere's hut, windows blacked, built on platform. No sound inside. Generator wired to hut, not on. Go leff from intersex, go twinny-five, t'irty yard, find two platforms with what looks like freezers."

"Freezers?" Denninger queried.

"T'ree of dem. Two on one platform, one t'other."

"You look inside?" Service asked.

"Touched nothin', sonny. Deys all got spinner locks. Guessin' nummers won't be no good. Have ta break 'em off, eh."

Combination locks. "The hut have a door?"

"Yep, spinner lock dere, too."

"Just one?"

"All I seen."

"Windows?"

"One in door, one on end, smudge wit' black paint."

"How big a structure?"

"Twelve by twinny-five."

"Hang here while I get the others up and briefed."

The old man didn't protest. Service checked his watch: *Just after 0400. Four and a half hours until sunrise. No snow or light inside the trees. The snowstorm will delay light.*

The others moved ahead with Treebone hanging back to secure their six. Denninger moved up to the cabin and came back. "Two feet clearance on both sides of the shack on the platform. Got a 6,800-watt Yamaha wired to inside controls. Twelve horsepower. Tank's full."

"Look for the fuel supply," Service told Willie Celt.

Willie went and Service moved up to the cabin door. *Locked tight, built tight. What's our probable cause? Ulupov had taken off in a hurry,* Service thought. *He knows about this place, too. Of course he does, a wood tick like him. Knows about it, and doesn't want any part of it.* Service turned to Allerdyce. "Three freezers?"

"Uh-huh."

"Let's take a look. You lead."

They got to the first one and stood there in silence, Service looking and thinking. *Huge, GE, six feet by three feet high. Deep sucker.* He used his red penlight.

Built-in manufacturer's lock under the handle, and a second lock, a Yale attached to bolted steel plates. Does opening something without provable PC soil the rest? Damn law is always a tiptoe, latest interpretation by some damn court here or there. Latest he knew, PC could be based on a "fair chance of criminal activity." Private land here, or State?

Service called Friday on the 800. "Your AVL working?"

"Yep."

"You know where Jen is. Public or private?"

"Probably public," she said.

"We're about a half or three-quarters of a mile west of her. What about us?"

"All public in your direction. Any private land is east, and not that close. Got something?"

"Tree house on a platform and some freezers on platforms. Trail from where Jen is leads almost directly to here, but I don't want to piss in our punch bowl. Gonna take this slow."

"Names on anything?" she asked.

"Negative."

"Ask me, you've found illegal structures and abandoned goods on public land. That equals a free pass."

Service went to Noonan. "You've got more experience with building entry and room clearance than some of us. Go check the cabin, tell me if you think anyone's inside."

Bluesuit was back in five minutes. "Ain't nobody. It's clear. And ain't no booby traps. I did once around perimeter, no trip wires or triggers."

"Sit on the place," Service told the Detroit detective. "We're gonna deal with the freezers."

Treebone felt all around the first freezer for booby traps. "No trip wires, but that ain't sayin' there ain't no trigger on the internal lock mechanism."

Shit. Think. This place is as remote as remote gets. Somebody felt secure enough and was skilled enough to build all this shit. The Yale locks are after-thoughts, peace-of-mind dissuaders. If an internal lock is set to an explosive, why add a second lock? Mind game? Nah.

"We're gonna blow the combo locks," Service told the others. He took the shotgun from Tree. Allerdyce stepped up and jammed a stick into the combo lock to stabilize it, then stepped away.

"Everybody back but Tree and me," Service told them. Tree lit the lock with his penlight. Service knelt below, lined up the barrel, touched off a round.

The lock disappeared. His ears were ringing, though the trees seemed to have eaten most of the sound. *Weird.*

Tree leaned over him. The built-in lock was a long thin handle in the middle of the top. "Get that from below," he said, using his light to show the angle.

Service put another slug in the shotgun, lay down on his shoulder, lined up the barrel again, squeezed.

A chunk of freezer evaporated. Treebone grabbed the top and opened it, shining his light inside. "*Fuck!*" he yelped.

Service stood up, saw human hands in baskets inside the freezer. He immediately called Friday. "Parts in the first container."

"Parts?" she asked.

"You know the kind I mean."

"Varhola is at the L'Anse post. They told him he's not under arrest, just there for questioning. He's not objecting."

"We're gonna check the other freezers, then open the cabin."

Venison in the second cooler, fish in the third. Service blasted the handle off the hut door on the platform and went in with Treebone. Another freezer. Long white table under a hanging fluorescent light in the middle. There was a body on the table, covered with a black neoprene apron. The all-white table had one blue leg, which was now going to always stick in his mind. Noonan slunk from one end to the other, whispered, "Clear."

Service didn't move. Used his eyes to look around, saw a rifle hanging on the wall, guessed the caliber at .30-06 or .308. An uneasy feeling began to grow inside him. *Something's off here; something not right.*

Service lifted the apron from the body, felt his knees buckle: Kelly Johnstone lay there, fully dressed, her throat cut, head nearly severed, heart removed. No blood.

Noonan found a crowbar hanging near the rifle, used it to break open the freezer, opened the top, pointed. Service looked. Frosted human heads in baskets. No dark cop humor, deathly silence, the heavy presence of true evil crushing them all.

He went outside, told the others to stay there to preserve the site, asked Willie Celt to alert and fetch Jen Maki.

Then he radioed Friday. "Another freezer, more parts, and Kelly Johnstone's here."

"Here as in *there*? She talk to you?"

"That ship has sailed."

Silence.

"Natural causes?"

"Nope."

"I'm sending more help. Let the Troops and Jen take over. You want to interview Varhola with me?"

"I'll head that way."

"No hurry. Let's let him stew for a while."

The 800 came alive with Troop traffic.

"The Troops will take it from here," Service told the others. "Varhola's been detained." Service looked at Denninger. "Tree and Suit, you and Willie stay with this until Jen and the Troops get here."

"Got it. This Varhola is one sick fuck," Dani said to no one in particular.

Service took a deep breath. *This is not over yet. All this has to be sewn together, somehow.* "Allerdyce and I are heading to L'Anse to meet Friday."

They stopped to touch base with Jen Maki on the way out. "Dust everything in the tree house for prints, even the generator."

Out in the Tahoe, Service said to the old man, "Good job."

Allerdyce grinned.

Should feel near to closure, Service thought, *but I don't. Something's wrong here. I can feel it. We've missed something big.*

72

Tuesday, January 20

L'ANSE

"I want to move him to Marquette," Friday told Service as soon as he walked into the post. "More facilities."

"Did you call Pincock?"

"I did. She's flying in this afternoon, landing at Sawyer. She'll meet us at the jail. I talked to Quigley. No charges until Varhola lawyer's up. Quigley doesn't want to lose this one on a technicality."

"Is he talking yet?"

"Nope. Just sitting there like a bump."

The L'Anse post, Number 88, had been in place since at least 1938. Friday confided, "Major cases may want in on this."

The state police had a major case unit. Service could never figure out how they judged what cases they would take. "That a problem for you?" he asked.

She shook her head. "I just want to make sure we have the right guy."

Is she having doubts, too?

Varhola was in a gray room. He wore faded blue jeans, a gray sweatshirt, faded Chuck Taylor high-tops, white star on the ankle. He showed no emotions when they walked in and sat down. "Need any coffee, water, pop?"

"What is this about?" Varhola asked immediately, his voice tight but even.

The delay doesn't seem to have worked. Why?

Friday took a card from her pocket, read the man his rights. They hadn't discussed this, and he guessed she assumed the fake priest would be dulled and not thinking, and might not yell immediately for a lawyer.

"Am I under arrest?" the man asked, still no alarm in his voice.

"No, this is just some housework to let you know your rights," she explained. "Do you understand your legal rights as I read them to you?"

Varhola nodded.

Friday asked, "Why do you think you're here, Mr. Lakotish?"

The response was immediate, including a blush that rose to his ears, eyebrows pinched by stress, sweaty forehead, licking his lips. "I assume you brought me here to assist you. I was in bed; did they tell you that? I don't sleep well since the war."

Aiming for victimhood? This should be good. No verbal reaction to the name.

"You didn't correct me on your name," Friday told him.

Service saw him look upward. *Decision time.* "No need. I assumed this day would eventually come."

Damn unexpected immediate yield, an almost precise and calm quit-claim.

Friday followed up directly, but in an almost matter-of-fact tone. "You, Samuel Lakotish, assumed the identity of Clement Varhola in Vietnam and have used his identity ever since."

"I always wanted to be a holy man," Lakotish said.

"So you created an opportunity."

This got his attention. "No, no, the opportunity came, sad as it was, a gift from God, and I took it."

"God arranged for Father Varhola to die so you could assume his identity?"

Lakotish smiled thinly. "One does not, *must* not, contradict *Him*."

Service saw an opportunity. "Infantry before you were transferred to Special Services."

"Yes," Lakotish said.

"You were in the shit in '66."

The man nodded. "Daily, for weeks."

"How did the transfer come about?"

"Casualties, new officers; my platoon sergeant didn't like my style."

"You mean, your chopping up women and children?"

"It was war. Arty, bombs, napalm—all killed civilians and toasted or ripped them to pieces. How does face-to-face differ?"

Service said, "I don't think pilots land to collect heads."

Lakotish gripped the table. "War. Some of us were perhaps overzealous. My platoon leader encouraged me."

"But he's dead."

"Yes. God's will."

"Why did they ship you to Special Services?"

"Path of least resistance," Lakotish said. "Out of sight, out of mind. It wasn't what it appears to be from this vantage point."

Service expected some follow-up explanation, but none came. "You don't deny the allegations?"

"No. Heat of battle, fog of war."

Friday intervened. "You'll understand then, given what you did over there in the fog of war, we naturally see you for what's going on around here: mutilations, your secret Volvo garage, your tree house, and the freezers with body parts."

Hardly a ripple of reaction. "I've done nothing here. What Volvo? What garage, tree house, freezers?"

"Kaisick Holes," Service said.

"The giant sinkholes south of church property, on national forestland? I don't go there. Too easy to get lost. I have a terrible sense of direction."

Understatement on multiple levels. "But you use the church land," Service said. Statement, not question.

"Of course. The church is covered under nonprofit corporation acts, and in Michigan property must be owned and occupied. I split my time between Assinins and camp, spring through fall."

"I went to Nett Lake. A man there told me about the false Lakotish, told us Wendell John Bellator came here to hunt you. Kelly Johnstone summoned him."

"Hunt *me?* Why would Chairman Johnstone do that?" He seemed clearly astonished by this.

"Maybe she believed you're a windigo?"

"Nonsense! I'd like to hear that from her!"

"That will never happen," Friday said. "Mrs. Johnstone is dead."

He was clearly startled by this, impostor priest's eyes wide with astonishment. "I didn't know," he said, with palpable anguish.

"We have reason to believe you're responsible."

"Why!" he screamed, slamming the sides of both fists on the table. "We had a *deal.* When the Ridge clan earns federal registration, the new tribe will buy the church land, nine hundred acres for two million dollars."

Curveball? Service thought.

"Is that in writing?" Friday asked.

"It was verbal, but there was a note of discussion with the deputy register of deeds."

"When?"

Lakotish looked exasperated. "Four years ago. I can't believe this," he added.

Friday nodded, and Service stepped outside the room with her.

He said, "Seems obvious he's been preparing himself for the identity switch, not the killings and not Johnstone. That's my read. Even the Vietnam thing is clear and justified in his mind. He made no attempt to deny or evade any of it. Your thoughts?"

"Leaning your way," she said. "I know something feels off in all this, something missing. Maybe the feds can help us sort it out, but I see no point in prolonging this. I'll arrange to move him to Marquette," Friday concluded, "identify-theft charges pending."

They walked into the canteen room to find Treebone sucking one of his fingers. "What happened to you?" Service asked.

"Digging in back of your Tahoe for something to eat, stuck myself on a damn knife." Treebone held it out to him. "You need to take care of your damn junk."

Service stared. It was the *puukko* he had taken off Ulupov. The handle, he now saw in the light, was made of glory pine, same workmanship as the tool handles in Varhola's workshop. *Jesus.* It had not been apparent in the snow and dark.

"Did you watch the questioning?"

"We just got in."

"How'd you get into my truck?"

"You forgot to lock it. You're getting old, man."

"Ulupov," Service said. Friday looked at him.

"I smell a rat. This has been suddenly too easy, too fast." He set the knife on the desk. "I took that knife off the Czech when he pulled it on Limpy."

Friday looked at the knife for several seconds. "The workshop."

"Same," Service said. "We're going back there to talk to Mr. Ulupov. We need a BOLO, person of extreme interest, probably armed, and potentially dangerous. Describe as mid-sixties, slight frame, faint accent, long hair."

"I'll get more," Friday said as Service headed for the door.

73

Tuesday, January 20

L'ANSE

The State Police forensics people were still at the Kaisick Holes site, but Service managed to get one of Jen Maki's tech assistants to go to Ulupov's with them. Denninger brought the female assistant, Lauren Sestina-Gould.

Allerdyce seemed to get on pretty well with Tree and Noonan, a real two-Mutt, One-Jeff trio.

They provided all the information they could remember about the property to Willie Celt, who called it in to L'Anse to arrange for a search warrant for Ulupov's property and surrounds. They would hike in and await a call from Willie. If Ulupov was there, Celt would have to bring the paperwork. If not, they would make their search. Ulupov had pointed to Lakotish-Varhola, given them the Volvo and garage and all the rest, and inadvertently had also given them the knife. Had Tree not nicked his finger, Service knew he might have overlooked it. *What would the Czech do when he remembered that Service had his knife?* Luck and serendipity played scary roles in some criminal cases. Always had, always would. Denninger had taken the knife in an evidence bag to Jen Maki for comparison to Varhola's unique tool collection at the workshop.

Service didn't bother to look for Ulupov's snowshoe tracks coming back, but followed their own trail, wending their way through the woods to the cabin on the shoulder ridge.

No smoke, no dogs; silence, snow falling softly. Willie called and said he was being met by somebody from the court in Alberta, would take possession of the warrants and head for Corbin Lake, follow their tracks in on foot. They all stood back while Allerdyce crept the area to see what he could find. Having the old poacher with them was like having the world's best sniffing hound.

The wind began to gust. Allerdyce came back and waved them over. "Nobody dere," he reported. "He took off, but t'ink he left dead body."

They all found places to sit to wait for Celt to bring the warrants. When Celt got there, his face was flushed from exertion. They read over the warrant and decided they were good, headed in with Allerdyce leading them, crossing through an aspen field where he pointed the others toward the camp. Allerdyce took Service aside and waited for the others to move past.

There were snowmobile tracks not ten yards away and a body beginning to be covered with snow: Johnstone's son, multiple gunshot wounds stitching his torso in front. Speedoboy was on snowshoes, one of them still attached to his boot. The snow machine had to be Ulupov's. The dead man had no pack and no weapons, and Service figured the Czech had stripped them.

Allerdyce found a spent 7.62 x 39mm cartridge. "Full metal jacket," he said. "T'ink dis jamoke got 'er full auto, eh."

Service grunted, looked at the body again, agreed. A fully automatic Kalashnikov was a dangerous thing to contemplate. The corpse was stiff, no way to judge how long it had been there in the snow. "What do you think?" he asked the old violator.

"Snow like dis overtop 'is tracks quick even if we jump on 'er now, eh."

"If you were him, where would you head?"

"Youse t'ink I'm 'im?"

"You know the country."

"Me, I allus got plan, go udder camp deep in woods. I hear dis Chenk run traps all way down Manitou Gortch, below big falls."

"Sturgeon Falls?"

Allerdyce nodded firmly. "'Speck he have line shacks for traplines all over place, hided real good. Run to where he know best, feel safe, eh?"

About the same as Service figured. "How far to the gorge?"

"Eight mile crow, 'speck, go foot figure like snake, two mile make one mile, mebbe fifteen, sixteen not crow-straight."

Service closed his eyes and tried to imagine the map and real distance. "He'll have to cross a lot of back roads and two-tracks."

"Load sleds, scout roads, jump track by an' by," the old man said quietly. "Got wait snow stop." The old man glanced upward. "Two more day wind make howler. We wait 'er oot, eh? No bloody 'urry. I t'ink he hunker tight."

"Maybe he has another vehicle stashed," Service said.

"Could, won't," Limpy said. "Feel safe here, knows land good, places ta hide."

The old man was right. "Let's go on down to the camp and help the search." His instinct was to get on the track and push until he overtook the Czech, but this was winter, and the old poacher was right. Discretion was in order. *Gather more evidence, think it through, make a plan, then act.*

74

Wednesday, January 21

MARQUETTE

Pincock had been delayed overnight by the storm, got to Green Bay, and drove the rest of the way north. The tech had gotten prints from Ulupov's cabin, but whatever weapons he'd had were gone. Little food. *Planned run? Other camps, like Limpy said?* The sweat lodge was bugging Service. Not the typical sauna, but an old Indian lodge, constructed on a north-south alignment, made of red willow ribs, covered with a plastic tarp and heavy felt blanket material to keep heat inside. The floor was covered with cedar shavings, fairly fresh. He knew something about the lodge should connect to something else, but it refused.

Later that morning, after they had cleared out of Ulupov's and got the techs back to their truck, Jen Maki called to tell him some of the frozen meat wasn't venison but appeared to be human remains packed in heavy-duty freezer paper. The stuff was packed well; no freezer burn. Service had decided to keep this from the others for now, a detail for later. Allerdyce rode home with him.

• • •

Service, Noonan, and Treebone drove to the three-story Marquette County Jail, which could house eighty prisoners, with ten federal units. Lakotish was still in a holding cell, not yet officially charged, and segregated from the general jail population.

Friday met them. "Pincock says the feds will want him when we're done. DOD and the FBI both want to talk to him. Pincock said we should mention the possibility of Murder One, because everything was on national forestland."

"How's he acting?"

"Flatline," she said. "Resignation, I'm guessing."

"Resigned to what?" Service said. "*That's* the question. Pincock bring other feds?"

"She's alone."

Service gave Friday a thorough briefing on Ulupov, excluding nothing, and as he talked he had a thought: *The tree-house kill room was not nearly as clean as Lakotish-Varhola's workshop.* The last thing he described was Kelly Johnstone's body. Throat cut, heart removed. The prints on the .308 hanging in the shed in the trees matched Varhola's.

"Like Lamb."

"Jen found human tissue mixed among venison packages."

Friday grimaced and asked, "What makes you think Ulupov will hunker down?"

"Hunch," he said, checking his watch.

"There's a multiple-state BOLO."

Service grunted. *What was it about that sweat lodge?*

Pincock joined them, went into the interview room with several water bottles, and asked Lakotish how he was doing. Friday introduced the federal agent.

"Am I under arrest?" Lakotish asked without emotion.

"We want to talk to Eldar Gavrilovich Ulupov," Pincock said. "You know him?"

"The Czech isn't the kind of man one gets to know well."

"Did he know about the pending land deal?"

Lakotish stared at a wall. "It's possible," he admitted quietly.

"You've met him?"

"Rarely."

"Why?"

"He came to my camp. I had never seen him before, never heard of him, or anyone like him. I got the impression he was a hermit. He said he lived not far away, out back."

"Back of where?"

"He never said."

"He came to your camp. What did he want?"

"Not sure, then or now. I cooked trout for us."

"When was this?" Pincock asked.

"Last May."

"Whose fish?"

"Mine."

"You shared a meal. What did you talk about?"

"My people. He knows a lot about the *Anishinaabe*—our history, our beliefs."

"That was it?"

"Pretty much."

"And then he went away?" Pincock asked.

"Yes. I got sick that night, drove myself to the hospital in L'Anse."

"In the Volvo?" Friday asked.

"*What* Volvo? A neighbor woman, Mrs. Asheguance, has an old Jeep she loans me. She looks after the rectory when I'm not around."

"Did the hospital admit you?"

"Overnight. They pumped my stomach and kept me for observation. Mrs. Asheguance and her husband picked up the Jeep, and me, and took me home."

"What was the diagnosis?"

"They weren't sure. Food poisoning, or an allergy. Never had the problem again."

"What kind of symptoms?"

"Terrible," Lakotish said. "I saw things, heard things; there were voices."

"How soon after you ate did your symptoms set in?"

"Not long."

"You supplied the fish. What did Ulupov bring?"

"Wild leeks and brown sugar."

"For the fish?"

"He fried the fish, and I made potatoes and onions."

"Was Ulupov still there when you got sick?"

"I'm not sure. I think I remember hearing his voice."

"Saying what?"

"Not my land. God's land."

"That's it?" Pincock asked.

"What I remember."

"And then you drove to the hospital."

"I woke up there. I don't remember the drive."

"When did you see him again?"

"Never."

"When did you get rid of your car?"

"I've never had one, I told you. I always borrowed, used a bicycle, or walked."

"There was a tire behind your workshop," Friday said. "Can you explain that?"

Lakotish said, "I don't know about any tire. People up here throw things wherever they please. They're getting better, but they still do it." He exhaled deeply. "I made mistakes, but I've tried to be a good shepherd, a good priest for my parish, I really have."

Friday left Pincock and Service with the prisoner and went out to call the hospital. Pincock and Service came out after a few minutes, and Friday reported, "The way he tells it: stomach pumped, held overnight and released, no sequelae, no tox panel, probable food poisoning or allergic reaction. He was fine five hours after admission."

Service told Pincock, "Ask him about the .308. His prints are all over the weapon."

Pincock went back inside. "We found a .308 with your prints."

"The Czech had a .308. I don't own guns . . . I use a bow."

"How do you explain your fingerprints?"

Lakotish pondered this. "That day, he had a rifle with him, insisted I try it."

"Which you did?"

"He's a difficult man to refuse."

The FBI agent came back outside. "You two better take a seat," she said, opened her briefcase, and took out a folder. "Ulupov was heavily involved in the '68 uprising against the Soviets. He fled to Austria, showed up at our embassy in Viennna, and asked for political asylum. He was one of many at that time, all claiming to be freedom fighters. Ulupov was a professor of anthropology at Náprstek Museum. He was part of a group of academics who began to study Native Americans in the early '60s, with a focus on how the Indians had tried to resist assimilation. The subject apparently became quite popular in certain circles and remains so today. A lot of Czechs love Indians, know a lot about them—because of Ulupov."

"Asylum granted?" Service asked.

"Czech communists then were under a reformer who was losing the reins. Moscow sent troops from five Warsaw Pact countries, smashed the uprising, and removed the leader, per the Brezhnev Doctrine. Ulupov played a key role as a commando leader. The CIA verified his claims. They brought him to Atlanta, set him up with a position at Emory University, teaching anthropology, and gave him a new identity."

"He come out alone?" Service asked.

"Just him. The CIA learned later he had been the driving force behind the Native American movement in Prague. He graduated from Charles University and did three years in the Czech Army in the early '50s. Earned advanced degrees after that and joined the museum faculty. He was the only Czech refugee to make it to our embassy, refused to say how he crossed the border. The CIA took this as a red flag. It seemed possible he had been sent by the Soviets as an agent provocateur. The agency took him to Germany and debriefed him for two years. He knew a lot about the Soviets. He landed in Atlanta in mid-1972."

"But he's here now," Service said.

"He disappeared from Atlanta in 1975. No trace of him since, and no national search undertaken. In his home country he often lived in the woods and off the land. He was obsessed with outdoor life, rugged individualism, all that. There was some effort made to look for him in North Georgia, but no leads came from that. Something must've spooked him, but nobody knows what. It was hypothesized that he went off the grid."

"U.P.," Friday said.

"Appears that way."

Service said, "We have prints on the gun and on a knife."

Pincock nodded. "We'll know, then." She added, "We have a psychological profile on him. Highly resourceful and intelligent, prefers to operate alone, unlikely to be found in a heavily populated area."

"Our tax money paid for this?" Service asked. "Say this is our guy, and now he's spooked again. What's the prediction?"

"He's seventy-five, and this is *his* turf. He'll dig in and disappear."

"If we confront him?"

"This is the end of his road. He'll fight."

"We have a shot at finding him," Service said, "but we may need some bodies."

"Agents?"

"Not where we think he might be headed. My own people, some conservation officers. If it's him."

"We'll have fingerprint data back by late today," Pincock said.

"You get any feel for Ulupov?" Friday asked.

"Not sure he's your guy," the special agent said.

• • •

Service and Allerdyce drove to the DNR regional office called the Roof.

Ulupov's identity was confirmed by fingerprints, and Pincock shared the prints with other federal agencies.

Allerdyce looked uncomfortable sitting in Service's old work cubicle.

"Dis bird," the old man said, "he sit tight like a pat, hold breat', honkered down, won't flush lessen get stepped on. Send shitload pipples, he jumps, mebbe kills bunch, or runs, an' we chase again. No good. Better few pipples, move slow, read sit'ation, grab 'im by surprise where he honker down. Give 'im no chance ta run. 'Member, dis guy real good in woods."

Service hauled out 7.5-minute topographical maps, spread them on a conference table, and anchored the corners with books. Allerdyce stood over the maps, mumbling. "Chenk won't be in da deep; come summer, too many pipples, Lebanese backpackers, downstater, outstater, weirdos with kittles." The man made a sour face. "Chenk, I t'ink he be up west side in feeder crick draws, some old camp, no pipples, hard get dere, straight-down cliffs, t'ick bush, hard slog. Hear way back was trapper ladders 'ere, 'ere, 'ere," he said, emphatically tapping a finger on a map.

"Trapper ladder?"

"Find place by cliff got high trees, cut branches, use like ladder or steps. Never make where easy ta see. Hide so udder trappers not find so good."

Service had never heard of this and once again wondered how big a storehouse of knowledge lay inside the old man's brain.

"Here's deal, sonny. I go now, find track, scout. You come later, just you, den we get sumbitch."

"I want Noonan and Tree with us."

"Dat li'l city dick?"

"He's with us—end of story. He's tough, and his instincts in the shit are unmatched, even by you." This ended the discussion. "How long before you want us?"

"Satitty, late day, youse run Forest 2210 up 2227 to end, den nort' one hunnert yards, look for my sign. Follow hit till see small red ribbon, I put on top small ridge, twinny yard off track. See dat, wait dere. No fires. Pisspot burner okay make tea. No fire smoke. Stay till Limpy come fetish."

Come "fetish?" All the marbles on Limpy? I couldn't imagine this ten years ago. Even a year ago. Hell, yesterday.

"Las' t'ing," Allerdyce said. "Dress all-white duds, eh. Face, gun, glove, ev't'ing."

Service nodded. "If he gets past us, where do we post backups?"

"Spread on 2210, 1360, wherever we end up. No radio talk."

There had been no evidence of electronics or communications gear in the Czech's camp. "You leaving now?"

The old man nodded.

"You got a firearm?"

"Youse know law say no, and gun jes' get in way. Whole life, Limpy learn how not get see', smelt, 'eard. I learn hide so good Limpy can't find Limpy."

Preemptive Allerdyce logic, meaning no response was possible. The two men shook hands.

"Satitty," the old violator said, and cackled. "Dis what it feel like when you chase me?"

"Sort of." *What a strange man.*

Service telephoned Friday. "Well?" she asked.

"It's this Ulupov."

"I don't see a motive," she said.

"We've seen this before. Somebody has a little plot of private land surrounded by state or fed, or other private, rarely visited, and they begin to think of it as their own turf, and sometimes something else happens to tip them to take action. Case down south of Kalamazoo where a guy shot two deer hunters on the same day. Took a cold-case team fifteen years to solve it. Turned out the perp was even a good DNR informant."

"Ulupov?" she asked.

"My opinion? If the casino comes in, he loses his land. He's not about to let that happen. Russians drove him out of Czechoslovakia. He's done being pushed."

"This is sick," Friday said.

"This is the world we live in," Service reminded her.

||||||||||||||||||||||||||||||||||||||||||||||||||||||||||||||||||||||||||||||||||||||||||||||||||||||||||||||||||||||||||||||||||||||||||||

75

Saturday, January 24

STURGEON RIVER GORGE WILDERNESS, HOUGHTON COUNTY

The past three days had been spent in planning and preparation, making contact with officers Service wanted to help with the manhunt. He had even made a call to the chief to fill him in and seek his blessing. Yesterday at noon, WLUC-TV had reported that a suspect in the killings had been taken into custody, another suspect was at large, and a manhunt was being organized. The report pissed him off.

Friday had called and told him she was hearing reports of vigilantes in Marquette, Baraga, and Houghton Counties, and that out-of-state and downstate license plates were filling area motels, and restaurants were full. Service thought he recognized an opportunity, quickly outlined his thinking to her, and after a long silence got an "I guess."

Friday had handled an impromptu press conference at the jail yesterday afternoon. TV queen Bonnie Balat had tried to hog the spotlight with inflammatory statements disguised as questions.

The conference began with Friday reading a prepared statement: "We have an individual in custody, but not charged with the killings. A second individual is being sought as a person of extreme interest. A BOLO has been issued, and you will all be given a copy before you leave. We believe this second individual to be in the Silver Lake Basin area, and the search will center there. We are asking civilians to stay out of the area unless they are there to work, or live there. Anyone caught there who doesn't belong will be asked to leave, or will be arrested for interfering with police and charged with conspiracy. The hunt could last forty-eight hours or more. We apologize for any inconvenience, but public and officer safety are paramount," she told reporters.

"We have also established an anonymous toll-free tip line. We ask you reporters to make it public. Callers will get a recording. Leave a message of less than one minute, your name, and phone number. We will have people screening the messages, and we'll call you back if your information appears relevant."

Service grinned when he saw Friday on TV. Messages would be taken, but not checked. Silver Lake Basin was almost eighty miles east of the main hunt. He had picked the site for misdirection because it was close to where Lamb Jones had been found. Calculated disinformation. He could tell Friday wasn't convinced when he talked to her with the idea, but her performance was professional and convincing.

"Questions?" she had asked after reading the statement.

Balat out-elbowed and out-shouted her competition. "Detective, you have no power to declare martial law."

"This isn't martial law, Bonnie. Martial law means the military governs, and there are no military personnel involved in this operation. Next question."

Balat again. "Has the governor authorized this?"

"This is a local law enforcement matter being conducted by the county, assisted by the Michigan State Police."

Balat was as insistent as an infection: "Why no charges?"

"Procedure," Friday said calmly.

"But the windigo!" Balat shrieked.

"There is no such thing," Friday said calmly. "You need to stop spreading fiction and stirring up kids and old people with outrageous, irresponsible, and unsupportable claims."

"*Someone* has to warn the public," Balat countered.

Friday paused for effect. "Bonnie, you are doing your audience a huge disservice by fanning the flames of some half-baked fantasy. You're either in the hard news and fact business, or you're someone who wants to make up things to create an audience to bring in more advertising. Right now I think your viewers have a pretty good idea which group you belong to. Next?"

The room was silent. Balat shut up and the other questions were perfunctory and polite. She had taken the wind out of Balat's sails.

Grady Service was proud of her poise, and when she called and asked what he thought, he told her: "Perfect."

"Balat called me a cunt when the cameras were off," she said.

"And you said?"

"Takes one."

Service laughed.

"The governor called me before I could call you," she added.

"Really?"

"She asked me if *you* had authorized this. I told her it's my investigation, and she didn't argue."

Damn the governor. What the hell was wrong with her?

"Newf and Cat miss you," Friday said. Both pets had been at her place for a long time.

"Just them?"

"Shigun, and Litle Maridly too."

"Not you?"

"Nah, we cops get it. Be safe."

"Always the goal," he told her.

"You honestly think this Silver Lake Basin ruse will work?"

"I don't know, but I hope so; if it does, it will help us."

"And if it doesn't, and everyone lands on our parade?"

"We'll tell the truth. We needed space, and thought this was a good way to get it."

• • •

Planning was done, and it was late Saturday afternoon. Service found Allerdyce's marker where Forest Highway 2217 and the USFS road ended, splitting into two trails, one veering southeast, the other angling due north. The old poacher's trail was a hundred yards behind the ribbon marker, and even then Service had to walk some to find it. The old man had brushed his trail clean from where Service had parked his truck to where the trail became readable. *Unbelievably cautious, with thorough woodcraft.*

Allerdyce's snowshoes eventually merged onto an old trail, badly overgrown, almost unnavigable on snowshoes. Three miles north, he, Treebone, and Noonan found the red ribbon in a spruce by a steep gully, with Stretch Creek to their west.

"You fuckers actually *like* this shit?" Noonan groused. He had maintained pace and never complained until they stopped.

"Your legs okay?"

"Burning like motherfuckers."

Service set up the rocket stove and melted snow. The burner weighed less than three ounces, but could boil a liter of water in less than four minutes. He dropped tea bags into insulated paper cups, handed Noonan packets of honey, and waited for the water to boil.

"This Allerdyce, he one of your bad guys?" Noonan asked.

Tree laughed out loud.

"Was," Service said. *Still could be. How can you know?*

"He's damn good out in this shit," Noonan said.

No response necessary. The voice in his head said, *I hope.*

"How will we know when he's coming in?"

"I'll know," Service said.

Noonan shrugged off his pack. There was a long white object tied to it. "What's that?"

"Close-in closer. Caught punks whaling on an old fella one night, up from Kentucky to see his grandson. He sent me an ax handle, made from musk wood. Works real good in close, poking or bashing," the retired detective said. "I wrote a manual one time: *How to Use an Ax Handle in a Fight.* My division commander liked to rip my head off, said he never wanted to see it again. Ax handle helps you stop the biggest bastards flying on speed or dust. They can maybe fight through the lightning, but not the handle, man. I sold maybe a thousand copies of the manual over the years, five bucks a pop."

Noonan was one very strange and intense bird.

Service sensed motion and heard a muffled sound. "Squirrel alerting call—sounds like a small crow with laryngitis," he told Noonan. "That's Allerdyce."

Soon thereafter there was a whispered, "Slow."

"Roller," Service replied softly.

Allerdyce came out of the dark and sat down. Like them, he was decked out in white. "Youses got tea for a chum?"

The old man was wearing night-vision goggles.

Service made a quick cup for him, gave him four packets of honey and a 400-calorie Mainstay energy bar.

"Find him?" Service asked as the old man loudly slurped his hot tea.

" 'Bout mile an' a 'alf nort', where Dry Wash, Little Silver, and Mountain Creek meet up. Dis trail youse on run along ritch, drops down to 'nudder finger ritch, where Dry and Little Silver meet. Steep drop dere to da east. He got him shack built just nort'. All cliffs to wess. Hard to get at 'im."

"You see him?"

"Could smell 'im, eh. No smoke. He's honkered, tight and quiet."

"How close *did* you get?"

"Close 'nuff. Found catch wit white gas he hid."

Service immediately guessed what the old man was thinking.

"Volatile," Service said.

"Put a match on 'er, drive 'im out right quick, 'speck."

"But not light us up in the process."

"Fill water bottle wit' white gas, make maltoshop contrail, pinhole in bottom, drop bottle down stovepipe."

"We can get to his stovepipe?"

"She angled down a bit, but not enough. Be easy drop. Bottle first, den drop lit' rope-wick behind 'er, cover pipe, *boomph!* Oot he comes!"

"We'll have to try to talk him out peacefully first," Service said.

"Youse talk, youse lose surprise," Allerdyce said. "Dis chenkist polack jamoke fight, I t'ink."

"Got to be this way, Limpy."

"Got porch, overlooks crick. Bears, wolfies, deer walk down dere. He got baits. Only one door in, one door out. One window, side of door, smoked like pimp-car window."

Noonan chuckled.

"Best time?"

"Four, five morning, when 'eads not so good."

"If he gets away?"

"Won't get far. Find trapper ladder built over near dere. He goes down to crick dat way, he have us on top 'im quick. I put traps in branches, chained dere. Pow-ful, take time get off, we hear ruckus. Two ladders, one next camp, udder couple hundred yard. He take dat one."

Service leaned to Noonan. "You following this?"

"Yep."

"You know white gas?"

Treebone intervened, "Naptha, flashpoint below thirty-two, heavier than air, vapor spreads fast but doesn't persist. Makes one helluva pop. Water bottle will scorch his ass. A quart would probably kill him. We use white gas, he may not make it out," the retired vice lieutenant said, and added, "It sucks to be him."

Allerdyce cackled.

"Don't forget, he got 'is Russkie pop gun," Allerdyce said. "He come out *bipbipbip*, need have cover either side porch, heads down when he come out."

"Let the others know what we're doing?" Noonan asked.

"Not yet," Service said. He wanted time to think, made more tea, and sat down. White gas could be deadly to use even when you knew what you were doing. He closed his eyes, tried to visualize events. *Fuck!* His mind hit a wall.

He whispered to the other men, "There could be evidence inside. We can't burn out the place."

"Won't," Allerdyce said, "Pipe go down to little woodstove, I t'ink, gas flatch dere, won't spread much."

"I don't know," Service said.

"Trust me, sonny."

They each ate another energy bar before heading out, leaving their snowshoes stashed in some trees. Service was feeling some doubt, but decided the approach held the best chance for their own safety and getting Ulupov out of hiding. He'd know more when he actually saw the setup. He could adjust then.

"When we get set up," he told the men, "stash your NVDs so you won't be blinded by flashes or fire."

• • •

The setup had been almost perfectly described by Allerdyce, and events happened fast. Service stood to the side of the door, knocked on the window. "Mr. Ulupov, Conservation Officer, DNR! We need to talk to you. You've got three minutes to come out, unarmed, hands up!"

Limpy was uphill at the pipe. Bluesuit was opposite Service. Tree was above near Limpy, and Noonan was crouched on the other side of the plank porch, down on a knee, bent at the waist, ax handle at the ready.

No response. Maybe he's not here. Time.

"Limpy!" he shouted.

The wall left of the door, closest to Noonan, shattered, and an AK-47 ripped the air as the wall shredded. Service saw star-shaped muzzle flashes as rounds came his way, cracking over his head like slaps on the ass. Then came a bright light and loud *pop*, and blue-red fire leapt out of the opening that the man had made. A long tongue of fire flared up from the stovepipe, and Service heard the sound of bone cracking and a voice screaming, "*Di-ben-ind-is-o-win!*"

More shots sounded as Service rose and crossed the porch, until something smacked him in the upper arm, spun him, and knocked him off his feet.

Silence. Bite of cordite in the air, which means old ammunition, definitely the AK. He'd heard just the one gun-voice.

"Didn't s'pect that!" Noonan said with a snarl.

"Up here, youses," Allerdyce said.

They joined him. Ulupov was on the ground, facedown, a full wolf pelt stretched from his head to his waist, down his back. Service lit the man with his penlight and turned him to his side. His head was shattered like a melon. A stick protruded from his chest. Service took off a glove, checked for pulse. *None. Why's blood running down my left arm?*

"You hit?" Tree asked.

"Nicked maybe, never went numb, burned like hell right away. Check for fire inside, Suit."

Allerdyce took on a tone of voice Service had never heard before. "Put yore butt on ground, sonny!"

The old man helped him remove off his outer whites and his coat, shone a light on his shirt, then split the shirt with a knife. "Went t'ru good. Let's stop bleedin', eh."

Treebone was working alongside the old man. They weren't arguing.

"First-aid kit in my pack," Service told the old man.

Noonan came back. "No fire, stove confined it, mostly." The retired detective handed Allerdyce a sterile bandage and antiseptic. The two men wrapped the arm and tied it off. *Hurts.*

Treebone triggered his 800. "We have him. Twenty Five Fourteen is down. You can see our rig on AVL. Trail's a hundred yards behind the truck. Bring a snowmobile, call for EMS."

Denninger's voice. "Bus or wagon?"

"Wagon."

"Stay put," Treebone's voice thundered. "Cavalry's coming."

"Sound the bugle," Service quipped.

Service looked at the wood protruding from Ulupov's chest. It was a foot-long sliver of two-by-four. Noonan said, "AK must've shattered it when he came through the damn wall, stuck him coming out. I didn't even need to use the ax, I bet."

Limpy stayed beside Service, not moving, talking quietly. "Youse 'member time youse an' yore ole man stop by da bar, at Gwinn? Youses wass bellied up to bar, yore ole man knocking down beers, and somebody down way say, 'What good's a game warden?' You come off stool like bottle rocket, smack guy right in da kisser, nose blow up blood, his buddies start punch youse up, yore old man jump in, screaming like jungle ape. I jes' walk in when all happen, jump in help youse two. Youse were mebbe twelve, I t'ink, big dumb kid. We put all dem jamokes down on floor. Yore ole man cry that night, say he so proud, you gon' be damn good man, not lush like him."

Why the hell is he telling me that story? "Am I dying?"

"No, sonny, jes' 'membered, is all."

Service heard Noonan on the radio. "Better move your sorry asses," and then it was dark and silent.

76

Monday, January 26

MARQUETTE

It was night when he was awake enough to make sense of his surroundings. He felt loopy and confused. "What the hell is going on?" he asked to no one in particular, but a second later he had Allerdyce and Noonan and Treebone in his face.

"You dumbass," Tree said. "You kept yelling 'flesh wound,' but you lost a *chunk* of flesh and some muscle. Damn near bled out on the way here. Fragment of bone clipped blood vessels or something. They may have to do more surgery."

"Bullshit," Grady Service said. "I'm good to go."

"Not your call," Friday said, wading in. "Your door guards here have intimidated the whole damn nursing staff and *all* your doctors. They couldn't do anything without the approval of the three musketeers."

"I don't feel so good," he said, slumping into his pillow.

• • •

He woke up to "You've been shot *again!*" It was Vince Vilardo, his doctor and friend from Escanaba, looking down at him.

"Lucky shot," Service mumbled.

"For him, not you," Friday said. "Ten inches to the right and you'd be . . . not here."

"I wore my vest," he said.

"Hapless," Friday told Vince Vilardo.

"When do I get out?" Service wanted to know.

"End of the week, earliest. They want healing to begin, and to make sure there's no sepsis," Friday said. "And when you get home, you *will* rest."

"I've heard this stupid speech before."

"Not from me, you haven't," she said. "This time you will do as you're told."

Bluesuit Noonan stood at the end of the bed with a hangdog face. "My fault. Hit that motherfucker in the side of his head and he buckled, foot slipped in snow, spun him your way as he started spraying rounds. I'd hit his spine, he'da dropped right there. My fault."

Service felt a hand on his shoulder, looked up. Tree was there, solemn, no words. Brothers didn't need them.

77

Thursday, March 5

SLIPPERY CREEK CAMP

Captain Lisette McKower came to see Service, and they sat in front of the TV.

He said, "Guess what: No smokes in forty days."

She shook her head. "Like Lent; brag this time next year." Lis was an old friend, lover for a very brief time, his sergeant, lieutenant, and now field captain for lower Michigan. "Easier ways to quit than getting shot, lunkhead."

"I expected an attaboy."

"Attaboy. I heard you mailed your badge and ID to the governor with a note."

"What of it?"

"Quote: I refuse to be a political football again. You panicked. No governor can panic, ever. Good thing you'll be gone in a year. End quote. That's damn harsh, Grady, even for you."

"She put me into something I didn't belong in."

"She also sent fifty officers to help after Katrina, one-third of our whole field force, and they didn't accomplish shit. She's the governor. The people elected her. She can do these things. Listen to me, Mr. Self-Righteous: You could have told her the case was Friday's, not yours. You didn't. Don't whine now."

"She ordered me to hunt an animal," he said.

"And you did," McKower said. "A felon and two retirees for partners. You call *that* a team?"

"We break any rules?"

"I probably can't count that high."

"Lawyers got their snouts in this?"

"They tried, but Governor Timms stepped in and told them to back off. You're all cleared, even Allerdyce."

Service looked at her. "Listen to me, Lis. Limpy was the difference in this deal. Without him—"

"Understood," she said. "I read the reports. What was the Czech yelling when he came out shooting?"

"*Di-ben-ind-is-o-win*. Freedom. Apparently the asshole convinced himself he was Indian."

McKower set his badge and ID on a tray table. "You'll need these things. You had a second surgery," she added.

"Just cleanup; the cutting's done. It's all rehab from here on."

She cocked her head. "They don't have a rehab for the likes of you. No duty until April first, light duty until the last Saturday in April, start the day after the trout opener, full steam ahead. You get the trout opener off. Think of it as a reward." McKower held the flat of her hand to his face, turned, and marched out smiling.

Biologist Cale Pilkington visited later that day. "Krelle's coming back from Oregon, April first, here through June. She wants to track and monitor the new wolves, monitor breeding. She's guessing these aren't new. Allerdyce has signed on as her scout. Feds pay real good."

"Wolf DNA?" Service asked.

"Gray wolf; not a crossbreed unless it's so close to *Canis lupus,* the genetic markers don't show it. Krelle hypothesizes this is a mutant: wide body, shorter legs, and with no inherent advantage, such a mutant will die out, the fruit of evolution at its starkest. Krelle wants to see it through for science. First thing Allerdyce did was hire young Donte DeJean as his assistant."

Service smiled. *At least the kid won't be shooting deer or moose calves to feed the wolves. I hope.*

78

Sunday, April 26

MOSQUITO RIVER HEADWATERS

Allerdyce had stopped by the night before, had a beer, muttered a few things, loved on Newf and Cat, and left. Yesterday had been the trout opener. Grady Service fished Slippery Creek for an hour and quit, wanting to save his energy for today.

How many years since he'd worked the Mosquito Wilderness?

At zero nine hundred, Service found the Peterson brothers, Dovey and Booby, with twenty brook trout each. The brothers were longtime violators out of Rock.

"Heard you was retired," Dovey said when Service stepped out on them.

"You heard wrong," he said. "Who told you that?"

"Old Man Allerdyce," Booby said.

Service wrote tickets, explained what they had to do to pay, and took their fish, which were over limit and undersized. Back in his truck, he laughed out loud. It had been Allerdyce last night who told him where the daffy Petersons would be. The sneaky old sonuvabitch had set them up and given him a gift.

The Mosquito River ran vodka-pure and clear, light dancing in the riffle. Service lowered the tailgate, sat on it, and let the music of the river and wind through the trees engulf him.

Home, he thought, and grinned.